Linda Fairstein is a former prosecutor and one of America's foremost legal experts on crimes of violence against women and children. For three decades, she served in the office of the New York County District Attorney, where she was Chief of the Sex Crimes Prosecution Unit. In 2010 she was the recipient of the Silver Bullet Award from the International Thriller Writers association. Her Alexandra Cooper novels have been translated into more than a dozen languages and have debuted on the *Sunday Times* and the *New York Times* bestseller lists, among others. She lives in Manhattan and on Martha's Vineyard.

Also by Linda Fairstein

The Alexandra Cooper Novels

Non-Fiction

Terminal City

LINDA FAIRSTEIN

sphere

SPHERE

First published in the United States in 2014 by Penguin Group (USA) Inc.
First published in Great Britain in 2014 by Little, Brown
This paperback edition published in 2015 by Sphere

1 3 5 7 9 10 8 6 4 2

A CIP catalogue record for this book
is available from the British Library.

ISBN 978-0-7515-5048-1

Typeset in Adobe Garamond by Palimpsest Book Production Limited,
Falkirk, Stirlingshire

Printed and bound in Great Britain by Clays Ltd, St Ives plc

Papers used by Sphere are from well-managed forests
and other responsible sources.

MIX
Paper from
responsible sources

FSC® C104740

Sphere
An imprint of
Little, Brown Book Group
100 Victoria Embankment
London EC4Y 0DY

An Hachette UK Company
www.hachette.co.uk

www.littlebrown.co.uk

For Michael

Good can imagine Evil, but Evil cannot imagine Good.

W. H. Auden

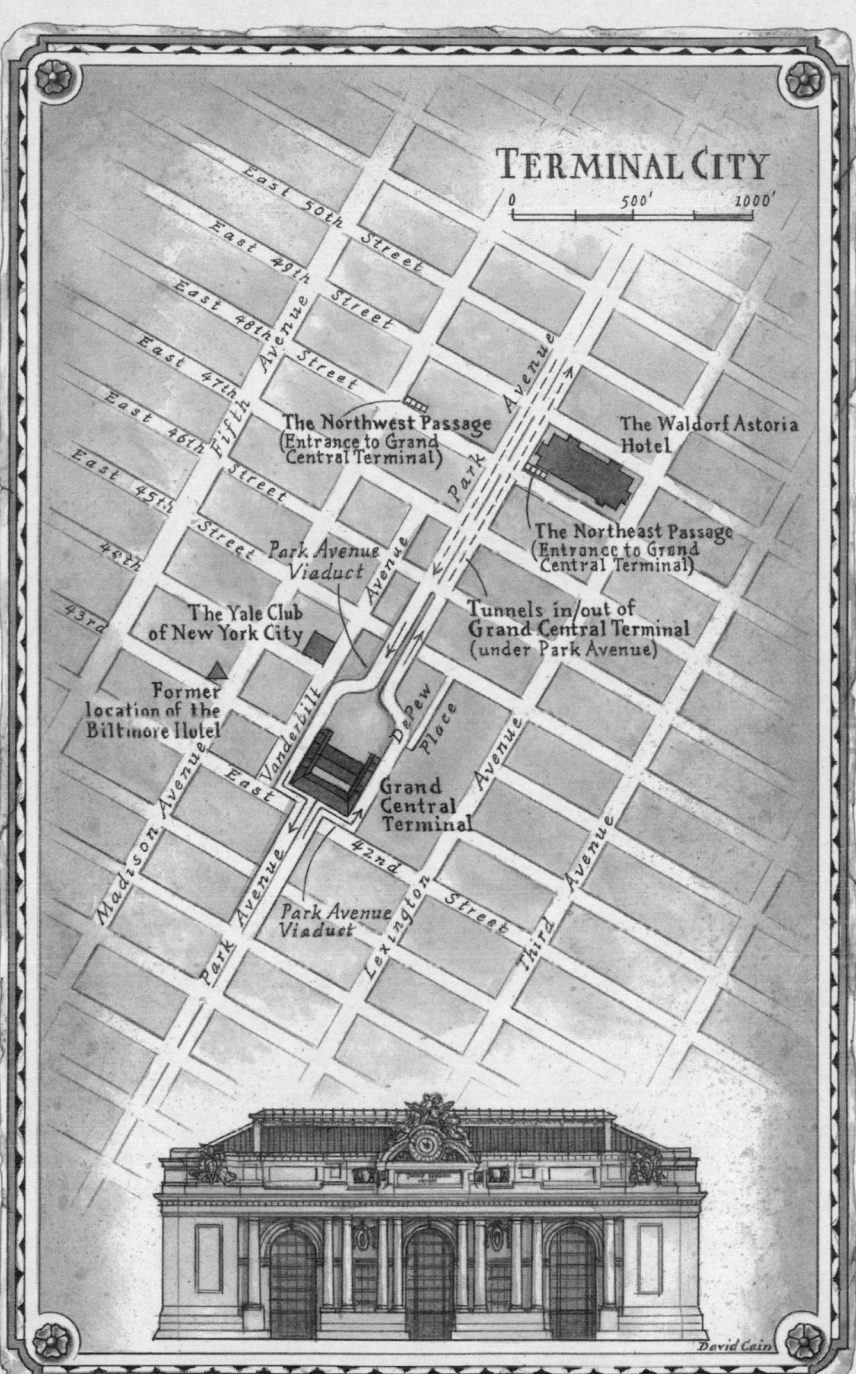

TERMINAL CITY

0   500'   1000'

East 50th Street

East 49th Street

East 48th Street

East 47th Street

East 46th Street

East 45th Street

44th Street

43rd Street

Fifth Avenue

Avenue

Park Avenue

The Northwest Passage
(Entrance to Grand
Central Terminal)

The Waldorf Astoria
Hotel

The Northeast Passage
(Entrance to Grand
Central Terminal)

Park Avenue
Viaduct

The Yale Club
of New York City

Tunnels in/out of
Grand Central Terminal
(under Park Avenue)

Former
location of the
Biltmore Hotel

DePew Place

Grand
Central
Terminal

Madison Avenue

East Vanderbilt Avenue

Park Avenue

42nd Street

Lexington Avenue

Third Avenue

Park Avenue
Viaduct

David Cain

One

'Not a pretty way to die, Alexandra.'

The lieutenant of Manhattan South's Homicide Squad opened the door to the luxury hotel suite on the forty-fifth floor at the Waldorf Astoria on Park Avenue.

'You know of one, Loo?' I asked, following him through the elegantly appointed living room. 'I mean a pretty way.'

Rocco Correlli shrugged his shoulders and shook his head. He had been on the job for almost thirty years and seen more corpses than most guys in the bureau could now lay claim to, as the city's murder rate continued its dramatic decline.

'Mike Chapman's got one.' Pug McBride was behind me, practically stepping on my heels in his effort to stay close to Correlli. The short detective, square-bodied with a wrinkled face like the dog for which he was nicknamed, was as annoying as he was good-natured. 'Says he'd like to die in bed with Gisele Bündchen's body double – fourth down, goal to go.'

Correlli stopped short at the open bedroom door. 'Shut it, Pug.'

'Yeah, I guess that's why Mike got jammed up. In the wrong bed at the wrong time.'

I was wedged between Correlli's back and McBride's barrel chest. His warm Marlboro-laced breath hit the back of my neck each time he opened his mouth. I trusted that neither man could see the color rise in my face at the mention of Chapman's name.

'I got the DA here,' Correlli said to someone standing with the body inside the room.

'Better buy him a cocktail first.'

I saw the flash of a camera go off. The speaker was Hal Sherman, one of the great pros in the Crime Scene Unit, whose voice was all too familiar to me.

'She's already had one, Hal.'

'Was it Scotch?' Hal said. 'Does that mean I actually drew the Coopster?'

'Hey, Hal. You going to let me in?'

Sherman framed himself in the archway of the open door. 'Good evening, Alex. I'd hoped you had better things to do tonight than come out on this one. You gotta learn to delegate, girl. Can't always be a control freak.'

'I did delegate, as a matter of fact. Had one of the new kids in the unit on the chart.'

The Special Victims Unit of the District Attorney's Office, which I had headed for more than a decade, used an on-call system, just like the prosecutors working homicides. That meant we rode investigations 24/7 in partnership with the NYPD – going to crime scenes, running lineups, interviewing suspects on video after the initial police interrogation – all designed to enhance the viability of the legal case that developed from the evidence collected.

'What was the matter? No booties or gloves that fit her?'

I glanced down at my outfit. Rocco made me glove up before I got on the elevator in the lobby. 'She's three months pregnant.'

'Probably throws up enough every day without having to see this crap, too,' Pug said.

I rolled my eyes. 'When Mercer called me, he was figuring she'd be on maternity leave by the time we'd need to go to trial.'

Rocco Correlli stepped to the side. He had straight silver-gray hair, a bit too long around the edges, and strong features that complemented his lean, angular build. 'That's assuming we catch the bastard.'

'Alex always assumes that,' Hal said. 'It's why she pushes us so hard.'

Mercer Wallace was the best Special Victims detective in the city and one of my closest friends. He had worked homicide for years – the highest-ranking African American in the squad and one of the few to be promoted to first grade – but requested the transfer to SVU because he preferred working with survivors of violent crime to handling murders. His compassion and gentle nature had helped scores of women and children in their recovery from the trauma of sexual assault.

'Are we waiting for Mercer?' I asked.

'He's downstairs with hotel security,' the lieutenant said,

'setting them up with a team of detectives to watch video surveillance tapes from the last seventy-two hours. No telling when he'll get back up here. This place is vast.'

'But there are so many cameras in the Waldorf, Loo. We could get lucky in a few hours,' I said.

'From your lips.'

'Now let me see the girl.'

'Take a deep breath, Alex.' Hal waved a licorice sucking candy under my nose. I opened my mouth and accepted it like a Communion wafer, even though it was small protection against the powerful odor of death.

I walked behind Hal, careful to avoid the areas of thick beige carpeting that were stained a dark red. The heavy silk drapes, rose-colored with a rich brocade trim, were drawn shut. Lamps on the dresser and night tables were lighted, and Hal's auxiliary spotlight equipment was directed at the unmade king bed. I skirted the chaise and sofa, then saw the body of the young woman, sprawled on her back on top of the rumpled sheets.

My eyes arrested on her neck. Her head was turned to the side, away from me, but there was a slice deep into her flesh that extended from behind her ear down to the top of her throat and then across her slim neck till it disappeared out of my line of sight. Beneath the far side of her head the blood had pooled and seeped into the bedding. The killer had deposited drops – large globs of the thick dark stain – as he walked away from his victim. Those were the markings on the carpet that led out of this death chamber toward the front door.

'Had anything like this, Alex?'

Rocco had given me time to take in the scene. The well-toned body of the woman was exposed to all of us, memorialized in photographs that would be studied in a courtroom if I overcame an adversary's cry of prejudice, and soon to be dissected by a first-rate medical examiner in the grimmest room in New York City.

My first instinct – anything but prosecutorial – was to restore some of her dignity and lift the sheet over her torso. Instead, I bit my lip and studied the position of the lower body – legs splayed to reveal a patch of dark, curly pubic hair.

'No,' I said. 'Nothing.'

The lieutenant wanted to know whether I had encountered any victims who had survived a similar assault – raped and left for dead with a deep knife wound to the neck. Rocco Correlli would not have received reports of survivors from the Special Victims Unit, but my team would have known of anyone operating with a similar modus operandi.

I folded my arms and stared at the body again, from the tips of her manicured toes to the lines that appeared to have been sliced by a sharp instrument into her upper thighs, past the gaping wound that killed her, to the top of her matted brunette hair. 'I'm sure you've checked with North.'

Rocco's superb team of homicide detectives covered the southern half of the island of Manhattan, responding to all the unnatural deaths that occurred from the lower border of Central Park on 59th Street to the tip of the

Battery. Manhattan North had the rest of the real estate – the park itself, the Upper East and Upper West Sides, Harlem and Spanish Harlem, to the border created by Spuyten Duyvil Creek, looking across to the Bronx. It was Detective Mike Chapman's turf, run by a veteran lieutenant named Ray Peterson, with whom I'd worked dozens of cases.

'Nada. It's like a monster that emerged from the deep and decided to commit a very professional job of slaughtering a broad smack in the middle of town, at one of the most prestigious addresses in Manhattan. No priors like it, nothing to suggest escalating from a pattern of serial rapes. It's like he came out of nowhere.'

'Nobody comes out of nowhere, boss,' Pug said.

'And disappeared back into nowhere,' Rocco said, ignoring Pug McBride.

'Who is she?' I said.

'No ID yet. You've asked me that three times. Impatience isn't your best feature.'

'How about the suite? Who's it registered to?'

'Nobody. That's the thing. It's been empty for four days. Housekeeper came in around five P.M. to ready it for an arrival tomorrow.'

'You thinking inside job? Hotel employee?'

'Start there. Management made an effort to shut down the place – well, slow it down anyway – as soon as the 911 call went in.'

'How is it possible to function if they do that? How many rooms have they got?'

'One thousand five hundred and seven, including these suites in the Towers.'

The Waldorf Astoria occupied an entire square block, with a grand entrance fronting on Park Avenue, and rear doors – several of them – facing Lexington. Over time it had been home to Cole Porter, Bugsy Siegel, Marilyn Monroe, and General Douglas MacArthur. Its large ballroom was nightly the site of black-tie dinners for every New York City charity, national political fund-raiser, and rubber-chicken corporate event.

'So it's impossible to close the place off, Loo.'

'They've been extremely cooperative. The night manager has called in all his supervisory staff, and they're trying to account for everyone's whereabouts the last three days. The entire employee list is online, so we'll be doing background checks throughout the night.'

'How long has she been dead?'

It wouldn't matter how intently I stared at the body. I couldn't help the woman, nor did I have Rocco's expertise in estimating things like time of death.

'I'm thinking day and a half, maybe more.'

'No medical examiner?'

'Johnny Mayes. I thought he'd beat you here.'

'Mercer caught me on my way home. I wasn't far from the hotel.' The District Attorney's Office was in Lower Manhattan, just north of City Hall. My apartment was in a high-rise only twenty blocks north of the Waldorf. Most days I drove downtown to work, parking on the street, with the laminated plaque that identified me as a prosecutor.

I was only five minutes from the hotel when Mercer reached me at 7:20 this evening. 'I'll wait for him.'

Mayes was one of the best forensic pathologists in the country. I learned something every time he examined a body, explaining the damage each weapon had caused or the kind of force necessary to result in death. It was extremely comfortable to work with him, to know the deceased was in his capable hands, to witness how he teased so much information from a silent, often reluctant corpse.

'Take your last look, Alex.' The lieutenant was fidgety, anxious to get me out of the way.

'The marks on her thighs, you make anything of them?'

'Leave it to the doc. They seem sort of superficial to me.'

'I get that. I mean the cuts, you think they form any kind of design?'

'Hal made photos,' Rocco said, taking his gloved hands out of his pockets to lean in, his head directly over the girl's flat abdomen, peering down at her scarred legs. 'Two parallel lines, kind of even, inch and a half long. With short strips going crosswise, like the rungs of a ladder.'

'I mean they're really even. They look so deliberately drawn.'

'Carved, not drawn. You've seen that before?'

'I told you no, Rocco. I'm just thinking that here comes this killer who gets into the hotel, maybe he encounters his victim here – in the hallway or even the bar – entirely by chance.'

The Bull and Bear was a fixture in the New York scene,

regularly crowded with businessmen and lawyers, conventioneers and tourists, highbrows and hookers.

'Maybe she works here,' Pug said.

'They're scoping that out. There are thousands of staffers here. Must be ten at the front desk alone,' Rocco said. The check-in area was so large it took up half the length of the lobby. 'You got housekeeping, kitchen and room service, engineering, reservations, maintenance, security, administration, a beauty parlor, a barber shop, a jewelry store that sells diamonds as big as the Ritz. Who'd even miss one girl?'

'I tell you what,' Pug said, with a sideways glance at the bed. 'That particular one I'd be missing.'

'What I was saying is that somehow the killer gets in. Like he just walks in off the street. He meets the girl, Rocco.'

'Or he comes in off Park Avenue with her,' Pug said, interrupting again.

'That should show on the surveillance tapes. But it's a crime of impulse, don't you think?'

'Why's that?' Rocco said, pointing the way back to the living room.

'Because he didn't stop to take a room, did he? He never checked in.'

'Nope. But how would he have known this suite was empty?'

'Easy to get that information if he works here,' I said. 'Or maybe he just got lucky trying doors. Could be he's a scam artist, burglarizing rooms with a master key card.

My point is that if this was a rape – an impulsive act – and the girl resisted, the perp might have gone berserk and slit her throat to shut her up.'

I turned back to look at the body again, but Rocco made it clear he wanted me out. 'If you're waiting for her to wake up, Alex, you're out of luck. Move on, now.'

'But what doesn't fit with that kind of crime of opportunity are the marks he etched on her thighs,' I said. 'Too neat. Way too carefully drawn.'

'You can't have it both ways, Alex,' Pug said.

'I'm just saying it's odd. The fatal wounds are inconsistent with the careful markings on her thighs. Disorganized killer versus very meticulous artist.'

'Maybe he did the legs first,' Rocco said. 'Maybe he tortured her.'

You couldn't look at the young woman's body and not think torture.

I crossed the threshold into the living room. Rocco directed me through the door and across the hallway, into another suite that management had given him to use as a mini command center. Several uniformed cops nodded at me when I entered. Before too long it would be swarming with detectives from the local precinct and Major Case.

'Want some coffee?' Rocco said.

'Sure.'

He poured us each a cup, then proceeded to tell me what his men would spend the night doing.

'Have you put out a photo of her yet?'

'No way, Alex. Her clothes are gone, there's no form of

ID around, and I can't release a picture until Johnny Mayes cleans her up.'

'Are they doing a vertical search of the hotel?'

'Waiting on Commissioner Scully to give me a platoon of guys to do that. There must be thirty elevator banks, staircases everywhere, and all those thousands of doors to knock on.'

'It's Pug's case?'

Rocco Correlli took a sip of the hot coffee, scowling as he put it to his lips. 'Scully wants someone with more polish as the front man. Pug's too likely to step on his own dick when the first reporter goes after some off-the-record lead. Mercer's on loan till we come up with a better idea.'

'That makes it easy for me.' Mercer and I had partnered more times than I could count.

'The word "easy" isn't in the mix, Alex. I've got to put a face and name to the body, quell the public hysteria about a murder in a Midtown landmark, and figure out who this madman is and where he came from.'

'Not to mention where he went.' I thought of the images of the two ladder-like designs on the victim's long legs. 'And who's at risk going forward.'

'I've got less than a week to deliver.'

'Scully understands what a massive job this will be. It will take that long to study the hotel's surveillance tapes, top to bottom of the building. He can't be serious about a deadline.'

Rocco Correlli rested his mug on the silver tray the

manager had sent to the room. 'It has nothing to do with the commissioner, Alex. In less than a week, three floors of suites in the Waldorf Towers will be filled to capacity. The president of the United States will take up residence here for an emergency special session at the United Nations.'

Two

'Maybe the White House ought to find POTUS another place to stay,' I said, refilling my cup with strong black coffee and sitting back on a yellow flocked love seat, flanked by a pair of cops in deep-blue uniforms.

'Every president since Herbert Hoover has been put up at the Waldorf Towers. The whole entourage. Secret Service and NYPD make the run from here to the UN like clockwork, and they've got every inch of this place figured out,' Rocco said. 'Besides, Scully's dep checked with all the major hotels in the zone. Mid-August? Every tourist and convention has a lock on all the acceptable places in town.'

'But you won't even be done processing this one, will you?'

'Crime Scene was here by five thirty tonight. Did a thorough job on the two rooms but—'

'Find anything?'

'It's a hotel suite, Alex. You know how many frigging fingerprint overlays they got? Hundreds of 'em. Not a clean lift in the place. Not even a partial in blood. Nothing on the porcelain surfaces in the bathroom. It all suggests a total pro.' Rocco put his coffee down and started for the door. 'Forget your impulsive rapist.'

'Don't blow me off like that.' There were detectives and supervisors who welcomed the insights of my senior colleagues, men and women who had worked the toughest cases shoulder to shoulder with their NYPD counterparts for many years. Rocco wanted to pick my brain about the sex crimes aspect of this case, but he didn't care for guidance in his hunt for a murderer.

'You interrupted me,' he said sharply. 'What did the guys find in the room, you want to know? No prints of value. Some trace evidence to be analyzed, probably from the maid service or a recent guest. Blood on the bed and on the floor – most likely the killer had spatter on his clothes. Didn't stop here to wash up, though. Got away somehow, and may have left with the deceased's belongings, too. Cool character. Maybe two of them.'

'Crime Scene must have a ton more work in the building,' I said, leaning forward.

'Second team was pulled in from the Bronx. The hotel is like an anthill full of cops. You know how many people – guests, visitors, employees, deliverymen – have pressed elevator buttons for the forty-fifth floor in the last two days? They're dusting and scraping and looking for specks of blood, but it's crazy, Alex. Give me a perv who likes to do his business in a small walk-up or a tiny boutique hotel or even a flophouse on the Bowery.'

'Not so many flophouses left down there, Loo.'

'Yeah, well, this killer could have targeted the Surrey or the Carlyle, some fancy digs farther uptown in Manhattan North. He had to do this on my watch?'

'Peterson doesn't need another headache,' I said.

The city's last high-profile homicide had taken place in Central Park, almost two months earlier, in June. It left me shattered for several weeks and resulted in Mike Chapman being suspended without pay for twenty-one days. He'd been burned by the embarrassment of his punishment for a personal transgression, then added a month of vacation to the rip imposed by the department to visit family in Ireland.

'Like you do?' Rocco said. 'Kiss your weekend plans good-bye. No jaunting up to Martha's Vineyard on Friday.'

'Guess not.' But I had already ditched plans to fly up to my house, even though August was high season and many of the friends I didn't get to see all year spent part of this month at the beach.

Mike was coming home at the end of this week, and he had asked me to have dinner with him on Saturday night. Our ten-year friendship, marked by an intense professional partnership that had circled around the prospect of personal intimacy for so long, had taken a slight turn on a June night, in the middle of Central Park. Mike's suspension, and his European travels, had given me far too much time to think about what might be next. My anxiety level was high.

'You got anything from Mercer?'

'Sorry? What did you ask me?'

'Don't zone out on me, Alex. The night is young.'

I checked for a text. 'He'll be up here within the hour. Before nine o'clock.'

In between that last murder investigation in Central Park and this one, the sweltering summer heat had added to the volatility of feuds. Drug gangs in Brooklyn were responsible for three shootings in July, the usual domestics left six women dead citywide, and an array of road rage, drunk drivers, deranged psych patients for whom there was no place in mental facilities had spiked the murder rate. The Manhattan District Attorney's aggressive and creative crime strategies had taken the figures to a dramatic new low, but the recent blip in numbers had everyone questioning whether the cycle was trending up again or if the brutal weather patterns had simply ignited violent tempers.

A detective appeared in the doorway. 'Excuse me, Loo. The medical examiner's on his way up, and I just got a call from the housekeeper over in the ER. She's stable, and they're sending her home.'

'What's wrong with her?' I got to my feet and walked toward Rocco.

'Palpitations. Totally freaked out by finding the body,' Rocco said. 'Thought she was having a heart attack. Two of the men from the Seventeenth Precinct who got to the scene early took a good statement from her. We did elimination prints and swabbed her mouth for DNA.'

He turned back to the detective. 'Tell the housekeeper we might need her to be available for a reinterview tomorrow. See if her memory improves once she calms down.'

'Memory problems?' I asked.

'I'll show you the notes. Saw nothing, heard nothing. I'm not sure she was so clueless, or that she just doesn't want to be involved. You can take a run at her when you're ready.'

I slipped past the detective and let Rocco give the man his next orders. I paced the hallway in front of the elevator bank, waiting for Johnny Mayes to step off. At forty-five, he had established a solid reputation as a brilliant pathologist who worked well with the senior prosecutorial staff. Once he finished his site exam, the young woman's body would be removed to the chief medical examiner's office, where Mayes would perform the autopsy, probably tomorrow.

'Johnny,' I said, greeting him as he stepped off the elevator, wheeling his equipment bag behind him.

'Alexandra Cooper,' he said, bowing at the waist. 'Did they shoot you out of a cannon? Have I kept you terribly long?'

He was about the same height as I – five feet ten – but his stout build was a distinct contrast to my slim frame. Mayes was a wine enthusiast whose refined tastes and interests seemed to lift him out of the dark world in which he spent an inordinate amount of his time.

'Not at all.' I pointed the way to the suite, and we walked the long corridor together. 'I'm waiting for Mercer to come back up here so we can make a plan, and everyone's terribly curious to hear what you have to say. The manager brought up fresh coffee if you need a jump start.'

'I'll take it,' he said. 'Who've we got? Rocco?'

'And Pug.'

Johnny smirked as he turned his head to me. 'Seriously? And who'll do damage control for his mouth?'

'That falls to me, I'd guess.'

'You have thoughts on this yet?'

'Waiting for your observations, Doc.'

Mayes unzipped his bag and reached in for a gown to wear over his long-sleeved shirt. He turned so that I could tie the strips behind his back. He leaned on my shoulder while he covered his brown leather shoes with booties, then fitted himself into a pair of gloves.

'Lots of blood, I understand.'

'Understatement.'

'You game for a forensic adventure, Alex?'

My office had pioneered the courtroom introduction of some of the most advanced scientific techniques since we first attempted to use DNA technology – unsuccessfully – in a 1986 homicide. Paul Battaglia, the longtime district attorney, had thrown his support behind unconventional approaches to solving crime. Biologists at the Office of the Chief Medical Examiner's lab gave us groundbreaking tools, from familial searches of genetic matches via blood relatives of a suspect to my recent Frye hearing on the use of an FST – Forensic Statistical Tool – to evaluate evidentiary material with low mixtures, rather than complete profiles, determining the probability the substance contained the perp's DNA.

'I'd like to try a homicide with just a straightforward cause of death for a change. And a blood-soaked perp fleeing the scene who's in custody before he hits the pavement.'

'Come ahead then, girl. I might be able to give you the former.'

'What's the adventure?' I asked as he tapped on the door of the victim's suite.

'A hyperspectral imaging device that can date blood samples, perhaps to within an hour of the time they were deposited,' Mayes said, as Rocco opened the door. 'The holy grail of forensic technology.'

'Hey, Johnny,' Rocco said, 'how've you been?'

Hal Sherman and Pug McBride came out of the bedroom.

'Hot. How about you, Lieutenant?'

'Just got orders to cancel my vacation. Hot and bothered is how I am. The dead girl's in the other room.'

'Anybody move her? Turn her over?' Mayes pointed a gloved finger at Rocco Correlli, then Pug and Hal.

'You crazy? Of course not,' Pug said. 'Scout's honor.'

'I know how it is when you're looking to identify a body, gentlemen. Objects have a tendency to shift in flight.'

An impetuous detective had screwed up a homicide of mine by rolling the body over before the medical examiner arrived, hoping to find a driver's license or wallet in her jeans pocket, making it impossible for the pathologists to know the exact pattern of the bloodstains.

'I didn't think she'd be lying naked on top of her library card, Doc. No problem waiting for you.'

'May I—?'

'Stay out here, Alexandra, will you?' Mayes said. 'Let me do this with Pug. I expect Dr Azeem will be here shortly. He can explain to Rocco and you what our experiment will be.'

'Don't be experimenting on my scorecard, Johnny,' the lieutenant said.

Dr Mayes walked to the threshold and peered into the room. 'I'm going to guess that someone sliced this young woman's jugular vein. I will trust your most excellent men,' he said, with the formality of speech that characterized his style, 'to find the executioner as quickly as possible. The more difficult issue will be figuring how this victim was led to slaughter, and precisely when it happened.'

'Azeem?'

'I heard him lecture in England in the spring. Teesside University. He happens to be here this week presenting his findings at Columbia. He offered the opportunity to give me a firsthand sampling of the prototype.'

'What does the device do, exactly?' I asked.

'She means what's so frigging holy about it,' Rocco said.

'The imaging scans for the visible spectrum of hemoglobin with extraordinary levels of laboratory accuracy. The only effective way of dating blood currently is centuries old, my friends,' Mayes said, his gloved hands clasped together on the bulge above his waist. 'Dr Azeem may be able to tell us, right here in this room – within the hour – what the time of death was. I assume if we pinpoint that, it might save your men a huge amount of time.'

Rocco whistled. 'And spare them endless hours of looking at videotapes of revolving doors and cement staircases.'

'Let me get to work. And you might tell the manager that when I'm done, I would prefer a fine glass of Montepulciano to chase down this lukewarm coffee on his hospitality cart.' Johnny Mayes disappeared into the bedroom.

'Go figure,' Rocco said, leading me back to the suite across the hall. 'Come out of there and drink a glass of blood-red wine? I'll stick to my vodka, and it can't come soon enough.'

I walked to the window and stared out at the dusky sky, at the last bit of light from behind the tall buildings to the west. I looked down at the tiny figures on the sidewalk so far below – pedestrians, making their way to trains or subways or restaurants nearby. Even though the rush hour traffic had abated, the strip fronting the Waldorf, Park Avenue between 49th and 50th Streets, was one of the busiest crossroads in Manhattan.

'Missing Persons have anything to say?'

'Give it a break, Alex. She might not be missing all that long yet. Dr Shazam—'

'Azeem.'

'Whatever. He and his amazing machine are supposed to solve that piece of the puzzle, aren't they?'

I sat back down on the couch and put my feet up on the coffee table, checking my BlackBerry for emails and texts.

Blood expert on the way, I texted to Mercer. *You might want to be here.*

Pug crossed over to stand in the doorway. 'Confirmation on the seminal fluid in the pubic area, Alex. Mayes asked me to tell you.'

The doctor had used a blue LED to fluoresce the dried fluid on the victim's skin and matted in her hair.

District Attorney Battaglia wasn't into electronic communication. He wanted to hear the news the old-fashioned way – catching hesitation in his lawyers' answers if they were uncertain of facts, picking up on the tonality of the voice of the reporter, allowing him to cross-examine before you had time to think of a response that could be abbreviated by a few keystrokes.

I called Paul Battaglia to tell him that I was at the Waldorf and that initial observations supported the view that this was a rape-homicide of an unidentified woman, probably in her late twenties, whose jugular vein had been severed by the sharp blade of a knife.

He had the usual concerns. Not the condition of the woman's body or the quality of our investigative work, but how this murder would impact his political standing. He'd want to know what church her mother attended so he could plan to be at Sunday's service, and whether there would be any victims' group rallies that might disrupt his schedule, requiring his attendance at a candlelight vigil, or something that might deprive him of a chance to golf with his son-in-law on Sunday morning.

Hal Sherman joined Pug McBride in the corridor. His voice boomed and I whipped around, ending my phone call as Hal shouted, 'Look who's back from the dead.'

I knew he wasn't talking about the body on the bed.

'Who is?' I asked.

Hal backed up and a short gentleman with dark skin, straight black hair and wire-rimmed glasses entered the room.

As he stepped toward me with an extended hand, introducing himself as Fareed Azeem, Mike Chapman came into view, slapping Hal's back as his old friend embraced him.

Then Mike led the others into the suite where Rocco and I were working. 'Hey, Loo. Here's the magician Johnny Mayes has been talking about.'

Azeem smiled and greeted Rocco Correlli.

'Nobody said Chapman was dead,' Rocco said as he shook hands with Dr Azeem. 'He just needed an attitude adjustment. And a lock for the zipper on his private parts.'

There was no mistaking my full-on blush for the warmth of the August night now.

'What about you, Coop?' Mike asked, running his fingers through his thick black hair, flashing his best grin. 'Miss me?'

'Once a week at least, Mike. Maybe twice. Whenever I thought it had been too long since anyone had taken a jab at me. I – uh – I hadn't realized you'd come home.'

I didn't want to squirm in front of this crew of professionals, but I was steaming because Mike hadn't called me to say he had returned a few days earlier than expected.

'Need-to-know basis only. I told you that, kid. Taking it slow.'

That last phrase was Mike's, the one he had used when he kissed me on the rooftop of the Arsenal on a pitch-perfect June night.

'Taking what slow?' Rocco asked.

I reached for a legal pad in my tote bag. Anything to avoid playing out this stilted reunion in front of the Manhattan South Homicide Squad.

'Am I interrupting something here, Alex?' the lieutenant asked. 'Or is this just the usual Chapman foreplay?'

'Sorry, Rocco. I've been waiting for Mike to get home so we could tie up some loose ends on a pending case.'

'She hates to be the last to know, Loo. Bad habit of hers.'

I turned to Fareed Azeem. 'I understand you're going to help Dr Mayes establish our victim's time of death, Doctor.'

'I don't want to get in the way, Ms Cooper,' he said, nodding his head in my direction. 'But I believe I can assist with that.'

'It could be critical in this case, if we can limit the window in which the perp committed the crime and escaped from this – this fortress. It would save the detectives days of wasted hours canvassing or sitting in front of video screens.'

'Yes, ma'am. It's rather a mammoth hotel.'

'Dr Mayes is across the hallway. Let me take you over to him,' Hal said.

He motioned to Azeem to follow as Rocco Correlli charged ahead. Mike moved back to let them through, while I tried to stay close on the heels of the highly touted forensic guru. I didn't see any point in being alone with Mike.

'So really, Coop, did you miss me?' he said, playfully poking me in the side as I passed him.

'Any day now I might have started to.'

'You look skinny, kid. How much weight did you lose pining away for me?' Mike grabbed my arm to try to hold me in place.

'Neither weight nor sleep.' I broke loose and kept walking.

'Hey, Coop. Turn around a minute.'

'What is it, Detective?' I worried my annoyance – and hurt – were palpable.

'Death becomes you, Ms Cooper,' Mike said. 'It brings color to your cheeks.'

Three

Johnny Mayes sipped a glass of wine as the rest of us settled into place in the mini command center on the Waldorf's forty-fifth floor. Mercer was beside me on the love seat, while Mike leaned on the mantel over the gas fireplace. Hal and Pug pulled up armchairs near the coffee table, and Rocco and Azeem were on opposite ends of the long sofa. It was 9:15 and there was no sign that the business portion of the evening would end soon.

'It will come as no surprise to any of you that this young lady died as a result of exsanguination,' Johnny said. 'The instrument of causation – the knife or other cutting tool – had an extremely sharp tip. A needle point, I might say, which perforated the skin quite easily behind the right ear. There is a very regular and steady path sliced across her neck, which severed the jugular vein and occasioned the outpouring of blood onto her body and the bedsheets.'

I swallowed hard and stared at a spot on the wall above Johnny Mayes's head.

'I say regular because it is so even, so unfluctuating, that it would appear that this victim offered no resistance to the assailant. She seems not to have struggled or moved during the time of the cutting, nor are there any defensive wounds on her hands or lower arms. Her fingernails are all intact. Polished a pale pink and not even chipped.'

'But it's the neck wound that killed her,' Pug said, 'or the blood flow wouldn't have been so dramatic.'

'She was alive when he slit her throat, Pug. Drugged, perhaps, but alive.'

'Why do you say drugged?' I asked. 'You think she's a junkie? Any marks on her body?'

'Nothing to suggest that, Alex. Several things make me think you won't find any photographs of her on the hotel videos. I don't think she came in here under her own steam.'

'How then?' Mercer said.

'It's her back, my friends. Her back and the skin on the rear of her thighs and legs. Two things of note,' Johnny said, stopping to sip his wine. 'There are more of those so-called ladders you saw on her thigh, Alex. All on her lower back. Four of them.'

'I'll have a set of photos to you tomorrow,' Hal said to me.

'Did they cause any injury?'

'None at all. I see you're wincing, Alex. I'm sure the young lady was too intoxicated – involuntarily – to know. There is also a pattern – not in high definition – but sort of vaguely apparent on her skin. Especially her shoulders, her buttocks, and the rear of her legs. You want a guess about why I think she didn't walk in through the lobby? All I can give you is my hunch.'

Mike started to pace. He rarely stood still when his mind was in gear. 'Shoot.'

'There's a faint imprint – it's actually on her forearms, too. Just on the surface of her skin, not dug into it,' Johnny turned to me as he spoke. 'It looks like a lining of some kind, a motif from the interior of a box or container. Imagine a wallpaper design in a faded red pattern that stamped onto her skin because it was wet. In this heat, enclosed in some kind of container, moisture from her sweat would have collected quickly.'

'Any ideas?' I asked.

'I'm thinking of something large enough, obviously, to conceal a body. Something used to transport or move an object or a piece of furniture.'

'You're supposed to be helping us, Johnny,' Mike said, one hand in the pocket of his jeans and the other waving in a circle over his head. 'You got an enormous square block of Manhattan real estate with exits and entrances on all sides and its own parking garage underneath. Deliveries are made every hour, day and night. Enough food to stock all the restaurants and room service, pallets filled with linens and laundry, boxes full of flower arrangements the size of small trees, and musicians hauling instruments of every conceivable size and shape up to the ballroom.'

Johnny Mayes tried to get a word in. 'But there is—'

'That's before you start with the guests and the transients. D'you ever get held up in Park Avenue traffic by a minivan unloading a family of five with suitcases and backpacks and duffel bags that look like they could hold Mercer's six foot four inches? I did a security detail two years back—'

'Should have been your last one, Chapman,' Pug said, enjoying the chance to lob a crack at Mike. 'You could have saved yourself some embarrassment.'

None of the rest of us laughed with him.

'Nice having you at my back, Pug. Like I was saying, I had this detail with one of the Saudi princes. Picked him up at JFK in an SUV and we needed a caravan to get his luggage here. Right to the Waldorf. Could have had a camel, a two-humper even, in one of the trunks he was carting around.'

'Stick with the idea of trunks for a minute,' Johnny Mayes said, placing his glass on the tray. 'I'm quite sure we're not dealing with something commercial, like a wooden packing crate. The markings would have been entirely different – strips of wood several inches thick, and certainly unlined. I would have expected to find shavings or splinters in the girl's hair or on her body. A cardboard one, perhaps, but that wouldn't be likely to have any design on the inside, would it? It would be a far cheaper product than wood.'

'You're saying she might have been carried into the Waldorf inside a trunk?' Mercer asked. 'You're all so quick to buy into this.'

'She didn't walk,' Johnny said. 'I'm betting good money on that.'

'Wheeled,' Pug said. 'Wheeled in, not carried. Fits with

Crime Scene findings. They think there were indentations in the carpet. We actually disregarded them, figuring it was a room service cart from a few days ago.'

Mike slapped his palm against his forehead, but Pug was oblivious to the gesture.

'Not all the way into the bedroom, but in the entryway to the suite. That's where they picked up some of the trace evidence. Dirt and debris.'

'It's not the wheeled versus carried that stops your heart,' Mercer said. 'This girl was alive, then stuffed inside a – a box or container of some kind for the purpose of getting her in here? To die in a suite in one of the most luxurious hotels in the world?'

'I don't begin to know the purpose,' Johnny said. 'I'm just telling you that the endgame was in that suite. I'd say she was drugged to unconsciousness – although toxicology results may take weeks to tell us with what – her body folded practically in half to be concealed in a large suitcase or trunk, and that she was brought to the forty-fifth floor of this hotel to be raped and murdered. She died right on that bed.'

'Why?' I said. 'Mercer's right. For what possible reason?'

'I won't pretend to be of any help on that count.'

'Any preliminary estimate of when she died?' Rocco Correlli asked.

Johnny lifted his glass again, tilting it in the direction of Fareed Azeem. 'I'd say "the game is afoot," my friend, but it would be in such bad taste. A pathologist outside his morgue versus a chemist with his portable new filter. I'm at such a disadvantage, Fareed. Shall I go first?'

Azeem gestured his consent with both hands.

'It's now Tuesday evening, after nine P.M. I'd put the time of death at somewhere between noon and six P.M. yesterday. Of course that's before I get to gastric contents and all that. The rigor, the appearance of the body, the color of the blood.'

'That's the best you can give me?' the lieutenant asked. 'Half a day? That costs me a dozen men stuck on more than a hundred video monitors in real time.'

'They can always fast-forward 'em, Loo,' Pug said. 'Bores me to tears to look at those empty corridors on surveillance tapes.'

'Hence my introduction to the amazing Dr Azeem. I'll come closer after tomorrow's autopsy, but let's see what he can tell us.'

'No insects,' I said softly. 'I didn't see any activity, or any obvious decomposition, despite the intense heat. You'd think if it were more than twenty-four hours ago . . .'

'The air conditioner was on full blow when uniform responded,' Pug said. 'It was like a meat freezer in here, Alex.'

'Let me go back across the hall and check my camera,' Azeem said. 'I'll give you a reading of the machine and explain the result.'

He stood up and walked out of the room.

'This imprint you've described on the girl's back,' Mike said. 'Is it distinctive enough to give us a clue?'

'The design may be fairly common,' Johnny said. 'Sort of chevron-shaped print, perhaps on a linen cloth that lined a piece of luggage. But there are also letters, some of which are quite easy to make out. There's an uppercase *G,* followed by an *a* or an *o.* In some instances the next one appears to be a *v* or maybe a *y.* It hasn't left the same impression in every place because of the natural protrusions of the bonier parts of the body. It's clear on the hips and on the shoulder blades, but then you lose the markings in the small of the victim's back. The curvature there obviously didn't make contact with the patterned fabric.'

'Any other specifics?' I asked. I was playing with the first few symbols on my pad.

'Seems to end with the letter *d.'*

'Goyard,' I said, filling in the blanks and sketching the familiar design that adorned all the company's products. 'Probably the oldest trunk maker in existence. Nineteenth-century Parisian.'

'They teach you that at Wellesley, kid?' Mike said. 'Give me a broad with a little class, an inherited fortune, a lot of foreign travel to see her old flame, and I'll show you a prosecutor right in her element. Voilà. Could be the murderer's a French chef, with a suitcase full of carving knives, out to avenge a broken heart. I'm telling you, Coop's going to crack this case. She'll get her personal shopper right on it.'

I was trying to laugh at Mike's digs rather than take umbrage. I wondered whether he was back to his old ways of putting me down just to save face in front of Rocco Correlli, or if his extended vacation had cooled the affection he had finally expressed two months ago.

'Hard not to be noticed with a friggin' trunk,' Pug said.

'In the Waldorf Astoria? Everybody's wandering through the hallways with a wheeler bag,' the lieutenant said. 'What's this Goyard stuff, Alex?'

'Very pricey. Used by half the royals of Europe and tons of celebrities. The Duchess of Windsor never went anywhere without a flock of their steamer trunks. Luggage like that would be perfectly in place in the Tower suites, the bigger the better.'

'Too much trouble for a rape,' Mike said, waving me off.

'What is?'

'Let's say the girl was drugged. She was clearly someplace remote enough when that happened that this perv could have—'

'Or pervs,' Hal said.

'Whichever. They were able to stuff her into a huge trunk. Why not just rape her there, wherever they were? Wherever "there" was. Finish her off. Why all the drama of staging a scene in the Waldorf?'

'Because there's a much bigger picture, you think,' I said, following Mike's lead.

'Exactly. How fast can you solve that puzzle for the commissioner?'

'So if this is a one-off, we're looking for a serial killer – or a pair of them,' Mercer said, jotting notes in his steno pad. 'Bold setting, the Waldorf. It would be too intimidating for an amateur, so they've likely done this before. You've got to check all the big metro hotels around the country.'

'Maybe it has nothing to do with the fact that this is a fancy hotel,' Mike said. 'Maybe it's a political statement. The president on his way here. Some high-level meeting at the UN a month before the annual General Assembly deal in September. A chance for the killer to make big waves. To make a tsunami, actually.'

'Unlikely this has political blowback,' Rocco said, shaking his head. The presidential invitation and setup was last minute. 'The White House pooh-bahs are pulling the man back from his vacation in Yellowstone. Swept the reunion of brain surgeons or whatever hot-shit group had these rooms blocked off over to a downtown Marriott. If this murder was so well planned, it had to have been set in motion before this special session was confirmed. So there could be another target in the Waldorf. Could be a setup to embarrass some other head of state or business leader. I got two guys going over that list with the assistant manager right now. What we need is a make on the dead girl.'

'I'll have her stitched up for a photo you can use by tomorrow afternoon,' Johnny said.

Fareed Azeem came back into the room, removing his vinyl gloves and tossing his booties in the trash can.

'What can you give us, Dr Azeem?' the lieutenant asked.

'All indications are that the young lady died between two and three P.M. yesterday. Well within the time frame Johnny targeted, but I can pinpoint it to that hour, if that is of any help.'

'Tremendous help. That will streamline what we're looking at.'

'I might add, Mr McBride, that your team may have missed some blood in the room where the body was found.'

'Not likely, Doc,' Pug said defensively. 'Fine-tooth comb and all that. You found a stain you think they missed? Show me where.'

'Not a stain, sir, but rather a spot.'

'A spot? Get real, Doc.'

'A spot on one of the panels of the curtains.'

Rose-colored curtains draped the windows of the room. How could one see a microscopic amount of blood against that backdrop?

'I think the lab will have more than enough blood from the vic to work with.'

'It isn't her blood, Mr McBride. It might well be the killer's. It was left on the curtain at least an hour after the girl was slaughtered.'

Four

Rocco Correlli was on the phone with one of his sergeants who was downstairs in the IT center of the Waldorf with senior staff and a slew of detectives. 'We might have this narrowed down. You got two scenarios we're looking at. Get this right, Huey.'

Hugh Tatum must have asked for a minute to write things down.

'We got no clue when the girl came to the hotel. It's possible she was packed unconscious into a trunk or a crate,' Rocco continued. 'Might even be fancy luggage. One, two, three guys – don't know the size of the entourage. She died between two and three yesterday, and it's possible someone was still in the room with her an hour later. So from three P.M. on, look for luggage going out, assuming no one found anything yet in a stairwell or closet. Am I right? So you can start them watching tape from three P.M. on. Like hawks, got that?'

A uniformed cop ducked in from the hallway. He was a fresh face, reinforcements no doubt sent in from the

Seventeenth Precinct after eight P.M. 'Excuse me, Lieutenant Correlli? My boss said to tell you that Commissioner Scully is on his way to the hotel. Stand-up press conference in the lobby at twenty-two hundred.'

'Press conference my ass. Fifteen minutes? We got nothing to give them.'

'It's a zoo downstairs, Loo,' Mike said. 'Gotta feed them something.'

'You better tell me how your magic box works, Dr Azeem,' Rocco said. 'Make sure I understand it, *capisce?*'

Fareed Azeem cleared his throat and moved into position by the fireplace mantel, as though it was the front of a small classroom. 'As you all know, the identification of blood at a crime scene can be difficult to detect and certainly hard to rely on to pinpoint the time the bleed occurred, without months of laboratory analysis.'

'And this is what you've tried to do right there in the room?'

'Yes, Lieutenant. The techniques currently in use are actually a century old. Instead, our project involves hyper-spectral imaging—'

'Explain that to me. I have to sell it to the media in a few minutes.'

'Certainly. So this imaging is done by a liquid-crystal filter – a tunable filter – that can provide immediate results.'

'How?' Mike said.

'The filter isolates different wavelength bands within every color. And because blood changes color over time

– from a bright crimson to a very dull brown – our device is able to put an exact age to a sample.'

'This works in the UK? This wavelength band isolation?' Rocco asked. 'Your murder teams use it?'

Fareed looked at the floor. 'I remind you that this is a prototype machine. We're still field-testing it. We've had remarkable levels of accuracy at home.'

'That's what Johnny meant when he asked me if I was in for a forensic adventure,' I said.

Rocco removed a cigarette and matches from his jacket pocket and lit it. 'So I'm a test case? Let's leave your best guess out of the equation.'

'No smoking in here, Loo,' Pug said. 'The manager reminded me.'

'I'm fresh out of heartburn medication, McBride. This is all I've got to calm my nerves.'

'Scully knows this is a crapshoot,' Mike said. 'He's gonna want to go with it.'

'What got your inner circle access back, Chapman? Last I knew you were headed for the rubber gun squad.'

Mike answered the lieutenant but looked at me. 'It's the latest thing, Loo, or hadn't you heard? They try to rehabilitate miscreants these days. Give us a second chance. Were you hoping they'd administer a lethal injection?'

Pug chuckled. 'Yeah, a quart of vodka.'

'It's Scully himself who brought Mike into this,' Mercer said. 'Once the medical examiner got word to him tonight that Professor Azeem was lecturing at Columbia this week and had this very promising device, he sent Mike to pick Azeem up and get him to you.'

The Manhattan North Homicide offices were uptown, much closer to the Columbia University campus than the South detectives or even the hotel scene. Keith Scully and Mike Chapman went way back together. It made sense that Scully would find a way to ease one of his smartest detectives into action again. This couldn't be Mike's case to run with, because his official assignment was the North, but he would be a valuable asset to have on a high-profile murder investigation.

'So Scully's got your back, huh? On loan to me for this nightmare?'

'I'm not working a full tour, Loo. My mother's in the hospital.'

I took a deep breath, anxious to ask why Mike hadn't told me.

'If I may break in,' Fareed said, 'I think the blood spot is an important factor. Perhaps every bit as important as the time of death. Not for the public, perhaps, but to inform the commissioner.'

'Yeah,' Pug said, scoffing at the reserved chemist. 'Was it like a spot or a speck? Scully's gonna wanna put his job on the line for that tidbit.'

'Tell me about it,' Rocco said.

'When your men worry about missing something with the naked eye, they paint the suspected area with luminol. It reacts with the iron in hemoglobin to produce a visible result.'

Television forensics had imparted that information to every viewer of *SVU* or *CSI*.

'But they missed a small area on the curtains today, which happens often when the fabric is in the very range of blood colors. These were what you might call rose. I imagine they just overlooked that area of ·the room as unimportant or uninvolved, since there was already so much blood on the bed and body.'

'So your camera scans the entire scene for the presence of blood?' I asked.

'Precisely. That avoids the assumptions that humans make, just applying the luminol where they expect to find evidence connected to the crime.'

'We may have enough of the killer's blood to work up a DNA sample?'

'That would be my hope, Ms Cooper. If the murder weapon is as sharp as Dr Mayes described, he may have just nicked his finger on it while packing up to leave.'

'Let Scully sit on that factoid. He shouldn't give it out to the public,' Rocco said, jabbing his cigarette at Fareed. 'I'd like you, Pug, and Mercer to come downstairs with me to stand with the commissioner. Don't open your mouth unless I tell you to.'

Pug nodded. Mercer didn't need any instructions in dealing with the media. His dignity and wisdom had guided me through every hot-spot situation we'd encountered together.

'And you, Chapman,' Rocco said, pointing his cigarette tip, 'keep out of the limelight.'

'I'm a new man.'

'I kind of liked the old one,' I said.

'What do you say, Loo? Welcome to our world, right? Probably the first time there's ever been a murder at the Waldorf, wouldn't you think?' Pug asked, straightening his shirt collar and reknotting his tie.

'Fifth,' Mike said. 'Best I can tell.'

Mike had an encyclopedic knowledge of the city's crime history, almost as thorough as the amount of military history he had absorbed throughout his youth and in his studies at Fordham University. His father, Brian, had been a tremendously respected homicide detective who died of a massive coronary within twenty-four hours of turning in his badge and gun. Brian had taken Mike, his only son, to crime scenes and on ride-alongs in unmarked cars as early as Mike could remember.

'Back in '82 there was a bank executive killed in a stairwell. Robbery gone bad, and boy did she bleed like a stuck pig. My dad caught the squeal. I'm not sure anyone was ever charged with that. And in '99 a tourist – from Brazil, I think – had his throat slashed by someone he brought back to the room with him after a week of gambling in Atlantic City. Known perp.'

'A slasher?' Rocco asked. 'Better have someone pull those files tomorrow. Never can tell.'

'Not even close, Loo,' Mike said. 'This was an execution.'

'Call Huey for me, will you, Mercer? Let's get a plan for the midnight tour and tomorrow morning.'

Mercer called Sergeant Tatum and told him to get up

to the command center, while Rocco began handing out assignments. 'What have you got in the morning, Alex?'

'I have to see Battaglia at eight thirty.' That appointment hadn't been made yet, but the district attorney would want as complete an update as I could give him before he started his day. 'Then a quick court appearance. I'm all yours by ten fifteen.'

'I want you to work out of the hotel. I'm going to run this right here.'

'Makes sense.'

'The sergeant will be up in five,' Mercer said. 'I'll meet Alex here in the morning and we'll handle this together.'

I looked at Mike to jump in with us, but he was staring at the lieutenant.

'You two are on the sex crimes angle,' Rocco said. 'Every contact you have in the other boroughs and across the country, every cold case you can get your hands on, every parolee who's hit the streets in the last year, every junkie who's AWOL from his program. And, Alex, look into every one of those trunks that's been sold – when, where, to whom.'

He searched in vain for an ashtray, then tapped the ashes from his cigarette into a vase of flowers.

'Hugh will oversee all the employee and guest interviews. Night Watch will kick in at midnight, and by morning we'll have help from all the local squads. As long as it takes. Any of the weepy broads – I can't stomach that stuff – anyone squirrelly or acting nuts we'll sweep right over to you, Alex. You'll have backup?'

'I'll reach out for someone tonight. Not a problem.'

'Pug, I'll throw you all the support you can handle. You'll have four guys around the clock with you for starters. More if Scully gives me what I ask for. Homicidal maniacs from here to Nome, anything that smells like this, you find 'em. Call in chits on any snitches you've got,' Rocco said. 'Who owns this joint anyway?'

'It's part of the Hilton chain, I think,' Mercer said.

'Get their lawyers in on this. Any litigation? Anybody trying to sabotage this place for commercial reasons?'

The uniformed cop stepped back into the doorway. 'Excuse me, Lieutenant Correlli? Just got word that the commissioner is about to pull up on the Lexington Avenue side. You're to head downstairs to Peacock Alley to brief him.'

'A briefing in a bar,' Pug said. 'Off and running.'

'Johnny? Professor? Anyone have anything to add?'

'The commissioner would like you to bring Ms Cooper, too,' the cop said.

'I – uh – I can't say anything to the press, Rocco. Battaglia would have my head. There's no point in taking me down with you.'

'You know Scully as well as I do, Alex. He doesn't want to be hanging out there all alone. He just wants the visual of you standing behind him. If anything gets screwed up,' Rocco said, smiling at me as he plunged his cigarette tip-down between the stems of the yellow roses, 'he can always say the district attorney was leading the charge.'

'He won't need Coop to take the fall,' Mike said. 'If

you haven't solved this within forty-eight hours, the feds will be in here, setting up shop for the president's pilgrimage. You want to see a complete professional fuckup? Put the feebies to work on a homicide.'

Five

Keith Scully stood at the makeshift podium in the fashionable lobby of the five-star hotel. He was an enormously well-respected commissioner who had risen through the ranks to the top job, keeping the admiration and affection of most of his men along the way. He was about my height – five ten – with the ramrod-straight bearing of an ex-marine. His short-cropped hair had grayed throughout his tenure, and he tolerated far less nonsense now than he had in his youth.

Rocco Correlli was a step back, at the commissioner's right shoulder. Pug, Mercer, and I stood several paces behind both of them and off to the side, where I attempted to keep out of camera range while the focus was on Scully.

The deputy commissioner for Public Information, Guido Lentini, was trying to control the unruly crowd of reporters who had surged past the patrol guards on Park Avenue and up the staircase to the lobby. We all knew the locals from print and broadcast well; most had a long familiarity with police work and knew how to ask questions and when to mine their favorite detectives for well-placed leaks. Others were drawn in from feature work about traffic accidents and consumer frauds and limited their inquiries to the color of the deceased's hair and whether next of kin had been notified.

This group was unusual. I recognized some national reporters, cable and network, thrown into the mix, perhaps anticipating that this was more than a gruesome street crime.

'When you guys settle down,' DCPI Lentini called out, 'the commissioner will get started.'

One of the reporters had slipped off to my side, whispering into his microphone as his cameraman scanned the art deco interior and the carefully placed potted palms lining the gilded archways into the main lobby. He seemed to be doing a setup for tomorrow's *NBC Nightly News,* talking to Brian Williams, in case the story grew into a national one.

'We're here, Brian, in the historic Waldorf Astoria – an early New York City skyscraper built over the air rights of the New York Central Railroad – yes, the train tracks run directly below us on Park Avenue to all points north of the city – and opened in 1931. It's actually the second site of the famed hotel,' the young man said, vamping to fill time while other teams elbowed for space, setting up tripods and mikes. 'If you know your history, Brian, you'll recall that it was an Astor family feud that led to the construction of the original Waldorf-Astoria, on the site of what is now the Empire State Building, Fifth Avenue at 33rd Street.'

The reporter looked around to see if Scully was ready to speak. The commissioner was listening to Rocco Correlli, who moments ago in the empty bar had given him a quick rundown – more of what we didn't know than what we did – and was now whispering something else in his ear.

'William Waldorf Astor built his swank establishment in 1893, naming it the Waldorf, next door to his aunt's home after a nasty battle with her, and when she moved away it was her son – John Jacob Astor IV, later to perish on the *Titanic* – who replaced her mansion with the Astoria Hotel. There was only a tiny strip of pavement, known as Peacock Alley, which separated the two structures, so the cousins soon after joined them together to create the Waldorf-Astoria, which at the time became the world's largest hotel and the very first to offer room service to its upscale clientele.'

Scully stepped to the microphone and silenced the press corps.

'Brian,' the reporter whispered as he turned to face the podium, 'Commissioner Keith Scully, after a briefing in Peacock Alley – now a bar in this legendary venue – is ready to tell us about this most unusual murder, in the Waldorf Towers, a boutique hotel within a hotel, on the eve of a presidential visit.'

I couldn't think what made this homicide unusual, except to someone who had never covered crime stories in Manhattan. People had been killed in every landmark location from Central Park to Madison Square Garden to the Metropolitan Opera House at Lincoln Center. The stories rarely made national headlines – housing projects, school playgrounds and abandoned buildings held no interest for news desk editors – unless the victim was prominent or the setting was one that resonated with the rest of America.

'Good evening, ladies and gentlemen,' Scully said, beginning with the routine assurances about the safety of the Waldorf Astoria and the full cooperation of management and staff.

He might have been talking about another body than the one I saw. The unidentified victim had been stabbed in the neck. No need to alarm the public by disclosing that her throat was slit from ear to ear. Uncertain about how she came to be in the Waldorf. Uncertain about which day and what time she died. Uncertain about whether she had anything to do with the hotel itself, either as a former employee or regular guest.

'How about a photo of the lady, Commish?' a tabloid reporter yelled out. 'What'd she look like? How old is she?'

'You'll have that tomorrow afternoon.'

'How long was she registered at the hotel?' another voice called from the back of the pack.

'There is no evidence that she was a registered guest this week.'

'A hooker, maybe?' That was the *New York Post*'s veteran crime reporter, Mickey Diamond.

The NBC correspondent's jaw dropped when he heard the question. The city's crime beat set the low bar for gentility.

Keith Scully gave Diamond his best 'drop dead' expression and pointed to one of the women who'd been sent by MSNBC.

'What do you intend to tell White House officials in preparation for the president's upcoming stay here?'

'That the Waldorf Astoria is the safest place in town. I'd be more worried about the grizzlies in Yellowstone than the likelihood of running into anything dangerous in New York. That we hope to have this matter solved within days. We're asking for everyone's help, in calling the TIPS hotline and remaining anonymous if you choose to do that. The hotel is offering a' – Scully looked off to the right at the management representative to confirm the amount – 'a one-hundred-thousand-dollar reward for information leading to an arrest.'

'Is that all?' Mickey Diamond shouted. 'Mr Hilton can do better. And would you tell us, Commissioner Scully, if the lady was sexually assaulted? We got a serial rapist on the loose?'

'This is a homicide, Diamond. That's all you need for now. OCME will conduct an autopsy tomorrow.'

I knew Scully's thinking. This news would be shocking enough. Let the medical examiner deal with the more sordid crime elements before making the panic message public. He was about to step down from the podium.

'But you've got Ms Cooper warming up in the wings, Scully,' Diamond continued. 'Is there something you're not telling us?'

Keith Scully stopped himself in time to grab my elbow,

rather than leave me alone and stupefied in the spotlights, and escort me off the platform, signaling to the corps that this was his last statement for the evening. 'Battaglia sent us his on-call bureau chief. Just happens to be Ms Cooper. We're ready for anything.'

Uniformed cops led the commissioner, Pug, Mercer and me through the hastily assembled group of reporters, past a few dozen startled hotel guests who were being questioned by detectives as they emerged from elevators, and took us back into Peacock Alley. At this hour, the stately room would normally be full of thirsty New Yorkers, throwing back late-night martinis or dining on the signature Waldorf salad. But the NYPD had closed down the chic bar early, depriving the hotel of a significant amount of revenue – as this entire tragedy would doubtlessly do. I looked wistfully at the bottles of Scotch lined up behind the empty bar.

'Anything else to do tonight, Alexandra?' Scully asked. His next meeting would be with his top commanders and the mayor.

'Just a late supper and a good night's sleep. Rocco gave us all our marching orders.'

'I'm taking off. See you tomorrow.'

Scully's security detail guided him out through the lobby, past the windows of the expensive jewelry store within the hotel – the scene of an armed robbery a few years back – and down the escalator toward Lexington Avenue.

As soon as he was out of the way, Sergeant Tatum began to usher in those of his men who were interviewing guests, turning Peacock Alley into a makeshift squad room. Several gents in black tie were separated and taken to tables in the rear, while two young couples dressed for a casual summer city night were squawking about being inconvenienced by the police stop.

I waited till Pug busied himself with some of his colleagues before taking Mercer aside.

'Where does a girl go to get a drink around here?'

'I hear you.'

'I'm not sure I could put down any food after that scene upstairs, but I'm having a nightcap here or at home.'

'This place isn't an option. Start walking.'

We took the same route as the commissioner. The reporters had all scattered to the sidewalk on Park – a far more scenic shot – to do their stand-ups beneath the glittering gold lettering of the hotel name carved into the stone facade, flanked by two giant American flags.

Mercer got on the down escalator backward, looking up at me as he rode to the ground floor. 'Mike's waiting for us at Patroon. At the rooftop bar.'

I tossed my head back to avoid locking eyes with Mercer.

'It's his mother, Alex. He flew home early because she's in the hospital.'

Mercer was Mike's best friend. They had worked together in homicide for years, until Mercer asked for a transfer to Special Victims. Like me, he enjoyed trying to put the pieces back together, restore dignity to those witnesses least likely to expect it from the system, and see them triumph in a court of law.

Mike, on the other hand, held his emotions close. It

was more natural for him to unravel the mysteries surrounding a dead man's dilemma than to try to comfort someone alive but traumatized by an assailant.

I bit my lip and nodded that I understood.

'You think he dissed you? Is that it?'

Still on the long descent to street level, I could look straight ahead and not make eye contact because Mercer was below me on the moving staircase. 'It's been almost two months.'

'Then think how Mike feels. Gets a very public whooping from the department,' he said, glancing over his shoulder to step off the moving staircase, 'just when he's breaking a major case that seemed impossible to crack.'

The hot air blasted my face like the exhaust from an oven when we walked onto Lexington Avenue. Patroon, my favorite restaurant, was a short walk – only three blocks from the Waldorf – with the most fantastic rooftop bar that was truly an oasis on a steamy Manhattan evening.

'For some reason, Mercer, he turned a three-week rip into a two-month odyssey abroad.'

'Feeling sorry for yourself, Ms Cooper? Sounds like a slight whine dripping into that sultry, rarely-on-the-losing-side-of-an-argument, jury-box delivery.'

'But—'

'When's he ever going to get a chance – or the time – for a trip like that?'

'Not till he retires, I guess.'

'And that's a word you can't say to him.' Brian Chapman had been determined to see that his son had a college education and didn't wind up in uniform. Within twenty-four hours of retiring, he died of a massive coronary. Mike got his degree but immediately applied to the NYPD and started at the academy. Police work was as much a part of his DNA as the physical traits he inherited.

'Ten years of carefully balancing our relationship, I go out on a limb and all I wound up doing with Romeo was having a go at footsie in a rowboat, chaperoned by half of Manhattan North and a flotilla of EMTs.'

'The man is all nervous about you. You get that, don't you?'

'About *me*?' I reached out and grabbed Mercer's handkerchief, dabbing my own forehead after he wiped his brow.

'Other-side-of-the-tracks thing going on. Upstairs, downstairs. Mike's blue-collar as far back as the family tree roots grow in county Cork, and you've got a trust fund that so far as I can tell could have helped with the Louisiana Purchase.'

'*Et tu*, Mercer? That really stings.'

He pulled me back to the curb as a taxi swerved toward us when I tried to cross Lex against the light.

Mercer knew my family well. My maternal grandfather had been a fireman, and my mother – descended from Finnish immigrants who were farmers – had been a nursing student with a great head for medicine, green eyes that caught everyone's attention, and long legs that she passed on to me. My father, Benjamin – whose ancestors had fled Russia a century ago – was a brilliant physician who, with his partner, had invented a plastic tubing device that was used worldwide in a certain type of cardiac surgery. The Cooper-Hoffman valve had been a godsend to patients and had provided my family with a financial cushion that not only paid for my college education, as well as that of my brothers', but also allowed me the privilege of dedicating a legal career to public service.

'Just sayin', Mike's finding it all a bit intimidating.'

'It's not like he doesn't know me better than I know myself.'

'Hey, girl. Vickee and I assumed you'd road tested and rejected all the warm and fuzzy types, the Latin lovers like Luc who *darling*'ed you to death. You have deliberately chosen new territory. Going Wolverine on us. Brooding, moody, and pound for pound the toughest creature out in the wild. You ought to realize you've settled on the most solitary animal I know. Anybody else in your world live in a black box?'

Mike's studio apartment, not very far from the high-rise co-op in which I lived, was such a tiny walk-up – dark and short on décor – that he had long ago dubbed it 'the coffin'.

We were approaching the front of Patroon. The owners, Ken and Di Aretsky, were dear friends of mine who made us comfortable whenever we arrived, and I had a mad crush on Stephane, the maître d' who saw to it that my glass was never empty.

'Why is it we women always think we can change guys?'

Mercer pulled open the heavy red door. 'I know you

like a challenge, Alex, but there'll be no turning this dude into something he isn't.'

The super-efficient hostess, Annie, kissed me on both cheeks before turning me over to Stephane, whose French accent charmed all comers. 'Very late for you two, no?' he asked. 'Monsieur Chapman is waiting for you on the roof. Ça va?'

'Très bien, Stephane,' I said, as he led us to the small elevator.

On the fourth-floor rooftop, a smartly designed space featuring an enormous wraparound bar cooled by a canopy holding large overhead fans, Mike was in an animated conversation with Ken Aretsky. The gaggle of thirtysome-things that made this site such a popular attraction was still three deep, many of them sipping pastel-colored confections while hatching hookup plans.

'This looks too serious for me,' Ken said, holding up both hands and yielding his stool to me as Mercer and I approached. 'Mike was just telling me about the murder. You three have your work cut out for you.'

Ken caught the bartender's attention and circled his finger in our direction before tapping his chest. The first round was his treat. He moved on to greet other customers as we started to talk.

'Dewar's on the rocks for me,' I said.

'Double down on Blondie's drink, will you?' Mike said, ordering another Ketel One martini for himself and one for Mercer.

I had an elbow on the tall mahogany bar, and Mike stood

a foot away, his back against the brick wall of the building.

'I want to explain—'

'Not necessary,' I said to him, watching the bartender pour.

'Peace between you two before I get back from the men's room, okay?' Mercer said, walking away.

Mike reached for my hand and turned me toward him. He crooked his forefinger and wiggled it, summoning me to come closer to him.

I laughed. 'You actually think I'll respond to your silent commands?'

'It used to work for me. Have I lost my touch?' Mike put his hands on my arms and drew me toward him, picking my head up to kiss me on the mouth.

I broke away and smiled, licking my lips. 'They make a good martini here. Do I only get that little taste?'

He pulled me close again and we kissed. Then I rested my head against his chest.

'I've missed you, Mike. Seven weeks is a long time.'

'For me, too. I didn't mean to put you in the middle of things tonight. In the hotel suite with Rocco and the guys, to just show up like that. Scully sniffed me out, heard I'd come back to town and—'

'I get it. I didn't think you were flying in until Friday, so I was just totally off guard. We still on for Saturday?' As much as I didn't want to be the one asking that question about our long-awaited romantic dinner, I was too anxious about the time gone by not to know.

'Sure we are. Sure,' he said, stroking my hair, which had

curled into ringlets around my neck. 'It may be sandwiches in the squad room till Pug collars the bastard who did this, but—'

'Your mother,' I said, pushing back. 'Tell me about your mother. That's the most important thing.'

'She's going to be okay. Bad scare, and my sisters called me to come home.'

'What is it? Her heart again?'

'Yeah, it's the ticker. Aortic fibrillation.'

'You should have let me know. I would have been happy to take a shift by her bedside.' Growing up as a cardiac surgeon's daughter, I probably knew as much about A-fib as any amateur. And I adored Mike's mother, to whom he was devoted.

Mike smiled his best grin at me. 'She'd have liked that, Coop. I just didn't think to do it. No surgery, though. They just changed her meds. Another forty-eight hours in ICU to monitor her and she goes home. You can call her next week.'

Mercer was making his way back to our side of the bar. We picked up our glasses to clink against his.

'That's a happier sight,' Mercer said as I stepped out of Mike's embrace. 'I almost hate to break it up.'

'Don't be silly,' I said, savoring the cold shot of Scotch and thinking of a warm night on top of the Arsenal in the park. 'I just needed a little TLC from Detective Chapman. Rooftops are a good place for us, don't you think?'

'I wasn't afraid of intruding on your intimacy, Alex. I just had a call from Pug. A couple of transit cops found some derelicts hauling around a beat-up piece of luggage, a couple of blocks from the hotel, on Madison Avenue. It's big and it's empty—'

'Anything inside? Any potential evidence?' Mike asked.

'Seems to have been doused with Clorox or some kind of bleach, the kind of thing that would destroy any residue of DNA or prints.'

Mike swallowed more vodka. 'I'm traveling with you, Mercer. Where'd they find it?'

'The Northwest Passage.'

I knew he wasn't talking about the open sea route through the Arctic from the Atlantic to the Pacific. 'Where's that?'

'You spend entirely too much time in turban town,' Mike said, referring in his politically incorrect way to the headdress of many of the city's yellow cab drivers. 'Public transportation wouldn't kill you, you know.'

'It's the northeast corner of 47th and Madison,' Mercer said. 'A thousand-foot-long corridor that leads to Grand Central.'

'And to the subways going in every direction out of this hood,' Mike said. 'However the killer got this broad into the Waldorf, I'd say he's comfortably on his way back home.'

'But it sounds like he left us a trophy,' I said, referring to the trunk.

'What are the odds it's of no forensic value?' Mike asked. 'Saddle up, Mercer, and let's check it out. Northwest Passage to nowhere.'

Six

Mike and Mercer walked me to my SUV, which I'd parked between Patroon and the Waldorf. The drive home took only six minutes. I used the interior staircase to get into the lobby from the garage, picked up my mail, and said good night to the two doormen on duty.

It was late enough, almost midnight, to forget topping off the night with a cocktail, since I'd left most of mine behind on the bar. But my empty stomach was growling and the liquor was likely to knock me out and prevent nightmarish flashbacks to the image of the young woman in the hotel suite.

A hot shower, no matter the weather, always helped to wash away the detritus of the day. I scrubbed myself, then toweled off and carried my drink into the bedroom.

I often had trouble sleeping, but never more so than after witnessing the kind of brutality I'd seen today. Soft music, relaxing scents, an excess of alcohol, and even the knowledge that I would be working around the clock until this case was solved rarely calmed me enough to do the job. I was fearful of dreaming, fearful of where my subconscious would take me. Eventually, though, I stopped tossing and nodded off.

I was out of bed before six, showered again – cool water this time – to get a fresh start on the day.

It was early enough for me to have a car service take me to Bay Ridge, wait for me while I ran in to say hello to Mike's mother in the Lutheran Medical Center, and then deposit me downtown at the DA's office well before Battaglia would be in for his briefing. I dialed the service and asked for a pickup in twenty minutes.

I dressed, made a cup of coffee, and toasted the last remaining piece of food in my refrigerator – an English muffin. There would be no flowers allowed in the intensive care unit, so I sketched a bouquet on a note card with an IOU for a dozen roses to be delivered when Mrs Chapman got home.

The newspapers were on my doorstep and I picked them up on my way out to read in the black car on the way to Brooklyn. The *Post*, never known for its good taste, had a banner headline: ASTORIA HYSTERIA – WALDORF TOWERS TRAGEDY. No surprise that I had to dig inside the Metro pages of the *Times'* first section to find a story, below the fold, about the body on the forty-fifth floor of the landmark hotel.

Someone had managed to leak a few details to the *Daily News* reporter – either a hotel staffer or one of the first responders: SLASHER SOUGHT IN SOCIETY HOTEL. The article had a grisly account of the victim as I saw her – deep wide slit in her throat, bathed in blood, and completely naked. I dropped the papers to the floor of the car.

I emailed Mike and Mercer, without telling them about my surprise detour. I asked what they had learned about the abandoned trunk, in preparation for my meeting with Battaglia.

Shortly before the car pulled up in front of the medical center, Mercer replied. *Trunk is at least sixty years old. Sort of a burgundy leather exterior, with brass fittings. Must have been pretty snazzy once. Interior has that name brand you mentioned in a few scattered places, but the bleach wiped out most of the design. It's at the lab now. By the way, reported stolen a week ago, with all its contents. From the Yale Club, on Vanderbilt Avenue, just a few blocks from the Northwest Passage.*

Those facts saved me the exercise of finding out when and by whom the trunk was bought. It would be easier for the cops to interview the Yale alum to learn how it went missing.

I told the driver that I didn't expect to be in the hospital more than fifteen minutes. There weren't many visitors in the rotunda when I entered, so I stopped at the desk and asked for the ICU. The only people in the elevator with me were medical personnel who appeared to be changing shifts.

I pushed through the two heavy doors to the unit. There was an administrator at the nurses' station, sitting amid the beeping and flashing monitors.

'Good morning. I'd just like to say hello to Mrs Chapman, if she's awake.'

'Mrs Who?'

'Chapman. Margaret Chapman. I'll be really quick. I just want to give her a hug and leave this note.'

The woman lowered her reading glasses and scanned the patient names on her clipboard.

'Honey, I hate to ruin your morning, but we don't have any Mrs Chapman.'

'But she was here last evening. Admitted a couple of days ago. She didn't—?' The word stuck in my throat. What if something had happened to her during the night?

'This is my fourth midnight shift in a row. There's been no Mrs Chapman in ICU. She didn't die. She didn't disappear,' the woman said, shaking her head at me as she scrolled down the computerized list of names on her desk. 'Hon, she just never was in this hospital.'

Seven

I was sitting in the anteroom of Paul Battaglia's office by 8:10 A.M. Even Rose Malone, his trusted executive assistant and my good friend was not in yet. I started up the large coffeepot and tried to control the range of emotions that had overtaken me with the thought that Mike had betrayed me.

Rose was only a few minutes behind me. 'I just spoke to the boss, Alex. He'll be on time for your meeting.'

'Thanks so much,' I said, pouring a mug for each of us.

'It's going to be another brutal day, isn't it? And you've got this horrible new case.'

She didn't waste a minute setting up the papers on her desk and triaging them for Battaglia's attention.

'Yes. He wants to be brought up to speed.'

'Go on in and turn on the lights. I'll hold all his calls.'

I settled into the wooden chair opposite Battaglia's over-sized desk. The original campaign poster from his first run for DA more than six terms ago occupied the wall space behind his desk. The slogan 'You Can't Play Politics with People's Lives' had become rather oxymoronic, since the man spent much of his day doing exactly that. His plush green leather armchair beneath the poster was a reminder that he expected to be more comfortable than anyone sitting where I was, in the position across from him.

I smelled the district attorney's cigar before I heard him trumpet his greeting to Rose. No one was actually sure whether he brushed his teeth at night or just kept the last expensive Cohiba of the day clenched in his mouth until he got out of bed.

'Who did Scully think he was fooling by not answering the question about rape at the press conference?' Battaglia said as he entered the room.

'Just trying to keep the reporters out of the trash bins till the ME confirms the findings. The guys are also trying to figure whether it's a known perp and if she had sex before she was killed. Always that possibility.'

'Glad you kept your mouth shut, Alex.'

Of course he was. Battaglia got credit for having one of his troops visible, in the fray early on, but no chance for a misquote yet.

'I had nothing to say, Paul.'

'What don't I know?'

I described the scene in the hotel room to him, told him about Fareed Azeem, dropped in the fact that Mike Chapman was back in play, let him know Johnny Mayes's theory about the trunk, the late-night discovery of the luggage, and the fact that it was stolen from the Yale Club.

'Holding back on anything?' the district attorney asked me, one hand poised on his telephone.

Battaglia wanted a juicy tidbit to dangle in front of the mayor. He would ask Rose to dial City Hall before I was ten feet away, just to show how in touch he was with events.

'You've got it all. I'll be working out of the Waldorf for the next few days. I'm going to grab Ryan Blackmer to second seat me on this.'

'Regular updates, okay?'

I walked out the door, told Rose where I'd be, and headed across the corridor to my office. Laura Wilkie, my longtime secretary, was already fielding calls.

'I guess you never made it to dinner with your law school buddies last night, did you? I saw you behind Scully on the late news.'

'Slight detour on the way to the restaurant.' Five of my closest friends from the University of Virginia tried to meet once a month. Tales from the civilized lands of mergers and acquisitions, corporate litigation, estate planning and mogul management were occasionally trumped by an intrusive felony.

'Did you ever get fed?'

'Watered is more like it. I'll survive.'

'You've already got some messages,' Laura said, following me to my desk and handing me the slips with numbers written out. 'And Mike, too. You must be glad he's back in town.'

'Over the moon,' I said. I knew my dry delivery would

disappoint Laura, who was Moneypenny to Mike's droll James Bond imitation.

'Guess I'll keep my nose out of that one,' she said. 'Do you have plans for the day, after the nine thirty court appearance?'

'Setting up shop with Mercer and Pug at the hotel. Could you please hunt down Ryan and see if he's available to work with me on this case? And ready me a folder to take along when I leave. Ask Catherine and Marisa to check cold cases for a throat-slitting rapist, maybe someone who sketches ladders on the bodies.'

'A fireman? A house painter?'

I groaned.

'Just trying to be useful.'

'I count on that. Tell them, too, to start checking SVUs in all the big cities for anything like this. A guy who might conceal a body in a piece of luggage.'

'I didn't see that fact in the *Times*.'

'Keep up with the tabloids online. They'll get the best leaks.'

'Will do.'

'Check with McKinney's secretary. Find out when he's back from vacation.'

My direct supervisor, chief of the Trial Division, was a prickly colleague named Pat McKinney. A total ass-kisser to the district attorney, he was most often found at my back, ready to plunge a knife if he thought I was being favored by the boss.

'You're good for two more weeks.'

I smiled at Laura. 'That's a relief.'

I gathered the case file and got on my way to the thirteenth-floor courtroom of Judge Alvin Aikens. He'd been newly appointed by the governor and was still feeling his way through the practicalities of his judicial role, after more than two decades as a Legal Aid attorney.

The large room was practically empty when I walked in at 9:25 A.M. The defendant, Gerardo Dominguez, was seated in the front row beside his mother. He was dressed in a dark suit and tie. Like many of the psychos I had prosecuted for sexual assault, the thirty-two-year-old looked benign and respectable when not searching cyberspace for his prey.

I took my seat at counsel table in the well of the courtroom. My adversary, David Drusin, was also prompt. He slapped his client on the back and ushered him to the defense table. I took Dominguez's measure, since it was the first time I saw him in person, and turned away only when he met my stare with a smile.

'All rise,' the chief court officer said. 'The Honorable Alvin Aikens entering.'

Aikens took the bench, signaling us to be seated. He appeared still to be self-conscious in his black robe, tugging at its folds as he pulled his chair into place.

'Ms Cooper, Mr Drusin. Good to see you both. You'll forgive me if I haven't quite found my groove yet.'

'Just so long as you don't let the district attorney walk all over you, sir. Those spikes she's got on can leave quite an impression on your rib cage.'

'Mr Drusin doesn't tread so lightly, either, Your Honor. I'm sure we'll all do fine.'

'Shall we call the case into the record?'

The clerk leaned back in his chair. 'People of the State of New York against Gerardo Dominguez.'

'You may sit down, Mr Dominguez,' the judge said. 'Counsel, would you two like to come up and discuss this with me.'

Drusin started to move to the bench.

'Actually, Your Honor,' I said. 'I'd like all of this to be on the record. No disrespect intended, but it's not the proper case for a sidebar.'

'Jesus, Alex,' Drusin said, slapping his palm on the table directly in front of his client. 'Why does it always have to be hardball?'

The court stenographer threw up her hands. 'What is it, guys? Are we on or off?'

'On, please. This isn't hardball, Mr Drusin. It's just that there will be no secrets on this one.'

'What have we got here?' the judge asked.

'It's an arraignment. It's an unsealing of an indictment on the charges of Conspiracy to Commit the Crime of Kidnap in the First Degree and Illegal Access of a New York State Database.'

'Just a chance for Alex to grandstand, sir. I'm sure she's alerted the press hounds to be here any minute now.'

'I arranged your client's surrender, didn't I? No media, no perp walk. Totally under the radar. There's not a prayer of a reporter showing up here.'

'What's the fuss, then?' the judge asked. 'Sounds like serious enough charges. Let's get Mr Dominguez arraigned and then you two can go at it.'

The clerk read the charges from the indictment, now public record. Dominguez pulled on the collar of his shirt and shifted his feet. When asked how he pleaded, he opened his mouth and practically shouted, 'Not guilty.'

'Are you requesting bail, Ms Cooper?'

'Yes, Your Honor. We're asking for one hundred thousand dollars.'

'Have you lost your mind, Alex?' Drusin said, now feigning total outrage. 'Judge Aikens, my client is a police officer.'

'What?'

'He's a cop. Gerry's a cop. Ten years on the job.'

'Suspended, as of the unsealing of this indictment, Judge. Suspended without pay.'

'He's got roots in the community, then, wouldn't you say? Family?'

David Drusin flung his left arm in the direction of Dominguez's mother. 'Right here in court with him. He's got an eighteen-month-old baby to support. His father's sick—'

'The baby lives with him? He's got a wife?'

'Mr Dominguez has a lovely wife, Your Honor,' I said. 'Unfortunately for him, she's the complaining witness in my case. She has the baby and she's in a very safe place for the moment, but I'd like the bail set to ensure his return to face these charges.'

'What's the allegation, Ms Cooper?'

'Judge,' David Drusin jumped in. 'I've got to object. There's no need to make a spectacle of this man. May we approach?'

Alvin Aikens motioned for Drusin to step up, but I held my ground. 'The courtroom is empty, but for the defendant's mother, the arresting officer, and some stragglers from the rest of your calendar. Both the district attorney and the police commissioner have asked that all of our remarks be recorded.'

Aikens didn't know which way to go. 'What are you charging? Where are the coconspirators, Ms Cooper?'

'Mr Dominguez is a sexual sadist, Judge. He has been seeking advice online and then communicating with two others who were arrested last evening – one in Westchester County and the other on Long Island – about how to abduct, torture, rape—'

'Don't say it, Alex, okay?' Drusin interrupted. 'You sound nuts. Leave it off the record for now.'

'Wait a minute. Your client's trolling online for live victims to boil in oil and I'm nuts?' I said. 'Judge Aikens, what Mr Drusin would rather whisper in your ear is that Dominguez was conspiring to rape, kill, cook and eat the women he targeted.'

The judge took a deep breath, Dominguez clasped his hands together and looked at his shoes, while behind me I could hear his mother sobbing. Most perps had a family full of collateral victims.

'Are you serious?' Aikens asked. 'You think you can prove this?'

'Your Honor, Alba Dominguez was one of her husband's intended victims. It is she who found the evidence on their home computer, in Washington Heights. Hundreds of photographs of dead and mutilated women—'

'He's a police officer, Judge. They're crime scene photos.'

'The defendant walks a beat on the Lower East Side. They're not his work product, if that's the angle you're taking. There are scores of pictures of women being sexually assaulted, there are chats – we have all the transcripts of them – that have sickening details of what these three men planned on doing, and there are even recipes that involve the preparation of human meat.'

'We're talking thought control here, Your Honor. Alexandra Cooper is the standard-bearer for what men are allowed to think? If that's the case, it's going to be a pretty restricted airspace, because her view of sexual norms must be as healthy as someone who's lived a lifetime in a cave,' Drusin said, thoroughly wound up in his spin. 'Maybe Ms Cooper doesn't understand that men – that men, uh – like to fantasize, and in the privacy of his own home, my client was fantasizing . . .'

With Mike Chapman's latest episode of lying to me, I was beginning to think that there was some truth to my inability to understand men.

'When one of his coconspirators was arrested last evening, at his security job at a shopping mall in White Plains, the man assumed he was meeting with a Dominguez victim-in-waiting, rather than the female undercover agent who showed up,' I said. 'That defendant brought to the engagement a Taser gun, rope, a meat hammer, duct tape and cleaning supplies in his backpack. That's taking fantasy to a new level, Judge.'

'These are death fetishists, Your Honor,' Drusin said. Apparently, he thought his argument would help his client's case. 'It's just fantasy role play, and the tools – none of which are illegal to possess, I might add – just bring a little spice to the stories they tell each other.'

'Alba Dominguez thought her husband was serious enough about his plans to kill her, and to make good on his threats to boil her body in a pot of oil after dismembering her, that she took their baby and fled to relatives who live on the West Coast before reporting this to our office. She had the additional fear of not being able to call the local precinct because her husband is a police officer. She came directly to us instead.'

'Your Honor, my client's record with the NYPD is unblemished. He's had commendations for bravery, he's taken the test for promotion, and at the base of all this is the fact that he just wants to clear his name and get his job back. He wants to be a cop.'

'He *was* a cop, Mr Drusin. What he wants is to be a cannibal. Maybe a cannibal cop.'

'You're way out of line, Alex Cooper,' Drusin said, turning to see if any reporters had entered the courtroom. 'I mean, that comment is just screaming to make you the poster girl for tonight's headlines. Is that what you want? Dragging my client into the gutter with you?'

'Tonight's headlines are taken, David. Some girl who

wasn't quite as fortunate as Mrs Dominguez didn't get away from the guy who was fantasizing about doing her harm. Your client won't even be a footnote in a crime story.'

'Hold off, you two,' Judge Aikens said, banging his gavel repeatedly. 'You just asked me to set one hundred thousand dollars bail, Ms Cooper, am I right?'

'Yes, sir.'

The defendant's mother's sobs rose up again over the sound of my voice.

'I think that's inadequate, actually, for the facts that you've laid out and the idea that coconspirators have been identified and arrested. I'm going to set bail in the amount of two hundred fifty thousand, and of course there'll be an order of protection for the wife and child, in the event he posts that bail. How much time do you want for motions?'

'You can't prosecute people for their thoughts, Alvin. I mean, Judge Aikens. Have you lost it, too? That's what she's trying to do here. Next time some poor slob thinks about getting an erection, Alex'll probably slap cuffs on him. That's what we're coming to?'

'It sounds like Ms Cooper thinks she can prove that your client took the overt steps necessary to go from thinking about criminal activity to committing a crime.'

'Man, Alvin, it didn't take you long to go over to the dark side. Six months ago you would have been standing right where I am, making these arguments even more ferociously than I am.'

'Don't make this personal, Mr Drusin. Not toward your adversary nor to me. May I have dates for a motion schedule, please?'

'Set whatever dates you want. I'll have a motion before you by Friday asking you to dismiss the indictment. You remember the First Amendment, Judge, or did you leave your copy of the Constitution in your desk back at Legal Aid? You might want to get ready to give some thought to that one. And don't think out loud because Alex will try to control your decision.'

'Did you hear me say I don't want this to get personal, Mr Drusin?' the judge asked.

'Tell that to Alex. To Ms Cooper. It's all personal to her.'

I shook my head. David Drusin didn't like to lose.

'Some guy threatens her life – or at least she *fantasizes* about that, if I'm not mistaken – and because my client made one mistake in his distinguished career, Ms Cooper gets this professional hard-on—'

'Watch yourself, Mr Drusin,' the judge said, pointing a finger at his friend.

'She takes this professional hard line, Your Honor. That's all that I was going to say. She goes after my guy for some imagined mind game just to punish him, making it look like legal eagling, because it personally affected her. My next motion is going to be to have you recuse her from the case, if she lacks the good sense to do that herself.'

'I have no idea what he's talking about, Judge.' I was getting short with David Drusin. He had no business making up nonsense to spin the court.

'No idea, Alex?' Drusin said, stepping toward my table, wagging a finger in my face. 'Raymond Tanner. That name doesn't ring a bell?'

That name was capable of stopping me cold, and Judge Aikens saw the freeze.

'Who's Tanner?'

'A rapist, Your Honor,' I said. 'A man I prosecuted several years ago, who—'

'Who was found not guilty. Cooper's been wrong on more than one occasion.'

'Not guilty because he's insane, Your Honor. He's not only extremely dangerous, but he's crazy, too. He escaped from a locked psych facility on a work release.'

'And threatened your life, Ms Cooper?'

I had no idea what Drusin knew about Raymond Tanner or why his name had come into this. I glanced over at Dominguez and saw that he was sneering at me. In June, when Tanner attacked a woman in Central Park, he was sporting a bold tattoo on the back of his hand, inked for him in the psych ward, that read KILL COOP.

'That's the least of it. He's on the loose and responsible for at least two rapes – maybe three – since June. This has nothing to do with the case before you, so I'd ask you to disregard Mr Drusin, who – for the record – seems to be foaming at the mouth . . . and—'

'You know damn well, Ms Cooper, that Officer Dominguez did a stop-and-frisk in late July. That he did his job well, that he resisted racial profiling, and that he happened to let Raymond Tanner slip through his fingers.

My client did the right thing, and because of that you and the department have been out to get him.'

'I have no idea what David is talking about, Judge.' I was stunned and started to move to the bench to get the Tanner information off the record.

'You wanted this all preserved for the commissioner, Alex,' Drusin said. 'You stay right where you are. No going sidebar on my client now. I'll give you some words to think about.'

I had subpoenaed Gerardo Dominguez's personnel files from NYPD Legal. There was no mention of this stop in any of the papers.

'There's simply no truth to the connection that Mr Drusin is trying to make.'

'Calm down, Ms Cooper,' Alvin Aikens said.

'I'm perfectly calm,' I said, resting my left hand on the table to stop it from shaking. 'Mr Tanner has been the subject of an intensive manhunt by the NYPD. Someone at headquarters would have brought this to my attention immediately had there been a sighting of Tanner and a mistake by Officer Dominguez. And most especially if there was anything more sinister in this coincidental connection between the two of them.'

'There she goes again, Judge. Another of her wild imaginings. The queen of would-be mind control,' Drusin said, fishing in his briefcase for a slip of paper. He found it and passed it to the court officer to hand to Aikens.

'May I see the document, Judge?'

'You have a copy for her, Mr Drusin?' the judge was frowning at me now.

'No, Your Honor. I didn't think you'd take this nonsense seriously.'

'It's the two-fifty, Ms Cooper,' Aikens said, referring to the name of the report officers must file after a stop-and-frisk that didn't result in an arrest. 'July thirtieth of this year, signed by Police Officer Gerardo Dominquez, after he detained one Raymond Danner, who was carrying some kind of pipe – not a per se weapon, not against the law to possess – that he dropped to the ground on the officer's approach. Looks like Mr Dominguez got the spelling wrong.'

'How convenient for Mr Danner.' I suspected that once the 250 form was entered electronically in the police data bank, the dots had been properly connected by other descriptive information – including the distinctive tattoo – and the point made that the dangerous escapee had been fortunate in his close encounter. 'The pipe has long been Tanner's weapon of choice. Unfortunately, this is the first I'm hearing about the stop.'

'That's simply not credible, Judge.'

'What's not credible is that Mr Dominguez didn't recognize Tanner,' I said. 'His wanted poster has been on display in every precinct for two months. He's been discussed at every muster and roll call since June twenty-first.'

My mind was spinning with conspiracies that I had better sense than to believe. Maybe Tanner and this perv of a police officer knew each other. They certainly shared violent propensities toward women. I was scrambling to remember where each of them had been raised and gone to school, whether there was any relationship I could cobble together before the judge's attitude toward the defendant took a detour.

'Expect a motion from me tomorrow, Judge Aikens. Ms Cooper needs to step down from this prosecution. She wouldn't be so uncharacteristically rattled if there wasn't such a clear conflict of interest between her involvement and this officer's chance for a fair trial.'

'If it's my credibility you're attacking, Mr Drusin, you'd better examine your own conscience. Or don't you have one any longer?' I said. 'How about September tenth for the next appearance, Judge? That should give Mr Drusin time for all the frivolous motions he intends to make.'

Aikens nodded as the clerk recorded the control date for the case. I picked up my papers and turned to leave the courtroom.

David Drusin pivoted to whisper to me. 'Don't let your imagination run away with you, Alex. You might start seeing Raymond Tanner's ugly face everywhere you go. That'll give you something to prosecute.'

Eight

'Do we have a temp office?' I asked Mercer, when he met me in the lobby of the Waldorf at 11:15 A.M.

'In the basement. A cubicle next to the homicide guys. Where's Blackmer?'

'He'll be up in the afternoon. He's interviewing a vic in that Columbia date rape.'

Mercer was leading me to the service elevator. 'Did you drive?'

'No. Took the subway. I had a stop to make on my way in. Went to check on a sick friend.' I looked at Mercer to see if he got what I meant.

'All good?'

'Apparently not as sick as I thought,' I said, but he didn't blink. 'Mike here?'

'Don't know what Rocco has him doing, or whether it's his mother. I wasn't expecting him yet. You've got to lose some of that edge, girl. You two will be okay.'

'My edge, such as it is, has nada to do with Detective Chapman. I've just come from the arraignment of Gerry

Dominguez, and it was a bit contentious, to say the least.'

'You got rattled at an arraignment?' Mercer said, chuckling out loud as the elevator doors closed. 'Miles to go, Alex.'

'I called the squad,' I said, referring to the SVU on upper Broadway. 'Gerry Dominguez responded to a 911 call last month. Suspicious-looking thug carrying a lead pipe. Seventh Precinct.'

The DA's office and courthouse were in the Fifth, so it was uncomfortably close territory.

'Lots of lead pipes around town.'

'This one was ours. Raymond Tanner. Fits the scrip to a tee, only Dominguez claims not to have known Tanner was wanted. Had his mitts on the mutt but misspelled the name by one letter in the two-fifty. Does that make any sense to you?'

'The sergeant hear anything about it?' Mercer said, referring to his boss at SVU.

'The only people in the know seem to be the giant computer brain at One Police Plaza and Dominguez's lawyer, David Drusin. Something wrong with that picture, right?'

'There's a whole task force looking for Tanner. They'll jump on this.'

'So in the meantime, since Drusin's shtick is that Dominguez is just playing mind games about chowing down on his wife and all the other ladies on his list, I can use my free fantasy time to worry about Tanner hunting me around town.'

'And I have no doubt you will do that, Alex, looking over your shoulder everywhere you go. So I'm going to put you to work instead.'

We had turned into a long corridor, dimly lit, with just enough air-conditioning to make breathing tolerable.

'You couldn't find anything more cheerless than this?' I asked.

We passed several open doors. I recognized a few detectives in each of the rooms, interviewing men and women I assumed to be hotel employees.

Halfway down the hall, Mercer turned in. There were four desks in the barely furnished space, with an old lamp on each and a ceiling fan that looked like an original artifact.

'Best we were able to do. The presidential suite's reserved.'

I dropped my tote on the floor, sat on a desktop, and began fanning myself with a manila folder. 'Tell me the news.'

'Autopsy's done,' Mercer said. 'No surprises, and details to follow. The lab says that spot of blood that Dr Azeem picked up on the curtain is sufficient to profile, so that jumps to the head of the line, along with our deceased.'

'Could it be hers?'

'Spatter? Sure thing. But it's either hers or the perp's, because Azeem's camera says it was deposited the same time of day. It's not some traveling salesman from a month ago who cut himself shaving.'

'So we're likely to have two DNA patterns by tomorrow

and a photo to put a name to the dead body anytime now. What's up with the video surveillance?'

Mercer pointed to the far end of the hallway with his thumb. 'They're working two angles. Because Azeem put an exact hour on the murder, Rocco has one team working all the videos starting at two P.M., the earliest time he thinks she died. They're looking for whoever left the room with the trunk, working off photos of the luggage we found last night, which is a huge help. That's about fifty cameras' worth.'

'Tedious job. Why wouldn't they have just left the trunk in the hotel?'

'The killer clearly wanted to bleach out the insides and make sure it wasn't traceable to him, and besides, it's not bad cover walking out with luggage. We're interviewing bellmen now to see if he was brazen enough to get help, even though someone had already attached wheels to the old thing long before it was stolen.'

'And what's the other angle?'

'The second group is working in reverse, going backwards to try to catch the killer or killers coming into the hotel.'

'Any sign of the feds yet?' I asked.

'Nope. Just an advance team on site to see if they can secure the area they need for the executive group arriving this week.'

'Maybe Scully's idea of lowballing this investigation to the media will work — making it look like an ordinary street crime, I mean.'

'I got the porter from the office building opposite the Yale Club in the next room. Let's finish up with him.'

'How about the owner of the suitcase?'

'In London. Private equity guy who was here for a few weeks but lives in London. His wife was using the luggage to pack up a lot of her stuff and ship it over. Says he bought it at the antiques market on Portobello Road, with wheels already attached.'

The Yale Club was located at 50 Vanderbilt Avenue, a handsome neoclassical building from the early nineteen hundreds, directly opposite Grand Central and sited – as Yale legend had it – on the very street corner on which their famous alum, Nathan Hale, was hanged by the Brits for espionage during the Revolution.

'How did it go missing?' I asked.

'Nobody at the clubhouse had an explanation,' Mercer said, motioning for me to follow him into the adjacent room. 'The guest insisted on having it outside on the sidewalk while he waited for a car service that was taking him to the airport. He went inside to use the men's room and ten minutes later, the trunk was gone.'

'Hardly a surprise.'

'He thought the club's doorman had an eye on it, but the entrance got busy, so nobody was watching.'

'And the porter?'

'Works in the building across the street,' Mercer said, tapping before he opened the door. 'Alex Cooper, I'd like you to meet Mr Johnson White.'

The slim gentleman, African American with skin as dark

as Mercer's, braced himself on the desk beside him and stood up briefly to shake my hand. He appeared to be in his late sixties, with close-cropped gray hair and beard. He was wearing a navy-blue jumpsuit over a white T-shirt.

'Pleased to meet you.'

'Good to meet you as well,' I said.

'How much longer will you have me here, Mr Wallace?'

'Don't you worry, sir. Your supervisor is fine with this.'

'It's not him I'm worried about,' the man said with a smile. 'It's my lunchtime.'

'We'll try to be quick,' Mercer said. Then to me he explained, 'Officers canvassing the area around the Yale Club found Mr White. They think he can put some pieces together for us. I had just started talking with him when you arrived.'

'I don't have many pieces, if that's what you're thinking.'

'Let me be the judge of that. Why don't you tell us about yourself?'

Johnson White was relaxed and talked easily. 'I was born sixty-eight years ago. Right here, in Harlem. Finished high school. Served in Vietnam. Married the first girl I saw when I got home,' he said. 'Have two daughters, three grandchildren. And I got one job I've had since 1974. Short story, Mr Wallace.'

'Short and sweet, sounds like to me. You're a porter, they tell me.'

'That's a polite way of saying it. A custodian. A porter. I'm a janitor, Mr Wallace.'

'You work in an office building?'

'Yes, ma'am. Right there on Vanderbilt Avenue, 43rd to 44th Streets. Bank of America building.'

'Since 1974?' I asked.

'I guess you're too young to know, but it wasn't a bank when I went to work there. It was the grandest hotel in New York.'

'Grander than the Waldorf?' I couldn't help but make the comparison because of the dead girl whose murder was driving our investigation.

'Oh, I would have to say yes to that. It was called the Biltmore.'

'I've heard of it, of course, although I don't remember it.'

F. Scott Fitzgerald had glorified the Biltmore in his stories, associating it with Jazz Age luxury and style. He and Zelda had honeymooned there – briefly – until they were ejected for their rowdiness. In countless movie romances, couples reunited under the famous Biltmore lobby clock.

'My father worked there long before me. Got me the job when I came home from 'Nam. In those days it was still connected to Grand Central. In fact, I used to meet passengers registered at the hotel on our own private arrival platform in the train station. It was called the Kissing Room,' he said, winking at me. 'Brought them back to the Biltmore underground – never had to deal with foul weather or the riffraff who used to hang around the station. Got them right up to the hotel lobby in a private elevator.'

'I didn't know that.'

'Bet you didn't know we had a roof garden in between the two wings of the hotel, either, and in the winter we turned it into a skating rink. Now is that grander than the Waldorf or not?'

'Sounds like it was.'

'All that's left of the Biltmore today is the old clock and the baby grand piano that sat in the lobby. You can come see them inside the bank building.'

'Mr White and I had just started talking about how he used to carry luggage for railroad passengers,' Mercer said. 'That's why he's got such a good eye for expensive bags and trunks.'

I knew there was a point that Mercer was making with the narrative.

'The police came around early this morning with a copy of a photograph of that big leather suitcase. I recognized it right away.'

'Because—?' Mercer asked.

'I'd never seen that kind before, if that's what you mean. But I knew it was fine.'

'Fine?'

'Not from my days hauling garbage and shredding documents in the bank, but from the time my daddy and I were helping fancy people from the train station into their hotel suites. This was a fine piece of leather luggage, a big trunk back when people traveled in style if they were rich. Not with all the wheely bags and backpacks and aluminum stuff that they jam into the airplane overheads today. Not that kind.'

'Where did you see it?' I asked.

'I was standing out in back of my building, on the loading dock area, on a break. Hot as hell the day was. And the brass fittings on the case? The sun was hitting on them, making them shiny like they were new, looking good against the dark leather of the trunk. Caught my eye is all.'

'Was there anyone with the trunk?'

'Not when I first saw it,' Johnson White said. 'Strange for people in this city to leave so much as a soda bottle on the street for fear it'll get snatched. A big, fat old suitcase? Really careless.'

'Did you say anything?'

'To who?'

'Well, did you see the people who put it out on the sidewalk?'

'Don't know when that happened. Didn't see anyone close to it at first. It was just standing there in that slice of sunlight, all by itself.'

Johnson White stopped talking and leaned his head down, taking out a handkerchief to wipe his neck. 'You got some kind of sweatbox going on in here, Mr Wallace?'

'Can't help it, I'm afraid. We're making do.'

'You're not thinking I had anything to do with that trunk, are you?' White was stern-looking now, as he lifted his head to ask Mercer. 'I've seen movies where police do this to people.'

'You're helping us, Mr White. The heat is just what it is down here.'

'How long were you watching the trunk?' I asked.

'I wasn't watching it at all. Don't go putting words in my mouth.'

'Sorry.'

'It caught my eye, is all. Then some guy walked across the street – you know, from the exit of the train station – walked right up to it all boldlike, and just wheeled it away. It was as though he was supposed to be doing it.'

'One guy?'

'All I saw was him.'

'Did he talk to anyone at the Yale Club?'

'I didn't see him say a word to nobody, and wasn't nobody paying attention to say a word to him.'

'What did you do?' Mercer asked.

'I kept on doing exactly what I'd been doing. Resting up.'

'Did it seem unusual to you, the guy taking the trunk?' I asked.

'For all I knew, young lady, he was the very guy who left it there. Didn't you listen to me? I don't know who put it out on the sidewalk in the first place.'

'So you didn't alert anyone at the club, or look for a patrolman?' Mercer asked.

The porter wiped his brow with the handkerchief. 'Nothing out of the ordinary, Mr Wallace. I'm not looking for any trouble, anytime.'

'What did the man look like?'

'White. He was a white man with dark hair, is all I can say.'

'C'mon now,' Mercer said. 'You can do better than that. Was he a kid? Was he your age?'

'Somewheres right in between. Maybe thirty, maybe older.'

'Tall? Short? Fat? Thin?'

'Regular.'

Johnson White was beginning to show his annoyance with all the questions.

'Tall or short, I'm asking you.'

'About as tall as this lady here,' he said, pointing at me. 'Tall for a lady, but kind of regular for a guy.'

'Well, did he look like a man who would have owned a fine piece of luggage?' Mercer said, leaning over to try to get in the witness's face.

'Now I'm supposed to be the judge of that?'

'You told us you had lots of practice at it. Grandest hotel in New York,' I said, trying to reignite a spark in the man.

'So long ago I've forgotten everything except how pretty the place was.'

'The man,' Mercer said, 'did he look clean? How was he dressed? Give me something to work with, Mr White.'

Johnson White was sweating profusely. 'Can't think in here. You gonna let me up for air?'

'Soon as you tell me what I want to know.'

'Pants. Shirt – not a T-shirt. Noticed the collar because he had on a baseball cap and I saw dark hair hanging out the back of the cap, over his collar.'

'Keep going.'

'That's all I took in. Man walking like he didn't have a

worry in the world, rolling that big trunk across the street.'

'You saw where he went?' I asked. 'Back into Grand Central?'

'I never said he came out of the train station. Just crossing from in front of it. And I saw exactly where he went.'

'Tell us,' Mercer said, leaning in again.

'There's a ramp that comes from the street on the 44th Street side.'

'What kind of ramp?'

'For vehicles. Cars and such,' White said. 'Has a special ceiling in it. A real pretty place.'

'Ceiling?'

'You two ever been to the Oyster Bar?'

White was talking about the famed seafood restaurant, one hundred years old, which still anchored the lower level – once the hub of all commuter traffic – of Grand Central.

'Sure we have. You never met the oyster Ms Cooper here didn't like.'

'Then you know the ceiling? The beautiful tiles?'

'Guastavino tiles,' I said. The terra-cotta free-span timbrel vaults, the invention of a Spanish architect named Rafael Guastavino, were landmarked in the famed restaurant as well as in sophisticated building designs throughout the city. 'Fancy tiles on a ramp? Ramp to what?'

'Used to be that ramp led to the basement of the Biltmore Hotel, miss. That's how come it was all spiffed up back in the day. I spent a lot of time going in and out there,' White said. 'But it doesn't go anywhere anymore. It's just a parking garage under there now.'

Nine

By one fifteen, Mercer and I were standing under the spectacular tiled ceiling of the Acme Garage on East 44th, almost kitty-corner from the Yale Club. The Catalan vaulting, as it was known, had once been a gateway to a luxurious hotel but was now as dirty and grim as any underground commercial parking space in the city.

The young man in charge was as surly as befit someone spending all his hours below the street, inhaling gas fumes and jockeying cars to get them as close together as possible without scratching fenders or sides.

'A guy with a trunk? Nothing unusual about luggage.'

'A big old leather trunk. You might notice,' Mercer said. 'Maybe think it wouldn't fit in a car.'

'We got vans, we got SUVs, we got pickups and panel trucks. I park 'em, I don't pack 'em.'

'How about surveillance cameras? You must have them in here for security.'

Garages were easy targets for armed robbers because they did so much business in cash.

'We got 'em. They're just on a loop, though. They record over themselves after twenty-four hours. No reason to save tapes if nothing happened,' the garage attendant said, pausing to spit on the floor. 'And nothing happened.'

'We'd like to go through receipts with you. See if anyone charged their parking fee or one of you jotted down plate numbers.'

'You told me you don't have a date. How you gonna do that?'

'We've figured it within a day or two,' I said. 'Will you let us into your office to check them out?'

'I don't keep 'em here, lady. The owner has eight garages. All the stuff gets forwarded next day to Queens, where he operates. Go there if you want, or call my manager. I've only worked here two months.'

A car nosed down the ramp and squealed to a stop a few feet away from us. The attendant walked over to the machine on the wall that dated and timed the receipts and handed a ticket to the woman who got out of the car.

'How long you gonna be, lady?'

She told him she planned to retrieve the car at five. As she turned to walk away, he gave her sculptured body a thorough top-to-bottom once-over, then spit again.

'What's in here besides a garage?' I asked. I was wondering if there was a place for someone to conceal himself – or a large trunk – for any period of time. Whoever stole the piece of luggage could not have been certain the opportunity to grab the object would present itself on a busy Manhattan street in the middle of the day.

'My cage,' he said.

I looked over at the glass-enclosed booth, which had a stool for the attendant, a small desk, and a cash register, and space for little else.

'Restrooms around the corner. Help yourself to a look.'

I walked thirty feet away and found the doors to two unisex bathrooms. The narrow stalls held a toilet and sink. With an occupant, there would be no room for a steamer trunk.

'Any other way out?' Mercer asked, as I was on my way back.

'Used to be this was connected to a hotel that was demolished,' the man said. 'Long before my time or yours. The ramp swings around to a lower level. Holds a load of cars down there.'

He turned away from us to take the receipt and payment from a man in a business suit who had come for his car.

Mercer had been excited to follow this lead. Now it appeared to be as much a dead end as the garage with a once-elegant history. 'I'll get uniform to come over and sweep the place. Check out the basement, too.'

'Look, it's possible the man who swiped the luggage just came down the ramp from the street to get out of sight for a while,' I said.

'With a steamer trunk? Somebody in here would have noticed that.'

'So there are a bunch of other employees the guys will have to talk to. I mean he may have just waited till he thought the coast was clear. Put the trunk in a corner at the rear of the garage. Tucked it next to a van in the basement and waited a few hours.'

We walked up the ramp and back out into the sweltering afternoon sun, a sliver of which seemed to find us in between the tall buildings.

'You want lunch?' Mercer asked.

'A bucket of water and something light.'

'We'll pass a takeout place on our way back to the Waldorf.'

We squared the block and started walking north on Park Avenue. The wide boulevard carried traffic north- and southbound, three lanes each divided by a median that was maintained as a garden throughout the year. The begonias were a great touch of color in August, the only plants seemingly able to withstand the intense heat and direct sunlight.

'So nothing from Mike this morning?' I was unable to suppress my curiosity and anxious to confront him about his deception.

'I'd tell you to chill, but it's too hot for that word to have any meaning.'

'You want to know what happened this—'

'I most distinctly do not. Got that, Ms Cooper?'

I stared ahead at the sidewalks filled with pedestrians for as far ahead as I could see. Boxy glass office buildings lined both sides of the broad avenue, eventually giving way to some of the priciest residential real estate in Manhattan.

'I thought you and Vickee were in favor of our – uh, flirtation.'

'I'm in favor of minding my own business. It's my wife who's in the advice-to-the-lovelorn business. Don't put me in the cross fire between you and Mike.'

Mercer had been a rock throughout many of my most difficult moments in the last ten years, and I understood completely that he did not want to be caught in the middle of this complicated relationship that Mike and I were attempting to work out.

We found a salad and sandwich place off Park on 47th Street and stopped to pick up some lunch. We had almost reached the Waldorf when Mercer's cell phone rang.

'Hey, Rocco. We're two blocks away.' Mercer listened to the lieutenant for more than a minute, looking at me as he responded. 'Alex and I will do that. We'll be ready to go.'

'News?'

Mercer pocketed his phone. 'The ME gave out a photo of our vic two hours ago and it went viral immediately. She's been identified.'

I pushed my sunglasses on top of my head, squinting at Mercer. 'A name? It's reliable?'

'Her father called it in. Saw the photo in a news bulletin on TV. Doesn't get more reliable than that.'

'Or more devastating.'

'Corinne Thatcher. Twenty-eight years old.'

I didn't know which was worse. A corpse that lay in the morgue unidentified for more than a week – like my last case – or the instant a loved one put a name to the body that was still on the steel table in the autopsy room.

'What does Rocco want us to do?' I asked. The girl who had died such an unthinkable death was exactly ten years younger than I.

Mercer put his long arm around my shoulder. 'He's got cops bringing the parents into town from their home on the North Fork. He wants us to talk to them.'

I bit my lip and nodded.

'Rocco wants us to figure out,' Mercer said, 'why somebody wanted to torture this girl to death.'

Ten

Mercer and I entered the lobby of the morgue in the Office of the Chief Medical Examiner. It was not the ideal setting for an interview of the victim's family, but I couldn't imagine asking them to sit in the hotel suite in which their daughter died.

The sign that greeted us was probably the first thing the Thatchers saw when they arrived half an hour earlier, at four P.M.: LET CONVERSATION CEASE, LET LAUGHTER FLEE. THIS IS THE PLACE WHERE DEATH DELIGHTS IN HELPING THE LIVING.

There was a faint, bitter odor of formaldehyde, which seemed to have seeped into every crevice of the building, an unnecessary reminder of the work that went on here.

The head of the Identification Unit had offered us a private room in which to meet. We were pacing the small space until I heard the wails from a woman approaching in the corridor.

Mercer opened the door and started to introduce himself. Bill Thatcher held out his hand, but his wife was inconsolable. She turned away from us and collapsed in her husband's arms. I followed Mercer out of the room and closed the door.

Fifteen minutes passed before Mr Thatcher opened the door to start the introductions again.

'I'm Alexandra Cooper. Please call me Alex. I'm the assistant district attorney who'll be working on Corinne's case. Mercer and I have partnered together for more than a decade.'

Bill Thatcher appeared to be as puzzled as he was pained. His eyes were bloodshot. He had no doubt been crying since he saw his daughter's photograph several hours ago. His wife was unable to compose herself, with good reason. She was trying to stifle her sobs with a wad of Kleenex tissue.

'We're going to try to answer all the questions you have,' I said, after I expressed my condolences. 'And while I know this is an impossible moment to impose on you, there are things we are hoping you can tell us about Corinne. We need to catch the person who killed her.'

I didn't believe in euphemisms. The harsh reality was that their daughter was dead, and as difficult as it was for them to absorb that, they would have to deal with the fact that she was murdered – not just 'hurt' or 'harmed' – and do it at warp speed.

'You have a job to do, Ms Cooper. But I'm not sure we're ready for that.'

Readiness wasn't a choice Mercer or I could give them.

'The lieutenant has a detective waiting to take you to

your home. But we do need to start with a bit of information about Corinne.'

'No offense, Ms Cooper – Alex. You don't look old enough to be responsible for my daughter's life,' Thatcher said. 'And you seem to be very nervous.'

'I *am* nervous, Mr Thatcher,' I said. I'd been brushing my hair away from my face and twisting my pen in my hands. 'I don't like this part of my job.'

Telling family members about the brutality of a loved one's death never got easier, nor did probing their lives to sniff out any undercurrents of darkness.

'I'd like to talk with the district attorney. Get someone more able to do this.'

Most prosecutors' offices were, as Mike liked to say, a children's crusade. Idealistic graduates just out of law school vied for the handful of jobs available with the Manhattan DA, the best training ground for litigators in the country. Before moving on to private practice or other careers in public service, they were tested with the most serious crimes in the city. I had prosecuted dozens of felonies to verdict, handling major cases by my third year in the office.

'We'll get you in to meet Mr Battaglia whenever you are up to it, sir,' Mercer said. 'You have to trust me that Alex has more experience handling these crimes than most lawyers twice her age.'

'What crimes? What crimes do you mean,' Bill Thatcher said, backing up and sitting down, placing his head in his hands. 'I don't understand what happened to Corinne.'

I wanted to tell him that no one understood what

happened. It was obvious to me that the family had not yet been informed about the details of the attack.

Mercer took the lead in describing the manner of death, omitting the fact that she was likely drugged and tortured before she was cut. Thelma Thatcher's body slumped against her husband's. I would have to make sure her physician was notified before she left the ME's office. She was not likely to get through the coming weeks without medical care and perhaps sedation.

'Was she – was she violated?' Corinne's father asked.

'It appears that she was,' Mercer said. 'We'll get more facts from Dr Mayes when his tests are done.'

'What kind of a man—?' Bill Thatcher couldn't finish his sentence.

'There's no good answer for that question, sir.'

'Corinne wouldn't know anyone like that,' he said. 'It must have been a stranger. Some kind of psychopath.'

'That may well be. That's why we need you to tell us about her.'

The Thatchers were both retired schoolteachers. They were in their late sixties, and Corinne was the youngest of their three children.

Corinne Thatcher had grown up in a small community in Suffolk County. Like her older brother and sister, she attended college at Hofstra University. We let her father talk about her most special traits, the goodness and generosity of spirit that had won her so many friends along the way. She had struggled with career choices, deciding not to follow in her parents' footsteps, nor to apply to nursing school as she had originally planned. But she had spent most of the last three years working on disaster relief with the American Red Cross before becoming overwhelmed – and perhaps disillusioned – by the emotionally charged work.

'Was Corinne an employee of the Red Cross?' I asked.

'Not anymore. She spent six months as a volunteer, when one of those tornadoes hit Oklahoma a few years back. Most of the workers are volunteers. But after her training and the time she spent on the job, they hired her to lead some of the major projects.'

'What wonderful work to do.'

Bill Thatcher continued to talk as his tears flowed. 'My cousin was from Enid, so when he lost his home in the storm, she flew out. Didn't know the first thing about saving lives, but they taught her everything from CPR to getting blood to people who needed it.'

Mercer threw in all the platitudes about the good dying young. How violently she died was better left unspoken.

We let Thatcher talk about Corinne's work for as long as he wanted to, his wife occasionally blotting her tears and adding a few words about her child's extraordinary kindness to others.

I waited until he seemed to have exhausted himself listing her good acts. We needed to know whether anyone in her orbit could have been responsible for this tragedy. 'What did she do for the Red Cross, exactly?'

'The disaster relief work took her all over the country. All over the world, actually. Anywhere there was a flood or a cyclone or a fire that destroyed a community. Supplying people with food and shelter and medicine, that's the kind of thing that Corinne did.'

'Not tonight, of course, but can you put together a list of the places she lived and some of the people at her job?'

Thelma Thatcher spoke. 'My son can do that.'

Corinne's father started reeling off a list of cities in the Midwest and on both coasts.

'What did she do abroad?' I asked.

'She lived in Okinawa for a while. It was Red Cross work, but it was with the air force in particular. I think it was called communications liaison.'

Mercer took over. 'So she had to handle emergency messages between military personnel on the island and their families back home?'

'Yes. She didn't mind it that much, but when there was a death that she had to report – like telling an officer that his dad had died, or even an ill soldier needing to reach out to relatives, it really took a toll on her.'

'I understand.'

'From there she went to Dubai.'

'Really?'

'It was a promotion, actually. Corinne learned how to issue grants to families to get them immediate assistance in an emergency.'

'Related to war in the Middle East?'

'Some of that, Mr Wallace. Yes, sir. But she was pretty miserable living there, so she asked to come back home.'

'Is that when she quit?' I asked.

'No. No, it wasn't. She got assigned to the support resources operations for post-deployment.'

'Sorry,' I said. 'I'm not familiar with what that is.'

Thatcher sighed as he began to explain the duties to me. 'Obviously, ma'am, there are always challenges when service members come home from war. Their spouses may have assumed new responsibilities or taken jobs. Some adjust quickly and easily, but many have trouble reestablishing relationships or handling depression.'

'I thought those were issues for the military to deal with.'

'I don't know for how long the Red Cross has been involved, but they are very much in the mix. That was Corinne's job.'

'Here in New York?'

'Yes, most of her work was here in the city.'

'Did she have direct contact with ex-military men?' I asked.

'And women.'

'One-on-one?'

'Some individually, others with their families. She had to deal with post-traumatic stress issues and often with TBIs.'

'I don't know—'

Bill Thatcher cut me off. "Traumatic brain injuries. A lot of our soldiers have long-term health problems. There's a good bit of reunion adjustment.'

'You said that Corinne became – well, overwhelmed by the work, is that right?'

'Yes, ma'am. It got to her, seeing how much some of these young people gave to their countries and how hard it was for them to get on with their lives.'

Mercer followed with a list of questions that suggested we were both on the same wavelength. Were there any ones in particular with whom Corinne had bonded? Or about whom she was most worried? Or who had threatened her well-being? We also needed to know if she had become intimate with any of them.

The answer to every question was no.

'Who knew Corinne best?' I asked.

Bill Thatcher flinched. 'Knew her?'

He still wasn't able to think of his daughter in the past tense. That might take months to happen.

'With whom was she closest? Her brother?'

'No. Not so much anymore. Maybe her roommate?' He turned to his wife.

'Lizzie. Elizabeth Angler,' Thelma Thatcher said. 'But she's on vacation. I think she went abroad to visit family.'

'We'll need that contact information,' Mercer said.

'Did Corinne quit her job?' I asked.

Her father answered. 'Yes, back in June. She's just taking some time off this summer. Starting at NYU in a few weeks with some grad school courses, so that she can teach. She decided she wants to teach school after all.'

'Did she have a boyfriend, Mr Thatcher?'

He paused before answering. 'Corinne was dating a young man through the winter and spring. She ended that relationship about the same time she quit work.'

'Was he also involved with the Red Cross?'

The Thatchers stared blankly at each other.

'Sir?'

'I don't think so,' he said. 'My wife and I never met him. For some reason, Corinne never wanted to bring him home. She didn't think we'd approve of him.'

I glanced across at Mercer.

'What do you know about him?'

'Precious little.'

'What was the reason for your disapproval?'

Bill Thatcher swallowed hard. 'He wasn't educated, this fellow. And Corinne knew how important that was to us. Now I hate myself for it. For being so small-minded.'

'That was the only issue for you?' I asked.

He thought about my question for a few seconds too long.

'Did he have a criminal history?'

'I have no reason to think so. Thelma knows his name, I'm sure.'

'So, you didn't even know that much,' I said.

'What is it, Thelma? Pedro, or is it Pablo? Something like that.'

Mercer grimaced as he nodded to me. *Something like that*. The boyfriend's background was 'something other' than the Thatchers'.

'He was Dominican. I didn't feel he was right for our daughter.'

The bold fact of Thatcher's prejudice didn't seem to slow him down at all.

'Because of his ethnicity. Just that?'

The father was silent. He avoided making eye contact with Mercer.

'Or was he ever violent toward Corinne? Did she mention any inappropriate behavior?' I asked. 'I mean when she broke up with him.'

The choice of separation by one partner is the leading cause of violence in a dating relationship, when the other one doesn't want to end the connection. Repeated efforts by the victim to escape the escalating attacks led to fatalities with astounding frequency.

'Nothing like that.'

'Do you know what he does for a living?' I asked.

'I – I don't.'

'Was he ever in the military?' Mercer asked, with mounting urgency.

'I wouldn't know,' Thatcher said. 'But look here, why are you so interested in the man she dated?'

'We have to check into everyone in Corinne's world,' I said. 'Friends, coworkers, people she might have been intimate with.'

The likelihood that a young woman was killed by someone she knew – rather than a stranger – was tremendous.

'I've met the man our daughter was dating,' Thelma Thatcher said softly, lifting her head.

'You've *what*?' her husband said, practically shouting at her.

'His name is Paco.'

'When did this happen?' Bill Thatcher asked.

'In the spring. I came into the city to have lunch with Corinne.'

'You know how I felt about this. You betrayed me, Thelma. You've made a fool of me.' Thatcher's face turned beet red as he tried to restrain his anger.

'What can you tell us about him?' Mercer asked.

'That Corinne liked him very much. That he was quiet and didn't speak a lot,' she said.

'Details,' Mercer said. 'We're going to need as many details as you can give us, Mrs Thatcher. We'd like to try to find him tonight.'

'You need to call my son. He has more information than I do. I just remember Corinne telling me she had ended the relationship because her friend – because Paco – was angry. That he was angry all the time.'

Bill Thatcher looked more puzzled than Mercer and I. 'She told you all this?'

'Why was he angry?' I said. 'Did Corinne tell you the reason?'

She nodded her head up and down as more tears streaked her cheeks. 'Paco's brother had come back from Afghanistan. He lost both legs. His tank was blown up by an IED.'

'That's a good reason to be mad.'

'He didn't hurt her, Mr Wallace.'

'But she told you Paco was always angry.'

'That was her world, Detective. Good people, but many of them damaged, many of them struggling, many of them deeply unhappy. This boy wasn't taking out any hostility on my daughter,' Thelma Thatcher said. 'He directed his anger elsewhere.'

'Do you know—?'

'Paco's brother isn't a citizen of this country. He joined the army to fight in this war and came home without his legs and half his face missing. Corinne told me she couldn't get her friend to focus his – his venom, she called it – into something more constructive. Paco's anger, according to Corinne, is directed at the president of the United States.'

Eleven

'You can't be that unhappy to see me,' Mike said.

'Perfect end to a truly miserable day,' I said, closing the door to the conference room of the morgue shortly before 7:30 P.M. 'You here to top it off?'

Mike's feet were up on the long table. He had obviously been examining autopsy and crime scene photographs. Mercer and I had just put the Thatchers in a patrol car for the ride home. I didn't imagine there would be much conversation on that long, sad drive.

'The commissioner thinks I'm presidential material. I mean, not presidential but—'

'I wasn't confused for a nanosecond. He's asked you to be part of the task force when the feebies show up.'

'Scully heard that the dead girl's wacko ex—'

'Nothing to suggest Paco is wacko, okay?'

'What did you feed her that's got her snapping at me, Mercer?'

I raised my arms and held them out to both sides. 'You guys talking about me? So very sorry. I'm just out of sorts 'cause I'm so distressed about Mrs Chapman's health.'

'Relax, Coop. She's doing much better.'

I looked for the slightest sign of deception or discomfort in Mike's demeanor but saw neither.

Mercer didn't skip a beat. 'I called Corinne's brother. He's got—'

'Do you mind giving us a few minutes, Mercer?' I asked.

He looked at Mike before he answered me. 'You can have whatever you want, Alex, but this doesn't seem like the time—'

Mike took his feet down and sat up straight. 'I've got no secrets from Mercer, kid. You got a beef with me, shoot.'

I stared straight at Mike. 'If you don't mind, Mercer. Five minutes.'

He turned and saluted me before walking out of the room.

'Don't go acting all crazy on me, Coop.'

'You know I adore your mother, Mike,' I said. 'My father helped you get her the best doctors, the best care when she was first diagnosed. There's nothing I wouldn't do for her.'

'And she's coming along fine. I just told you that.'

'You also told me that she's in ICU for a few more days of observation.'

Mike's expression didn't change. 'Like I said. So what's got you so smoked up about my mother, Coop?'

'Just the fact that I went to visit her in the hospital—'

'Whoa. No visitors but family.'

'Excuse me. She always says I'm just a shadow away

from family. I went to say hello to her this morning – just a smile and to blow a kiss – perk her up a bit. Funniest thing is, she wasn't there. Not this morning. Not this week.'

'So—'

'So your bullshit is wearing thin with me, Detective Chapman. I don't care that you make a fool of me, but just give it to me face-to-face. Are we done?'

Mike was talking over me. 'What hospital did you go to?'

'What does that matter? She wasn't there.'

'Where?'

I was overtired and overwrought, practically wringing my hands to keep them from flailing while I talked. 'Lutheran. The Medical Center.'

'Well, that's the problem.'

'No, I'm obviously the problem, Mike. What is it? Margaret's always been treated at Lutheran. Why are you being so – so evasive? It's about us. It's about me, isn't it? It's not about your mother at all.'

'I got no issue with you, Coop.'

'Then what?'

'Don't go crying on me, okay? Just dig those two chunky central incisors – the uppers, right there in the front of your mouth,' Mike said, stepping toward me and grabbing my shoulders tightly. 'Just dig those two big teeth into your lip. Thatta girl. Bite down.'

I looked at Mike. I wanted him to put his arms around me and explain the long absence and the nonsense about his mother.

'Not here, Coop, okay? I know that look in your eye. Don't even think about it,' he said, releasing me and taking two steps back, running his fingers through his hair. 'Not in the morgue, okay? Creeps me out to think about even touching you while we're a hairbreadth away from an autopsy table.'

'I wasn't thinking about touching you.'

'Sure you were,' he said, flashing that irresistible grin. 'You wanted a piece of me, didn't you?'

'Where is your mother? Would you just tell me that?'

'You never heard of HIPAA Security Rule?' Mike said, still clowning around.

'HIPAA, my ass. I'm not violating Margaret's privacy by asking where she is.'

'Yeah, but—'

'Just *your* privacy, Mike. Am I violating that?'

'Listen to me for a minute, Coop,' he said, turning dead serious on a dime, leaning on his arms on the table between us. 'When are you going to understand that I would sooner stick a shiv between the fifth and sixth ribs on the left side of my chest cavity than—'

'You mean, the place where most people have a heart? Are you able to say the word "heart"?'

'—than hurt you. Do you get that?' he asked, jabbing a finger toward my face. 'Will you ever get that?'

I inhaled and looked down at the table. 'I don't think you'd do anything – intentionally – to hurt me.'

'What did you just say?'

'You heard me.'

'It's not enough for you, is it?' Mike said. 'For Christsakes, we're in the morgue, Coop. My testosterone kind of chills down in here. It's about all I can give you right now.'

I picked my head up. 'Then just tell me where Margaret is.'

'Margaret is under a doctor's care. You want to see her on Sunday? Come to church with me.' Mike had taken his mother to Mass whenever he could for as long as I'd known him. 'We let heathens in.'

'Can I visit with her?' I asked, softening my tone.

'Course you can.' Mike walked around the end of the table and stood face-to-face with me. 'Sometimes you just have to trust me, kid.'

'Hard to do when you go off the way you did for so long. Hard to understand.'

'What happened to the gray matter up there?' he asked, tapping the side of my head. 'Asleep at the wheel?'

'Distracted.'

'Use your brain, Coop.'

'If I think too much, it takes me to a bad place,' I said. 'It's one thing to have a three-week rip, but then a vacation on top of that?'

Mike hesitated before speaking. 'Scully's giving me a big break, taking a real chance. You think I just disappeared on you? Is that what you think?'

'I don't exactly have a choice, do I? Or has there been another temptress?'

Mike threw back his head. 'Just because your peepers are green, kid, don't fall into that trap and become some green-eyed monster. There's no other woman. No competition.'

'What then?'

'Scully sent me on a mission, okay? If I tell you about it, I'll have to kill you,' Mike said, grinning at me as he walked back toward the chair he'd first been sitting in.

'You're killing me anyway.'

'Will you give me a week?'

I shook my head. 'Tell me now.'

'No can do.'

'I see,' I said, walking toward the door. 'I'm supposed to trust you, but you can't—'

'It's not me. It's the commissioner,' Mike said, pivoting to cut me off at the door.

'Scully trusts me implicitly.'

'He thinks you have too many friends. That you gossip.'

'That I – I—?' That one was hard to dispute.

'We'll have this all out, Coop. Believe me. Next week.'

'What about Saturday night?'

'We're still on.'

'But you won't tell me your secret?'

'It's not mine to tell.'

'So your mother? That's all some line you fed me?' I put my hand on the doorknob.

'Keep your temper under check, Coop. I wanted her out of harm's way,' Mike said, gripping my wrist and pulling it off the knob. 'Very same place I want you.'

114

Twelve

'So you were starting to tell me about Corinne's brother,' Mike said to Mercer.

'Yeah. He's as broken up as you might guess. Pug's going to talk to him. Corinne's brother gave us all the contact information for Paco, as well as his family. Rocco's got somebody going out to pick Paco up. Did you divine anything from the photographs, Detective?'

'Corinne's not talking to me yet, Mercer.'

'Dead girl winds up in the very hotel where the president is coming to stay, and her ex-lover has a grudge against the top dog.'

'That's a major leap to make,' Mike said, reaching for the remote control and turning on the television set hanging above the whiteboard across the room.

'Well, we've got a major case and nothing else that even smells like a clue,' Mercer said, throwing his pad on the table and pausing to look at the pictures. 'Turn the volume down before you wake the dead.'

For as long as I could remember, Mike had an addiction

to the Final Jeopardy! question on the popular long-running television show. The location didn't matter – morgue or steak joint, crime scene or courthouse – he'd find a way to the nearest television and tune in to test his own bottomless well of trivial information against whoever was in his company.

The three of us bet against one another every time we were together. Mike's strength reflected his deep knowledge of all things military – and, like me, great affection for old movies and Motown music. Mercer's upbringing by a single father who was a mechanic at Delta Air Lines had infused him with a love for world geography and modes of transportation, even in the most remote locales. I had majored in literature before law was ever a career path I'd considered, so I knew a lot about works from *Beowulf* and *The Decameron* to the romantic poets and Victorian novelists.

'That's Alex Trebek rattling the bones downstairs in the autopsy room. Not me,' Mike said. 'And don't tell me "not I" again, Coop, like you're always doing. I can see you're in that kind of mood – grammar police on patrol.'

'I gave that business up while you were away. Can't change the spots on this leopard, that's for sure.'

Mercer laughed. 'Wolverine. I told you wolverine.'

'I get the feeling I'm missing something here.' Mike unmuted the television as Trebek stood in front of the board with the final category.

'Twentieth-Century Words,' the TV host said. He repeated the category, and as the three contestants picked up their pens to write the question down, Trebek reminded viewers that there were new words entering the lexicon all the time. 'Your *Oxford English Dictionary* won't help you with this one, I don't think.'

'I'll throw in my twenty bucks,' Mercer said, 'but this has Ms Cooper written all over it.'

'Just because the kid's got a sharp tongue doesn't mean she's on top of all the street jive. I'm good for twenty.'

The category screen disappeared and was replaced by the Final Jeopardy! answer, right after I had agreed to join in with the guys.

The answer appeared in the giant blue-background box on the screen: COINED IN 1979, THIS WORD MEANS ROMANTIC ATTRACTION THAT RESULTS IN MANIC, OBSESSIVE NEED TO HAVE FEELINGS RECIPROCATED.

Mercer started to laugh again as Mike's feet dropped to the floor with an exaggerated bang.

'How stupid could I have been, Mercer? Of course she knows this.'

'Don't go there, Mike,' Mercer said, wagging a finger at him.

'I wouldn't have the slightest idea what the word is or what Mike is talking about,' I said, picking up my case folder. 'And now I'm really hungry and I need a stiff drink.'

The first two contestants drew blanks, as had I.

Mike pointed at the screen, as if trying to get the attention of the third player. 'C'mon, lady. What is *Coopster-itis*? It'll be in all the psych write-ups before too long. Emphasis *manic*. Emphasis *obsessive*.'

'None of you have this?' Trebek asked, then tsked them for not knowing the question. 'Not even venturing a guess?'

'What is *limerence*?' Trebek said, repeating the word twice.

Each of the contestants groaned.

'Obsessive love, folks. An infatuation that's not necessarily reciprocated,' the host continued. 'Coined in 1979 by a psychologist named Dorothy Tennov,' Trebek said. 'I guess that was a tough one.'

'I got to say, Coop, that's a word right out of your playbook.'

'Never heard of it.'

'But you live it, girl. Infatuation. Not necessarily reciprocated. Like first there was this investment banker type, then the newscaster dude, then the Frenchman with the frying pan.'

'You are so close to the fire, Mr Chapman,' I said, 'you might get scorched if you don't keep your mouth shut.'

'Don't knock my girl off her game,' Mercer said, crossing behind Mike as he tried to playfully muzzle him. 'I need her positive energy beaming in on finding a killer.'

'So buy us dinner,' Mike said, flashing his best grin at me. 'I'm all tapped out after being suspended without pay for three weeks. Oh, and then there's the dimes I blew on the rest of the vacation.'

'Dinner it is,' Mercer said. 'That'll give Rocco's guys time to get to the Bronx and see if they can bring Paco in for questioning. I can flip back down to talk to him after we eat.'

'Let's shoot up to Primola,' I said. My favorite Italian restaurant was on Second Avenue near 64th Street, a ten-minute ride from the morgue and an atmospheric world away, part of the Upper East Side scene. The food was consistently good and the staff took great care of me and my friends. 'I'm obsessing about prosciutto and figs and maybe a half order of pasta. Positively manic about it. My limerence for food is so much more rewarding than a romance.'

'I wouldn't know,' Mike said.

'Now that's a joke. You've probably sublimated more with food than anyone on the planet,' I said.

'Another twentieth-century word I'm not familiar with. Sublimating? What are you suggesting, exactly?'

'She sort of means you eat all the time instead of hooking up with the ladies,' Mercer said.

'Guaranteed less agita in chowing down,' Mike said. 'Anyway, I don't have my car.'

'Neither do I. Mercer's the wheelman.'

The three of us said good night to the security guard and walked around the corner to Mercer's car. I climbed into the backseat and rested my head. Mercer filled Mike in on our day, including my story about Raymond Tanner.

We parked near the restaurant and were greeted at the door by the owner, Giuliano. The bar was crowded and busy, packed with well-dressed Upper East Siders who liked the scene as much as they enjoyed the food.

'Ciao, Signorina Alessandra,' the big man said, sticking out his hand to Mike and Mercer. 'Nice to have you here.'

'You have a quiet table in the back?' I asked.

'Right here,' Giuliano said. 'I'm going to put you right here at table two, by the window, so Dominick can take care of you. Just give me a minute.'

Giuliano wanted us to have the best service in the front of the always-crowded room, but the seating was too visible for a serious catch-up with Mike.

'The usual, Alessandra?' Dominick asked.

'No Scotch tonight, thanks. Something light and refreshing.'

'I'll bring you a nice pinot gri, okay?'

'Perfect.'

Mike ordered a dirty martini, super dry, with onions and olives. Mercer, who was counting on going back to work, asked for a large bottle of sparkling water.

'You ready to order?'

'Not yet, Dominick. We just need to relax for a while,' I said.

In the three minutes it took for the drinks to arrive, we were already back in conversation about Corinne Thatcher's death.

I told Mike about the work she had been doing with returning vets, and Paco's vituperative rage at the president for his brother's injury.

'Then she broke up with Paco,' Mercer said.

'So you can't rule out limericks, can you?'

'*Limerence*,' I said, correcting Mike.

'See, I knew all along you had that word in your vocabulary.'

'I just heard it for the first time tonight.'

'Obsessive love. Paco makes mincemeat of Corinne.'

Mercer looked at his watch. 'I should have a handle on that before midnight.'

We were all aware the clock was ticking and the FBI would be on board by midday tomorrow to do the presidential advance work.

'But why the Waldorf?' I asked. 'Too much drama, and he couldn't get it done alone.'

'I've been thinking about those drawings on her skin,' Mercer said.

'The ladders?' Mike asked.

'The double helix is constructed on a ladder,' Mercer said, sketching one with his finger on the tablecloth. 'Suppose it's someone with a familiar DNA profile. A killer who's already in the data bank, taunting us to figure out who he is. The ladder is the frame for his genetic fingerprint, which is in the system.'

'Has to be a really sick motherfucker to plan one this big. If there were fava beans in her belly at the autopsy, I'd be looking for Hannibal Lecter.'

'No fava beans. Just a lot of green salad,' Mercer said. 'And we don't know this guy, because his turf is some other part of the country.'

'It's a thought.'

'But your SVU buddies have been checking serial killer cases all day,' I said.

'So they need to go international,' Mercer said. 'Maybe Canada, maybe Europe.'

When Dominick saw a break in the conversation, he approached us to take our order. I went first, followed by Mike's *spaghetti alle vongole* with a grilled veal chop, and Mercer's salad with a chicken paillard.

It was almost ten by the time we finished eating dinner. I had sipped two glasses of the chilled white wine and was thinking about whether to top it off with a third.

Mercer dialed Rocco Correlli's number and waited for him to pick up. Mike was staring across the room and seemed miles away from both of us.

'Loo? I'm hanging close, hoping I can do the boyfriend's interview tonight.'

I couldn't hear the lieutenant's answer but saw the expression on Mercer's face change.

'When did that go down?' he said, listening again. There was a long pause while Mercer took in information, motioning to Mike for a piece of paper and pulling a pen from his jacket pocket. 'What street? Say that again. What kind of track marks?'

Mercer ended the call. 'You want the bad news first, or the really bad news?'

'The bad,' Mike said.

'Corinne's boyfriend took his brother home today.'

'Home?' I asked.

'Yeah. They flew to the DR at nine A.M. Two one-way tickets. *Hasta la vista,* Paco.'

'So the good news is we can have another round,' Mike said, waving his hand at the bartender. 'What could be really bad about that?'

'The really bad news is that the cops just found another body.'

'A woman?' I asked. 'Another mutilation?'

'Not this time. It's a guy, actually,' Mercer said. 'And you'd better make that cocktail a roadie. We ought to take a look.'

I didn't get the link to our homicide. 'The hotel again?'

'No. A deserted alleyway in the East 40s. What we've been calling ladders? First cops on the scene looked at the same lines and saw them as tracks.'

'Track marks?' I asked. 'Like a junkie?'

'Railroad tracks. We've been looking at the marks on Thatcher's body like little ladders, just because that's how Rocco described them to us the first time he talked about them. That's the power of suggestion. But these cops find a body right outside Grand Central and they make a different connection.'

'Railroad tracks,' Mike said, repeating Mercer's words. 'What the hell does Corinne Thatcher have to do with something like that?'

'Maybe the killer first saw her on a train,' I said. 'Maybe the madman's a trainspotter. Maybe he . . .'

'Your *maybe*s can fill a trash can, Coop. As usual,' Mike said. 'Who's the dead man?'

'Thirty years old or so. Caucasian,' Mercer said. ''Bout as filthy dirty as can be. Single stab wound in the back. Could be homeless, 'cept he's got some decent clothes on. Labels and all that.'

Dominick came over with the bill, and Mercer stood up to pay.

'Found on the loneliest piece of pavement in Manhattan,' Mercer said. 'DePew Place.'

Thirteen

At 10:30 P.M., in the pitch black of a hot summer night, I was standing in a desolate alley in Midtown Manhattan. The city street sign marked it as DePew Place.

Mike and I had often jousted over the existence of old roadways on our island. I figured if I'd never prosecuted a crime that occurred on an obscurely named motorway in my dozen years on the job, then it probably had been obliterated by developers. I was wrong about DePew.

I spotted the salivating dogs before I saw the dead man's body.

Four guys in civvies were each holding leashes — two with Jack Russells straining against their owners' grip and two others with small terriers as well.

'Gentlemen,' Rocco Correlli said to Mercer, Mike and me, 'I'd like you to meet Toby Straight. He's the man who found the vic.'

'Actually, it's Bertie here who did the deed,' Straight said, commanding his pet to sit.

'Mr Straight runs a little club called Rats,' the lieutenant said. 'Guess all the classy names were taken.'

'What's that?' Mercer asked, keeping one eye on the medical examiner's team, which had set up a spotlight over the deceased.

'It's an acronym, really. Rat Alley Trencher-Fed Society.'

'RATS, obviously,' Mercer said. 'So help me out.'

'We had our first go at this here in DePew Place,' Straight said, gesturing at the narrow alley just east of the 45th Street piece of the landmarked train terminal, running north-south for the length of one city block. 'We come back at least once or twice every year.'

'I know where we are,' Mercer said. 'You'll have to help me with *trencher-fed.*'

Mike had both hands in his pants pockets as he stepped closer to the body. 'Probably in the twenty-first-century dictionary, m'man.'

'Afraid not, Detective,' Straight said. 'The word comes from a much earlier time. It refers to the keeping of hounds to hunt.'

'No wonder you lost me. Granddad wasn't from the hunting-hound Chapmans. Must have lost ours in the potato famine. What's your deal?'

Toby Straight looked like a fish out of water in this urban cul-de-sac. His long-sleeve shirt, rolled up at the cuffs, had initials monogrammed on the pocket. His jeans were perfectly clean and neatly pressed, and his tasseled loafers seemed impervious to scuffs. He wore a tweed cap and carried a walking stick or fancily carved cane, despite the fact that he appeared to be younger than I and wasn't limping.

'We started meeting almost fifteen years ago, right after I got out of graduate school. When I lived in town.'

'You don't live here now?' I asked.

'No, Bertie and I drive in from Darien,' Straight said, bending over to pick up his dog and stroke his belly. 'The group meets once a week.'

'Here?' I looked around the dark alley, which had none of the familiar trappings of a city street – no traffic lights, trash bins, or pedestrian crossing lines. Wedged between the edge of the terminal building and bordering the west side of the US post office that fronted on Lexington Avenue, DePew was now a dead end, filled with loading docks and truck bays.

'Anywhere there's garbage, Ms Cooper. Ryders Alley downtown, Bayard Street, the walkways in Riverside Park.'

'What's the attraction to garbage?' Mike asked.

'Where there's garbage, Detective, there are rats. And the hunt for rats is what indulges the basic instincts of these terriers.'

'Sorry?'

'These dogs were bred to chase small game – to chase vermin, if you will,' Toby Straight said. 'It's sort of like a twofer. In a city with a rat population that's out of control, we may not make a noticeable difference, but we do our bit. And the dogs have a good time at it.'

The other Jack Russell was yelping now, tugging against his leash and posing like a pointer. A homeless man came out of a doorway at the rear of the alley, below the Park Avenue Viaduct that circled the majestic terminal, now a century old. The dog barked again, practically howling, as the man dragged a huge plastic bag that clanged along the street as though it was filled with empty soda cans.

'Watch this, Mike,' Rocco Correlli said, lighting a cigarette. 'Let your dog go, Mr Straight.'

'Are you crazy, Loo?' I said. 'There's a dead body twenty feet away and some helpless vagrant stumbling around, not expecting any police activity.'

Straight bent down, holding Bertie over the ground while we argued.

'You'll see. He doesn't want either of them.'

When Straight let go of the terrier, he scrambled faster than a racehorse out of the gate, past the ME crouched over the deceased and around the startled homeless man. The other three dogs barked furiously.

Bertie disappeared out of sight for almost a minute before returning with a rat in his jaws, shaking the rodent vigorously from side to side to make sure he was dead.

Toby Straight seemed pleased with the kill. I was revolted.

'We've offended you, Ms Cooper,' he said.

'Hard to do,' Mike said. 'I've been trying for years.'

'Bertie's exercising his brain. It's a form of mental stimulation. It's in the nature of a terrier.'

'And what does this have to do with the dead man?' I asked. 'This – this urban fox hunt.'

'I never think of you as having such delicate sensibilities,

128

Alex,' the lieutenant said. 'Or else I wouldn't have invited you here tonight.'

'Let it be, Rocco,' Mercer said. 'I'm the one who invited her.'

'I'm not sure what it means,' Toby Straight said, cocking his head in my direction, 'that the sight of a dead man doesn't bother you, but a dead rat does.'

'I could give you a solid answer to that one,' Mike said, 'but I'm hoping to hang on to my private parts.'

Straight turned away from me, gloved up like a Crime Scene investigator, bagged the creature that Bertie deposited at his feet, and then rewarded the dog with a treat. 'The Department of Health actually pays us for ridding the streets of these creatures.'

'So you guys,' Rocco said, referring to Straight and his friends, 'you call yourselves—?'

'Ratters, Mr Correlli. We're ratters.'

'You came in here tonight – when was it?'

'About eight forty-five, sir. Right after dark.'

'You didn't see the body at first.'

'Not at all,' Straight said. 'We know DePew well. As you're probably aware, it's owned by the railroad company – Metro-North – and it's mainly used for mail trucks and as a freight loading area, so there's no automobile traffic to endanger the dogs.'

'That makes it the perfect free zone for rats,' the lieutenant said. 'Workmen create garbage during the day, throwing away remains of sandwiches and food and tossing soda cans. There's a couple of Dumpsters towards the rear.

The rats come out of the sewers and subway gratings at night and go hog-wild.'

The three other men were talking among themselves, watched over by a uniformed cop.

'I walked to the end of the alley,' Straight said, lifting his walking stick and jabbing it into the air, waist-high. 'This cane isn't an affectation. I lead off by pounding on the Dumpsters and stray piles of debris.'

'And that stirs up the vermin,' I said.

'Exactly. Tonight a stream of them came shooting out the big hole in the bottom of the Dumpster. And the stick protects me if any of them decide I'm fair game. Then we let the dogs off the leashes and they hunt,' Straight said, smiling at me as though to test my reaction, 'like they were born to do.'

'The dead man,' I said.

'When the rats came running out of the Dumpster, there weren't many places for them to go. Bertie and I were closest to them, and he was pretty agitated. Farther up the alley were my friends, and three other excited terriers. So they scattered, looking for a safe way back underground or out onto the streets of Manhattan.'

I shuddered. Popular lore was that in New York City, where the rodent population matched the size of the human population, one was never farther than thirty feet away from a rat.

'Bertie kept pointing to that last truck bay on the left,' Straight said, lifting his stick. 'I let him take me there. That's where the body was.'

'And rats?' Mercer asked.

'Some of them must have smelled blood – or death – and found it irresistible to stop and explore. But when Bertie turned the corner he was within six, seven feet of them, and they were gone in a flash.'

'Any damage to the body?' Mercer said to Rocco.

The lieutenant shook his head. 'I don't think he was there very long. Might be a scratch on his eyeball, but that's about it.'

'But he was moved?'

'My fault entirely,' Straight said. 'I knew if I left the man in that dark cul-de-sac, they'd be chewing on him in minutes. I dragged him out here, where you see him now, and yelled to one of my buddies to call 911.'

'You flipped him?' Mercer asked.

'I did. If he were still breathing, I'd have tried to resuscitate him.'

Rocco crooked his finger at me and walked away from Toby Straight, telling him to stick around. Straight tipped his cap, kept a tight rein on Bertie, and rejoined the other hunters.

Mercer and Mike followed us toward the deputy medical examiner.

'How's that for a bunch of sick fucks?' Rocco said. 'The rat brigade.'

'Tell me the truth, Coop, was that guy at your deb ball? Your coming-out party? Tallyho and all that?'

'Sorry to disappoint again, Mr Chapman. Never was a deb,' I said. 'I would, however, dearly like to take Mr Straight's pants off.'

'Here and now?'

'Didn't you see the blood on his pants leg? And his shirtsleeves?'

'He dragged the dead guy, who's oozing from a stab wound,' Mike said. 'Or maybe it's rat blood. What's your point?'

'Who are these men and why are you treating them so lightly?' I said. 'Because they're rich white boys from the burbs?'

Mike was standing behind the deputy ME, who was on his knees next to the corpse, looking over the young doctor's shoulder.

'Anybody home? They're into blood sports, Mike.'

'Relax, Alex,' the lieutenant said. 'We've got all their names and numbers.'

'What's with those marks?' Mike asked the doctor.

'Postmortem scrapes. No active bleed.'

'Never helps when somebody moves the body before you see it,' Mike said. 'The man's stabbed in the back. How come the blood's on his sneakers?'

'The fellow who found him,' the deputy doc said, 'told me he dragged him out of that passageway over to here while his friends called 911. Turned him over first to see whether he was still breathing, so the blood got all over his hands. I had to get him facedown again to examine the wound. Then one last turn so Crime Scene could photo his face.'

It was impossible to know what amount of trace evidence had been lost in all that movement. That, coupled with the fact that the outdoor location – impossible to scour in the dark – would be teeming with commercial workmen by daybreak and any efforts to retrieve more clues of value would be futile.

'The fingernails?' Mercer asked.

'Chipped and full of dirt to begin with. I don't think there was any kind of struggle.'

It looked as if the man's pants legs – the only thing the deceased was still wearing – had been pulled up to his knees during the move, and his skin had abrasions from being dragged across the pavement.

'I'd like to get the body out of here.'

'We need to see the marks on his skin,' Mike said.

'That means I have to roll him again?' the doctor asked.

'I'll scope it when you lift to put him in the body bag. How's that?'

'Better for my purposes. Would you call in the attendants to get to work?'

Mike signaled to the uniformed cop who was standing with the ratters. 'The morgue van out on the street? Get those guys in here, stat.'

'Are you swabbing the hunters for DNA?' I asked, seemingly to anyone who would listen to me.

'Last thing on my mind, blondie,' Mike said.

The two attendants trudged in from the street with the large vinyl sack that would carry the remains to the autopsy room.

'You want to see the clothing before I pack it up?' the

doctor asked, unfolding a stack of brown paper bags, each one of which would hold a separate item.

Mercer stepped in. 'What have you got? The jeans look pretty raggedy.'

'He was wearing this,' the deputy ME said, holding out a dirty men's sport shirt, pale yellow with long sleeves and a button-down collar. 'I had to cut it off him to get at the wound, but otherwise it's in pretty good shape.'

Mercer put the tip of his pen under the shirt collar and held it up, turning it around slowly so we could look at it. The rear panel was blood-soaked, and there were some pulls in the fabric that had probably been caused when Toby Straight pulled him out onto DePew Place.

'Looks almost new otherwise, unlike the denim, which is full of holes,' Mercer said. 'It's got a Gap label.'

'And this,' the doctor added. 'A baseball cap. Mr Straight says it was on the body when he first saw it but fell off while he was dragging the man.'

I looked at the shaggy brown hair that reached the dead man's shoulders. There seemed to be the slight indentation of a cap mark.

'What's his team?' I asked.

Mercer, having put the shirt in the paper bag and closed it, held up the cap with his pen. It was navy blue but didn't bear any sports logo.

'Poor guy didn't even have this long enough to get grease marks in the lining,' Mike said. 'Looks like one of those generic hats from a tourist stand in the city. At least we didn't lose a Yankees fan.'

The attendants got in place on either end of the corpse. As they lifted him to put him into the bag that would lie on the stretcher for the ride downtown, the three of us squatted.

Mike shined a light on the man's back. The wound was wide – probably deep – and had caused blood to spurt and drain all over the skin. Then, in an almost v-shape design leading down to the waist, were a series of evenly sketched ladders – or train tracks – just like the ones on the body of Corinne Thatcher.

'Got it,' Mike said. 'He's all yours.'

'Hey, Officer,' the doctor called out to the uniformed cop who'd been standing beside Toby Straight and his friends. 'Would you mind giving us a hand?'

The cop walked over to help lift the stretcher into place as the taller attendant was pulling the zipper up to the top of the bag.

'Holy shit,' the cop said, as the man's face disappeared. 'I think I know this guy.'

Mercer raised his hand like an officer stopping traffic on a freeway. 'Hold on.'

The attendant stopped and opened the bag again.

'That's Carl,' the cop said. 'I've been on this beat for more than ten years. Known him the last three or four.'

'You're sure?' Mercer said. 'No ID on him. We were thinking homeless. But you know his name?'

This was a great stroke of luck – for the dead man and for our work. One of the traditional reasons for cops working neighborhood patrols was about to pay off. The beat cop knew his territory and knew the people who lived and worked in it.

'Carl. He once told me his name was Carl. So my partner and me, we called him Carl Spackler.'

'Carl Spackler?' Mike said, the irrepressible grin reemerging on his face. 'The same name as the Bill Murray character in *Caddyshack*? The guy who killed gophers on the golf course?'

'Yeah, that's why we called him Carl Spackler.'

'You mean that's not his real name?' I asked.

'Like I said, it's how we knew him. First-name basis, and my partner likes to goof with all the characters we meet around here. This Carl guy, he's sort of homeless.'

'I don't understand. What do you mean he killed gophers? What does that have to do with the fact that his name is Carl?'

The cop was as impatient with me as Mike was. 'I mean he's *like* a gopher, Counselor. We don't got gophers in the city.'

'And this guy,' I said. 'This – this – Carl?'

'He lives underground, Ms Cooper. He lives in the train tunnels right below us,' the cop said. 'Pops up every now and then from underground. That's how come we know he's one of them moles.'

Fourteen

At 6:45 on Thursday morning, I met Mercer and Mike at the information booth on the main concourse of Grand Central Terminal. As directed, I was dressed down in my shabbiest jeans, old sneakers and a polo shirt.

Sergeant Hank Brantley of the Transit police had been assigned to accompany P.O. Joe Sammen – the cop who had recognized 'Carl' the evening before – and us into the community of tunnel dwellers referred to as 'mole people.'

In the pecking order of the homeless in New York City, moles had been given the most pejorative name. They were likened to animals, while others who slept in church doorways or on park benches were not.

Hank was stationed in Grand Central, with a specific duty to do outreach to homeless people in the area.

'Take a look around, guys,' Hank said. 'You won't see too many people dressed for success where we're going.'

Morning commuters were beginning to swarm past us. They came up from subways that deposited them on the lower-level concourse, and from suburban trains north of Manhattan.

I grabbed Mike's arm so I didn't get separated in the flow. 'How many people pass through here every day?'

'Seven hundred and fifty thousand of them daily,' Hank said. 'Maybe half a million going in and out on trains, and the rest just tourists, now that it's been restored. After Times Square, Grand Central is the most popular tourist attraction in New York.'

'That's a staggering number of people. I remember coming here as a kid,' I said. I had grown up in Westchester County, and riding to the city with my mother for adventures – to see the Christmas tree at Rockefeller Center, ice-skate in Central Park, visit the great museums, savor an ice-cream soda at Serendipity, and shop in the wonderful stores that lined the broad avenues – was always a memorable experience. 'Grand Central was our gateway to Gotham.'

'It was built as the Gateway to the Continent, more than one hundred years ago,' Hank said. 'You weren't the only one to find this place magical.'

'There's almost a choreography to this flow of people.'

'You nailed it, Alex. During the morning and evening commutes, everyone's making a beeline for an office or rendezvous, everyone's in motion. They know exactly where they're going and how to crisscross this place to get there. In between, we've got the tourists. Almost as crowded but moving at a much slower pace. Two entirely different dances, depending on the time of day you're in here.'

'The ceiling has always been my favorite.'

'If you slow down to look up, Coop, you'll be trampled,' Mike said.

The aqua-colored celestial ceiling with its golden constellations and stars stretched across the entire vault of the terminal. As a child, I'd been mesmerized by the sight of it whenever I emerged from the train. I had declared it my favorite work of art when I was six years old – the familiar signs of the zodiac played out above me but close enough to see in detail. I loved it.

Hank was leading us across the floor, to a wide ramp that led to the lower concourse. 'Take a last peek.'

I looked up and practically gasped again. Artists had restored the enormous scene to its original vibrant coloration, and it sparkled above us like the heavens.

'At some point,' I said, 'I remember visiting here and the ceiling was entirely black. I guess that's what decades of railroad traffic did.'

'Turns out it had nothing to do with soot from the trains or steam engines,' Hank said. 'It was completely the result of nicotine from the millions of cigarette smokers hanging out here.'

'Seriously? Nicotine blackened the painting?'

'All those mad men smoking while they waited for the last train to Scarsdale. Slurping down shellfish and martinis in the Oyster Bar, going through half a pack at the end of the day. That's what did it.'

'Well, it's glorious again. The entire station is,' I said, looking around.

'Ten constellations up there – the zodiac. Twenty-five hundred stars in an October night sky scene,' Hank said. 'The only catch is that it's all backwards.'

'What?'

We had lost sight of the great barrel-vaulted painting now, down on the lower level. 'When the painters created the ceiling back in 1913, they misinterpreted the design, which was meant to reflect the sky from above.'

'You mean it's a mirror image of what it should be?' Mike asked.

'First day the place opened, a commuter who was an amateur stargazer looked up and saw they got it wrong. He even wrote to the Vanderbilts, who owned the joint, to complain.'

'That must have gone down well.'

'They didn't bat an eyelash. Told the media that they'd planned the whole thing that way – backwards – so it would be the view that God had, looking down at Grand Central.'

'I guess when you're the richest family in America, you can plan for God, too,' Mike said. 'You're telling me Pegasus should be flying the other way?'

'For sure. The winged horse is prancing to the west, when he should be going east, in the other corner of the sky,' Hank said, stopping at the bottom of the long ramp. 'So this is how we get into the tunnels, lady and gentlemen.'

'What about the trains?' I asked.

'Here's the deal, Alex. When the station was opened in 1913, all the long-distance travel originated on the main concourse, whether you were going north to Canada or west of here to Chicago.'

Mercer interrupted, his transportation 'gene' going into gear. 'Now those were the glamorous runs, my dad used to say. Twentieth Century Limited, right?'

'Grand Central to Chicago's LaSalle Street Station,' Hank said, 'starting in 1902 and advertised as the most famous and luxurious train in the world. The New York Central provided a red carpet every night when the rich people boarded, and that expression – *rolling out the red carpet*, which originated right in this spot – stuck as a fancy way to treat people.'

'Never knew that,' Mercer said. 'Wasn't there an Owl, too?'

'Overnight to Boston,' Hank said. 'I grew up on this stuff. The Yankee Clipper, the Detroiter, the Green Mountain Flyer, the Hendrick Hudson.'

'Used to be my old man could call out every train and all the stops it made.'

'Worked for the railroad?'

'No. For the airlines. That's what put these great iron horses out of business after the Second World War. My old man loved train travel and everything about it. Always made him a bit melancholy that the work he did for Delta helped kill long-distance train travel.'

'I get that,' Hank said. 'Like I was telling you, when this station was constructed, all the fancy out-of-town travel operated from the main concourse. This lower level was only for the commuter trains. Once those routes were shut down over the years, the locals moved upstairs. This area, as you can see, became a major food court and commercial zone, and most of the tracks down here have basically been closed off.'

We made our way around the various cafés and restaurants and the automated information booth that sat directly below the one on the main concourse. Hank Brantley had a plan and a path. The rest of us followed him.

We stopped in front of gate 100, its wrought iron grating shut tight. Hank had radioed ahead to get a Metro-North security guard to meet us and unlock the metal barrier. The guard had brought along four hard hats for us to wear.

'I need this?' I asked. 'What are we expecting?'

'I'd prefer it, Alex. Never know what's up ahead. Things leak, they drip, they fall from work areas above. It's precautionary, okay? Just humor me.'

I put the hat on, increasing my discomfort and making me sweat before I even left the shelter of the building.

Once inside, there was another long ramp that led off to the side of the railroad tracks, those thick dark lines that appeared to stretch out endlessly in the tunnel ahead.

'Stay close, mind you,' Hank said. 'There are loads of syringes and crack vials underfoot. And I heard you had your first close encounter with some track rabbits last night. We've got plenty of 'em down here.'

'Track rabbits?' I asked.

'Rats. That's what we call them in the tunnels. They're

so used to seeing moles – underground people – that they're more likely to run towards you than away.'

'Maybe this wasn't such a good idea.'

'You'll see some fires, too. Don't be alarmed.'

'Fires in the tunnel? I can barely breathe now,' I said.

'Lots of the moles scavenge for pieces of old wood. Keep fires lit even in this intense heat 'cause it keeps the rodents away.'

He started to walk along the narrow ledge to the left of the last set of tracks. Mercer followed, and I was next in line. 'I always thought the tunnel-people stories were urban legend. All the stuff about a city beneath the streets.'

Hank Brantley shook his head. 'I asked to work in this building thirty years ago, Alex. It was the height of the city's homeless problem. I came here because I loved trains, and then I had this awfully rude awakening. Grand Central was one of the meccas for the homeless.'

'The station itself?' I asked.

'There used to be a waiting room,' Hank said. 'A huge space that's completely empty now. In fact, it's rented out for private parties. But it was quite the sight in its time. Marble walls and oak flooring, with wainscoting around the entire room. Maids standing by for women who were traveling without help. When train travel hit the skids, that waiting room became the finest free hotel space for the city's homeless, sleeping on the long wooden benches that lined the room.'

'I can't imagine it.' Though the homeless – whether mentally ill, victims of domestic violence, or returning veterans without resources – were still a big problem in the city, there were now entire departments of government and nonprofit agencies that tried to work with the struggling population.

'Vagrants is what we called them back when I was a kid. Got here to find out that Grand Central's public areas were considered the safest places for them to seek shelter from the wild streets of the eighties,' Hank said. 'That was the city's decade lost to crack and homelessness.'

'They could remain inside all night?' Mercer asked.

'Yes, unlike today, the building used to stay open. There'd be regular police checks at one in the morning, and then again at five A.M., just before the commuter rush. In between, it was easy for them to close their eyes and get some real rest. During the day, they'd panhandle to get enough food to keep them alive.'

'How many homeless people lived inside the main station?'

'By 1990, the estimates were at least five hundred of them. And from the faces I'd see day after day, I'd say at least fifty of them lived in here for more than a year. Pretty ironic that this magnificent edifice was so full of human misery.'

The path was narrow, and the farther we got from the train platform, the dimmer the lighting became. Every now and again, over our heads, was a bare bulb throwing off a glow against the dingy black area of the tracks. There was the distant rumble of subway trains going by somewhere farther below us. It seemed to repeat every few minutes.

'Is this dangerous?' I asked. I was running one hand

along the wall to my left to keep my balance. 'Where we're walking now?'

'Not dangerous for you, Alex. More so for the poor souls who call it home.'

There were noises all around us in the long tunnel. Train whistles from nearby and far away, the occasional screeching sound of brakes, a dull pounding from a jackhammer, and voices too indistinct to hear from this distance.

'Is there still such a thing as an electrified third rail?'

'Sure there is. But not in a dead tunnel like the one we're going to.'

'Relax, Coop. Years of ballet lessons and you can't do a little balance beam here?' Mike said. He had latched his forefinger into the rear waistband of my jeans. 'You won't get electrocuted.'

'Actually, Mike,' Hank Brantley said, 'that's usually the way we discover where moles live. Someone rolls out of a cubby onto the tracks, while they're sleeping or high. Gets electrocuted. Those bodies even cause trains to derail. Happens every week or two.'

There was the sound of something scratching against the metal tracks up ahead of us.

'Quit tugging at me, Mike,' I said.

'Can't have it both ways, kid. I'm either hooked in your pants for life or not. Hear that noise?'

'Yeah.'

'Track rabbits. That's the sound their nails make when they're scampering across the railroad ties. Nails scratching metal.'

'I just changed my mind then, Mike. Don't let go of me.'

Hank turned on a flashlight to guide us ahead. In about ten feet, he came to a place where the path widened into a raised concrete square, and we all grouped around him.

'So the guy you're looking for, you know anything about him?'

Our heads all turned to Joe Sammen, the cop who'd recognized 'Carl.'

'Only that I've seen him around my beat for the last three, maybe four years. That he's a mole. 'Cause he told me that a few times, and I've seen him with other guys I know.'

'What's your sector?' Hank asked.

'Charlie-David. I got above 43rd Street, Third Avenue to the east side of Fifth, north to 50th Street. The body was in DePew.'

'Let me see his photo again,' Hank said, holding out his hand for Mike's iPhone. He looked at the picture of the dead man's face, grimaced, and shook his head from side to side.

'Not familiar to me, which probably means he didn't come into the station proper.'

'Is that uncommon?' Mike asked.

'Not for a real mole. I mean, there are at least six hundred people – men, women and the occasional kid – who live in the tunnels that burrow out of 42nd Street, below the concourse. Some of them come in to use the bathrooms and clean up in the sinks, but the ones who are really hard-boiled? They've got their own little apartments down here. And they're afraid that if they run into any of the homeless advocates in Grand Central, they're going to be scooped up and taken to the nut house. Last thing they want are the rules and regs of a homeless shelter, you know?'

I knew that fact from many of the vulnerable homeless with whom my colleagues had worked.

'I'm warning you guys. What you're going to see is unpleasant. These folks, they've got their own mayor, their own system of laws, and they live by their wits. Some of them cook food on the steam pipes that you hear hissing – food they beg for or take half eaten out of the trash.'

'How long has this been going on?'

'Hobos have lived along train tracks since the first steam engine was invented. Right here, I'd say the 1980s was the decade of the tunnels. The New York Central had gone bust, so a lot of tracks were shut down. At first men mostly used to come in to do drugs. It just kept growing,' Hank said. 'Okay, we're going to move along now. When we stood at the entrance to gate one hundred, I'd say we were almost directly underneath what would be 44th Street to the east of the building.'

'Sort of right below where DePew Place begins,' Mike said.

'Yeah. We're going to pass along here, and there are hollow areas under this walkway where people live. Don't disturb anyone if you hear noise. Most of them know me and will respond better than to strangers.'

'Okay.'

Hank Brantley was moving as he talked, turning to look back at us so we could hear him. 'There are also some cubbies overhead—'

'In the wall?' Mike asked. I stood still while he leaned his head back. 'Up there?'

'Pickaxed into the cracked concrete. Yup. That's what I meant by apartments. If you look for the areas with over-hangs, they're especially sought after,' Hank said, pointing the light up and craning his neck. 'That protects the moles from being seen by workmen on the platforms opposite the wall.'

'Do the tracks run straight out like this from the station?' I asked.

Hank held out one of his beefy arms. 'Not at all. The train tracks go due north, but the tunnels spread out and around like the veins on the back of my hand. Sooner or later they connect to the subway tunnels throughout the city, and eventually they lead over to Penn Station,' he said, referring to the city's massive but far less attractive train hub on the west side. 'They were never meant to be linked together, but as the systems spread and the infra-structure rotted, you can pretty much get from here to the Hudson River via underground tunnels.'

'Don't any of them get killed by trains just walking around?' I asked.

Hank Brantley shrugged. 'Not too often. They manage to navigate the rails incredibly well.'

'What's that smell?' We were deeper into a branch off

to the side, still walking on our narrow ledge. I pulled up my collar and buried my nose and mouth in the soft cotton material.

'We're coming up on one of the little communities,' he said, shining his light on an area below the platform and ten feet ahead of us. 'Twenty or thirty guys live in it at any given time. Human waste is a problem for them here in the condos, otherwise they've got it figured out pretty good.'

'Condos?'

'That's what they call them. Like a series of concrete caverns, so close to the surface that they're often an entry point to tunnel life, but just far enough away from routine police patrols. The condos are pretty upscale, compared to the rest of the area. There are enough sprinkler pipes scattered throughout to get water, and some electrical wire to screw in bulbs. Just hold your nose and walk on by me. Hand me your phone, Mike.'

We inched around Hank, though I almost gagged on the awful smell emanating from below. I took a flashlight from Mercer and moved forward, enough to get away from the direct line of the scent. More scratching noise, and out of the next hole ahead came four or five rats, two the size of piglets.

Hank Brantley had lured three men out of their condo. All were dark-skinned, two were bare-chested against the intense heat, while the third wore a torn undershirt. They stood inches from the long-out-of-use tracks, leaning on the edge of the platform to talk with the cop whom they regarded as a friend.

They looked at the photograph of the dead man on Mike's phone. None of them showed any glimmer of recognition. I couldn't hear their conversation, till the one closest to me called out and asked if we had any food.

Mike apologized and said he'd send some back in with Brantley.

The man thanked Mike and laughed, directing his gaze at me. 'Make mine a filet, medium rare.'

'Don't look at her, buddy. Can't cook to save her life. I'll see you get some red meat.'

'Well, how about she delivers it?' the man said, wagging a finger at me.

'Tell us how to find out who this guy is,' Hank said, 'and she'll bring you a six-pack, too.'

'Don't know. Not my neighbor.' He held up his arm, and Hank's light followed. The tunnel forked about twenty feet away. 'To the left, you're going west across 44th. The other one leads up to 46th Street. You say you found him in DePew? Then I'd stay to the right. There's some broken air vents near DePew you could crawl down if you know your way around here.'

Hank thanked them, then straightened up and rejoined us.

'Can we give them some money?' I asked. 'To eat? I mean it's no worse than paying informants, and I feel so badly for them, living this way.'

'Stone-cold junkies, Alex. Those three would trade it right in for heroin. Mike's got the right idea. I'll send one of my men back later with a few sandwiches.'

At the actual fork, the platform we were on ended. Hank guided us down a short staircase. 'Step lively. You're crossing an old track here. Keep your toes out of the ties.'

We paraded across the solid lines, our forward advance sending a dozen or more track rabbits scurrying out of our way. Up five steps and onto another ledge. We passed several more apartment units, with residents occasionally sticking out their heads to see who was trespassing in their hood. They all seemed to relax when they spotted Hank Brantley.

'Just look the other way, Alex, if we come upon a guy called Dirty Harry.'

'And I'll know him because . . . ?'

'He'll come out of his hole, expose himself, and start masturbating, okay?'

'That's her specialty,' Mike said. 'Nothing shocks Coop.'

'These tunnels might just prove to be the spot that does,' I said. 'Mentally ill?'

'First layer of hell here are the criminals and junkies. Second are the insane, those who have walked away from all the help that's been offered. You've seen a lot of homeless street people,' Hank said, 'but the moles are outcasts even within the homeless world of outcasts.'

We had just worked a case that involved the murder of a young homeless woman in Central Park. The way she and her friends existed in the city's woods and vast green areas seemed almost tranquil compared to the stifling, foul, airless space beneath the city streets.

Hank led the way again.

'How long are we going to keep this up?' I asked. 'How many tunnels are there?'

'Just coming out of Grand Central alone, there's thirty-four miles of track, which fan out and around going down seven levels below the street.'

'Seven stories?'

'Not kidding. So, tunnels? Impossible to know how many there are. The place has been dug and redug so many times for so many different reasons that no blueprints exist of the terminal area. That's why it's impossible to patrol.'

Two white men, both bearded and shoeless, soot blackening their feet as high as their ankles, greeted Hank, but he passed them by.

'Both crazy as loons. Not worth my time,' he said. 'Those seven levels funnel into twenty-six main rail arteries, which leave here going north, east, and west.'

I was getting nauseous from the smells and sounds as we burrowed deeper into the tunnels.

I knew the importance of what we were doing but should have let Mercer and Mike make the trip without me. Still, I wouldn't have believed what they reported to me.

Several steps ahead, Hank came to an abrupt stop. He stooped and braced one hand on the platform, then jumped down beside the tracks. 'You in there, Smitty?'

It took almost a minute for the bone-thin black man to crawl out of his cubbyhole. 'Officer Hank. What's the beef?'

'No beef, Smitty. I think one of your boys got himself killed last night.'

'Haven't heard a word. Can't be true.'

Other heads appeared above us, and a guy in only his undershorts started coming closer to Hank.

'Go back home, Harry,' Hank said, as the man rested one hand on his crotch and started rubbing himself. 'I got some police here with me. I got a lady, too.'

Harry ignored the officer but looked at the four of us – Joe Sammen bringing up the rear of our group. He became more excited and obviously aroused.

Smitty shouted at him. 'Get out of here, Harry. Respect yourself, dude.'

Dirty Harry didn't stop playing with himself, but he turned his back and walked off into a darkened strip adjacent to our platform.

'Thanks, Smitty,' Hank said, turning to the officer who'd recognized the deceased. 'You two know each other?'

Sammen screwed up his face and studied Smitty. 'I think I've seen you around, but not lately.'

'I don't go up much anymore. Don't have to. Got most of what I need down here.'

Mike's curiosity got the better of him. He lowered himself down to take a look at Smitty's lair. The man was intelligent and well-spoken. I couldn't imagine what had reduced him to life as a mole.

Mike motioned to me, and I slid down off the platform to stand next to him. Inside the hole in the concrete, extending back about eight feet, were the makings of a home. There was a mattress covered by a dirty sheet, a stack of crates that had been converted into a dresser, a bulb overhead, and a wall-sized sketch of Derek Jeter that dominated the space. On top of the bed was a dog-eared old paperback by Chester Himes.

'I'm Mike Chapman. This is Alexandra Cooper,' Mike said, making the rest of the introductions.

It was clear that Hank Brantley had a relationship with this man, who seemed to trust him. 'Smitty used to be a graffiti artist. He did that Jeter portrait himself.'

'You're so obviously talented,' I said. 'Why – what brought you—?'

'Why am I a mole? That's what you want to know, isn't it?'

'Yes, please,' I said, while Mike brought up the photo of the dead man on his phone.

'I spent a lot of time riding subways doing my art. That got me into the tunnels, and I kind of liked it here. I used to shoot heroin. Big-time habit, and I was stealing all the time. In jail and out, on probation and off. Finally tested positive for HIV and now it's full-on AIDS. I've been shunned for so long aboveground – lost all my family along the way – it's just easier for me to live down here. Not so judgmental. Not so painful.'

'But there's medical help we can get you for your condition. You don't need to live like this,' I said.

'Speak for yourself, lady. This happens to suit me fine.'

'Smitty used to be the mayor of the Grand Central tunnels.'

'No more politics for me,' he said, holding up both hands and smiling broadly.

'You know everybody, don't you?'

'Pretty much.'

'Need you to look at this picture,' Hank said, taking the phone from Mike.

'What you got for me? Something to eat or a good cigar?'

Hank took a pack of cigarettes out of his pants pocket. 'For starters, okay?'

Smitty took the Marlboros and opened the box, reaching into his pocket for a book of matches. 'Let me see.'

Hank handed him Mike's iPhone.

'Sure, I know him.'

I felt better immediately. 'What's his name?'

'Down here, Ms Alex, that's the last thing you ask anyone. Nobody wants to be known – not by his street name.'

'Officer Sammen had a nickname for him. Called him Carl. Did he have another name?'

'Not that I know of. You need to understand, there's groups of people down here. Folks who come in to get out of the cold.'

'Get in how?' I asked. 'Through the station?'

'That doesn't happen much. Security there is pretty tight,' Smitty said, punctuating his words with a few violent coughs. 'But there are ladders hanging on some of the walls throughout all the tunnels in the city, rusty old things with thin iron rungs that workmen have used for decades. Gets frigid enough on the street and some people just find a broken grating, a manhole in the street. Let themselves in for the night and maybe stay a week or two. We call them wanderers. Not likely to stay very long. Not worth bothering to get to know 'em.'

'And your – your constituency?' I asked.

'Like you hear. Moles. Full-on moles. This is home. There are Grand Central moles, Penn Station moles, Bowery moles, Riverside Park moles, Dyker Avenue moles. We're all straight out of the journey to the center of the earth, Ms Alex. Only it's not science fiction.'

Out of the darkness behind Smitty's back, the shadowy silhouette of Dirty Harry reappeared. He was fully exposed now and still touching himself. Smitty knew it from the expression on my face.

'I hear you coming, Harry. Now I've got company, and this fine lady has no interest in you taking care of your nasty business while she's talking to me. She's sent people up the river for less than that. You go on to Ms Sylvia's nest and maybe she'll tell you how pretty it is. Then you can put it away for an hour or two.'

Harry retreated, and Mike was back to pressing Smitty.

'So this guy,' Mike said, taking back his iPhone and shaking it in Smitty's face, 'he's not quite a mole and more than a wanderer.'

'That's right,' he said, drawing deeply on the lighted cigarette before coughing. 'This boy's a runner.'

'What's that?'

'Just what it sounds, Detective. Me? I don't like to go up to the street. Somebody might try to take me to a hospital or put me in some kind of sterile shelter. Cramp my style. Some moles, like Harry, can't go up, 'cause they'd land in the Bellevue psych ward, where he busted out from two years ago. Wants to go up – show his stuff – but he just can't. Ms Sylvia? She's got a load of warrants from when she used to have enough meat on her bones to turn tricks. Hank's good to her. He just looks the other way and lets her be, so she sits tight, too.'

'And runners,' Mike said. 'They're the go-betweens, right?'

'Yes, indeed. Mostly, they live down here because we let them. Don't plan to stay very long at first, but if their spirits are dark enough, compromised enough, they get used to our ways,' Smitty said, crossing his arms and resting his back against the platform. 'But some of them – like your dead man – they still like the night prowl. Go up to steal food sometimes. Maybe swipe some clean clothes out of a Laundromat when no one's looking. Take a shower in a summer rainstorm.'

'So this guy, who did he run for?'

'Anybody who asked him, Detective.'

'Someone stabbed him in the back last night,' I said, ratcheting up the urgency of our mission. 'It doesn't get more serious than that, Smitty. Was he a runner for moles, or for people above, on the street?'

'Stabbed to death, was he? That's sure as hell tied into his business.'

'What business?'

'Look, Ms Alex,' Smitty said, coughing up enough of whatever was killing him to spit it out onto the tracks behind us. 'When I was in charge of this tunnel – back when I had some juice – anything I asked the guy to get me from the street, he'd find a way to come back with the goods. Not my job to ask how, you understand? So you call him Carl or whatever you want, he was just a runner-boy to me. I had a craving for a Big Mac and fries? A carton of cigarettes? A new lightbulb or an old library book or a can of spray paint for me to draw with? He'd steal those things or hustle a few bucks to buy them. I don't know whether he sold his sweet ass or knocked over your aunt Tilly to steal her purse. He got it done.'

Smitty realized he was snapping at me and backed off. 'Now, he didn't bother me and I didn't know what he was up to. No doubt he was running up more regular in this heat. It's a good time of year to escape the tunnels.'

'You called it business,' I said.

'I'm out of office, Ms Alex. Kept my nose clean. Somebody on the street – your kind of people – somebody offered him a dime to do a job, that runner-boy's likely to say yes. He liked to hustle. There are others here who'd know what he was up to. I didn't much care.'

'So how do we find those moles?' Mike asked.

'Where runner-boy kept his crib,' Smitty said, taking the phone from Mike and staring at the lifeless image of his old neighbor.

'Where's that at?'

'Last I knew, this runner-boy lived where it was easy to get in and out. Third tunnel ahead on the left, above the platform. There's a great big hole in the concrete, almost gets you to the subway entrance if you can stand crawling through it, past the rodents and roaches. It's got one of those old iron ladders – missing a few rungs.'

'Can you take us to it?' Mike asked.

'I don't like to leave home. Officer Hank can find it,' Smitty said, turning to our underworld guide. 'It's near the wall where the concrete crumbled a few years back. Crushed that girl who was trying to get herself out. The city never patched it up, 'cause one less mole didn't make the least bit of difference in the scheme of things.'

'I can probably get us there.'

'You know it, Officer Hank. Just south of that entrance on 47th Street. It's the hole that connects to the Northwest Passage.'

Fifteen

I doubled back with Mercer, into the great train station, stopping in the restroom to scrub my hands and face before going outside and walking – first north on Lexington and then west to the corner of Madison and 47th Street.

The Northwest Passage was the entrance to the train system where the antique steamer trunk had been found – bleached out and abandoned.

Mike took the tunnel route along with Hank Brantley and Joe Sammen, hoping that Sammen might recognize other moles, men who were geographically closer to Carl's turf in their underground lairs. Mercer told them we'd find a coffee shop near the corner of 47th Street and wait for them.

I couldn't bear the thought of eating after what I'd seen belowground. Two cups of strong black coffee couldn't make my nerves feel any more jangly than they already did.

At 8:45 a patrol car dropped Mike in front of the coffee shop, and Mercer waved him inside to us. He looked more like an off-duty coal miner than a cop.

'Sit down,' I said. 'The girl will be right over with your coffee.'

'I gotta go home and shower first thing. I stink.'

'I'm going to shower in the office. The sooner I get there and fill Battaglia in, the better.'

'I'm with Alex. I got fresh clothes in my trunk,' Mercer said. 'What'd you see?'

'First of all, I could probably get to Philly tunneling underground. Maybe all the way to DC.'

'But did you find out anything about who Carl is?' I asked.

'Everything but a name, kid.'

'What do you know?'

'That was his crib, right below 46th Street. If Hank's coordinates are as accurate as I think, it's an easy crawl – if you don't mind feeling like you're in an episode of some Animal Planet show – to the Northwest Passage. Joe Sammen recognized a whole pod of Carl's friends.'

'What did they call him?'

'Runner-Boy. From the days when Smitty was in charge and dubbed him that.'

'Get anything useful?' Mercer asked.

'I went in to look at his space. All he had was a yoga mat on the floor, a couple of torn T-shirts, a pair of sandals and a picture of himself from a few years back. I grabbed that,' Mike said. 'I asked Hank to see if he could find a man to safeguard the joint till you can get a warrant to search it. Didn't want to get you riled up, but there won't be anything left of Runner-Boy's once the pals in the hood know he's dead.'

I reached across the table for the old photograph. 'We don't need a warrant. Carl wasn't paying any rent. No expectation of privacy. Call Hank and tell him to go in and grab whatever there is. Look for paper, for other photos. Grab it all.'

'Love it when you go rogue, Coop.'

'It's the law, Mike. Every now and then the law is your friend.'

'Clean-cut kid,' Mercer said, when I passed him the picture. 'Wonder what happened here.'

'At least it gives us another photo to go public with. Sort of before and after looks.'

'Does headquarters have the shot on your iPhone?' I asked.

'Yeah.'

'Then it's okay to forward it to Mercer and me now.'

'Will do.'

'Mercer, let's you and I stop by to see Johnson White before we go to the office.'

'Who's he?' Mike asked.

'The porter who saw a man make off with the Yalie's steamer trunk,' I said. 'You didn't find any other clothes in Carl's cubby?'

'Torn-up tees, like I told you.'

'So the Grim Reaper fetches him in a new sports shirt from the Gap,' I said. 'And a touristy baseball cap.'

'And long dark hair over the collar of the shirt,' Mercer said.

'But he's got no other clothes. What does that say?'

'That whoever he was running for recently bought him new duds. Suited him up for a job, like stealing a trunk while no one's looking.'

'Might get us a step closer,' I said.

'Then Johnson White it is,' Mercer said, paying for the coffee as we stood up.

'I'll be home till I hear from you two,' Mike said. 'Unless Rocco's got plans for me.'

'Call you later.'

We walked across to Park Avenue and down to 43rd, to the Bank of America building. I waited in the lobby while Mercer was directed to the basement to find White.

He returned five minutes later, shaking his head. 'Best he could say was that the shirt was light-colored, like the one Carl was wearing when he was found, and that the cap was darker than the guy's hair. But because the brim of the cap was pulled down so low, White couldn't make anything out of his features. Showing him the iPhone photo didn't give us anything.'

'Skunked. Might as well go downtown.'

'I'm parked on 45th Street, just east of Grand Central.'

We tried to make a game plan for the day, unable to factor in what would happen once Commissioner Scully made a public statement about the second murder.

'Did you ask Mike to have the dead man's face run through facial recognition programs in the Real Time Crime Center?'

The NYPD's dramatically effective 'real time' center

worked with more than thirteen million mug shots and arrest photos, scanning them against images of suspects sought for violent crimes.

'Rocco's on it.'

'Last count,' I said, 'there were more than four thousand closed-circuit TV cameras in the subway system citywide. There must be a few at the entrance to the Northwest Passage.'

'Same way the baseball cap pulled snug down prevented Johnson White from seeing the trunk thief's face? That would have foiled facial recognition software, too.'

We were almost near the courthouse when Mike called.

'We haven't even reached Hogan Place,' I said. 'Be patient.'

'Got a hit?'

'Not yet. The photo you took last night?'

'Didn't work. Rocco had it run against Universal Face Workstation,' Mike said, referring to the program with millions of criminal faceprints, digitally recorded representations of human faces, as individual as fingerprints. 'But the system works in part on the theory that faces are symmetrical. And our boy wound up a little cockeyed last night. The photo drew a complete blank.'

'Scully will go public by noon,' I said. 'That should help.'

'I stole his thunder, Coop. That other photo of him I swiped, that was taken a few years ago?'

'The one where he looks like a Boy Scout?'

'That one. Earned him a few badges they don't give out in scouting,' Mike said.

'A criminal history?' I asked.

'Smitty was right about our boy hustling. His picture comes up with three arrests for prostitution. About five years ago, in Midtown South, before he went down under and got too dirty to sell his flesh. And he was a frequent flier for petty theft, too.'

'Sounds like a runner for hire to me. Now what in God's name would a guy like that have to do with Corinne Thatcher?'

Sixteen

Laura printed out the two photographs Mike had forwarded to me of Carl the mole – dead and alive – while I went to the ladies' room and showered. The spare clothes I kept at the office to dress down when I had an unexpected reason to go out into the field were a huge step up from the tunnel-tour threads in which I'd left home.

'Mr Battaglia's waiting,' Laura said, when I returned to my office.

'Where's Mercer?'

'He cleans up faster than you do. Maybe better, too. Put a brush to that hair, young lady.'

I closed the door that separated her cubicle from my office and tried to make sense of my tangle of clean hair in the mirror that hung on the rear of the door.

'Mercer's out in the hallway waiting to go over with you. When you're done, Judge Aikens wants to see you on the Dominguez case. Drusin's filed some everything-but-the-kitchen-sink motions to get his client out of jail immediately and to get you off his back,' my efficient secretary said. 'And Mike asked me to print out the rap sheet on the deceased.'

I picked up both files – the Thatcher murder and the Dominguez papers – from her desk, and grabbed the rap sheet. Mercer was outside in the main corridor, fifteen feet from Laura's desk.

I handed the rap to Mercer. 'Carl Condon. Get familiar with the record so you can help me answer the district attorney's questions.'

We walked the gauntlet together, the locked executive wing hallway – lined with photographs of the stone-faced white men who had preceded Battaglia as DA – that led to his executive assistant's desk.

'He's ready for you, Alex,' Rose said, smiling at me. 'Pat yourself on the back for calling him last night, even though it was late. The mayor thought the boss was at the crime scene, he seemed to know so much.'

Paul Battaglia had no use for the new mayor, who had no understanding of the criminal justice system. It suited Battaglia's personality to walk all over a politician in whom he sensed a point of weakness, of vulnerability. New York City's latest leader wouldn't have a clue how to handle the DA and the police commissioner in front of the media, with all the frenzy surrounding a serial murderer.

The smell of Battaglia's expensive Cohiba at ten in the morning was like a breath of cool mountain air after the oppressive odors in the Grand Central tunnels.

The cigar was lodged in a corner of the DA's mouth when he said hello to Mercer and me, and he showed no intention of removing it. Words occasionally slurred as he talked around the brown stub, but it never got in the way of expressing his strong opinions.

'You two figured this one out yet, Alex?'

'This second kill has thrown us way off track, Paul.'

'You're sure it's the same guy?'

'Or team,' Mercer said. 'No doubt.'

'You've got a young woman in a top-tier hotel, throat slit and body violated. Good family, important job. Now tell me about this guy.'

Mercer had done a quick study of the criminal history. 'Carl Condon. Twenty-six years old. Originally from Apalachicola, Florida. Dropped out of FSU and moved here six years ago. Four collars for larceny and three for prostitution.'

'Common denominator?'

'Marks on their bodies,' I said. 'Drawings that might represent train tracks.'

'*Might?* I can't do a stand-up on *might*. The department never declares a serial case till there are three crimes. Why go on two?'

'I agree with the commissioner this time, Paul. People have to be made aware before the body count grows. Maybe these few clues will resonate with someone who knows the killer. They are especially brutal crimes.'

'There's a homicide that isn't brutal?'

'I'd say there's a good chance that Carl Condon was an accomplice in getting the Thatcher girl into the Waldorf. He might have stolen the trunk—'

'I get that,' the DA said, blowing me off and turning to Mercer. 'Did this guy really live in a hole in the ground? In a tunnel?'

'Yes, sir.'

Battaglia leaned forward, on the scent of a hit. 'Were you there? Did you see it yourselves? Am I safe in actually saying people make their homes down there?'

'Alex and I went in this morning, with an officer from Grand Central. It was only Chapman who actually saw where Condon lived.'

'But the moles Alex described last night,' he said to Mercer, 'they actually exist in numbers?'

'No question about it. We met a few dozen of them.'

'So the mayor's been in office almost nine months,' the sixth-term incumbent noted. The DA's office relied heavily on funding from the city, and the new mayor had not been Battaglia's candidate. 'He'll get pummeled on his homeless problem once this gets out, am I right?'

'In all likelihood, sir.'

Paul Battaglia leaned back, sensing a hole in the mayoral armor. 'All his blather about New York as a tale of two cities, and he hasn't done a goddamn thing about the homeless problem yet. It's an absolute disgrace on a human level, driving the murder rate back up after all the successes of my crime-strategies approach.'

'But, Paul—,' I said, trying to interject a thought.

'Cavemen lived underground, Alex. Troglodytes and other subhuman cultures burrowed into cliffside dwellings. Egyptian slaves lived and died in their mines. Cimmerian monks cut their cells into rocks, coming out only to minister to passing pilgrims.'

Battaglia was revving up a speech for his fall appearance at Riverside Church. I tried not to choke on his rhetoric as I stared at the sign hanging behind his head, reminding me that he couldn't play politics with people's lives.

'Scully and I may have two homicides to answer for this week, but City Hall has allowed the larger problem to exist, to flourish under this new leadership.' The cigar bobbed up and down furiously, marking the tempo of Battaglia's prattle. 'And if the mayor thinks that by spending all his time trying to raise taxes on my most loyal constituents while every John Doe Lunatic takes up residence in a train tunnel, he'll be a one-termer faster than you can say *Jimmy Carter.*'

'Is there a problem you want to tell us about?' I asked.

Paul Battaglia had known Mercer for almost as long as he had known me, and trusted him as the loyal NYPD partner that he was.

'My application to the city council for twenty million dollars for the international cyberbanking initiative I want to create – remember that?'

It was part of the program for my counterparts in the white-collar crime unit of the office, which was Battaglia's pet division. They did more intellectual work than street crime, cleaner and without any element of violence. 'It was discussed at the last bureau chief's meeting. That's all I've heard.'

'The Speaker called me yesterday and told me the mayor's

going to veto it. Straight-out veto. No discussion, no money for this office.'

If the mayor wasn't yet familiar with Battaglia's form of payback, he was in for a rude awakening.

'He and I – Keith Scully, too – have been invited to the reception for the president when he arrives for the special UN meeting. You need to solve these cases before that. Let the mayor be the one who's embarrassed about the homeless. His policies allow the situation in this city to deteriorate, while the commissioner and I tackle all the scum thrown our way.'

'You can't put these homicides in the middle of a polit-ical skirmish,' I said. 'That's way too transparent for your style.'

The district attorney of New York County rarely left fingerprints, but this mix of money and murder was a formula that could lead him onto the rocks.

'The reception is Monday night. Get everything else off your plate, Alex. Give Rocco what he needs to get this done. There's only one clown in town,' Battaglia said, 'and unfortunately for me he's running City Hall. I want results from you before the weekend's over.'

Seventeen

'Don't mess with him, Alex. Hand off the Dominguez case to Catherine or Nan,' Mercer said, referring to two of my closest friends in the bureau.

'Let me run up to the courtroom and see what Drusin is filling the judge's head with. It's just some motion nonsense, I'm sure. If there are immediate issues to deal with – substantive ones – I will put someone else on it.'

'I hear you.'

'Would you mind getting an update from the team at the Waldorf? Do we have any idea whether they've seen anything on the surveillance cameras they've been checking? We should certainly know more by now.'

'We'd have heard something for sure if they'd gotten lucky. I'll do the catch-up.'

Over the years, the route to the courtrooms from the DA's office had become more circuitous, even though we occupied several floors in the massive building. I jogged down the staircase one flight from the executive wing on eight, since the only direct entrance was by way of the lone security guard at the seventh-floor desk.

The thirteenth-floor hallway – which held eight trial 'parts', as they were called – was beginning to fill up with defendants, lawyers, families and friends of the accused, and some of the court-watchers who hung out, hoping for salacious proceedings to fill the long, quiet days of their retirement. Some of them were like Sex Crimes Unit stalkers who knew if one of my colleagues showed up, there might be enough references to sexual acts to keep them awake and engaged – better than the best soap operas on television.

I headed for Judge Aikens's part, although I saw no sign of my adversary.

As I pulled open one of the double doors, there was a sudden burst of laughter behind me. I turned to see a group of eight or ten men emerging from the restroom, led by Gerardo Dominguez. I didn't look long enough to study faces. One of the old men who followed my trials for all the wrong reasons – perverse sexual acts, foul language, and endless talk of body parts – was calling to me, coming at me from the other direction.

'Ms Cooper! Ms Cooper! I didn't see your name on any of the calendars today. What have you got going?'

I pretended I didn't hear him and let the courtroom door swing shut behind me.

David Drusin was standing at the bench, talking with the judge.

'Good morning, Alexandra. Thanks for coming up so

promptly,' Judge Aikens said. 'It's apparent from the news that you have a lot on your plate.'

'Not a problem, Judge. Thank you both for waiting. I see, David, that your client made bail.'

'COMET.'

'Did you say *comet*?' I asked.

'I did. Cannibals of Metro New York – Cooper Chapter. I formed a new nonprofit yesterday, to make it easier for you to find these guys. There are so many flesh-eating figments of your imagination out there, ready to chomp on the ladies, that they all chipped in to raise Gerry's bail. Dinner is at eight tonight, if you'd like to join them.'

I smiled at Drusin. 'Nice way to get rid of me.'

'You're too tough to eat, Alex. Though a bit of grilling might tenderize you.'

'Step back, both of you,' the judge said. 'Let's go on the record.'

Officer Dominguez had entered the courtroom. Half a dozen men sat in the front row as he made his way to counsel table to sit beside his lawyer.

I glanced around at the group. Each man had his police officer's shield flapped over the pocket of his sports jacket. I was not at all surprised that the solid blue line of cops would support a colleague in trouble. I was in for some stonewalling should I need anything from the precinct in which Dominguez patrolled.

'Once again, good morning to you all,' the judge said, after the case was called into the record. 'It appears that the issue of bail has been resolved, Mr Drusin. I'm going to remind your client that there are orders of protection for his wife and child. There is to be absolutely no contact between them. None attempted.'

Gerry Dominguez clasped his hands together in front of him, fidgeting in place, nodding his head to let the judge know that he understood the terms of his release.

The cops in the front row were whispering to one another, trying to unsettle me. Judge Aikens banged his gavel and demanded silence.

'I understand, Mr Drusin, that you've prepared some of your motions already. Quick work.'

'I told you I'd have them to you as soon as possible. First is the motion for the dismissal on First Amendment grounds. All we have here is speech, which is supposed to be free.'

'May I give you examples of the language, Your Honor?' I asked, pulling documents from the folder. 'Emails that said Mr Dominguez was looking forward to "cramming a chloroform-soaked rag" in his wife's mouth. A document titled "A Blueprint for the Abduction and Devouring of Alba Dominguez".'

'He was sending these emails as part of a fantasy, Judge. A game.'

'His cyber life was bleeding into reality. He wasn't just chatting with these men, he was the provocateur of the conversations. Mr Dominguez took overt acts,' I said. 'I will respond to these motions with all the supporting documentation so the court can see what the facts are.'

'On an expedited schedule, Ms Cooper,' Judge Aikens

said, playing to the cops in the front row. 'I'm not dragging my feet on this one. If Dominguez is a good officer – and if you cannot prove any overt acts in this conspiracy charge – then we need to get him back on our streets as soon as possible.'

There was applause from the defendant's supporters. I looked over my shoulder. My sole cheerleader was the elderly court-watcher, a staple in my small posse of regulars, who leaned forward in hopes of more specifics from me.

'Thank you for that, Your Honor. And most important, I would very much like to have you remove Ms Cooper from the prosecution of this case, as I mentioned yesterday. Let me give you some of the reasons I have to add to my preliminary remarks.'

My spine stiffened at the idea of Drusin throwing any more personal venom into the formal court record.

'Actually, Judge Aikens, I've just come from Mr Battaglia's office, as you know. Mr Drusin may withdraw his motion and keep his litany of personal peeves to himself.'

'But, Judge, I'm entitled to make a record about Ms Cooper in support of my application.'

'That won't be necessary. I've been assigned to handle a breaking double homicide that will require my complete attention, around the clock, until a suspect or suspects are apprehended and then swiftly charged. I'm in the process of reassigning the Dominguez matter to a colleague in the Special Victims Unit.'

'Very wise of you, Ms Cooper,' the judge said. 'I assume this won't delay the proceedings?'

'Wait a minute,' Drusin said. He seemed upset not to be able to throw some ad hominem attack about me on the record. 'I'm not finished.'

'No, but you're defanged on this issue, Mr Drusin,' I said. 'By noon today, there will be a new prosecutor handling this matter. And no disruption in the expedited-motion schedule. Anything else I need to deal with, or am I free to step out of the well?'

'We're officially adjourned,' the judge said, banging his gavel to underscore that point. 'Thanks for coming up, Alex. And, you, David, got half of what you wanted right off the bat. You ought to stop being so vituperative.'

I stepped away from the table and turned to walk out of the room as the judge left the bench.

The six officers stood up as I passed them, muttering epithets at me, causing my lone supporter to try to catch up with me.

'Ms Cooper,' he called after me, 'you shouldn't have to give up the case. You could nail this guy.'

I gave him a thumbs-up as I left the courtroom but walked faster to avoid the conversation he wanted to have. There was still a small pack of men huddled in the corner of the long hallway, and I assumed they were Dominguez supporters. I wanted to get away from the entire crew.

I pressed both DOWN buttons on each side of the elevator bank, hoping one of the eight oversized sets of doors would open before the old guy caught up to me and tried to bend my ear.

The one farthest from the corridor – closest to the

window – creaked apart, and I ran to get on it. There were several prosecutors and witnesses in it, descending from one of the higher floors. The heavy steel doors, several inches thick, started to close as I greeted the others and pressed for the seventh floor.

Before the doors could shut completely, a man whose footsteps I'd heard coming up behind me – I thought it was the overanxious court-watcher – thrust his arm between the two sides.

I reached for the OPEN button before the viselike grip of the solid doors could cause any injury to the man's forearm, which was too well muscled and too dark-skinned to be that of my elderly admirer.

The doors sprung several inches apart. The man withdrew his arm and the doors slammed shut again before I could see his face and apologize to him. But not before I saw the words KILL COOP tattooed on the skin of his hand.

Eighteen

'I'm telling you I came directly back here and asked Laura to alert security,' I said to Mercer. 'I wanted Raymond Tanner stopped before he got out of this building.'

'The guy must have moved like lightning. I came out of the conference room and everybody was scrambling.'

Mercer was out of breath, having chased the sociopathic rapist who had somehow gotten himself past security and up to the corridor where Gerardo Dominguez's case was being heard.

'Tanner's wanted for a handful of violent crimes and escape from his psych facility. Now he slips into the courthouse,' I said, 'to the very room where a cop who stopped him on the street and let him go has his own encounter with the law?'

'Not just with the law, Alex. With you, in particular. That's why this isn't any kind of coincidence,' Mercer said. 'And now there's not a sign of Tanner anywhere.'

'Did anyone think to horse-collar David Drusin? He may have set the whole thing up. Or try dragging Gerry

Dominguez over to Internal Affairs?' I was shaking, and both Mercer Wallace and Nan Toth were trying to calm me down.

'Dominguez is facing state time. You don't really think Drusin is going to let him talk to IAB, do you?' Nan asked. 'I'm taking the case. You going to let me in on the guy's recipes, or am I flying blind?'

'That would be a recipe for disaster, Nan. And I know you're trying to lighten me up, but this case is not for you.'

'Don't be ridiculous. It's mine.'

'That was before Raymond Tanner showed up today. It has to go to one of the men in the unit. Tanner adds a very sinister undertone of misogyny here. Both he and Dominguez clearly hate women, and touching these case folders is like bringing on a personal vendetta.'

'Alex is right. I got someone at Special Vic trying to dig up a connection between these two men – serial rapist and cannibal cop,' Mercer said. 'Till we find it and can prove it, best you stay out of the mix before you wind up in a microwave, Nan.'

'Give me the folder,' she said. 'What if I assign it to Evan?'

'Perfect.'

Evan Kruger was a senior trial lawyer, as smart and even-tempered as they come. He would dive into this case – as he had with many others of the toughest in the bureau – and master the facts and legal issues, steering clear of the baiting that David Drusin had stooped to with me.

'Are you going to be reachable?' Nan asked.

'We're off to the Waldorf,' Mercer said. 'Gonna clear her mind with some old-fashioned murder. Call anytime.'

'You might need to fill Evan in on the facts.'

'It won't take long to do. All the emails Dominguez wrote are in the file, and the grand jury minutes with his wife's testimony takes it the rest of the way,' I said. 'He's going to get slammed with a bunch of bullshit motions, but the facts hold up.'

'Case of first impression?' Nan asked. 'Not quite like the Donner Pass.'

'I was just beginning to research an online encounter. He'll find my notes. The only case on point is about a decade old, in Germany. A guy who trolled the Web looking for an adolescent willing to be butchered,' I said, stopping to brush my hair at the mirror behind the door – mostly an attempt to see if my arm had stopped trembling. 'Miewes is the perp's name. Cut off his victim's penis and then fried it. They ate it together before he killed the kid.'

'We don't need to go there,' Nan said.

'Judge Aikens will actually be looking for some support if he needs to be convinced this isn't just magical thinking. Drusin wants everyone to believe the eating people part is fantasy. Be sure to tell Evan that the website on which Armin Miewes found his victim is called the Cannibal Café. Check out the menu.'

'She's stalling, Nan,' Mercer said.

'Damn right. I want to be here when they haul Raymond

Tanner back in the courtroom. I can't believe he got very far.'

'He wasn't sticking around to get cuffed, girl. That little appearance was well orchestrated. You never saw him coming and you saw only the part of him that he wanted you to see, to scare the daylights out of you,' Mercer said. 'Seems to be working fine, that plan.'

'But you agree with me, then? Dominguez is behind this.'

'We'll sort it out. The last place you need to be is roaming the courthouse when we bring Tanner's sorry ass in here.'

'Too bad Mike's not back in town,' Nan said, smiling at me. The senior women in the unit were among my closest friends. They had followed the slow path of my relationship with Mike Chapman for years. 'Sounds like you're in need of a bodyguard. That could take your mind off work.'

'He is back, or did I forget to tell you? Besides, his last babysitting job was a disaster, or don't you remember?'

Mercer laughed. 'Good thing you didn't go into dentistry, Nan. I think you just hit a nerve.'

I tossed my hairbrush into the bottom drawer of my desk and held up my hands. 'I'm cool with it. The man's a wolverine.'

'Aren't they part of the weasel family?' Nan asked, poking me in the side.

'If they weren't, they are now,' I said as I passed by her. 'Talk later.'

I opened the door and told Laura that Mercer and I were off to the Waldorf.

'Rose called. She said Battaglia needs to see you. He's very unhappy that you went to court on Dominguez and set off this firestorm with the fugitive.'

'Tell Rose it's Evan Kruger's case. I don't have time for a dressing-down by Battaglia. Tell her you'll give me the message when you see me.'

'But I am seeing you, Alex. Don't cross the district attorney.'

'You thought you saw me, Laura. But it's just a fantasy.'

'I'll bring her back to you safe and sound,' Mercer said. 'Tell the boss I was ordered to get her out of the courthouse.'

We were downstairs in three minutes and in Mercer's car, headed uptown to the Waldorf Astoria. By one P.M. we had parked the car and entered through the rear lobby on Lexington Avenue, now well guarded by uniformed cops and additional private security.

We made our way to the basement of the great hotel, still the headquarters for the investigative team.

One of the Manhattan South detectives, Gary Stryker, saw me coming and cupped his hand over his mouth to shout down the hallway. 'Hey, Chapman? Your minder is here.'

Gary high-fived me as I walked past.

'He went out without his leash today, Stryker. I had to bring it along.'

'Mike's roughing up the video techs something awful, Alex. Better get in there and calm him down.'

'I'm fresh out of calm myself. What's the problem?

Mercer couldn't even get anyone to tell him what's the latest when he called.'

I reached the cubicle in which two men from the hotel's AV system were working with Mike and Rocco Correlli.

'I'll tell you what the problem is, kid,' Mike said, without even straightening up from his position, leaning over the shoulder of the video operator who was sweating bullets. 'There are more gaps in this surveillance system than there were between your front teeth before you got braces, Coop. It's a joke, this system.'

'How so?' I asked as Mercer crowded into the small room behind me.

'Dr Azeem narrowed the time frame for us. We actually pulled feed from fifty-two cameras. Decided it would double the work to take off every single floor, because the elevators and stairwells would catch the action going from one to the other. These men have been on this – with teams of six detectives backing up the work – for the last twenty-four hours. Not a thing to show for it. Half of them drew blanks.'

'Blanks?'

'Yeah. Either the cameras themselves weren't working or the software was so outdated that no images were captured. Not one single frame of any use.'

'Show me what you're talking about.'

'Bring up Monday afternoon for her,' Mike said, wiping the sweat off his forehead with the back of his hand. 'High noon, in fact. Show us the elevator that leads to the fortieth-floor suites.'

One of the techs had his nose so close to the monitor that it was practically touching the screen. Mike provided the sound track as the grainy video began to play. I could see Monday's date and time in the upper right corner.

'First of all, only the newest equipment – like the cameras in the main lobby elevators – have the latest technology. The hallways and stairs are mostly old-fashioned tape. They loop over again and again in twenty-four-hour cycles, and the images are so muddy there's not much to see.'

I stepped back so Mercer could get a good look. 'Useless,' he said. 'I can make out movement, and a couple of suited men from time to time, but nothing or nobody you could recognize.'

'Out of the fifty-two cameras we started with,' Mike said, 'more than a dozen of them are flat-out broken. Not working. Just there to rope-a-dope any would-be felons into thinking they're being recorded.'

'Exits and entrances?' Mercer asked.

'I can give you some clear shots of those,' the tech said. He played with the computer and brought up footage from the Park Avenue entrance of the hotel, midday on Monday. 'Your detectives have been over these films, reviewing the hours from noon to six P.M., dozens of times.'

'Why?' I asked.

'Different people see different things,' he said. 'Your brain gets fried pretty quickly watching so many hundreds of people coming and going. Then the bellman brings the luggage in ten, fifteen minutes later, so you can't possibly connect it to the people who might own it.'

'But big pieces? Anything like the trunk we think is involved?'

'Not so easy. Around two fifteen that afternoon a group of thirty people arrived from a cruise ship on some kind of package tour. There were trunks the size of my apartment,' Mike said. 'Once they got loaded on the luggage carts and hauled inside, it was impossible to see any of the individual pieces. Impossible to tell how and when they got to the rooms.'

'You think someone could have slipped one into the pile?' Mercer asked.

'Hand one of the bellmen ten bucks? You could slip a boatload of contraband right through the front door.'

'But the fancy-dancy suites in the Towers?' I asked. 'There must be a real effort at security. I mean, just for antitheft purposes, not expecting this kind of violence.'

'Give her the Towers elevators,' Mike said to the tech.

Again, the young man moved in so close to the monitor that I thought he'd leave some of the hairs from his goatee on the screen.

The tape started to roll. The images were the clearest I'd seen yet. We watched several elevator trips – a tedious task at best – with well-dressed guests going up forty flights, then others leaving their floors to return to the lobby. My yawns were so big they were audible.

Suddenly the screen went white.

'See what I mean?' Mike said. 'Is this lame or what?'

Mercer moved closer to the tech. 'How long does this go on?'

'I suppose it just died. Must go on this way to the end.'

'You mean no one has watched it all the way?'

'You'll have to ask the detectives down the hall,' the tech said. 'I have no idea.'

'Fast-forward for me. Can you do that?'

'What's the—?' I started to ask.

Mercer shushed me. We watched for several minutes while the tech kept us informed about the time.

'That's half an hour since it went dead,' he said. 'Now we're coming up on an hour. I don't know how long you want me to do this, but personally I think it's pretty futile.'

'Stick with it,' Mercer said.

At least fifteen minutes went by until the tech told us that the timer showed that three hours of this past Monday afternoon had elapsed.

'Give up the ghost, Mercer,' Mike said. 'It's dead.'

About two minutes later, as though suddenly resuscitated, the footage came on with perfect clarity.

Mike elbowed me out of the way. A couple had gotten on at the thirty-ninth floor and spent most of the ride down to the lobby kissing each other in the corner of the cab. 'It's not dead after all.'

'It never was,' Mercer said.

'Then how the hell do you account for three hours of a total eclipse, my friend?'

'The security camera was intentionally blinded, Detective Chapman.' Mercer pointed his forefinger at the light fixture above our heads and pretended to pull it like a trigger. 'It was temporarily blinded by a laser gun.'

Nineteen

Rocco Correlli moved us all into a slightly larger window-less room. The long table was half covered with trays of food that catering had sent down to the bleary-eyed detect-ives. The other half was covered with papers – police reports, hotel bills, records of the various tape recordings, and photographs of both victims and the antique steamer trunk. The tech guy loaded the software from the Towers surveillance equipment onto a larger computer at the far end of the room.

'How do you blind a camera?' Rocco asked.

'All too simple,' Mercer said. 'Remember when that Russian oil billionaire had his yacht in the city last year?'

'Ivanovic? Vladimir Ivanovic?' Mike said.

'Yeah. Well, there were some people walking on the pier, up near the *Intrepid*,' he said, referring to the steamship piers along the Hudson River, on the west side of Midtown Manhattan. 'One of them was a good friend of Vickee's. They tried to take photos of the mega-yacht, but they couldn't.'

'Why not?' I asked.

'First of all, his staff goes nuts when anybody gets too close to the boat. When the story hit the *Social Diary*,' Mercer said, referring to the hottest gossip page in town, 'it said that Ivanovic actually installed antipaparazzi shields all over the yacht.'

'So what do they have to do with this?' Rocco asked.

'They're lasers, Rocco. They sweep the area around the boat, and if anyone tries to take photos or videos, the lasers blind the cameras. The cameras simply can't take pictures.'

'You gotta be kidding.'

'Not for a second. You want to know how easy it is to do? For about twenty bucks – in case you're not a billionaire with a yacht – all you need is a laser from an old DVD player, a lens you can focus, and a couple of double-A batteries.'

'What made you think of that?' Mike asked, gnawing on a turkey sandwich.

'Because it wasn't the same as the other footage. It went completely white. It was never grainy or black. It didn't look like it had been recorded over.'

'Does it mean our killer's a high-tech operative?'

Mercer laughed. 'Not really. Wouldn't even need a second guy. It's one of those things you can search online, like I did when Vickee told me the story about her friends' attempts to take photos of the big yacht. Anyone can learn to do this – it's even easier than surfing for cannibal codefendants.'

'But how?' Mike asked.

'The laser can be the size of a tiny flashlight,' Mercer said, looking at the elevator interior on the image frozen on the screen. 'A piece of duct tape could hold it in place here.' He pointed to a spot on the elevator's ceiling, directly opposite the surveillance camera. 'All you need is a straight shot at the lens. The laser will actually cause some glare as it reflects off the end of the camera. Then – bam! The camera is completely disabled and the screen goes white.'

'But it recovered,' I said. 'It started working again.'

'Some do, some don't. But they're out of commission for several hours, at least,' Mercer said. 'That's for sure.'

Mike pounded his fist against the wall. 'So this adds another angle, doesn't it? Plus our guys have to go back over every one of these tapes and see where else this happened.'

'What for?' I asked.

'Look, we know Thatcher was taken to the Towers, but how? Which way into the hotel is still the big question.'

'Excuse me.'

I turned around and saw a man in the hallway outside our room. 'Yes?'

'I'm looking for Rocco Correlli?'

'I'm Correlli.'

The man in the khaki suit with the hint of a Southern accent extended his hand. 'Branson. FBI. I'm head of the team that's been sent in to work with you.'

'Work with us?' Mike said. 'I don't remember asking for help.'

I elbowed him in the side. Mike's attempts at humor about the traditional NYPD/FBI tension on cases that were clearly within city jurisdiction wore thin at a time like this.

'That's because we figured you'd have stopped watching cartoons by this time,' Branson said, pointing at the monitor, 'and put your hands on a murderer.'

'So you've got it figured out?' the lieutenant asked, shouldering Mike out of the way.

'I don't have any choice in the matter. We've been sent in to light a fire under your asses before the president arrives. I expect if we put our heads together, it'll be easier to solve than most of what my guys spend their time doing,' Branson said. 'I was told to ask for you.'

'Welcome to the Waldorf,' Correlli said, sweeping his arm down the length of the table. 'Everything we've got is yours. We'll bring your team up to speed.'

'Thanks. Commissioner Scully sent a summary of all the key points to my boss this morning.' Branson was sweating, too, but wouldn't even loosen the knot in the rep tie that was tightly in place around his neck. 'You find a connection yet between the derelict who was killed last night and the girl?'

Mercer shook his head.

'Nobody in his family was military?' Branson asked, stopping to pick up crime scene photos. 'He wasn't one of her flock?'

'The only living relative Carl Condon had seems to be

an aunt in Minneapolis, tucked away in a nursing home,' Mercer said. 'No link at all.'

'I'm going to go look for some more of the surveillance videos, Rocco,' Mike said. He was stuffing his pockets with chocolate chip cookies and brownies.

'I hear they're all blank,' Branson said.

'Some blank. Some blind.'

Branson dropped the photos back on the table and looked over at Mike. 'The difference being . . .'

'Oh, Lordy. This is going to be a steep learning curve. Loo, you want to fill him in? Coop and Mercer and me, we're on a roll.'

I hadn't realized we were rolling. Murder wasn't the feebies' strong suit, but maybe fresh, intelligent eyes would be a help.

Rocco hadn't realized we had a moving plan, either. But he knew Mike bolted at the thought of being under the thumb of the feds. 'Still trying to figure which way the Thatcher broad was brought into the hotel?'

Mike nodded. 'I want to recheck the cameras from the garage and the various loading docks. Commercial entrances. I want to see if the sequences on any of them went blind.'

'That should be easy to establish,' Branson said.

'How so?'

'I've got two agents up on the street now.'

I could see Mike starting to steam.

'Scully's report says the trunk Thatcher was probably brought here in was found discarded in the Northwest Passage to Grand Central. Am I correct?'

'Yeah. But that's over on Madison Avenue and 47th Street. That's a long chance to take, carrying a drugged vic through the city streets.'

'But there's a Northeast Passage, too,' Branson said. 'And it's just a corner away from here on Park. Park and 48th Street. It runs parallel to the tracks, all the way to the train station.'

I was looking back and forth between Mike and his newfound nemesis.

'I assumed you'd already been focused on the hotel entrance nearest to that point,' Branson said.

'We don't assume anything we can't prove. We've got nothing to connect Corinne Thatcher to the train station,' Mike said.

'Except another corpse who happened to live in a train tunnel and a neatly drawn set of tracks on her ass,' Branson said, pouring himself a cup of coffee.

Mike was not in the winning position. He was running his fingers through his hair and searching for a clever rejoinder, coming up short.

'C'mon, Mike. Branson's making a valid point,' I said. 'Let's recheck the entrances on that side of the hotel.'

'Do you mind, Lieutenant, if we do a sweep of the Towers?' Branson said, turning to Rocco Correlli. 'The Secret Service will be moving some of the president's top aides in on Saturday.'

'We've got it covered,' Rocco said. 'But feel free to check it out.'

'In fact, I found some old dresses that J. Edgar left in

one of the closets when he stayed here,' Mike said. 'Your men should feel right at home.'

'Curb your immaturity, will you please?' I whispered to him. 'Let's get on our way.'

Agent Branson took the high road and didn't even glance at Mike. 'I understand the Service will be responsible for the living quarters here, and you'll have the lobbies and doors.'

'That's the way it usually works,' Rocco said. 'We lead the motorcade back and forth from the United Nations and bring POTUS in from the heliport.'

'Heliport?' Branson said. 'Not happening this trip.'

'The commissioner briefed me yesterday. The president's flying in from the national park to JFK, then a chopper to the East River heliport.'

'He changed his mind last night. The president has decided to do an old-fashioned train ride, like a whistle-stop tour, so he can cross through more than a dozen states and shake hands off the back of the caboose.'

'Amtrak's Empire Builder,' Mercer said. 'Picks it up in Glacier National Park in Montana. Very smart. Gets him through scores of small towns with endless meet and greets – people who'd otherwise never have a chance to see the man.'

'But it's not an election year,' Rocco said.

'Every congressman from here to Missoula will be hanging out for a photo op,' Branson said. 'Good for the party operatives. Tough for the Secret Service.'

'Where does the Empire Builder stop?' I asked.

'Chicago,' Mercer said. 'Then they'll have to cobble together something else to get him here.'

'It's been cobbled,' Branson said. 'A series of private trains running through Indiana and Ohio and Pennsylvania, all put together by the secretary of transportation and the Homeland Security people. You think you guys can keep the bodies out of this hotel and away from the tunnels? Is that too much to ask?'

'I'm kicking right in, Rocco. You need me, I'll be doing overtime at the Oyster Bar. Two dozen Katama Bay bivalves, straight from Martha's Vineyard. That'll be our Saturday night soiree, Coop. Some chilled vodka, some chardonnay. We'll be making it safe for POTUS.'

'That's fine with me, Detective,' Branson said. 'So long as you don't screw it up. The president arrives in Grand Central on Sunday at five P.M.'

Twenty

'I accept.'

'What?' Mike asked.

'Dinner at the Oyster Bar on Saturday night. It's the prettiest room in the city. Those gleaming cream-colored tiles, that—'

'You're on.'

'Do I have to wear a hard hat?' I asked.

'Not if you leave your hard head at home.'

I smiled at Mike. 'I thought things would be different when you got back from the trip. I wasn't counting on a double homicide to get in the way of seeing you again.'

'Neither were the vics, kid.'

I caught myself, still uncertain about why Mike had lied to me. 'Or your mother's health.'

He didn't take his eyes off the monitor. 'She's coming along fine.'

'I had hoped we could fly up to the Vineyard for the weekend.' There wasn't a more romantic place in the world.

'Hold that thought. I've been dreaming about fried clams at the Bite and a steamed lobster courtesy of Larsen's.'

I'd been dreaming about a bottle of cabernet in front of my fireplace on an early fall night. But all that would have to wait.

We were back in our video cubicle, trying again to examine footage from the hotel entrance closest to the Northeast Passage. After leaving Correlli and Branson, I had been drafted to help interview two of the housekeeping employees who had become hysterical during questioning, fearful that they were being targeted as subjects of the investigation.

Mercer was talking to a police inspector in the Dominican Republic about looking for the family of Corinne Thatcher's ex-boyfriend, and reporters were texting me furiously because David Drusin had given his spin on the Gerry Dominguez arrest – and now my 'cannibal cop' phrase was gaining tabloid traction.

'We should have some word on Paco and his whereabouts by tonight,' Mercer said. 'What's next on your list for me?'

'I'd say we got thirty-two hundred employees upstairs waiting to be interviewed,' Mike said.

'Sounds like a job for some rookie looking for a gold shield. Get me out of this dungeon.'

'It's almost four o'clock,' I said. 'We need to find a link between Thatcher and Carl Condon.'

'The Real Time Crime guys have run them six ways to Sunday and come up cold,' Mike said. 'That one's going to take detective work. Pounding the pavement.'

'Starting now?'

'I'm good to go,' Mercer said. 'Get a jump on the morning.'

We told Rocco we were leaving. Two of his men, he told us, were working with Corinne Thatcher's brother. No one had come up with her laptop and cell phone, and the brother was trying to reconstruct contacts of both friends and professional associations for the detectives.

'Where are you off to?' I asked.

'I want to eyeball some of the garage workers,' Mike said.

The Waldorf's parking garage was on the 49th Street side of the building. If Branson and the feds were correct, that was closest to the Northeast Passage, which they assumed had been the killer's point of entry.

'It's been done,' Rocco said. 'Every shift has been interviewed.'

'Not by me,' Mike said.

'Like you know something my squad doesn't. Get real, Chapman.'

'Crack how the girl got in and we're halfway home,' Mike said, looking over at me. 'You and Mercer with me?'

'I'm in,' I said. 'Beats facing the music with Battaglia.'

The three of us made our way upstairs and found a cushy trio of armchairs in the main lobby in which we sat to make our calls. Mike checked in at Manhattan North with his lieutenant, Mercer called the SVU to report on the day and learn whether there was any news, and I avoided Laura – and the stack of messages she had undoubtedly been collecting from a district attorney who didn't like to be ignored – by calling Nan Toth.

'Where are you?' she asked.

'Still at the Waldorf. Nothing's coming together the way we need it to.'

'Same on this end.'

'Raymond Tanner?' I asked. 'Any sign of him?'

'Zero,' Nan said. 'There must have been a plan. Evan and I went up to talk to Judge Aikens. He's peeved, to say the least. You can't micromanage this one, Alex. You can trust Evan to keep his eye on the case and on the players.'

'Thanks. And if you don't mind calling Laura, please tell her I'm keeping her honest. She can say to Battaglia she hasn't heard from me since I left the office.'

I waited for Mike and Mercer to finish their calls. When I looked up after checking my texts, I saw Rocco Correlli sprinting from the basement stairwell toward the exit door that led to the garage.

'Rocco! What's the rush?'

'I was chasing after you guys,' he said, stopping to catch his breath. 'I figured you were outside in the garage.'

The three of us were on our feet, phones off, as we walked to meet him.

'Something clicked?' I asked. 'Progress?'

'Only if you think bad things happen in threes.'

'Another?'

'Corpse. Yeah. Another dead girl.'

'Where is she, Rocco?' Mike asked.

'On a train.'

'Subway or commuter train?' Mike said. 'You talking homicide?'

'I'm talking a broad with a slit throat, naked and apparently sexually abused. Train tracks marked on her thighs and tail. She's in a railroad car, Chapman. Some kind of private railroad car, sitting on an abandoned set of tracks right the fuck next to Grand Central.'

Twenty-one

'The feds found her,' Rocco Correlli said. 'They were doing a sweep in advance of the president's trip.'

The four of us were on Park Avenue, walking to the glass-sided entrance of the MetLife Building on 45th Street, headed for the tall escalators that led down to the main concourse of Grand Central.

'I didn't know there was any such thing as a private railroad car,' I said, waiting for the traffic light to change.

'That way of travel is mostly a thing of the past,' Mercer said, 'but there are still scores of old cars – antiques – that are in private hands.'

'And they just sit in the tunnels?'

'No, no. Amtrak actually lets the owners – or renters – travel on certain routes, for a hefty fee. There are some real beauties, and as long as you've got a siding – a short piece of track that connects to the main rail – you can pretty much travel around the country in one of these.'

'What do you know about the girl?' I asked Rocco.

'Pretty much like Corinne Thatcher's situation. No

clothes, no phone, no computer, no personal belongings. Her ID is the first mystery we have to solve.'

'Do they know who owns the railroad car?'

'Not yet. They only found the body fifteen minutes before I got the call,' Rocco said, holding out his arm to the angry taxi driver as we crossed against the light.

'Fresh kill?'

'At least a day old,' Rocco said, turning to address Mike. 'How come you didn't sniff this out during your early-morning tour of the tunnels, bright eyes? Were you looking to be stiffed by the feds?'

'It's a big hole in the ground, Loo. I didn't see any private cars.'

'There weren't any in the direction we walked,' Mercer said. 'I know what they look like.'

We had practically run the four blocks from the Waldorf entrance into MetLife, through the revolving doors, and down the moving staircase. Rush hour had begun, so we were jostled and crowded by end-of-day workers determined to make their return commute.

Two NYPD officers were waiting for us at the foot of the escalator. Passengers were streaking down staircases, crossing the concourse, and making their way to their designated departure gates. They were oblivious to our arrival.

The cops escorted us down the western staircase to the lower level. Instead of turning left, as we had in our morning excursion, we made a right and walked out onto another long platform. Trains rumbled in the distance, flashes of headlights occasionally penetrating the concrete archways in the darkened space.

Rocco and Mike were directly behind the uniformed officers. I tried to keep pace with them as Mercer brought up the rear.

Someone had turned on a row of overhead lights ahead of us. I could see an elongated railroad car against the black background of the interior space. It looked as though we were traveling back in time. The single coach was from a much earlier era, painted a bright red with black and yellow trim. It had to be more than one hundred years old but was restored to a high gloss.

'That's what they call private varnish,' Mercer said, expressing his admiration for the great-looking machine up ahead.

'What does that mean?'

He kept one hand on the small of my back, nudging me forward when he talked. 'Late eighteen hundreds, before rich Americans had cars, they used to travel around in private trains, like this one. They were made of wood, so it was extremely difficult to maintain the exterior condition of them because of weather issues. Most owners varnished them so they really gleamed riding along those rails. Poor folk in small towns? They got to know pretty quick that the shiny varnished trains were the private ones.'

'So who owned these?'

'Back then? All the great railroad tycoons first. Leland Stanford, J. P. Morgan, Archer Dalton.'

'Archer Dalton, of course,' I said, thinking of the case

we had just worked in Central Park, with miniature antique silver trains as clues in the long-ago murder of Dalton's only grandchild.

'Then the Vanderbilts and Rockefellers and Meriweathers. I'll take you on a tour when the next exhibition comes along.'

'And now?'

'Think of them as yachts on rails, Alex. Beautifully restored and as lavishly outfitted as you can imagine.'

'Then this car is here for a reason, right? Someone can tell us who brought it here.'

'They're all regulated by Amtrak. Won't be hard to do.'

Rocco and Mike were at the foot of the steps that led up to the platform at the rear of the car. It looked as if a couple of federal agents had staked out the railroad car itself as their turf. Men from the NYPD and Metro-North security were gingerly walking around the tracks on either side, carefully avoiding the intense orange paint that highlighted the electrified third rail.

I jogged the last few yards so that neither Mercer nor I would miss any of the conversation.

Rocco was climbing the ladder of the train. As I approached, Mike took one step up, then glanced back and held out his hand for me.

I looked down the exterior length of the bright-red car. Painted along the side, in burnished black letters almost two feet high, were the words BIG TIMBER.

'What's Big Timber?' I whispered to Mike.

'Some little paradise in the middle of Montana. We're

about to find out how kinky the rich dude who owns this must be.'

The agents led the way into the car as we tagged along behind them. We had been so close to Grand Central that we beat Crime Scene and the morgue team to the body.

I had never seen anything quite like the interior of Big Timber. It was decorated exquisitely, with a Western theme and strong masculine influence. There was a bar against one side – heavy with Noah's Mill and an assortment of other fancy bourbons – which was part of a lounge area, as if we were in an elegant country home. There were brown leather sofas – intentionally distressed to look as if they had some age on them – several armchairs, and between each of the windows an attractive array of black-and-white photographs, including some brilliant Edward Curtis images of Native Americans that were probably originals.

'Nothing looks even out of place here, does it?'

'No, ma'am,' one of the agents said.

'Any signs of a struggle? Anything broken or damaged?'

'No, ma'am.'

'Can you cut the *ma'am* thing for a change?' Mike said, passing out gloves to each of us. 'Makes her feel old. Just treat her like one of the guys. She gets off on that.'

'Then I hope she's ready for the scene in the bedroom,' he said, turning his back to us and moving forward.

A door to our right separated the lounge area from a

large bathroom – large enough to hold a stall shower, set up with a bench for steam treatments.

'Looks like some blood in the sink,' the agent pointed out to Mike.

They passed by the bathroom without going in. Three feet beyond was another door, the entrance to the bedroom.

The scene of Corinne Thatcher's murder had been repeated in this plush boudoir. This time, a girl who looked even younger than Thatcher – barely twenty, I guessed – was laid out across the queen-sized bed. Her throat, too, had been sliced from behind one ear almost to the other. She was naked, her legs spread apart. It was a sight I had hoped dearly never to see again.

'Crime Scene?' Mercer asked.

'They're on the way,' the second agent said.

'Either of you touch anything?' Mike said, starting a meticulous visual scope of the room.

'We took Homicide 101, Chapman. I know that surprises you, but we both passed.'

'Touch the girl?'

'No need to. I know dead when I see it.'

'So how'd you get into the car?' Rocco asked.

The second agent picked up the narrative. 'We're part of the New York office. Often help out the Secret Service when there's a presidential visit. When the orders came in with the change of plans from heliport to train station, we drew the short straw. Checking out this area. The White House on steel wheels is supposed to dock two tracks over in just about seventy-two hours.'

'How did Big Timber get here and when is she supposed to leave?' Mike asked.

The room was perfectly appointed. Forest-green curtains, again accented by Western décor – everything except deer antlers – and a slightly warmer shade of green on the upholstered headboard and blankets.

Dressers were built against the wall, under the windows on one side of the room. Mike opened the drawers and then the closet. There was a man's leather jacket and some corduroy slacks hanging up but nothing out of order.

Only the bed looked as if it had served as an abattoir for the same butcher who had taken the lives of Corinne Thatcher and Carl Condon.

'Seems there's this whole association of people who own railroad cars. This one belongs to a cattle baron from a town called Big Timber in Montana.'

'Long way from home, isn't it?' Rocco said.

'Planned the trip a year ago. Got all the clearances from Amtrak and—'

'I don't get it,' Mike said. 'The damn thing's got no engine. How does it move?'

'The owner pays, Detective. Not only a couple of bucks a mile to ride on Amtrak's rails, but they get coupled up to long-distance trains by a switch engine and crew. Takes an arm and a leg to finance. Then they get charged fees for parking at sidings at major facilities.'

'And this cattle tycoon, he did all that?'

'His office is faxing over the paperwork to prove it. The

Northeast Corridor – anywhere in the run from Boston to DC – that's the most restrictive route. And he's had A-plus clearance all the way.'

'What does that mean?'

'He's a good customer. Been here before and follows the rules,' the agent said, looking at his notes. 'Like you can't carry propane into New York, on account of all the tunnels in the city and under the rivers. They know this guy. He's not a risk.'

'Have you talked to him?' Mike asked. 'Maybe he's got a rough side they don't know about. Maybe he's got train tracks branded into his cattle.'

We were all thinking about the distinctive marks on the bodies of the three victims.

'He was expecting to be here this week, like I said, but flew down to a cattle auction in Texas at the last minute,' the agent said. 'Big Timber is parked here legally until Saturday. Been in town about ten days.'

'So now we've got to talk to all the engineers and conductors and security team and track workers to see whether anyone's come and gone from this machine,' Rocco said. 'Without pulling detectives off the Waldorf and the work on the first two homicides. Scully better come up with some manpower.'

'And the blood,' I said. 'There's so much blood. Could it all be from this poor girl? I keep thinking of that speck on the curtain at the Waldorf.'

'We should have a result on that Waldorf DNA by tonight or tomorrow. It would be great if it isn't Thatcher's.

Maybe something in this bathroom sink belongs to the killer,' Mike said.

'You have any movement on the Thatcher toxicology?' Rocco asked.

'You're kidding, Loo, right?'

'We'll have to do the same here, of course,' I said.

The analysis of biological tissue for toxicological purposes – the detection of drugs – was a lengthy process. Solvents had to be used first to separate the drug from the actual tissue. Then the purification of the drug was carried out by more extraction procedures, which used alkaline and acid solutions. The work was slow and time-consuming, and even when a positive identification of a specific drug was achieved, it couldn't be reported without confirmation by a second method of analysis.

'It might be weeks before we learn what was in Thatcher's system. The tox docs at the lab are flying blind,' Mike said. 'We have no reason to know what hit her.'

'Okay,' Rocco said, 'why don't you all step out till Crime Scene gets here. Maybe we'll get lucky with something our boy dropped on the floor.'

The lieutenant was talking to the two FBI agents and me. He was letting Mike and Mercer poke around the space, trusting their skill and ability to keep order till the team arrived.

The agents and I walked out past the bathroom, through the lounge, and started to make our way down the rungs of the ladder off the rear platform.

Murder always seemed to draw a crowd. A small group

of rubberneckers had already gathered around Big Timber.

Some wore the uniforms of Metro-North station employees, others were dressed in work clothes, a few commuters straggled behind, and some men and women who appeared to be moles completed the growing circle. I could see Dirty Harry on the far side of the third rail, excited to be watching an official police operation.

'This isn't going to work,' I said to the feds. 'I think you need to clear the area. It's neither smart nor safe till we know what happened here.'

'Let's get some names,' the first guy said to the second. 'It's like they say about arson. The pyromaniac sets the place on fire, then circles the block and comes back to admire his handiwork. Maybe we got our killer right here.'

They were right about many arsonists, who come back to the scene of the crime, masturbating as the flames they lighted engulf the targeted building.

'Do what you have to do,' I said. 'But that sort of deranged-looking guy back there, playing with himself? He's harmless. Lives in the tunnel. I'm going to wait inside the station. Here's my card, in case you need me.'

'Wish we could take your word for it, ma'am, but that's not our way of operating. We'll clear the area and set up a perimeter. Talk to everyone who's lurking around.'

I stepped through the small group that had gathered and walked back into the lower concourse. The Crime Scene detectives would have to pass me in order to get out to the platform and do their. work. I skirted the commuters and found a seat at a table in front of the Shake Shack concession, texting Mike and Mercer to tell them where I was.

More than half an hour passed and still there was no sign of the elite team.

The public service announcements boomed throughout the vast space – a woman's voice, like the recording of a car's GPS – urged passengers to report luggage or packages that were unattended, to stand back from the edge of train platforms, and to avoid slippery patches when wet. I half expected her to announce the news that there was a dead woman on the tracks at a nearby departure gate.

Fifteen minutes later, Mike and Mercer joined me after Mike bought himself a chocolate shake.

It was almost six o'clock when two Crime Scene detectives made their way down the marble staircase toward the departure gate to which they'd been directed.

'Yo, Hal,' Mike said, waving his shake in the air. 'You on a slow boat, or what?'

'Why, she going somewhere without me? Dead girls don't walk.'

'Yeah, but the train might just up and pull out of here.'

'Looks like you got a trifecta now. Two broads and a homeless guy. Scully must be pulling his hair out.' Hal and his partner were lugging large cases filled with equipment. 'Make yourself useful, Chapman. Go on back up to the car and bring down a load. Take one of the Metro-North kids with you.'

'I'll take you out to Big Timber first. That's where the body is.'

The automated voice boomed the MTA's latest mantra through the loudspeakers. *Remember, ladies and gentlemen, to mind the gap between the platform and the train. And if you see something, say something.*

'Who's the jerk who told me to go to Grand Central Station?' Hal Sherman asked as he walked away from us.

'Where the hell do you think you are?' Mike said, grabbing one of Hal's camera cases.

'First thing we did was go down to the Station. That's why we're so late.'

'Look, Hal,' I said, 'I know you've been whipped back and forth, but we're all too drained to be playing word games.'

'Listen to you,' Hal said, wiping his brow with his shirtsleeve. 'Grand Central Station is the name of the IRT subway stop that serves the 4, 5, 6 and 7 trains. I know you don't like traveling with all your perps and molesters on public transportation, Alex, but most of us have to. I dragged all this crap down into the subway station – which was packed to the gills with the great unwashed, bearing the sweet smell of a summer afternoon after a day at the office – and had a hell of a time getting it back upstairs.'

'So where are we now?' I asked. 'I stand ready to be corrected.'

'This building, which might just be the most beautiful crime scene in all the city, is a terminal. It's not a station. Its name is Grand Central Terminal.'

'What?'

'Trains terminate here. They don't stop and move on. Penn Station, Union Station – you get the picture – they're all just two-minute stops on the line. Trains come in. Unpack their passengers and reload, then keep on chugging along. Like the dictionary tells you,' Hal said, holding a finger straight up to make his point, before hoisting his heavy case, 'a terminal can be a station, but not every station is a terminal. *This* place was built as a terminal. Everything comes to a dead end right here.'

'Tell it to the girl on Big Timber,' Mike said. 'She's terminal, too.'

Twenty-two

We had trudged to the 42nd Street side of the great terminal, on a gently sloping ramp that ran from the lower concourse to the upper. Lieutenant Correlli, Mike, Mercer and I were being turned over to the acting president of Metro-North, Bruce Gleeson. One of the security guards led us to the elevator, which required keyed access to enter.

I studied the wall directory, but it offered no clues to our destination. There must have been offices built on top of the vast barrel vault of the ceiling above the main concourse, but it was impossible to see where they might be.

The directory listings were for floors one through six. The concourse – more than sixteen stories high – was all one could make out around and above us.

'When you get on,' the security guard said, 'press the button for the seventh floor.'

'It only goes to six,' I said, pointing at the directory.

'The public doesn't need to know the seventh floor exists, but that's where you're headed.'

We stepped into the elevator. It was a slow ride to the

top of the tall building. When the doors opened, we were greeted by Bruce Gleeson.

'Why don't you follow me?' he said. 'It gets pretty complicated up here. And just so you know, these hallways are dotted with NYPD surveillance cameras.'

'That's comforting,' Mike said.

The corridors we walked were narrow and long, snaking from one end of the vast building to the other, a circuitous route that was windowless, with peeling white paint on the walls. Bare pipes ran overhead, causing me to wonder how the huge space was ventilated and cooled down when it was constructed more than a century ago.

After three or four minutes, we reached a locked door, which Gleeson opened for us.

'C'mon in and take a seat,' he said, turning on the lights. 'This is our situation room.'

Unlike the hallway, this space had obviously been upgraded. It was the size of a large corporate office, with faux-wood paneling and a conference table in the center of the room. There were twenty chairs, large phone consoles in front of each one, and a spider-phone that made external communication accessible to all participants in the room.

'What happens here?' Mike asked.

'This is where we come to figure out how to run the railroads when something else shuts them down,' Gleeson said with a laugh. 'Hurricane Sandy in 2012, the great blackout in 2004. You can even go back to 9/11. It's our command and control center, for times when things are out of control.'

'I know your trains are running today,' Rocco said. 'But it's clear we've got a situation here.'

'And I'm not exactly sure what that is, other than the body that was found this afternoon. I've been given information about this, but I'm afraid I'm not a crime buff. I don't read the tabloids.'

'It's our third homicide in as many days, Mr Gleeson. Two didn't happen here, although close by, but they're linked to this victim because someone drew train tracks – at least, that's what we think the design is – on each of the bodies.'

Gleeson picked up a remote control and turned from the head of the table to a wall off to the side, where eight television screens were mounted in two stacks of four each. With a single click they were on. Each one was tuned to a different channel, and all seemed to be in the middle of the evening news cycle. Five of the screens showed reporters standing somewhere within the landmarked terminal.

'I guess the news is out,' he said. 'I'm a novice at this. Just holding a place while our terminal's CEO gets a bit of a sabbatical. Tell me what you need.'

'So our first victim was found Tuesday night. Fiftieth Street, in the Waldorf Hotel,' Mike said. 'A young woman who was probably drugged and kidnapped before she was murdered. No reason to connect it to Grand Central then. Now we've got this track thing going on – some kind of souvenir the killer leaves on their bodies, and like the girl in the railroad car downstairs, that one had her throat slit, too. Probably raped.'

Bruce Gleeson shook his head.

'Second victim is a guy. Stabbed in the back. Found up on DePew Place, right on the street, but we confirmed this morning that he lived in one of your tunnels.'

'That's a story we don't need to tell the reporters.'

'It's all hanging out there by now.'

'Actually, Mr Gleeson,' Mercer said, 'the deceased didn't seem to have anything to do with the station proper – I mean, with the terminal. By the accounts we have so far, he came and went by the Northwest Passage. He was more of a street hustler who burrowed in when he needed a place to stay.'

'So it's this body on the private railcar that brings everything under our roof right now, am I right?'

'Yes, sir,' Mercer said.

'This young woman,' Gleeson asked, 'does she work in Grand Central?'

'We don't know who she is yet. Not a whit of identification, just like the first one. We may not be able to answer that till we get her picture out in public tomorrow.'

'Do you think the killer could be an employee?' Gleeson's fingers were nervously tapping on the table.

'Until an hour ago,' Mike said, circling the table as he talked, 'we had no reason to connect this to the terminal. We don't know whether this guy is a train buff or a conductor, a mole or a commuter. But I don't like the direction the case is taking.'

'What direction is that?'

'Bodies getting closer to the terminal.'

'You've got a luxury hotel on 50th Street,' Mercer said. 'The body's found in a Tower suite, forty-five flights up in the air. Dicey because the president is due to take over that space in a few days, but it seems like the location is just a coincidence.'

Mike was running his fingers through his hair. 'No such thing as coincidence.'

'Next guy is on a dead-end street. Stabbed in the back. In our business,' Mercer said to Gleeson, 'there's no reason in the world to connect him to the first victim – who turns out to be a well-educated girl from a stable family with a work history and maybe dating a bad guy.'

'Emphasis on *maybe*,' Mike said.

'The boyfriend didn't like the breakup – that's often cause for violence,' Mercer said, 'and he happens to channel all his anger toward POTUS.'

'That's a far cry from being able to organize all this shit,' Mike said.

'He fled, didn't he?' Rocco said.

'Lousy timing, although I'm not sure he's perp material.'

'But not just a coincidence, in your book.'

'Never is,' Mike said, shaking his head.

'Only the design of the tracks on both bodies,' Mercer said, 'which we first thought was a ladder, is what connected them. I don't think any cops would have linked the two deaths otherwise.'

Gleeson was trying to divert the crimes from his turf. 'Could that be what they are? Ladders?'

'That's what Coop thought,' Mike said. 'Led us off

course, like she often does. We'd all be happy if they were ladders.'

'This new case changes the whole dynamic,' Mercer said. 'It happens in a railroad car that's sitting on a platform directly adjacent to your terminal, two days before the president of the United States, who'll be staying at the Waldorf, is due to arrive.'

'But we've got excellent security here,' Gleeson said, watching Mike as he did laps around the table.

'Like what?' Rocco asked.

'There's an NYPD presence, as you know. Well armed and patrolling all parts of the terminal. There's Metro-North police.'

'What, two hundred of them covering more than thirty stations?' Mike said. 'Not exactly reassuring. Especially if you remember the midnight cowboys.'

More than a decade ago, the Metro-North police force was rocked by a scandal. Videos surfaced of officers patrolling the concourse of the great terminal on the late shift, wearing only their hats, neckties, shoes, and holsters. The building was nicknamed the Wild West. Massive firings that resulted led to the slow growth of an entirely new crop of officers.

'They've got K-9 units – dogs that sniff bombs and others that are trained to detect poisonous vapors. And they can bring in assault weapons if needed.'

Homeland Security had long ago designated major transportation hubs for heightened security measures. Operation Torch established teams comprised of six detectives and a dog – all trained in counterterrorism techniques – to patrol on New York City subways.

'Are they in place now?' Mike asked.

'I know they're planning to saturate the terminal over the weekend, for the president's arrival,' Gleeson said, counting off a list on his fingers. 'Sniffers are installed all over, too.'

'You said that. Dogs.'

'No, I mean the electronic sensors. They're called sniffers.'

'Where are they?' I asked.

'I'm sure you've seen those metal boxes around the concourse, and the wires dangling from some of the arches?'

I shook my head. 'I've never noticed them.'

'That's part of the plan,' Gleeson said. 'They sniff the air for traces of poisonous gas or any kind of chemical that would signal a biological attack.'

'Someone actually monitors that?' I asked.

'No, Ms Cooper. The sensors feed data to a computer system that runs constantly and is primed to alert security if there's a positive result.'

'That's happening now?' Mike asked.

Gleeson hesitated. 'It's supposed to be. I'll have to check and get an answer for you. Occasionally the chemicals in the cleaning fluids set off the sensors, so they have to be readjusted from time to time. And we have surveillance cameras, as you know. With facial recognition capability.'

'Using that term very loosely.'

'Why? You've had a problem with it? Most of the officers think it's been very effective.'

'It has been, Mr Gleeson,' Rocco Correlli said. 'Chapman

doesn't like anything to slip through the cracks. Every now and then—'

'Face it, Loo,' Mike said. 'You don't want your mug on the camera? Anyone with half a brain can bypass the system. Head down, any kind of hat with a brim.'

'A wig, a fake mustache, a pair of large sunglasses,' Mercer said. 'Facial recog is not going to help us in the short run here.'

'What's this?' Mike asked. He had circled the conference table enough times to make me dizzy from watching him. 'What's behind these blinds?'

He was standing to the right of the table, pointing at a large panel of venetian blinds.

'It's – it's the operations room behind there,' Gleeson said. 'It has nothing to do with the issue of security inside the terminal itself.'

'Lift them, will you?'

Gleeson picked up one of the remotes and pressed a button. The white blinds glided up and rolled back, revealing another room twenty feet below us. There were two rows of men – ten per row – each in front of a desktop. Covering the entire wall in front of them was a giant board, run by a computer, with brightly colored lines that danced as the workers typed on their keyboards.

'What am I looking at?' Mike asked.

Bruce Gleeson stood up and approached the window to the operations room. 'Those men can tell you where every piece of equipment that's running is at any given moment. They're the rail traffic controllers.

'There are thousands of square miles – and hundreds of thousands of travelers – serviced by this system. There are two thousand switches along the rails the trains ride, going to the north and west of the city. Used to be there were men who stood in the switch towers all day to make changes on the tracks according to the signals they were sent. Now,' Gleeson went on, 'these guys you're looking at just right-click on the mouse and the change is made, whether the rail is in New Haven or Poughkeepsie. No more towers. No more men out there flipping the switches.'

'That's a lot of power for these guys,' Mike said.

'And a huge responsibility.'

'The lines on the big screen?'

'A train arrives at this terminal every forty-seven seconds, Mr Chapman. To the far right, you can see that there are only four lines. White lines.'

'Yeah.'

'That's because there are only four tracks that go in and out of the tunnel, once they merge from the departure platforms. Four tracks,' Gleeson said. 'Keep your eye on the white lines.'

'Will do.'

'As soon as the color changes – there you go – one of them is red now.'

The red neon streaked onto the screen. 'So that's an arrival,' Mike said.

'Yes. And when the four tracks reach northern Manhattan, they branch out. Soon there are eight tracks going in different directions. Then sixteen.'

'The green and yellow lines.'

'Exactly.'

'How about all that purple?' Mike asked, pointing to lines on the left.

'Those are tracks under repair,' Gleeson said. 'Or an indication that a VIP is going to be coming through, so they're left empty.'

'Is any of that clearance for this weekend? For the president?'

'I – I don't know. I'm in management, I'm not an engineer. I'll have to find out for you.'

'I'm getting ahead of myself. Following tracks up to Canada when I should be more interested in a bad guy heading this way.' Mike turned his attention back to the conference room. 'How many exits and entrances to Grand Central? To the terminal itself?'

'Twenty-six.'

'Are you kidding me?' Mike said. 'Twenty-six separate and distinct entrances? We'd need an army to cover those – and monitor every train pulling in or out – twenty-four/seven.'

Bruce Gleeson put his hand to his forehead. 'You've got the entrance on Vanderbilt Avenue, at the top of the marble staircase. Opposite the Yale Club.'

Mike nodded at Mercer. 'Where the trunk was stolen.'

'On the south side – 42nd Street – there are entrances on both corners – and of course the Grand Hyatt hotel is in the middle of the block. You can access the terminal and subway through a back corridor in the lobby.'

'Check.'

'Lexington Avenue has the long arcade entrance, past all the shops and food halls. It draws you right into the main concourse as well as down into the subway station.'

'Don't forget the Park Avenue Viaduct,' Mercer said.

That roadway above street level that encircles the building has an entry into the upper tier above the Grand Hyatt lobby, too, which I had used many times coming and going to ballroom events and avoiding the crowds at the bar downstairs.

'And from Park Avenue,' Gleeson said, 'through the MetLife Building, you come directly in here.'

'That's what we did this afternoon,' Mike said.

'I don't have to remind you that there are feeds from subway lines all over this building, so one could theoretically get in from any corner of the city by coming underground,' Gleeson said.

'Talking underground, you've got the opening from the commuter train tunnels – wider than the mouth of the Nile,' Mike said, 'that feeds into the concourse. You got your homeless, your employees, your odd sorts traveling in privately. Hundreds of miles of train tracks just waiting to be compromised.'

'Don't sound so negative,' I said, still thinking of the Grand Hyatt, built directly above the landmarked old terminal. 'There's a hotel right upstairs. If our killer was looking to make that kind of connection to the terminal, he could have murdered Corinne Thatcher right here.'

It had been a long day. I was exhausted and distressed

about Raymond Tanner. I didn't need Mike to overdramatize the already titillating events.

'So what're you saying?' Mike asked.

'I'm rejecting your "no coincidence" theory, Detective Chapman,' I said, twisting my hair to get it off my neck and banding it into a ponytail. 'I'm suggesting the fact that Thatcher's body was deposited in the Waldorf may be just that. A coincidence.'

Bruce Gleeson had moved to the window overlooking the operations room. He lowered the white blind covering the window that separated the two spaces before he spoke. 'I think you're wrong, Ms Cooper. I'd have to agree with Mr Chapman – much as I would hope otherwise, for the sake of everyone in this terminal – that the murder in the Waldorf is not likely to be a coincidence.'

'What do you mean?'

Gleeson bit his lip, then continued to speak. 'You know there's a city underground, right below this mammoth building?'

'The train tunnels,' Mike said, 'where the homeless people live. We get it.'

'That's not what I'm talking about.'

'What then?'

'When the design for Grand Central was sketched out in 1900, the master planners wanted to change the entire complexion of Midtown Manhattan. The area to the east of 42nd Street – prime real estate now – was made up entirely of slums and slaughterhouses.'

'Right here?' I asked.

'East Side slaughterhouses, Ms Cooper. Cattle used to escape from time to time and wander onto the old tracks, when they were aboveground, unlike where they are today. The buildings weren't skyscrapers and office towers. They were tenements and shanties.'

'I didn't realize.'

'You've heard of the White City?' Gleeson asked. 'The movement to beautify urban areas, which started at the exposition in Chicago.'

'Yes, I've heard of the White City, and the devil who lived in it. Dr H. H. Holmes, wasn't it? The serial killer who turned his home into a World's Fair hotel, complete with a gas chamber and a dissection table. That's not what you're thinking?'

'No, no. But the architecture that turned Chicago into the White City was the impetus for what the builders did here, in the Grand Central zone.'

'What's that?' Mike asked.

'They stood to gain a fortune from creating something that was not only safer in terms of train travel, but that would make this complex the center of the sprawling city. That would rid it of slums and shantytowns,' Gleeson said. 'The railroad tracks had already been sunk below street grade by the commodore.'

'Cornelius Vanderbilt?'

'Yes, Detective Chapman. But Commodore Vanderbilt died in 1877. Twenty-five years later, the chief engineer of the New York Central Railroad came up with the concept of air rights. Do you know what that means?'

'I think so,' I said.

'Vanderbilt dredged the area north of Grand Central that we now call Park Avenue – home to some of the world's most expensive real estate – and ran the trains below street level. Dug deep trenches in the ground to lay the tracks. Saved lives by doing that. Threw up iron fences and plotted patches of grass. That's when they changed the name of the street.'

'What do you mean?'

'Down below Union Square, where the road begins, it's still Fourth Avenue, named like all the numbered avenues. Once the trains were laid in and the flowers planted, they tried to class it up by dubbing it Park Avenue.'

'Seems to have taken,' I said, thinking of all the glorious flower displays in the meridians throughout each season and the sparkling Christmas tree lights.

'People used little footbridges to cross the avenue, and all the flying cinders from the steam engines stayed down in the ditches, no longer setting fire to everything around the old rails.'

'Clever,' Mike said.

'Then, with the introduction of electric trains after 1900, this fellow named William Wilgus – the chief engineer – took the commodore's concept a step further.'

'He covered the tracks,' Mercer said. 'They were already dug below the surface, and these gents figured that they could pave right over the damn things. Enclose them completely. Get them out of sight altogether and build on top of the train tracks.'

'Exactly. Not only did Vanderbilt and his successors buy up all the land around Grand Central for eventual development, but then Wilgus had the genius to envision great office buildings and private clubs rising on Park Avenue, right above the tracks themselves.'

'So this area that had once been such an eyesore,' Mike said, 'and so dangerous, was going to be converted into a canyon of high-rent profitability. They sold air rights to the properties that sat on top of the New York Central Railroad tracks.'

'Which not only led to the building of some of the most famous structures in New York City, but it also gave the Central enough income to pay for the conversion of its entire system from steam-powered locomotives to electric trains.'

'What does any of this have to do with coincidence?' I asked.

'It's this architectural plan that defies the coincidence among your murders, Ms Cooper,' Gleeson said.

'Architecture? I don't understand.'

'You must first be aware that a single entity, the New York Central Railroad, controlled a thirty-block area of Midtown Manhattan – as a direct result of Vanderbilt's entrepreneurial instincts. And all of that property was tethered to its magnificent centerpiece – this very Grand Central Terminal.'

'I'm following you.'

'So this complex of buildings was created, mostly in the nineteen twenties, after Grand Central was opened,' Bruce

Gleeson said, sketching an outline on the conference table with his forefinger. 'Over here, practically adjacent to where we're standing, was the Biltmore Hotel. Very fancy. A destination for long-distance train travelers.'

We all nodded.

'Beyond that, across Vanderbilt Avenue, was the Yale Club,' Gleeson said, drawing an imaginary line from point to point.

'You could reach that from this terminal, too?' Mike asked.

'Absolutely. Next came the Roosevelt and the Commodore, both grand hotels in their day. Then the US post office, because the New York Central carried mail, by contract with the government. That's on Lexington Avenue, back to DePew Place.'

I heard the words 'DePew Place' and looked at Mike, who was concentrating on the movement of Gleeson's fingertip.

'A civic center was created here, with the added feature that people could move from Grand Central to hotels and to office buildings within the complex without ever venturing onto city streets. At least twenty-five thousand of them every day.'

Mike picked up the narrative. 'Because there are underground tunnels and passages that connect this building to all of the others, am I right?'

'Not just tunnels and passages, but an underground city, Detective Chapman. Designed and executed as that,' Gleeson said. 'They named it Terminal City.'

I placed my palms down on the table and leaned in, tracing another line in the dust on the tabletop from the location of DePew Place, dragging it slowly up Park Avenue. 'How far north do these tunnels go, Mr Gleeson?'

'To 50th Street, Ms Cooper. The railroad owned the land up to 50th Street.'

The men watched as my finger crossed the pretend streets and came to a stop on the corner of Park Avenue. 'Right here?' I asked.

'Right there,' Gleeson said. 'That's why I'm afraid the answer to your problems can't be attributed to any coincidence, as you thought. Think of your first victim, Ms Cooper, and where her body was found. The last great tower built as part of Terminal City was the Waldorf-Astoria Hotel.'

Twenty-three

'Terminal City,' Mike said. 'You ever hear of it, Coop?'

'No.'

Bruce Gleeson had left us in the situation room while he went back to his office to try to find one of the old-timers who could talk us through the maze of underground links. Rocco Correlli was on his way to headquarters to give Commissioner Scully an update.

'Me neither,' Mercer said. 'I thought I knew every inch of Manhattan.'

'But don't you think I'm right?' Mike said, turning to Mercer. 'The perp starts his spree in the Waldorf, moves closer in to the terminal on DePew, then actually commits a homicide just yards from the lower concourse. Next thing has to be something explodes right inside the terminal. That's the way this bastard is moving.'

'You're talking a *bomb*?' I asked.

'Get a grip, blondie. I haven't taken it that far yet. They got sniffers downstairs, don't they? I'm not saying he's got – they've got – a bomb. But it's an explosive situation. I mean that this guy is intent on leading us right into Grand Central, with a dramatic purpose, is what I think.'

'He's clearly familiar with places we don't even know about. Gleeson better find us a guide to this behemoth.'

'Who's going to help us figure out what his grudge is?' Mike said, speaking to no one in particular. 'There's more ways into this building than into a wedge of Swiss cheese. And there's no single button that closes every entry in the joint. So it's impossible to do a total lockdown, if it came to that.'

'No way,' Mercer said.

'We don't know who or what we're looking for – perp or next potential vic. Scully needs to get this body ID'd,' I said. 'Carl Condon is probably collateral damage, especially if he was just hired to steal the trunk. The association – the motive we're looking for – has to be some nexus between the two women.'

'What if our bad boy used to work here?' Mike said. 'He's got a head start on the whole thing that will be impossible to overcome.'

'Or if he grew up around this place, like his old man used to work here,' Mercer said. I knew he was thinking about how his own father, a lifelong Delta Air Lines employee, had taken him out on the tarmac and into the hangars of LaGuardia as a kid, long before the restrictions of 9/11 became commonplace. 'He'll know more crevices and uncharted cubbyholes than we'll be able to find.'

'Rocco's right,' I said. 'Now this becomes a huge public safety issue. Scully's got to go to the media with the fact that somebody's targeted Grand Central for trouble. Big trouble.'

Mike started pacing again. He passed behind me and tugged at my hair. 'Don't we just all sound like jerks now 'cause we don't know what the trouble might be?'

'Or maybe the whole thing is a ruse,' Mercer said. 'Bring all the troops to circle the wagons at the terminal, and leave some other target exposed.'

'Like?'

'Like the United Nations, where the president is coming to town to speak.'

'So the perp wants us to think he's a serial killer,' I said, 'and we're working overtime to make the ladies safe, while he pulls the rug out from underneath.'

'How far does Terminal City extend to the east and west?' Mike asked. 'The UN is four blocks from here – due east.'

'Sit tight. Gleeson's gone to get us an expert,' Mercer said.

'Ironic that this neighborhood was known for its slaughterhouses,' I said. 'It's like déjà vu, with humans on the chopping block now.'

'Always looking at the bright side, kid.'

'Both of you need to be patient. We can manage this,' Mercer said. 'Girl gets ID'd tomorrow, that's my bet. We learn our way around. The motive becomes more obvious.'

'Yeah, like laying all those railroad tracks straight in a line,' Mike said, checking his watch, then picking up the remote and clicking it at the wall of monitors. 'The yellow brick road will take Coop right to Oz. What we need is a wizard to tell us the strategy.'

Eight television sets powered on. Mike played with the controls until he had all the screens set to the channel with *Jeopardy!*

In the early days, when we'd first worked together, I often took the high road and reminded Mike that there was a body in the next room, still warm, that made his obsession with betting on the final question rather chilling. There was no changing him, and the habit he relished was something that all of his colleagues tolerated. Mercer and I had actually grown to enjoy the competition.

'Right after the commercial,' he said, raising the volume.

'There's got to be some central place in here with surveillance cameras that capture the terminal interior,' Mercer said.

'Gleeson says there's a room with monitors that security staffs. But there are too many blind spots – staircases, ramps, archways – to capture every bit of the place at any given time.'

'So if you've got an insider's knowledge of the building, you might know how to avoid getting caught on film, right?' I said.

'No such thing as film, Coop.'

'You know what I mean.'

'Did you hear the man? The main concourse is thirty-six thousand square feet. That's just the start of things for us. It's not like looking for a needle in a haystack. More like a needle in an iceberg,' Mike said. 'Whoa. Here's Trebek.'

'Two of you are tied for the lead here, ladies,' Alex Trebek said. 'Let's see if we can break that open and find a winner.'

The 'card' on the large board flipped aside and crisp white letters appeared on the cobalt-blue field. 'Tonight's category, ladies, is Native American history.'

'I'm golden,' Mike said, as the three contestants screwed up their faces waiting for the answer to be revealed. 'I'll go forty on this.'

'Didn't know it was one of your areas of expertise,' I said.

'I've got a better chance than you, babe. The answer's not going to be some great piece of literature, is it? Or a Motown hit? Geronimo and the Miracles. Or a classic film noir? You'll be out of your element.'

'Sometimes the depth of your political correctness takes my breath away.'

'It's a realistic risk assessment,' Mike said, checking his pocket for cash. 'Just saying I can take you on Pontiac's Conspiracy or the Trail of Tears or the Yamasee War. Double or nothing, am I right, Mercer?'

Mercer laughed. 'I'm holding at forty.'

'Native Americans have known what terrorism is since 1492, Coop. I'm totally on their side. Manifest Destiny be damned.'

'Forty it is for me, too.'

'Yellow-bellied. Both of you.'

Trebek looked up as the answer to the night's final question appeared on the screen: OSAGE TRIBESWOMAN WHO

BECAME AMERICA'S FIRST PRIMA BALLERINA. Trebek read it aloud.

Mike rolled his money into a ball and threw it at me. 'Now that really sucks. That's a very misleading header. The question isn't about history, it's culture. And I don't know anything about culture.'

'Who is Maria Tallchief?' I said, flattening the bills on the conference table and counting them to make sure I had it all. 'I keep offering to take you to the ballet with me.'

'Too many swans, too little time.'

I had taken ballet lessons since early childhood, still preferring my hours in the studio every Saturday to a workout at the gym. I loved the discipline of dance, the way the music always elevated my spirit, and the grace of the movement.

Two of the three contestants, both in their sixties, were also right. The young computer programmer who had briefly been tied for first place had left the question blank.

'So you're the winner after all,' Trebek said, congratulating the woman on her third victory. 'Betty Marie Tallchief came out of Oklahoma, to star in New York, Paris, and Monte Carlo – both an inspiration to and wife of the great George Balanchine. Congratulations to you, Mrs—'

Mike shut down the televisions. 'If you spent half as much time on your back, Coop, as you do dancing on your toes, you'd be a much more interesting woman.'

'And you lose all your charm the minute you open your

mouth, Detective,' I said, pushing back my chair. 'It's not exactly like you're channeling Nick Charles, is it?'

'Chill, guys,' Mercer said. 'What we need are the keys to Terminal City.'

Mike's phone rang. It was obvious from the conversation that the caller was Rocco Correlli.

'The ME's going to stitch the girl up and get some photos ready for the eleven o'clock news. It won't be very good-looking, but we've got to know who she is.'

The door opened and Bruce Gleeson reentered with an older man, whom Gleeson introduced to us as Don Ledger. 'We got lucky,' Gleeson said. 'I grabbed Don just as he was leaving his office for the night.'

'Pleased to meet you,' Mike said.

'Same here, Detective.'

'Don's what we call our living history. He's worked in the maintenance department since he was eighteen. He turned seventy-eight two weeks ago.'

'Sixty years?' Mercer said. 'Hats off, sir.'

'You do what you love, Mr Wallace. If you're fortunate, that is.'

'Amen to that. Would you mind sitting down and letting us ask you some questions about the terminal?'

Ledger was shorter than I, with a slim build and a headful of white hair. He wore hearing aids and had reading glasses in the pocket of his work shirt, and I doubted that his teeth were his own. But he was warm and good-natured, eager to help us get a picture of Grand Central.

'Happy to try,' Ledger said, taking a seat.

Mike looked over his shoulder at Bruce Gleeson. 'Were you able to come up with a blueprint of the place for us?'

'Not yet.' Gleeson winced. 'The building was completely renovated more than a decade ago. There are a good number of interior structural changes that won't be accounted for in the original plans. But we should have copies for you to work from by morning.'

'You mean there have been changes big enough to make a difference in looking for people who are inside the joint?' Mike asked.

'Oh, yeah. There were entire walls taken down; there were staircases constructed. The one on the concourse that leads up to the Apple store? That didn't exist until a decade ago. It was part of the original plan but it wasn't built till the terminal was restored. The original builders ran short on money for the Italian marble, so the blueprints will only get you so far,' Ledger said, poking his finger to the side of his head. 'You got a few of us with institutional memory.'

'Good. Let's get started now, but then we'll meet you back here at eight A.M.,' Mike said. 'You hang with us for a few days, okay?'

'If Mr Gleeson frees me up to assist you, I'll be here.'

'Anything the police need, Ledger. That's what you'll be doing.'

'Thanks to you both,' Mike said. 'But I'm getting ahead of myself. Tomorrow the three of us – Mercer, Coop and I – will start the day here. The commissioner will undoubtedly have teams saturating the station. Feds, too. First,

Don, it would help if you give us some background. Help us figure how to get to know this place. We'll be tripping all over one another if we don't know half of what you do.'

Ledger leaned back in his chair and twisted the end of his white mustache. 'That could take most of the night.'

Mike pulled his chair closer in to make his point. 'We may not have that many hours, Don. Give us what we need to know.'

Ledger wagged his finger and practically put his nose against Mike's. 'You've got a colossus here, young man. One hundred years old and full of secrets. If you all don't know what you're looking for inside her walls, then how in hell can I pick out what's important? I'd prefer to start at the get-go, run through it as fast as I can, then let you gents decide for yourselves.'

'Secrets?' Mike said, half grinning at the old man's choice of words.

'Dead serious, young man. Don't mock me. There's basements you won't find on any floor plan, hidden staircases, isolated platforms for dignitaries, and enough mystery down below us that Hitler thought he could change the course of World War Two by penetrating Grand Central.'

Don Ledger had me when he uttered the words 'secrets' and 'hidden'.

'You're in charge, sir.'

Mercer handed me an extra steno pad, and Ledger got to work.

'The first rail line in New York City was laid in 1831, from Prince Street to Union Square. Until that time, steamboats ran passengers and freight up and down the Hudson, so no trains were allowed to operate on the west side of town near the river, as a matter of law.'

'Weren't allowed to compete with maritime traffic?' Mercer asked.

'That's right. It was such a primitive business that the first iron rails were shipped over from England – not even made here. And the man who owned the train line was Thomas Emmet. He had a younger brother you might have heard of named Robert.'

Mike smiled. 'The great Irish revolutionary, executed for high treason for plotting a rebellion against the British. One of my mother's heroes. And all the time his brother a wealthy entrepreneur over here? I never knew that.'

'The population of Manhattan was centered downtown then, as you probably know.'

The island had been settled at its southern tip, at the Battery, and had slowly moved northward with the influx of European immigrants.

Ledger went on. 'By 1851, when there were several rail lines – the New York and Harlem, the Albany, the New Haven – the builders had finally blasted through rocks to lay rails up to Yorkville and later extended them through Harlem and across the river into the Bronx. A year after that, a New Yorker could travel by train from City Hall to Albany.

'But because the steam locomotives were so dangerous

– starting fires, running over horses and people who dared cross the tracks to get to the other side of the street – they weren't allowed to operate below 42nd Street.'

'So how did people get uptown, no less to Albany, from City Hall?' I asked.

'The depot that was built on this site was the end of the rail. It was horse-drawn carriages that took folk from here downtown. Part old-fashioned and the other part newfangled.'

'Think of it,' Mercer said, 'it's these railroads that created suburbs outside the city. Gave men the ability to live up in Westchester or Connecticut with their families but travel into Manhattan every day. It's literally what made commuting possible.'

'But Cornelius Vanderbilt,' Mike said, 'didn't he make all his millions in steamboats?'

'The commodore, now there's a man for you,' Ledger said. 'Started life as a poor farm boy on Staten Island, descended from a Dutchman who came to America as an indentured servant. By the age of sixteen he had bought himself a flat-bottomed boat and was rowing people back and forth across the harbor to Manhattan. Just a kid with a long oar and a dream to make a buck. Twenty years later, he'd pocketed enough money to build his own steamboat.'

'When did he switch his interest to trains?'

'Began investing in them in the eighteen forties. While the Hudson River froze over in wintertime and steamboats couldn't get to Albany, railroad trains could deliver their passengers practically on time. Twenty years later, Vanderbilt owned two lines in Manhattan with separate terminals and finally became president of a third line – the most powerful, New York Central – which is when he decided to merge them into a single building.'

'On this site?' I asked.

'Oh, yes. The commodore spent more than one hundred million dollars of his own money to pay for the depot, buying up all the land around. A real visionary. He saw the railroads as the future.'

'What became of the original station downtown?' Mike asked.

'Vanderbilt sold it to a fellow named P. T. Barnum. Heard of him?' Ledger said. 'Remade it into the Hippodrome, for the circus and all his other spectacles. Till it became the first Madison Square Garden.'

'Where Harry Thaw murdered the great architect Stanford White,' Mike said, 'over the girl on the red velvet swing.'

'I guess you guys see murder in everything.'

'Afraid I do, Mr Ledger,' Mike said.

'Cornelius Vanderbilt came to understand that railroads were changing the face of America. Before the Civil War, we were an agrarian nation. We grew things, and we moved them around on horse carriages or by ships. It took five days to cross New Jersey by the Morris Canal in those days, from the Delaware River to the Hudson. Trains came along? It became a five-hour trip.'

'Moving people and freight at a new speed and efficiency.'

'Moving ideas, too. I think of the trains as the computer

technology of their time,' Ledger said. 'Now Vanderbilt's station opened in 1871, so keep in mind, because 42nd Street then was in the middle of nowhere, you still had to shuttle people on streetcars and horse-drawn carriages from 42nd Street to downtown. It was pretty much a mess up here at the depot, even though his ownership of the train lines – and all the real estate – paid off. When the commodore died in 1877, he had a fortune greater than all the money in the US Treasury. And just as he passed away, a blizzard shattered the glass roof of his train station.'

'Time for a new plan, I guess.'

'But it didn't happen quite yet, nor for that reason,' Ledger said 'Not till 1902. Just like today, there were only four tracks carrying trains down through the spine of Manhattan, even though there were sixteen million passengers a year by then.

'One January morning, a new engineer was making his first run piloting a passenger train – the local one-eighteen from White Plains. It was snowing out, the kind of thing that made the Park Avenue trenches especially murky, weather that left steam and vapors hanging in the air. The driver was speeding a bit, trying to make up for time lost on the route. Claims he never saw the train ahead of him – the Danbury express – that was parked on the same track, right up at 56th Street, waiting for a signal from the station to pull on in.'

'People died?' I asked.

'Fifteen. Most ever, to this day, in a train accident in Manhattan. The way the steam hissed and the smoke bellowed, the rest of the injured thought they'd be cooked alive,' Ledger said. '"Harvest of death" – that's what a reporter called it. A harvest of death under New York City streets. That's why this building's an accidental terminal.'

'Accidental?'

'Got built, Ms Cooper, because of that accident. Your colleagues indicted the engineer for manslaughter. The very next year, the plans for this building began. When the terminal opened in 1913, Grand Central was the highest-value piece of property in New York City. And then the entire center of gravity began to shift to this neighborhood. It's this colossus of a train station that *made* this part of the city "Midtown".'

'So tell us about crime, Don,' Mike said. 'You can't have an attraction like this without bringing in all kinds of crime. You must know stories that never reach the street.'

'I can't think of any murders, till this one today. There've been robberies over the years, of course. But that could happen anywhere, mind you. And the stuff that you do, Ms Cooper,' Ledger said, twirling the end of his mustache, reluctant like many others of his generation to use the word 'rape'. 'When the terminal was at its lowest ebb, back in the eighties, we had some bad cases out of here.'

I remembered as a young prosecutor when one of my colleagues had handled a case of a man who waited in prey for tourists getting off trains, offering to help them with luggage and taking them instead to remote platforms where he sexually assaulted them.

'Those crimes happen much more frequently in subway

stations,' I said, respecting the man's great pride in his terminal. We'd had cases that took place on moving trains, in deserted cars, as well as on platforms late at night when women alone were easy targets.

'What else, Don?' Mike asked.

'Over the years we've had more than our share of ransom demands. Are you old enough to remember when there used to be banks of lockers in the terminal?'

We all nodded. In one of my favorite novels, *The Catcher in the Rye*, the character named Holden Caulfield stored his belongings in one of the coin-operated lockers while he slept on a waiting-room bench.

'Used to be you could rent one for hours or days to store your things in. So the lockers were often designated drop spots in kidnappings. But that all changed after 9/11. No more temporary storage. You know about that better than I do. And mail train robberies. Looking back on things, we sure had a lot of those.'

'Of course,' Mike said.

'One day it's a funeral cortege with some head of state, or war heroes shipping out, or kids going off to college or a summer vacation,' Ledger said. 'Next thing you know it's a Code Black.'

'Code Black?'

Don Ledger looked to Bruce Gleeson before he answered. 'That's what the emergency system is called for our station-masters.'

'What system?' Mike said.

'Well, for terrorists and things like that.'

'Tell me.'

'Go ahead, Don,' Gleeson said. 'It's okay.'

'From the stationmaster's office and several other locations in the terminal, there are surveillance cameras that can zoom in on any part of the building – theoretically – if they're alerted to a problem.'

'Theoretically,' Mike said. 'If there isn't any visual obstruction – pillar, staircase, ticket booth.'

'Best we can do, Detective. This lets them direct emergency responders to the exact spot, as well as shut down exhaust fans to stop the spread of contaminants.'

'We'll need to see this equipment,' Mike said, straightening up and brushing back his hair with his hand. 'Make sure it's working. You've had a terrorist bomb in here before.'

Gleeson looked quizzically at Mike. He seemed as surprised to hear the news as I did.

Don Ledger nodded. 'Way before your time. All of you.'

'A cop died,' Mike said. 'Back when my father was on the job. 1976. You grow up in a blue household, you hear those stories instead of fairy tales.'

'Terrorists?' I asked. '1976?'

'The Croatian National Resistance. Wanted to be freed from Yugoslavian control. A group of them hijacked a TWA flight from New York, bound for Chicago. Made their demands and got a plane full of passengers to Paris.'

I didn't know the story at all.

'And the threat,' Ledger said, 'was a bomb in a locker.'

'Here?' I asked.

'A locker right here in the belly of Grand Central Terminal.

Could have taken out half of the five-fifteen to Greenwich.'

'So the negotiators met the demands of the terrorists,' Mike said, 'who told them exactly where the bomb was. The Bomb Squad retrieved it and took it to be detonated at Rodman's Neck.'

The NYPD Firing Range in the Bronx was a training ground where officers learned to shoot for operations, including the emergency response on September 11, 2001, and – in a large crater on the southernmost tip of the neck of land that juts out into Eastchester Bay – the place where the elite Bomb Squad took deadly explosives to be detonated. The Pit, as the crater was called, was the spot in which the bombs were rendered harmless. From crude to sophisticated devices, they'd been the handiwork of every radical group from the Weathermen to the Black Panthers to George Metesky – the Mad Bomber – and even Al-Qaeda.

'Only thing wrong was that when the squad tried to detonate the device by remote control, it didn't go off. So a young cop named Brian Murray was sent out to the Pit to find the problem,' Mike said. 'The damn thing exploded and killed him.'

No one spoke.

'RIP,' Mike said.

'I get your point, Detective,' Bruce Gleeson said. 'I got the call this evening, and I assumed we had a sexual predator on the prowl. You think it's bigger than that.'

'I think you can't make any assumptions. Transportation hubs are a natural target for terrorists. They've been here before, and someday they're going to be back.'

Twenty-four

'That's the very place I made my movie debut, Ms Cooper,' Ledger said.

It was after eight P.M. on Thursday evening, and Mike had asked Ledger and Gleeson to take us through some of the physical plant, to explain to us the size and scope of the terminal. It was a good time to do it, with rush hour crowds already dispersed to their homes.

'Maybe that's why you look so familiar to me,' I said, smiling back at him.

'You think I'm kidding, do you? Are you a Hitchcock fan?'

'My favorite.'

'*North by Northwest*? It was the first movie ever shot in Grand Central. 1959. My boss wanted a walk-on in a frame with Cary Grant, who was jumping on the Twentieth Century 'cause he was suspected of murder, so I tagged along in the shot.'

We were standing at the iconic information booth, which was crowned by an opalescent four-faced Seth Thomas clock, a priceless golden ball that had kept perfect time for a century.

'Good flick. Almost makes sleeping in the sleeping car of a train look sexy,' Mike said. 'What are we looking at, Don?'

'The main concourse, all thirty-six thousand square feet of it. Larger than the nave of Notre Dame Cathedral.'

I remember, as a kid, thinking this was the largest indoor space I'd ever seen. That still held true.

'Nowhere to hide out here,' Mike said. 'Wide-open.'

The room was enormous, with only the round information booth obstructing its center. The south side of the great hall, broken by the walkway to the old waiting room, was lined with ticket booths, most closed for the evening. Each one of them – if breached – could be a cubbyhole for someone looking to do evil.

The departure gates covered the north side.

'Yeah, but those gates are the portals to the unknown,' Mercer said, waving his arm across the length of that quarter of the room, a gaping mouth full of tunnels that led under- and aboveground to all of Manhattan.

We could see up the staircase on the west to the doors fronting Vanderbilt Avenue. The eastern end was much more troublesome. The staircase there, replicated in the restoration of the terminal, despite its grandeur, was a dead end, leading up to an Apple store that was one of the biggest revenue sources for the building. No exit.

But on either side of the staircases there were wide archways, one framing the entrance to the subway station and the other to an arcade of shops and services, then eventually to Lexington Avenue. Between the two sets of stairs was another one down to the lower concourse.

'*Portals to the unknown* kind of nails it, Detective,' Ledger said. 'This terminal and its train yards actually cover seventy acres of territory.'

'What?' Mike said.

'That's the amount of land that Vanderbilt and his successors bought up. Penn Station? That's got less than thirty acres. We go on forever, or so it seems. We control track up to 97th Street, all buried now under Park Avenue. Try keeping your eye on that.'

'And below us? Is there something under the lower concourse? What's the secret basement you mentioned?'

'The levels beneath are the deepest in New York City. Think of a ten-story office building turned upside down. We're talking the underbelly of Manhattan.'

'Isn't there a new subway coming in?' Mercer asked.

'Yes, the Long Island Railroad is building a link that will land even deeper. Sixteen stories down, not ready till 2019.'

'But digging right now?'

'Absolutely.'

'So there are men down there, connected to this terminal?'

'Every day. Hundreds of men working on that. It will enable another eighty thousand folks to come through here, from Long Island, without them having to go to Penn Station like they do now,' Ledger said. Penn Station was Amtrak's facility on the west side.

'So when trains "terminate" here,' I said, 'how does that work? Where do they go if they don't just pass through to the next stop, like all the other stations?'

Ledger told us. 'They're backed out onto another track, which takes them to a wheelhouse, where they turn around, make a complete loop underneath the terminal, and then get set up for the trip out.'

'And a wheelhouse is . . . ?'

'Exactly what it sounds like. The trains pull out and go around – used to be called a "roundhouse" – on a circular track underneath the building, and come back facing north again, for the next ride.'

Mike's eyes were scanning the room, now staring up at the zodiac figures on the celestial ceiling, until he shifted his gaze to the many-storied arched windows that stretched for the length of a football field above the concourse.

'Talk access up there,' he said. 'What's all that glass?'

I took several steps back to lean against the information counter and look up.

'Windows, Detective.'

'I know that, Don. But there's a helluva lot of them.'

'When the terminal was built, there was only one way to ventilate it. Fresh air.'

'You mean that those things open and close?'

On either end of the concourse, east and west, were three gigantic windows, hundreds of feet overhead. I don't think I had ever seen bays of windows as large as these.

'Had to be that way a hundred years ago. Light didn't come from anywhere else but the street. It was the primitive days of electricity, so lighting the terminal was a daunting task. Not a bad place to hide up top, if you don't get vertigo.'

'Hide? It's all glass.'

'A bit of an illusion, Detective Chapman. Those are actually catwalks up there. Glass boxes, if you will.'

I strained to see what Ledger was talking about.

'So there's one layer of glass, the windows that open over Lexington Avenue, many flights up, of course. Then there's actually a walkway, made entirely of glass brick, which runs across the entire width of the building. Look down through it and you'd think you're about to fall twenty stories to the terminal floor.'

I got queasy even listening to the description.

'But nowhere to hide,' I said, squinting to look up at the glass panes.

'You'd be wrong about that,' Ledger said. 'The second long pane of glass faces the interior, over the concourse. Those windows open, too. So natural air flowed through, as well as a great amount of light. But see those pillars in between each of the arched windows?'

The pillars extended from the top of the staircases on either end of the building up to the arch where the vaulted ceiling rose over the concourse.

'Sure,' Mercer said.

'The catwalks go clear from one side of the building to the other. Easy to hide a small posse behind those pillars. Give you a bird's-eye view of the entire floor, if your stomach doesn't get butterflies from standing up there.'

'Butterflies?' Mike asked.

'Standing on a piece of glass in the sky? I never liked it much. One of the architects walked me through ages ago. I got kind of nervous midway out when I made the mistake of looking down. "Form following function," he kept saying, to move me along. "All done for a plan, Don. Air and light. Now just keep walking." ' Ledger imitated the man's Southern accent, laughing at himself as he talked.

'But what do they connect? Why are they there, and how would one get up inside them?'

'Used to be several offices in the corners at the top, just beyond the windows. One end with desks for the station managers, another in which the engineers had a lounge. They could catch up on their sleep on cots. I don't think anything up there is used much these days, since the big renovation. It's too remote to be practical now.'

'Getting there?' Mercer repeated.

Ledger had to think. 'You need a key, any way you look at it. That situation room you were all just in?'

'The imaginary seventh floor, the one that's twenty flights up,' Mike said. 'Those dark, snaky hallways leading to it?'

'Yes. You can climb down to the catwalks from the situation room. And there's a stairwell that goes from landing to landing, but it's kept locked on every level, too.'

'Add it to tomorrow's list,' Mike said.

I took a few steps forward to turn around and look at the glass-enclosed, glass-bottomed catwalks on the other end of the terminal. A woman racing for a midevening train bumped against me hard and practically spun me around.

'Watch where you're going,' she said.

'Sorry.'

Two suits carrying briefcases and walking briskly passed on either side of me. The automated lady on the loudspeaker reminded people to take all their belongings with them and not litter the terminal.

'Those lightbulbs,' I said, holding on to Mercer's arm as I looked upward again. 'They're all bare. There must be hundreds of them.'

Where the celestial mural met the marble columns that held up the vaulted ceiling of the terminal, there was a string of bulbs that illuminated the entire circumference of the building.

'Four thousand of them up there,' Ledger said.

'But they're bare. No shades, no covers.'

'In 1913, gaslight was still the way most of this city was lit. The Vanderbilts were showing off, as well they could.'

'They had just converted all their New York Central trains from steam to electricity,' Mike said, 'and now they could make their grand terminal electric, too. Just leave the bulbs exposed. Was that the plan?'

'Indeed it was.'

'Somebody actually gets up there and changes them?' I asked.

'Not a job I want any more than you do,' Ledger said. 'What looks like a layer of crown molding beneath the bulbs, edging the marble columns? Well, you can't see it from this angle, but it would hold all of us inside that molding. You can climb out into those pockets – they're man-sized, all right – from the catwalk. Walk the length of the terminal. Unscrew every one of those bulbs and replace them when they burn out.'

'I'll pass,' I said.

'Where are all those people going?' Mike asked.

There had been a steady stream of walkers – not just businesspeople, but also teenagers and families with children, well-dressed travelers and scruffy-looking women and men – a typical cityscape in motion.

'I told you,' Ledger said. 'That's the way to the subway. Grand Central Station, the IRT line.'

Mike started off in that direction, to the southeast corner of the concourse, and we all followed behind him.

'How many ways up from that subway platform, from the station to the terminal?'

'A whole bunch of stairs, Detective. And elevators. Escalators from the lowest floors, too. Actually, the new LIRR feed is so deep it's going to take passengers four minutes to get up to this level.'

'And ramps,' Mike said. 'This place is full of ramps. Can't imagine anyone was thinking about handicapped people in 1913.'

'They weren't,' Ledger said. 'These wide ramps were the genius of the original architects.'

I was trying to keep up with Mercer's long strides, but it seemed I was constantly bumping against someone who was in a greater hurry than I.

'Think of it. A passenger gets off a train, whether a century ago, or today. It's possible to get from the door of the railroad car to any level of the terminal – or to the street and even to a hotel or office building – without encountering a single step,' Ledger said. 'It was ingenious for the period, and just as much so now.'

I'd been in this building thousands of times and made my way up the graded ramps, some as wide as a boulevard, to get to 42nd Street from commuter trains, without ever giving a thought to their purpose.

'This great terminal is all about movement,' Ledger said. 'It was not only designed to be seen as a huge monument to the glory of commerce and transportation in its day, to be appreciated for its beauty – which it still is now – but also to be the most glorious example of moving people through spaces to their destination.'

Mike had turned his head to listen to Ledger, colliding with a young man determined to catch up with his traveling companions. He picked up the lead again. A subway train must have just pulled in and disgorged its riders, who charged toward us from steps below.

I felt as though we were minnows swimming upstream against a bigger pod of fish. Guys on their way home or to a second job or dinner or a club or a romantic assignation brushed against me from both sides.

'Keep up, Coop. Your ass is dragging,' Mike called to me over his shoulder.

'You want to know why I hate the subway? This is part of it. It's not even rush hour and I feel like I'm caught in a whirlpool.'

Mercer was cool with it. 'Mike just wants to see how many exits there are. This would be the fastest way out of

Midtown if someone was up to something bad in the terminal. You wait here. We'll grab a look and be right back.'

I stepped to the side and tried to catch my breath.

I could still see the top of Mercer's head over the line of emerging subway riders coming from the opposite direction. Corridors led off three ways, like forks in a road. A large newsstand obstructed my view, so I started to move to the side of it.

From behind me I thought I heard someone call me. I knew Mike was several hundred feet in front of me, but I looked back to see who had said the word 'Coop.'

As soon as I swiveled around, the man who had spoken was on me, pressing my body against the cold marble wall under the archway leading to the IRT steps.

He ripped off the do-rag that had been wrapped around his head and tried to grind his hips against mine, whispering to me as I pushed hard back at him. 'Your time is almost here, Coop.'

I kneed him in the groin as dozens of people passed us by, probably assuming a suitor was keeping a rendezvous with me in the terminal.

I slapped him across the face, and he let go of me, laughing as he covered his forehead and eyes with the rag, and ran toward the same subway entrance that Mike, Mercer and Don Ledger had gone to check.

'Mercer!' I screamed as loud as I could. There was no one near me now. There wouldn't be a crowd till the next train deposited its passengers. 'Mercer! It's Raymond Tanner. Stop the bastard, will you? It's Raymond Tanner!'

Twenty-five

'How would he know I'm in Grand Central Terminal? How could he possibly figure that out?'

I was sitting at the counter of the Oyster Bar with Mike and Mercer almost an hour later. They were watching me drink a second Dewar's on the rocks. The first one hadn't touched me.

'Rocco says there's footage of us all over the six o'clock news,' Mike said, 'rushing into the building when we got the call about the girl's body.'

He and Mercer had taken off after Tanner, leaving me with a stunned and silent Metro-North officer on the subway platform. They thought they had jumped on the same train with the fugitive and rode a few stops, walking through the cars to search for him. But he had somehow given them the slip. On their return, they retrieved me from a police sergeant's room behind the row of ticket booths and walked me down the ramp to the Oyster Bar.

'Why would anyone have news footage? It wasn't a story then.'

'Mike and I were running with gold shields in hand. That attracted some tourist's attention.'

'Forgot that.' They needed to identify themselves as detectives so they didn't appear to be frantic citizens on a rampage, running into the terminal or any other building.

'Some lady from New Zealand filmed it on her smartphone and sent it in when CNN ran the story of the dead body shortly after that. At least one of the local news anchors identified you using your name, fingering the link to a crime — a sexual assault or homicide — that had you as part of our team.'

'And that brought the game out in Raymond Tanner,' I said, sloshing the ice cubes around in my glass. 'Apparently my time is almost up.'

'I could have told you that,' Mike said. 'Could have wrapped myself in a turban like a—'

'Don't go there.'

'Could have covered my head in a ninja mask so the facial recog software didn't match me, either. Maybe I'd be more appealing to you, kid. Never thought of coming on to you in quite so public a place.'

'Detective Wallace,' I said, lifting my glass toward Mercer while Mike inhaled his fifth or sixth Malpeque oyster, 'would you please tell your good friend that there was nothing the least bit amusing about being molested by Raymond Tanner?'

'You call that molested?' Mike asked. 'Sounds like foreplay to me.'

'You're the guy who lays on ten years of foreplay and

then freaks out after you kiss me once,' I said. 'I don't think you know the first thing about the subject.'

'Okay now, blondie. You're beginning to feel the glow of that cool amber Scotch. I love it when you get fired up.'

'The man wants to kill me, Mike. Tanner's a hideously dangerous rapist. An escaped felon, wanted for more violent crimes than I can remember.'

'He's jerking you around. You've got such a bad temper you rise to the bait too easy. He could have clubbed you with one of his lead pipes right here if that was his goal. Stuck a knife in your ribs. He prefers playing with you, kid. The cat tossing the mouse between his paws. He likes making it personal.'

'Well, it works. I feel so disgusting right now. I just want to shower and get the touch of him off me, the smell of him out of my nostrils.'

Too many women had told me too many times how violated they felt in the hands of an abuser. The idea that Raymond Tanner was stalking me – doubly ironic that the high visibility of the cases I handled made the task so easy for him – was chilling. He was skilled at evading capture, brazen enough to make his way into Grand Central just as it was about to be flooded with police.

'Know what would help?' Mike said, pushing his plate toward me. 'A bivalve. Pure protein.'

'I'm too nervous to eat.'

'You need to coat your stomach with something or that Scotch will bore clear through to your toenails, Coop.'

'Who's out on the street looking for Tanner?'

'Everybody but us,' Mercer said. 'And you need to slow down on the alcohol.'

'So he creates a complete diversion from the triple homicide, and I'm the patsy for it.'

'Maybe not complete,' Mike said. 'The A team stays focused on the triple. Scully can use minor leaguers to hunt for your lunatic.'

'Thanks. Very gratifying. Minor leaguers on the hunt for my stalker. Maybe Scully can bring in some wannabes as well. Boy Scouts or Dora the Explorer.'

'I just mean that the perv is making it easier for them to find him. Showing himself at the courthouse and following your every move in the media.'

'You'd think some Good Samaritan would have noticed a madman pinning me to the wall.'

'You're only the center of your own universe, Coop. Must've looked like you were pleased the guy was jumping your bones. You are such the image of a broad running home to her blond, green-eyed peeps in some white-bread part of Connecticut, saying good-bye to the inner-city dude who's got your number.'

'Sick imagination, Mr Chapman.'

'Tanner's breaking your concentration, Alex.' Mercer was also working his way through a dozen oysters while he tried to get me to chill. 'We need your brain back in the case.'

'It's out to lunch.'

'Stick on it, girl. I know that's easy for me to say right

now. We'll find that fool,' Mercer said, reaching over and taking my hand off the drinking glass. 'Vickee's got the guest room all made up. I told Rocco we'd stop and pick up your toothbrush and some clothes for the morning, and I'd keep your mind off things overnight.'

I looked at Mike. Why couldn't I just stay at his place instead of being the third wheel at Mercer and Vickee's comfortable home in Douglaston?

'Maybe Mike could just—?'

'Oh, no, kid. Can't have you pawing at me all night. I'm twenty-four/seven into my work right now.'

'And Logan will be out of his skull to wake up and see you in the morning,' Mercer said, tousling my hair.

'Yeah, it's not every four-year-old who has a full-on head case for his godmother,' Mike said. 'Just don't let him smell your breath when you give him a kiss. The fumes might kill him.'

The bartender told us that our table, a small corner one in the back, nestled under the vaulted white tile ceiling, was ready. There were still a few dozen diners lingering over their meals, many of whom seemed to be working their way through oversized seafood platters. The red-and-white-checked tablecloths added cheer to the room.

'You folks ready to order?' the waiter asked. 'Young lady?'

'I'm not hungry. Just a glass of white wine, please.'

'She'll have sparkling water,' Mercer said. 'And a bowl of clam chowder.'

'I'll have the chowder if I can have some sauvignon blanc, too.'

'Deal.'

'The Coopster's in no position to make deals, Mercer.'

'Wine has a very calming influence on me, guys.'

'And for you, gentlemen?' the waiter asked.

'I'll have the Maine lobster. I'd like a three-pounder,' Mike said. 'All the sides, okay? Fries and onion rings and coleslaw. And have you got Sierra Nevada Pale Ale on draught?'

'Yes, sir. And for you?'

'The grilled salmon, please. Another Grey Goose martini straight up. Three olives.'

'Now here's how you regain your center,' Mike said to me. 'Where are we?'

'The best seafood restaurant in Manhattan. Is that what you want me to say? Landmarked and all that?'

'Nope. I want you to channel your favorite place on the planet.'

Martha's Vineyard. My home on a hilltop in Chilmark. My escape from all things prosecutorial.

'Close your eyes for a minute,' Mike said.

I'd bought the old farmhouse with my fiancé, Adam Nyman, who'd been a medical student at the University of Virginia during my law school years. The night before our Vineyard wedding, on his drive from New York to the romantic island, another driver ran him off a bridge into a riverbed below and Adam was killed in the crash.

'Okay. I'm thinking the Vineyard.'

'Then take some deep breaths. Imagine the clam chowder you're about to eat is from the Bite,' Mike said, referring to the tiny shack in the fishing village of Menemsha where the Quinn sisters served up the most spectacular chowder and fried clams. 'And that Mercer's oysters and my lobster are from Larsen's Fish Market. You almost home, Coop?'

I opened my eyes and looked at Mike, who was naming my favorite island haunts. 'Almost there. But my recurring nightmare is that Raymond Tanner will be along for the ride.'

'He's got Mercer and me to contend with. And over your shoulder? Lieutenant Correlli's about to crash our little soiree.'

I looked around. Rocco was walking toward our table from the bar, carrying a glass of red wine.

'Safety in numbers, I guess.'

'I just want to apologize to you, Alex,' he said, as he lowered himself into the fourth chair at the table.

'You didn't do anything, Loo. No need to apologize.'

'I mean, this bastard keeps giving us the slip. I gotta say he's really good at it.'

'Serial rapists? If they weren't good at extricating themselves from every kind of situation, they'd be one-time offenders.'

'Scully talked to Battaglia,' Rocco said. 'I told Mercer—'

'Right. That's how you knew we'd still be here. The commissioner and the district attorney have got me under wraps for the night.'

The waiter arrived with a steaming bowl of New England clam chowder. The restaurant's air-conditioning – and the chills I'd had since Tanner put his hands on me – made the soup a welcome sight, despite the temperature on the street.

'Just till we nab him, Alex,' the lieutenant said, gnawing on an unlighted cigarette.

'I hear you've got your best guys on the hunt. So I guess I should just hibernate until Groundhog Day? Don't want to be a strain on your resources.'

'Don't lose it now, Alex.' Rocco Correlli leaned in and clinked his glass against mine. 'We figured out the link. Like Mike says, nothing's a coincidence.'

'What link?'

'Between the sociopathic rapist who's stalking you and the cannibal cop.'

I almost gulped a helping of my wine. 'What's that?'

'Gerardo Dominguez and Raymond Tanner,' Rocco said. 'They both grew up in the same project. Fulton Houses, on 17th Street.'

I didn't know whether to be relieved or more nervous. 'How did—?'

'Scully had someone go back practically as far as the maternity ward. We're with you, Alex. I promise. The pair of pervs have been linked together since childhood.'

Mike Chapman cracked the claw of his lobster. 'Two scumbags under the same roof, Coop. Must have been something in the water over at Fulton.'

Twenty-six

'Some days I'm simply more trouble than I'm worth,' I said.

I got into Mercer's car and slammed the door shut. It was 7:05 in the morning, and Vickee wanted us out of sight before she got Logan out of bed.

'Sorry.'

'Everybody keeps apologizing to me. Cut it out, Mercer.'

'Vickee thought it would be too disruptive for Logan to get all juiced up if you surprised him before she put him on the bus for day camp. You'll see him tonight.'

'Why tonight? Is this a long-term exile? Scully's sending me to Elba?'

'Don't start my day like this, Alex. Could be they'll have Tanner in custody by then, and you just might choose to have dinner with the three of us because we haven't seen much of you.'

Vickee and I had stayed up late into the night, talking and catching up on personal things. She was as smart a detective as anyone on the job and had used her skills –

and our long friendship – to try to soothe and distract me.

The clothes I picked up when we stopped by my apartment were perfectly suited for a day exploring the nether regions of Grand Central Terminal. I had on a man-tailored shirt with rolled-up sleeves, hanging out over my jeans, and my running shoes. Don Ledger had told us we'd be covered in dust and soot by the time we had satisfied our curiosity.

'I'd like to do dinner,' I said. 'Anytime. But on my own terms, not because I've been exiled.'

'Understood.'

'You hear from anyone this morning?' I asked, as Mercer drove through the quiet streets of Douglaston, a section of Queens known for its upscale suburban feel, despite its New York City address. The homes were good-looking and spacious, many of them set on large pieces of land.

'No calls. And there aren't any news reports of bodies found.'

'We're meeting Mike at Grand Central?'

'Eight o'clock.'

We were both pretty quiet on the ride in. I emailed messages to my team at the office, since it was unlikely I would see them today, depending on how things went at the terminal. It was summer Friday hours, and many of them would take off early for weekends in the Hamptons or on the Jersey Shore.

'Calls about the victim on the private train should start coming in,' I said. I was surfing the internet for stories about the murder and saw that her photograph had been released late last night with an announcement by Scully.

The *New York Post* led with the banner headline TERMINAL! above a grainy shot of the murdered girl, and a caption described her last train ride through the century-old landmark as a FAST TRACK TO DEATH.

'Rocco's ready.'

The highway traffic was relatively light until we reached the Triborough Bridge. Mercer navigated the lanes and made his way to the 42nd Street exit on the FDR without using lights and sirens, which was always my temptation when with him.

We reached Don Ledger's office within the terminal at 8:15 and found him and Mike waiting for us. Muscling through the crowd of commuters to get to him seemed more dangerous than battling traffic on the city streets.

'I've got permission to take you down to the sub-basement,' Ledger said, after we finished the coffee he offered us.

'Is that a big deal?' I asked.

'Very big, Ms Cooper. And not a bad place to start if you want to wreak some havoc here.'

'How could someone get in if it's so mysterious?' Mike asked.

'Like I said, this room doesn't exist on any blueprint of Grand Central. If I wanted to hide, it's the perfect spot to be.'

'But off-limits to the public.'

'Course it is. My boss tells me the man you're looking

for seems to know his way around Terminal City. And I'm telling you that in the one hundred years since this place was built, no one knows where all the holes in this building are today. Or all the keys.'

'Let's get moving,' Mike said.

The four of us began our march out of Ledger's office and onto the main concourse. He weaved his way through the masses to the western staircase and down to the lower level, then gathered us around him at the bottom.

'We're going to M42, the deepest basement in New York City.'

'M42?' I asked.

'Shorthand for the main substation under 42nd Street.'

'You mean that's not where Lex Luthor's lair is?' Mike said. In the 1978 movie version of *Superman,* the villain lived in an elegant apartment deep in the bowels of Grand Central.

'No, sir. But this one is totally off the charts, and if you wanted to bring New York City to a standstill, you'd head right for this spot in the terminal.'

We walked another three minutes to get to a deserted corridor, stopping in front of a narrow elevator door that looked too obsolete to move. Don Ledger had a chain that dangled from his belt, packed with twenty-five or thirty keys. He shuffled them to find the right one for the unmarked elevator.

There was only one button to press, and the descent was slow.

'How deep are we going?' I asked.

'Terminal City was blasted into the bedrock of Manhattan, but nothing goes farther down than this. Not the basement of the old World Trade Center, not the bullion vaults at the Federal Reserve Bank. We're going more than ten stories under the train tracks.'

'Kind of like the water tunnel that's being built across town,' I said, recalling the treacherous time that the three of us spent with the city's sandhogs. I swallowed hard to clear the blockage in my ears.

'Does anyone work down here?' Mercer asked.

'Just a small crew. The original equipment has been updated, so it pretty much runs by itself.'

The doors creaked apart, and we stepped off onto a small platform to begin our hike, one by one, down a winding steel staircase. Ledger reminded us to watch our step. I held on to the railing, needing no reminder.

Three flights down, he opened a heavy door, and we were all inside M42, a concrete bunker that I guessed was at least the same size as the main concourse above us — eighty thousand square feet.

The room was sealed closed like a giant burial vault, airless and oppressive.

'You all right, Coop?' Mike asked. 'You're white as a sheet.'

'It's so hot down here I can barely breathe,' I said, fanning myself with my notepad. 'What's that buzzing noise?'

'So this is the room that powers Grand Central Terminal,' Ledger said. He led us into the center of several rows of massive machines. The ones to my left looked a century old, and the ones to my right seemed much more modern.

'The noise, Ms Cooper, comes from these rows of transformers.' Ledger was pointing to the new machines, which emitted a loud monotonous humming sound. 'What transformers do is convert alternating current – you know, AC? – into direct current – DC.'

I nodded my head, although the subject had been beyond my grasp since high school.

'Most power is delivered in AC, which moves back and forth, while DC is always going in one direction. So it's a much more efficient way to run trains.'

'I think I understand,' I said to Ledger, before turning to whisper to Mercer. 'At least I understand well enough that I want to get out of this hotbox. I'm suffocating.'

He wiped his brow with his handkerchief and then handed it to me. 'Be patient.'

'What happens if you stop these machines?' Mike asked.

'You bring to a halt every train going in and out of the terminal. Five hundred and thirty-eight of them a day.'

'Back-up generator?'

'Not a chance, Detective. There is no way to power up this operation if all this stops.'

'What are those antiques?' Mike asked, pointing to the older equipment and walking away from us, between the machines.

'The original rotary converters.'

Each one was the size of a small building, cylindrical in

shape with a rust-colored coating on top of both. We followed Mike in between the machines, our footsteps falling like leaden weights on the concrete floor, echoing throughout the room.

'So this is what Hitler was looking for,' he said, patting the side of one of the silent giants. The machine dwarfed him. That seemed to be the scale of everything in the terminal.

'You know that story?' Ledger asked.

'Mike,' I said, 'it's way too hot in here. Let's get out.'

He waved me off, walking away to the far side of the converter.

'What about Hitler?' Mercer asked.

'He wanted to disable the rail service along this route,' Mike said. 'He figured he could disrupt troop movements for all the Eastern Seaboard embarkations by bringing the trains to a complete standstill.'

'Grand Central Terminal,' Mercer said. 'One-stop shopping.'

He was as fascinated with the giant converters as Mike was.

Don Ledger pointed over at the door through which we had entered. 'I'll tell you this much,' he said. 'If anyone unauthorized, so much as peeked through that entrance during World War Two, the orders were to shoot on sight. There were armed soldiers on duty here around the clock.'

I heard footsteps across the room, or thought I did. 'What's that noise?'

'One of the workmen, I assume,' Ledger said.

'Why would they have shot at anyone coming in?' Mercer asked.

'All it would have taken to disable that sucker was a bucket of sand thrown at it. The converter would have come to an immediate stop – they're very fragile devices, despite their size – which would have brought the trains to a halt. So the orders were not even to let anyone explain the purpose of their visit but simply for the soldiers to take aim and shoot.'

'Did you hear that?' I was looking over my shoulder and then kneeled to peer under the converter, but I couldn't see anyone.

'What Mr Ledger just said?' Mercer asked.

'No. There's someone walking on the far side of the room.'

'You're so jumpy, Alex. People work in here, girl.'

'Saboteurs,' Mike said, paying me no mind. 'They almost made it, didn't they?'

'Came pretty damn close, too close for my taste,' Ledger said.

'Pay attention, Coop. This is stuff you ought to know.'

'I'm riveted, Mike.' I rolled my eyes at him, then kept looking back to see why the footsteps had died off and why this workman didn't show himself to us.

'In 1942, a German sub landed four spies on the beach in Amagansett. They were actually intercepted by a young coast guard officer who saw them and questioned what they were up to. One of them, who spoke good English, told him they were fishermen. He didn't buy the story, but he was unarmed, so he let them go.'

'I had no idea any of them landed on our beaches,' Mercer said.

'The kid called in the news, and the four were arrested a few days later, with all their plans and maps. They were determined to blow up strategic sites, like rail bridges, including the one over Hell Gate.'

'I know you're trying to get my attention, Mike,' I said, noting his reference to the scene of one of our major investigations, at the point along the East River where the mayor's residence sat in Manhattan.

'Pastorius.'

'What's that?'

'I'll save your butt, Coop. It'll be a Final Jeopardy! question one of these days and you'll score big.'

'Not if it's military. And not if it's against you.'

'Think long-term. After you dump me.'

Mercer and Mike were examining the machine as we talked.

'Blow me off and that will be sooner than you think.'

'Admiral Canaris,' Mike said.

'Head of German intelligence. The Abwehr,' I said.

'Not as dumb as you look right now, Coop. How about Operation Pastorius?'

'Clueless.'

'Francis Pastorius was the leader of the first German settlement in the US,' Mike said. 'So Canaris named his attempt to cripple troop movements and implode the economic system here after Pastorius. It was his hope to target a major transportation hub.'

'World War Two-style terrorism,' Mercer said.

'Yeah,' Mike went on. 'Paralyze the trains and put the fear of God in the civilian population.'

I bristled at the sound of someone running, reverberating on the concrete floor.

Don Ledger had heard the noise, too. 'Who's there?'

Mike's voice was so loud that apparently he hadn't heard the footsteps that Ledger and I did. Ledger stepped out from behind the large converter and started to retrace his route toward the entrance.

'Mercer,' I said. 'There's someone in here, and Ledger doesn't like it any more than I do. Don't let him approach the guy alone.'

Mercer turned on a dime and overtook the older man.

I could see the back of a tall, slim figure dressed in black, a hoodie pulled up on his head, opening the door of M42.

'Who are you?' Ledger called out again.

And just as loud, Mercer yelled for the man to stop.

But the heavy door slammed shut behind him and I was frozen in place, sweat dripping from my pores.

Mercer jogged to the door and pushed on it. 'It's locked.'

'Can't be,' Ledger said. 'The lock's on our side.'

Mercer threw his body against the exit, but it didn't give. He twisted the knob and thrust at it a second time. 'It won't budge.'

'Then he's barricaded it from the outside,' Ledger said. 'He's locked us in.'

Twenty-seven

Don Ledger was sitting on the floor with his back against the wall. He had undone his necktie and unbuttoned the top buttons of his shirt. Not only was he terribly over-heated, but he also had a chronic heart condition and was experiencing palpitations.

I was crouched in front of him, wiping his brow with Mercer's handkerchief. His distress had put my own concerns in perspective.

'We'll be fine, Mr Ledger. It's just the heat and the lack of fresh air. The guys will have you out of here in no time.'

'Water,' he said. 'Do any of you have water?'

'We didn't bring any, sir. Would there be any around?'

'I don't know. I – I haven't been down here in months.'

Mike and Mercer had taken turns manipulating the doorknob and trying to dislodge it, but something was holding it in place.

Cell phones were useless. M42 was too far underground and encased in solid steel foundations to get any service. The cords to the receivers of the two in-house phones that were attached to the wall near the exit had been sliced and rendered useless.

'How long till someone misses you, Mr Ledger?' I asked.

'Nobody misses old men like me. They'll think I've wandered off to cool down in some bigwig's air-conditioned office.'

Mike was jogging away from me, down the long row of machinery. I assumed he was looking for something he could use as a battering ram, or some other way to contact the world above us.

'Are you okay if I leave you for a couple of minutes?' I asked Ledger.

He held one of his hands out to me. 'Do what you have to do, young lady.'

I gripped it tightly and forced a big smile. 'Somebody must have to oil one of these converters every now and then. We just need to breathe deep.'

I stood up and watched for a few seconds as he put his hand on his chest, as though to measure his own heartbeats. Then I walked to the next aisle of supersized devices and got out of sight of Ledger before starting to trot in pursuit of Mike.

He heard me coming and turned around to wait. 'How's Ledger?'

'Scared more than anything, I think. He's anxious and very dry, and he's mostly feeling guilty that he led us into this desolate basement.'

'There's a secretary up there, in the office next to his. I'm hoping she starts missing him soon.'

'Then I suppose I should be grateful you flirted with her.'

Mike wiped his forehead with the back of his hand before running his fingers through it. 'A little bit long in the tooth for me, but she liked the blarney. I got there before Ledger got in. She clearly has a soft spot for him.'

'Are we screwed here?'

'D'you see the size of this place, Coop? It's not like we're going to run out of oxygen.'

'But—'

'I'm just going up and down the aisles to see what's around. I'm not expecting anything lethal,' Mike said, holding on to my elbow as though to steady me. 'Look, I know you're claustrophobic, and I wish—'

'I feel like I've been sealed into one of the pyramids,' I said, trying to make light of the situation.

'You picked a place that might actually hold all of your worldly goods, babe. Smart move. You can stack all your boxes of shoes over in that corner. And if you play your cards right, you could go across the River Styx after a three-way with Mercer and me.'

'My dream come true, Detective Chapman. Till then what do we do?'

'You're doing it. Keep Ledger preoccupied,' Mike said, turning away from me, 'and see whether Mercer needs anything.'

I started back toward the door. Mercer was pounding his large fist against it from time to time and yelling at the top of his lungs every minute or so. I didn't think there would be anyone or anything out there to hear him, except for a passing track rabbit.

I took my position again next to Don Ledger. I started to tell him stories about adventures that Mercer, Mike and I had been through together – lighter ones than murder – and how they had always managed to get me out in one piece.

Almost ten minutes elapsed before Mike shouted to me from the farthest corner of the room.

'Hold your calls, ladies and gentlemen, we have a winner.'

'I'll be right back, Mr Ledger. Mike must have found something.'

I sprinted in the direction of Mike's voice and saw him kneeling at the end of the first row of antique converters. As I got closer to him, I noticed a dark blanket spread out on the floor. Mike pulled a pair of vinyl gloves out of his pocket and put them on.

'Looks like we've got a nester,' he said.

The blanket was doubled over to create a makeshift sleeping bag.

'I can't imagine anyone getting in here.'

'We have a Houdini on our hands, Coop,' Mike said, lifting a corner of the blanket with two fingers. 'He got a steamer trunk packed to the gills with a body in and out of the Waldorf, probably knows these tunnels better than the rats, worked his way onto a private varnish to murder another vic, and knows as much about M42 as Nazi saboteurs. That should limit the cast of characters.'

'What's that?' I asked.

'What?'

'The piece of paper under the edge of the blanket, Mike. See it sticking out from underneath?'

He reached for the small gray card that almost blended in with the concrete flooring. He flipped it over and we could both see the photograph of the dead girl on Big Timber.

'Shit,' Mike said. 'Lydia Tsarlev. Nineteen years old. Student ID from Westchester Community College.'

It was becoming harder to breathe by the minute.

'These assholes really like their souvenirs, don't they?' He got to his feet and put his arm around my shoulder, staring at the picture as we headed back to Mercer. 'They really like their trophies from a kill.'

Twenty-eight

It was almost eleven A.M. when I heard banging and scraping against the metal door. It was Pug McBride's voice calling for Mike that first penetrated the space.

'You inside there, Chapman?'

Mercer was still beside the door. 'We all are. Open up.'

I helped Don Ledger to his feet, and we waited as the objects wedged under the doorknob to prevent it from moving – which turned out to be lengths of old steel railroad ties – were dragged aside and one of the workmen pulled open the door.

As hot and steamy as the tunnel area surrounding the staircase was, it was refreshing after the stillness of M42.

'Everybody okay?' Pug asked.

'Get a bus to take Mr Ledger to the ER, will you?' I asked. There were EMTs and firemen who worked inside the terminal who could carry him up the winding staircase and load him into an ambulance. He needed to be checked out. 'He needs water as soon as possible, and I think we all do.'

'Good work, Pug,' Mike said, patting McBride on the back. 'I keep telling Rocco you're going to find a real perp one day, if you keep looking hard enough.'

'You were easy. I just followed the scent of your vodka through the station.'

'Odorless, Pug. That's why I drink the stuff.'

'And that's why I'm such a brilliant detective. Caught the teeniest whiff of it and dogged it through the entire terminal.'

'Thanks, Pug,' I said. 'Another hour and I would have melted.'

'You already look like you did,' he said, giving me the once-over.

'How'd you find us?' Mercer asked.

'One of the summer interns overheard Ledger talking. Said he was taking some cops down to M42. I got kind of antsy when we got a hit on the dead girl's ID at about nine this morning. Didn't get an answer from Mike when I called his cell to let him know, and then Rocco couldn't bring up any of you on your phones, so he sent us here to look.'

'Lydia Tsarlev,' Mike said.

Pug's entire face screwed up in puzzlement. 'You got a TV set in there but no cell service? You know her name already?'

Mike took the girl's ID out of his pocket and held it up to Pug McBride's face. 'I just told you her name, didn't I? Now let me out of here. Whoever was using this as his crib has at least a two-hour jump on us.'

Mike started up the spiral staircase, but Pug was pulling at his shirt.

'You sat on this information since last night?'

'Don't be a jerk, Pug. I just found it inside this basement,' Mike said, taking the steps two at a time. 'Scully's got to saturate the terminal with uniforms. Get Crime Scene in here to dust for prints and pick up the blanket for trace. Meet you in Ledger's office.'

'I'll stay put till the guys come for Ledger,' I said.

Mike called down over the railing. 'This entire area – M42 and whatever abuts it – has to be secured, Pug. Nobody gets access unless they're cops. And nobody touches nothing.'

'I'm taking orders from you, Chapman?'

'For now you are. And keep your eye on the blonde. She's as fragile as an old rotary converter.'

'Yeah, she looks like she got hit by a bus,' Pug said.

It was only minutes until four men from the Grand Central fire station clambered down the staircase. Don Ledger tried to insist that he walk up under his own steam, but two of them managed to lock hands and carry him, despite the steepness of the steps and the great height. A wheelchair was waiting for him at the elevator landing, and by the time we emerged on the lower concourse, the ambulance crew had taken him out.

Mercer and I were on our way to regroup with Mike in Ledger's office.

'Give me five minutes,' I said.

'Not alone.'

'Then come along.'

He followed me up a ramp, past Posman bookstore and a doughnut shop, to a small Banana Republic in the retail area of the terminal. I bought a shirt for each of us to replace the ones we'd been wearing, which were soaked with perspiration.

'You think I smell bad?' Mercer asked when I handed my money to the cashier.

'I know you do. And I can't stand myself this way. There's a bathroom in the stationmaster's suite. You can either shower or just clean up a bit.'

We walked back to Ledger's office, where Mike had taken over the man's desk and mouthed to us that he was on the phone with Rocco Correlli. I took the shirts out of the bag and he gave me a thumbs-up before slamming down the receiver.

'Here's the deal,' he said. 'Scully's calling in every unit he can get. NYPD, Metro-North, National Guard, US Army, feds, state troopers. You name 'em, we'll have 'em.'

'When?' Mercer asked.

'He can't control that, but he said we'd be seeing a flood of cops. He'll divert a lot of details from the four-to-twelve shift, and then more at midnight.'

'I thought Grand Central closes its doors at two A.M.,' I said.

'It does. The plan is to get as much law enforcement in here as a presence as soon as possible. Uniforms and guns everywhere.'

'That won't catch the killer,' Mercer said, 'but it will comfort the commuters.'

'Exactly. The only reason the terminal shuts down between two and five thirty A.M. is that it prevents the place from becoming a homeless shelter again. Gets everybody to clear out. So that gives us an opportunity to have investigators from any or all of the agencies go through here with a fine-tooth comb.'

'If we haven't put our hands on the killer by midnight, they can penetrate every crevice of the terminal and the tunnels.'

'From what we've seen,' I said, 'that doesn't even seem remotely possible. Each level leads to another level beneath or above it, or a tunnel that leads to another part of Terminal City or a wheelhouse or a room that isn't on the blueprints.'

'Losing heart, sunshine?' Mike asked. 'It doesn't sound like you.'

'Whoever this guy is, he's done his homework. Wherever we go, he's been there first. Yes, I'm demoralized by it.'

'And you're sweaty, and maybe a tad hungover?'

'All of the above,' I said.

'So the manpower is the first order of business. Next is Lydia Tsarlev.'

'They've found her family?' I asked.

'No. It's several of her classmates who called in. She's an exchange student, here on some kind of visa. The lieutenant has a team going to White Plains to search her apartment. He needs to contact her parents, check her computer if there is one. Routine stuff.'

'How about Corinne Thatcher's parents? Or her brother? I can get Ryan to work on that with your squad.'

'He's on it, kid. Looking for any connection between the two vics. Where have you been all morning? In a black hole?'

'Very black. I'm about to clean up.'

'Before you hear the DNA results?'

'The lab got a match?' Somehow the adrenaline was pumping again.

'Not a perp, Coop. Not yet. Just case to case.'

'So the speck of blood on the curtain at the Waldorf wasn't Corinne Thatcher's after all?'

'All cred to Dr Azeem and his fancy camera,' Mike said. 'The killer must have cut himself.'

'And it matches some of the blood in the Big Timber train car?'

'Yeah. Case to case. Confirms the killer of both women is the same guy.'

'If you didn't know any other way.' I crossed fingers on both hands. 'Now tell me he's in the data bank.'

'Weren't you listening? There's no profile for him in either the city or the state banks.'

'But they haven't tried NDIS yet?' I asked. I was referring to the National DNA Identification System maintained by the FBI.

'Going in as we speak. Should have results later today.'

'It's like Pug said when we were first at the Waldorf.' I was removing the tags from my shirt with renewed spirit and energy. 'Nobody comes out of nowhere. Not with a killing style like this.'

'I'm with you, Alex,' Mercer said. 'This bastard has killed before. He's got to be high profile in somebody's data bank.'

Twenty-nine

We had each cleaned up as best we could, put on our new shirts, and were back in Ledger's office. Mike had brought in sandwiches, suggesting we eat now because there was no telling when we would have the chance again.

'Where to?' I asked.

'We're going to the Waldorf.'

'Something breaking over there?'

'No, we're taking the Terminal City path,' Mike said. 'We're going underground. We need to see if our perp could have found his way in through this route.'

'I'm assuming however we're going is a path without a blueprint,' Mercer said. 'There's got to be a reason no one was aware of this connection.'

'Better than a blueprint. Hank Brantley, the cop whose specialty is the tunnel homeless population, is going to lead us through.'

'So much for a fresh change of clothes.'

I was hungrier than I thought and washed down half a turkey sandwich with a full bottle of water. Brantley arrived within minutes, handed out our hard hats and flashlights, and we were ready to take off again.

He led us down to the gate on the lower level – number 100 – which a Metro-North patrol officer was guarding.

'Same rules apply,' Hank said. 'Stay close. Walk on the platform as far as it goes. It gets pretty narrow up ahead, and this time you will have a third rail off to the far side of the tracks. That's what electrifies the trains. It'll light you up pretty good, too, if you give it the chance.'

We headed down the first ramp away from the departure gate, a slight incline that took us away from the brightly lit terminal into the dark, subterranean maze of tunnels.

I would never get used to seeing people huddled in holes in the concrete walls or foraging for scraps between the railroad ties, but on this trip I was slightly less shocked than I had been a day earlier.

The live tracks were only a dozen feet away from our platform. As a train approached, headlights glaring through the arched openings in the wall between where we stood and where the train was slowing to a stop, I froze in place, unable to stabilize my footing. We were in a single row – Indian file, as Mike called it – with him behind Brantley, then me, then Mercer last in line.

'I can't get you there myself,' Hank said. 'It's not exactly a straight line any longer, so I took a walk out just now and asked Smitty to meet us at the point this platform stops.'

'Great,' I said to Mercer as I flapped my arms to regain my balance. 'What's wrong with starting out up in the daylight on Park Avenue? Taking the Northeast Passage? I'm beginning to feel like a troglobite.'

Mike got half of what he heard right. 'Troglodyte?'

'That's you, Detective. Somebody whose thinking is out of step with the times. A throwback to Neanderthal thinking.'

'What's the difference between *bites* and *dytes*?'

'Troglo*bites* are animals who spend so much time in caves that they're practically blind, but their eyes adapt to seeing in the dark.'

'Bite me, Coop.'

'I would, but you're walking too fast.'

Our presence in the tunnels, now at least one city block away from the terminal, had stirred up some of the population. Heads poked out above us and below. Huge rats – seemingly unafraid of us – played on the tracks while roaches the size of small rodents crunched under Hank Brantley's feet.

Smitty, the former mayor of the Grand Central tunnel system, was waiting for us in the shadows of an enormous steel girder. I figured we were somewhere near 45th Street, in our slow trek north of the terminal.

Hank handed him a small plastic bag. 'Three sandwiches and sodas and a carton of cigarettes. We appreciate your help.'

'The platform ends up ahead about fifty feet,' Smitty said, now leading our pack.

An outbound train made so much noise as it passed by us that I couldn't hear what Hank said back to him.

'What happens when the platform ends?' I called out.

'We go the rest of the way on the tracks,' Smitty said, 'but it's a dead line. No trains running on it these days. It only goes so far as the siding up by the hotel you're going to.'

'That makes no sense,' I said to no one in particular.

The walkway ended abruptly. There were two large steps down to the tracks. I didn't question Hank Brantley, who seemed to have complete faith in Smitty.

Three men and a woman were sitting on the old rail ties in our path, playing cards and drinking beer. They greeted Smitty and expressed surprise at seeing the rest of us.

I flinched as a locomotive, which seemed to be heading in our direction, rounded the corner on an adjacent track as it slowed on its final approach to Grand Central.

Smitty turned to face us, making sure we all made it past the cardsharps.

'You heard about the other body they found last night?' Mike asked him.

I couldn't take my eyes off the third rail, which was painted a bright neon orange and was painfully close to the trail we were taking.

'Yeah.'

'You know anything?'

'Like I told you, Mr Detective, it's not good to know too much down here. Private railcar, dead girl, big commotion. Anything that brings the man into the tunnels is a bad deal for us. We try not to bring trouble on ourselves.'

291

'That's two bodies in as many days, Smitty. Must be some kind of talk.'

Smitty started to cough, grabbing his chest as he did. 'Not so much. She wasn't one of us, is all I know. The whole NYPD wouldn't be taking such an interest if she was.'

'Not true. Carl came from your world.'

'So-so.' Smitty spat across the tracks, dislodging a gaggle of roaches. 'Half up, half down.'

'You'll let Hank know if you start getting information?' Mercer said. 'We can pay you for it. Feed you and your sources.'

Smitty laughed. 'That's a whole lot of food you'd be haulin' in. All I know so far is that the young lady here, she gave Dirty Harry a pass.'

'I – I didn't really do—'

'You're down with me, Ms Detective. He didn't hurt her.'

I was rethinking my own decision to tell the cops not to bother with Dirty Harry. My sympathetic instinct for a mentally ill man had overruled my usual concern about thoroughness.

Smitty had stopped talking and moved on his way again. We all had our flashlights on, stepping carefully on the tracks that skirted the active train line.

I thought of both young women, Corinne Thatcher and Lydia Tsarlev, and wondered whether they had been subjected to the torture of spending time in this underground hell. It was truly an inferno in this part of Terminal

City. Filth and stench, rodents and insects, the mad and the disenfranchised, all dancing around a third rail that supplied a constant flow of electricity to the hundreds of trains coursing through here every day. The throbbing vitality of Grand Central and its busy concourses was turned upside down in this strange underbelly of Manhattan.

The path forked once more, and we again took the western route, separating slightly further from the incoming and outgoing commuter trains.

We trudged on, occasionally rattling some living thing – large or small – that got out of our way.

'What's that?' I heard Mike ask, as he came to a standstill almost half an hour after we had started our exploration.

He moved to the left, one foot underneath the track and the other on one of the old ties on which we'd been walking. Then he reached back to grab my hand and move me forward so I could see – and Mercer behind me – what was directly in front of us.

'It's a railroad car, Detective,' Hank Brantley said.

'I can tell that for myself.'

The enormous, windowless train looked like an armored tank on steel wheels. It was dark green, like a military vehicle, old, and covered with layers of dust.

The tracks on which we were walking had broken ties and didn't appear able to support the weight of this mysterious train.

Mike approached it, running his hand across the side of it as though to remove a layer of grime. 'It's a relic, isn't it? It must have been sitting on this siding for decades.'

'That's because it was built for just one man, Mike.'

'The armored train?'

'The armored train and the special siding here. Track sixty-one.'

'Who was the man?'

'The president of the United States.'

Mike whistled. 'Well, if he's counting on this to spirit him out of Manhattan in case of a terrorist attack, he'd better send in a team to spiff it up. This iron horse isn't about to make a run, Secret Service be damned.'

'Not for this president,' Hank said. 'This train was designed for Franklin Roosevelt, during the Second World War. And so was this secret entrance to the Waldorf-Astoria Hotel.'

'We're right below the Waldorf?' Mike asked. 'And there's a secret entrance?'

Hank pointed to an unusually narrow elevator shaft. 'Terminal City ends here.'

Thirty

'This was originally a spur that ran below an old warehouse and a railroad power plant,' Hank Brantley explained. 'Those buildings were torn down to be replaced by a luxury hotel to anchor the terminal.'

'The Waldorf-Astoria. The Manhattan White House,' Mike said. He had disappeared out of sight, making his way around the presidential train.

There was a small platform between the train and the elevator shaft. Smitty sat on the edge of it, taking in all the conversation while eating one of his sandwiches.

Mike returned to the front of the machine and climbed the three steps to the door. He pulled on the handle, but it didn't move. 'Hank, how fast can you get someone to open her up?'

'There's supposed to be a Metro-North security head meeting us. He's just late.'

'Bad time to be late. We need to see whether Houdini made his way in here.' Mike kicked at the door and pulled the handle again, with no success. 'I knew there was an armored car built for Roosevelt during the war.'

'First passenger railcar built for a president,' Hank said.

'The second, actually. The War Department had a special one made for Lincoln. Just too bad he didn't take it to the Ford's Theatre and sit inside it. What else do you know about it?'

'I'm afraid I'll get it wrong, just like that fact.'

'I been on the tour,' Smitty said. 'I know about it.'

'You what?' Mercer asked.

'Metro-North has a PR guy. He gives tours to bigwigs and stuff,' Smitty said, devouring a bag of chips. 'I've heard his bit.'

'Like what?'

'This here is track sixty-one, like Hank says. Right through that hole is track sixty-three,' he said, pointing through an archway beyond the front of the train. 'See that blue boxcar?'

There was indeed another rusted machine, which appeared to have been abandoned just next to the presidential one.

'Roosevelt was crippled,' Smitty said. 'Y'all know that. But he didn't like anybody to see that he couldn't walk. So during the war, they made up this special train for him. Armor plating on the side and bottom and both ends. There's only tiny little windows you can barely see, done with bullet-resistant glass.'

Mike walked along the side of the train till he found the slits of glass, wiping them with his fingers and trying to look inside. 'Thick as mud. I can't make out anything.'

'The blue boxcar held Roosevelt's fancy automobile.'

'A Pierce-Arrow, if I'm not mistaken,' Mercer said.

'I'm impressed,' I said to Mercer.

'Whatever it was, that boxcar was coupled to this train,' Smitty said. 'Last time she was used was the fall of 1944.'

'Glad you listened up, Smitty,' Mike said. He was back on the front platform, climbing on the railing to get on the roof of the car.

'See these wide doors on the side of the armored train?'

'Yeah,' Mercer said. 'They look like they belong on the side of a barn.'

'They slide apart and a lift comes down. The president's limousine glided right onto that and got hoisted up into the railroad car.'

'So nobody got to see that Roosevelt couldn't stand up or walk unassisted,' Mercer said.

'There are actually gun turrets up here,' Mike said, pounding against the roof of the old railroad car. 'You gotta take a look at this, Mercer. This mother was really loaded for war.'

'What happened in the fall of '44?' Mercer asked Smitty. 'That was six months before the president died.'

'On this tour they were giving a couple of weeks ago, the man said Roosevelt spent the whole day in the city campaigning for local politicians. It was pouring rain, but he went everywhere in his fancy car, with the top down, so people could know he was okay.'

'Ebbets Field,' Mercer said. 'My old man was there in the crowd. He loved Roosevelt and the Brooklyn Dodgers both, even before Jackie Robinson took the field. It was the only time, he used to tell me, that the president – who was a New Yorker – had ever been to Ebbets Field.'

Smitty continued. 'Supposed to be that Roosevelt was seen by more than a million people that day.'

'I don't doubt it,' Mercer said.

'Now what happens,' Smitty went on, 'is that the whole train pulls into the tunnel here, and these last two cars are uncoupled on these tracks, while everyone else goes on ahead to the terminal.'

He gestured behind him to the elevator. 'The Pierce-Arrow gets lowered down from the armored car and drives the prez across this short platform, onto the elevator.'

'It looks so narrow,' I said.

'Built for the specs of the presidential limo,' Smitty said. 'Just wide enough to hold the car, and just tall enough to fit the Secret Service guys who stood on the running board. And nobody – nobody – ever saw that the big dude didn't have a pair of legs he could stand up on.'

I could hear someone hurrying down the metal staircase that ran to the rear of the elevator. The man had on a blue Metro-North uniform and was carrying a metal ring, six inches wide, with several dozen keys hanging around it.

'I apologize for being late. I had to get all the skeletons,' the man said, waving the wad of keys. 'What is it you gentlemen want to see?'

'Get us into this train,' Mike said.

'That's damn near rusted shut. All I can do is try,' he said, fumbling with the keys.

'When's the last time it was opened?'

'To my knowledge, it's been years.'

'Are you still expecting the presidential train on Sunday?' I asked.

'We certainly are. It pulls in end-to-end with this one.'

'Is it also armored?'

The man scowled at me. 'I can't tell you anything about that, miss.'

'Look, I'm the prosecutor who's working on these murder cases.'

'Do you have federal security clearance?'

'No, but I'm—'

'Then I don't care who or what you are, I'm not authorized to tell you anything about the president's train,' he said, mounting the steps to the platform of the armored car.

'You might be making a slip here, bro,' Smitty said with a laugh. 'I think that's the lady who's driving this operation. The dude sitting on top of your train? He works for her.'

'Used to be that was true, Smitty,' Mike said, lowering himself onto the platform. 'It's why I look as old as I do.'

The Metro-North security guard was at the door of the train. He was trying to manipulate the key in the lock, but he couldn't get it to turn.

Mike was at his back, expressing his impatience. The man became frustrated and passed the key to Mike, who rattled and rattled the knob until it finally gave out.

'Coop, you and Mercer walk it with me.'

I grabbed the railing and boosted myself onto the platform, followed by Mercer. Mike led the way, shining his flashlight into the dark, long-unventilated space.

The first part of the antiquated car was a lounge and dining area. Displayed on a shelf above the table was china bearing the presidential seal, and next to each chair – at eye level – was one of the slits that served as a window.

In the bathroom beyond the lounge was a small laminated sign that read ESCAPE HATCH, and directly opposite was a wheelchair, locked into place against the wall.

I knew Mike was looking for a murder victim, but the excitement of living history was what seized my imagination.

The next bay was the garage designed to hold the Pierce-Arrow. No car in place, but all the trappings to secure it, and a photograph on the wall – opposite the very large pocket doors and the lift – of the president and first lady riding in the smart silver machine.

Beyond that were two bedrooms – his and hers – that had taken on a very shabby look over the years. There were also small quarters for staff. To our great relief, none of the areas had been disturbed by our killer.

'I would have bet money our guy had been in here,' Mike said, 'but not a sign of it.'

He turned around and ushered me out of Eleanor's bedroom. 'We've got to go, Coop.'

The Metro-North security guard was smug. 'There are

some places one simply can't penetrate,' he said. 'That's why the president will be safe here.'

'You just never know,' Smitty said, grinning at me. 'All depends on who's around. I got peeps down here could be a greeting committee come Sunday and scare the crap out of the man.'

'Back off,' Hank Brantley said.

'How about the elevator?' Mike asked.

'Yeah,' I said. 'Does it go up to the Tower suites?'

'Now that would be foolish, miss, wouldn't it? A car inside the hotel.'

'Open the elevator for us,' Mike said. 'Ms Cooper is a lot of crazy-ass things, but foolish isn't one of them. Where does the damn thing go?'

'You've probably passed the elevator doors thousands of times on the street,' the guard said, fishing out the key – double-checking that he had the right one before he inserted it in the keyhole below the call button.

'What street?' I tried to imagine anything that looked like an elevator door but couldn't.

'Forty-ninth Street, miss,' the agent said. He pressed the button, and the doors slid apart. We said good-bye to Hank and Smitty, and the three of us stepped on with him. 'This was a pipe shaft before the siding was constructed for the hotel to receive its special guest.'

The conveyance was very primitive and slow to move up the shaft to its destination. The brick walls were exposed, and steam pipes still lined them from top to bottom.

'How often does this get used?' Mike asked.

'Never,' the guard said. 'Why would it be?'

'And who has keys? Who has keys to all these remote outposts? This elevator, the president's railcar, M42?'

'There are a good number of keys, Detective. There are occasional emergencies and many of us in senior positions have sets of skeleton keys.'

'How many and who are they is what he wants to know,' Mercer said. 'Whoever you work for, you call and say we need that complete list in an hour.'

'We'll be over in the stationmaster's office,' Mike said. 'Get it to us there.'

The doors slid back, and as they opened, the sunlight was almost blinding.

'Wait,' I said, shielding my eyes from the glare, 'there's something here.'

Mike's hand was already pressing against the small of my back. 'Step out, Coop. Where are we?'

I took three steps forward and spun around, telling the guard to hold the door for a minute.

We were on East 49th Street, in the middle of the block between Park and Lexington Avenues, the south side of the great hotel. The portal to the elevator doors was gleaming in gilded paint, dappled by the sun's rays. It looked more like the entrance to an exclusive spa than to a dilapidated railroad car siding and, yes, each of us had passed it by many hundreds of times.

'The president's car would come out right here,' the

guard said, 'and one sharp right turn puts you directly into the Waldorf-Astoria garage.'

The garage opening was fifteen feet from the gilded doors. The killer could have been in and out in seconds, without being seen on the street.

'Damn it,' Mike said. 'I got sidetracked when I was looking for the garage surveillance footage. That's when we got the call about the body in the private car.'

'I kept the team on it,' Mercer said. 'The camera was blinded, just like so many of the others. Your instincts were right.'

'One more thing,' I said, stepping back into the elevator with the Metro-North guard. 'Our killer was in this elevator shaft, so you'd better hurry up with that list of key-holders you're looking for.'

'How can you tell?' Mike asked, doubling back to study whatever I was looking at. 'He didn't drop anything. There's nothing on the floor.'

'Where's the best place to look for prints in an elevator?' I asked.

There was the clear outline of a fingerprint on the call button of the old cab, right on top of the letter *D*, which would have taken the man down. We didn't need powder to bring its detail into focus. It was patent – obvious to the human eye – not latent.

'My bet is that it will match the profile of the man who cut himself in the suite at the Waldorf Towers.'

Mike was trying to push me aside so that he could see

the smudge himself. 'What if anyone else pushed the same button after that? Impossible to get a clean lift.'

'No one can get in this elevator,' the guard said. But I wasn't listening to him.

'This one's in blood, Mike. Get someone from the squad over here to lift it ASAP. It's a fingerprint highlighted in the blood of the man who killed Corinne Thatcher, and it's giving us his escape route.'

Thirty-one

The three of us practically raced back to Grand Central in the afternoon heat, moving south on Park Avenue, caught in the early exit of many professionals also heading to the terminal for their weekend getaways.

Rocco Correlli was waiting for us in the stationmaster's office. We took over Don Ledger's desk after learning that he was resting comfortably at New York University Hospital and would be released after twenty-four hours of observation.

'I need you in the next room, Alex.'

'Sure. What's up?'

'The Tsarlev girl's roommate just got in. We need you to calm her down and get the story.'

'Of course. Was Ryan able to reach Corinne's parents and brother?'

'Yeah, but so far there's no obvious connection. Not by age or neighborhood or school or job. Total disconnect.'

'That only fits if he's picked them at random, Rocco,' I said, 'and there's way too much overkill for that to be.'

'What do you mean?'

'Rapists rape. Over and over again when they get good at it. They don't usually kill unless it's a grudge against a particular vic they know, or the woman resists the attack, the guy goes nuts and ups the force.'

'No resistance from a woman like Thatcher, who's been drugged.'

'Not to mention a master plan with three murders perfectly orchestrated.'

'Three, so far.' Correlli was constantly popping candy in his mouth in place of sucking on a cigarette inside the terminal offices.

'Tell your guys to keep working with Ryan Blackmer. They've got to drill down a few levels to find the common denominator. Feed him whatever they get so he stays on top of it,' I said. 'Where's the roommate?'

'C'mon,' he said, walking me out to an even smaller office a few doors down.

He knocked and opened the door. A sullen-looking young woman was sitting at a small table with her head on her crossed arms as though napping. She lifted her head when I stepped inside.

'Hi, I'm Alex Cooper. Thanks for coming into the city on such short notice.'

'It's okay.'

'I'm an assistant district attorney. I work on sexual-assault cases with the police. And on homicides.'

'Like *SVU*?'

'What?'

'Like the TV show. The Special Victims one.'

'Yes, except this is real.'

'Way cool. I love that show.'

'I'm so very sorry about your friend. About Lydia.'

She rubbed both eyes with her fists and yawned at me. I thought she'd been crying, but she was only tired. I didn't know why the lieutenant thought she needed calming down. She didn't seem the least bit agitated. 'We weren't really close or anything, but thanks.'

'What's your name?' I pulled out the chair opposite hers and sat down.

'Jean. Jean Jansen.'

'How old are you?'

'Nineteen.'

'Do you mind if I ask you some questions about Lydia?'

'Sure. But I don't know that much.'

'Do you go to the same college as Lydia?'

'Yeah. Westchester Community. It's a two-year school.'

'Where are you from?'

'My family lives outside of New Haven now, but I grew up in Yonkers, so I wanted to come back here to go to school.'

'You have a lot of friends from this area?'

'Sure.'

She was slightly overweight, with pudgy arms extending from the T-shirt she was wearing that proclaimed her love for the Kings of Leon.

'You shared an apartment with Lydia, is that right?'

'Uh-huh.'

'So you must have been somewhat friendly.'

'Friendly, yeah. But not like good friends. My roommate from first semester didn't come back to school, so we got together on Craigslist 'cause I needed someone to split the rent.'

'I see.'

'What can you tell me about her?'

Jean Jansen was picking the remains of an iridescent blue polish off her nails. 'Like what do you want to know?'

'You understand that Lydia is dead.'

'Yeah.'

'Murdered,' I said, hoping to get the girl's attention, even though she'd heard the story on the news. 'Her throat was slit, Jean, from ear to ear.'

She never took her eyes off her stubby fingers. 'Gross.'

'That's all you have to say about it?'

'I mean, I'll go to the funeral. It's just totally gross she died like that.'

'We're trying to find out why someone would want to kill Lydia,' I said. 'So if my questions spark any sort of answer that might help us – no matter how crazy it seems to you – just tell me what you're thinking.'

'Okay.'

'The police found Lydia's student ID, but there were no other papers with it. Nothing that tells us any more about her.'

Jean was silent.

'Well?'

The girl looked at me. 'Well, what? Was that supposed to be a question?'

Score one for the Sullen Teens team. I wanted to light a fire under her, but it didn't seem likely I could ignite it.

'When did Lydia move in with you?'

'It was February. A couple of weeks after the second semester began.'

'Did you share a bedroom?'

'No. The place is small, but we each have our own room.'

'Did she have a computer?'

'The cops already searched the place. Tore her room apart looking for stuff,' Jean said. 'Lydia had a laptop, but it isn't there. Neither is her phone. She took them with her when she went.'

'Went? Went where?'

Jean Jansen shrugged. 'To get herself killed, I guess.'

I sat straight up, surprised by the young woman's nonchalance.

'You think that's what Lydia did? Get herself killed?' I asked, spacing those last three words and barking them out, for emphasis.

'I mean, I don't really know. I don't want to be here, Ms Cooper,' she said, showing emotion for the first time. Unfortunately, it was about herself. 'My boyfriend is already so pissed off that I called the hotline.'

'Why? What you did has helped us enormously. It's going to prove a huge benefit to Lydia's family.' I'd save the boyfriend's problem for a later question.

Jean looked at me quizzically. 'Oh, really? Where's her family?'

'We know she's a foreign student. We were hoping you could tell us about them. About where Lydia is from.'

'All I know is what she told me, and we didn't talk that much. I know she's from Russia.'

'That's a good start. Do you know what part of Russia?'

Jean flaked off a good-sized piece of nail polish, which landed on the floor next to my sneaker. 'I can't remember that, if I ever knew.'

'We want to call her parents before they see this on the news or on the Internet. We could send the local police to her house, and it would be a much more humane way for them to learn about this tragedy.'

'That's a good idea. But you'll have to find her computer to figure out where her parents are. I know she Skyped with them every week or so.'

'Okay. That's helpful,' I said, even though the laptop and cell phone were not among the trophies the killer seemed to have saved. Pictures of prey – especially attractive young women – were usually what these perps held on to, and the ID card with Lydia's photograph was evidence of that. 'How about her friends? Do you know who she socialized with?'

Jean shrugged again. 'We didn't even go to class on the same campus, Ms Cooper. All my courses were in Yonkers, and hers were in Peekskill.'

'Did she have a car?' I asked, thinking of another place to look, another way to track Lydia's movement in the last days of her life.

'No way. She didn't have much money. Lydia took the

bus to school, then she worked after class in a coffee shop, I think it was. Took the bus home. Never brought anybody with her.'

Jean Jansen had gotten most of the blue polish off her nails. Now she was concentrating on expanding the hole in the knee of her denim pants, twisting and pulling at the loose threads.

'Never?'

'Maybe once or twice. But she didn't like my music, so she usually went into her room and closed the door. And my boyfriend didn't much like her – I mean, like he thought she was very snobby – so that was fine with us.'

'Your boyfriend, what's his name?'

Jean paused for several seconds. 'I've gotta ask him if he wants me to tell you. He doesn't want to be involved in this, really.'

That's not a choice he's going to have. 'Then help me with a few other things. Did you think she was snobby?'

Jean looked at me when she answered. 'Lydia thought she was smarter than me. High and mighty, a bit. Sometimes I felt it was 'cause this was a second language for her, stuff came out kind of stilted. She usually said what was on her mind, though, which could be kind of annoying.'

'Can you give me an example?'

Jean pursed her lips. 'Like she was always on me about my weight. You – you're skinny like she is, Ms Cooper. Like she was, I mean. Maybe I don't want to be that way. Maybe I'm happy with how I look. But she was always telling me I couldn't keep food that she thought was junk in the apartment. That I ought to join a gym. Sometimes she'd even throw out food that I'd left in the fridge, and when I'd call her out on it, she'd say it had gone bad and smelled. Which wasn't true, by the way. That kind of thing.'

So far, nothing I'd heard gave rise to a motive to murder.

'I'm sorry she did that, Jean,' I said. 'The couple of times she brought people home, do you remember who they were? Men or women? How recently?'

'I know there was another Russian girl who was in one or two of Lydia's classes. She came over a few times. I could hear them laughing a lot from the other room. They'd been Skyping friends back home. You should find her.'

'Good idea,' I said. 'We'll try to do that. No guys?'

'Lydia has a boyfriend in Russia. You'd better talk to him, too. She wasn't dating anyone here, as far as we could tell. She brought one or two guys home, but they were just friends. They stayed for an hour or two and then they left. You know what I mean? Nobody spent the night with her.'

'Did you meet them, these guys? How recently were they at your apartment?'

Jean gave the question some thought. 'One of them was here about a month ago. Like in the middle of July.'

'So maybe he knows something about her. Do you know how we can find him? Was he also a student?'

'She introduced me to him. I know he doesn't go to our

school, because he told me that himself. Lydia and I were in summer school classes, but he looked a little older, and he told me he didn't go to college.'

'Was he Russian, too?' I asked.

'How am I supposed to know?'

'Did you hear his name, Jean? Did he speak with any kind of an accent?'

She yanked on another long string and her plump kneecap popped through the gaping hole in the denim. 'Just normal is what he sounded. Like from here.'

'Okay.'

'They were fighting. Arguing really. Not fighting.'

Jean was giving this part of the conversation more thought. She stopped playing with her frayed dungarees and looked at me.

'How do you know that?' I think she sensed my heightened interest in her answer.

'Because it was the night of the All-Star Game,' Jean said. 'You know what that is?'

'Yes. Yes, I do.' The Midsummer Classic marked the symbolic middle of the Major League Baseball season. It would be easy to put an exact date on the night, if it proved to have any significance in the case. 'Could you hear the argument?'

Jean laughed. 'The problem was my boyfriend couldn't listen to the game because this guy got so loud. He was all like screaming at Lydia.'

'Do you know what he was screaming about?'

The girl turned serious again. 'Not really.'

'Tell me, Jean,' I said. 'You must have heard something. Some of the words.'

She was slow to respond. 'I think the guy was trying to get her to do something with him. Maybe *for* him, not just with him. He was yelling that she was wasting her time.'

'What time? With school?'

'Not with school, no. They weren't arguing about school.'

'What, then?'

Jean put her elbows on the desk and her head in her hands. 'I am so screwed,' she said. 'My boyfriend is going to go ballistic about this.'

'The detectives will explain everything to your boyfriend. Nobody's going to let you get bothered for talking to us,' I said. 'Why were they fighting?'

'Lydia is – well, she was – all into causes and stuff. Belonged to organizations, she told me, back home and then here.'

'Political organizations? Is that it?'

'No. Not like that. She was – what do you call it? An actionist?'

'An activist? Do you mean activist?'

'Yeah. For Lydia, it was all about animals. She couldn't stand seeing animals suffer.'

'I don't know who can,' I said.

'Not just cats and dogs, though. Like all kinds of animals. Lydia told me her mother had been arrested once, back home in Russia. Went to jail because she broke into some laboratory and saved the chimpanzees from the scientists.

314

I mean, like lecturing me that I didn't stand for anything. That's why she joined this group.'

'Is it a club at your school?'

'Are you kidding? These people aren't just students.'

'Does the group have a name?'

'It must, but I can't remember it.'

'Was it PETA?' I asked. 'People for the Ethical Treatment of Animals?'

'Nope. It wasn't that. I don't know, Ms Cooper. I think it was something with the word "liberation" in its name.'

'Were they planning violent acts, Jean? Is that what you don't want to say?'

'No way. Lydia was all about nonviolence. It was just saving the creatures. I showed the cops the poster on her wall. It says FREE THE ANIMALS. EXPERIMENT ON ME.'

'Okay. That's a good start. That gives the detectives something to work with,' I said. 'Did Lydia have animals? Did she have any pets?'

'She rescued a couple of dogs in the spring. But we're not allowed to have any in our apartment, so she got them all to good homes, like with other students.'

'So why was this guy fighting with her if she was doing decent things with her life?'

Jean shook her head, looking as though she hadn't thought of it that way before. She almost whispered her answer. 'I don't know. I just don't know.'

'I think you know more than you're telling me, Jean. I bet you heard what the guy said.'

She took a few more minutes to think, pulling her cell

phone out of her pocket to look for messages. 'Look, could I go soon? I've got to be home in time for dinner.'

'Or what, Jean? What will happen to you?' I said. 'Lydia's dead. You ought to think about what I'm asking you.'

'The guy must have been some kind of nut, Ms Cooper,' Jean said. 'He used to be in this animal group with Lydia. Like they were buddies, saving their monkeys and chimpanzees and baboons back in the spring. Then something switched off in him, like he was crazy.'

'Can you explain what you mean?'

'Only that he was yelling at her that night, during the baseball game. He told her he didn't care about animals anymore. That it didn't matter what scientists did to them, if they were cruel or not. That they weren't people, so what was the difference.'

'But you said he had something else he wanted her to do for him, right?'

'Yeah. He kept saying he had a more important plan.'

'This is really good, Jean. You're helping us out here,' I said. 'And what did he say the plan was?'

'That's the part I couldn't hear, 'cause of the television being on and all that. Or maybe he was just being more quiet when he talked to Lydia about it. The walls are sort of paper-thin, so you can hear way more than you want to.'

'You must have picked up part of it, didn't you?'

She shook her head back and forth, strongly indicating she didn't.

'But you just called him a nut. You said he switched off like he was crazy.'

'I swear I'm not making this part up, Ms Cooper. Okay? I'm going to say this to you, and you're going to have to believe me,' Jean Jansen said. 'The only part I heard after that was him saying he knew he was right because he heard voices.'

'Voices? I'm confused. There were other people in the room?'

'No, no. This guy was telling Lydia that she had to do what he told her because he was hearing voices inside his head. That someone was taking control of his mind, and he needed her to do whatever he ordered.'

Whether or not this visitor to the apartment was the killer, there had been a man with serious mental illness in Lydia Tsarlev's life.

'Now I understand you, Jean. Of course I believe you,' I said. 'Did you hear how Lydia responded to him?'

'Can we keep this between us, Ms Cooper. Just this part?'

'I'd like to tell you yes, Jean. But that wouldn't be very smart of me. It depends on what you say.'

Jean Jansen took a deep breath, then exhaled before she answered. 'I never heard Lydia talking to him at all.'

'Even though the walls were so thin? C'mon, Jean.'

'You didn't let me finish. She wasn't speaking by the time he finished screeching at her. She was just crying. That's exactly what I heard, Lydia crying.'

I gave Jean a few seconds to finish her description, but she seemed to be done.

'Did you – did you do anything then?'

'Yeah. I mean, my boyfriend listened to the whole thing, too,' Jean said sheepishly. 'This is the part I don't want everybody to know, 'cause like my boyfriend gets wild when he's angry.'

'Let me hear it.'

Jean looked at me for reassurance but I could give her none. 'Okay. He got up from the sofa and he went into Lydia's bedroom. I mean, it wasn't locked or anything. He just opened the door and went in.'

'So far so good, Jean. I don't blame him.'

'I was right behind him, like trying to stop him. I could see Lydia all balled up on her bed, just sobbing like a baby.'

'Then what happened?'

'The guy kind of freaked out when he saw my boyfriend. He's like six feet tall, much bigger than Lydia's friend.'

'What did your boyfriend do?'

'He – um – he told the guy to get out. Told him to stop screaming at Lyd. The trouble started when the other guy said he never yelled at her. That it wasn't him we'd heard.'

'Was that possible?'

'Oh, no. He was the one, all right. He told us – I was in the room trying to help Lydia get out of there and into the bathroom, so we could lock the door – he told us that there was another person inside him who was doing the yelling. I mean, how freaky is that?'

'Did he leave then?'

'Nope. He didn't want to leave until he saw Lydia again,

till he made sure she wasn't going to bad-mouth him to us. That's when it got physical.'

'How?'

'My boyfriend started pushing him out of the room. I could hear the commotion from inside the bathroom. They're kind of scuffling, although the guy was too wiry, too small to put up much of a fight. He was almost out the door, I think, when my boyfriend told him that if he ever comes anywhere near my apartment again, he'd be a dead man.'

'That's when he left?' I asked. 'That's the line you didn't want me to tell anyone?'

'Part of it. I mean, it doesn't look good now that Lydia's been killed.'

'Did the guy ever come back?'

'Not that I know of. And she never mentioned him again.'

I smiled at Jean Jansen. 'Then maybe your boyfriend did a good thing. Maybe that encounter has nothing to do with her murder.'

'But you can't talk to my boyfriend about it, Ms Cooper. You absolutely can't.'

'Why not? He might know the name of Lydia's friend or have some other detail.'

Jean looked me in the eye. 'Because he's already on probation.'

'For—?'

'You can't draw him into a criminal investigation. The judge will have him violated.'

'What did he do, Jean?'

She didn't answer me.

'Please tell me what your boyfriend did.' I said it more firmly this time.

'He assaulted me, Ms Cooper. Three months ago, he got mad at me one night and beat me so bad my jaw had to be wired.'

I reached across the table to take her hand, but she pulled away. 'I'm so sorry, Jean.'

'He's got a criminal record longer than your arm. I'm not the first woman he's attacked, either,' Jean said. 'And he had a real thing about Lydia.'

'What kind of thing?'

'He came on to her one night, just a few weeks ago, before I got home. She told me about it the next day, which I thought was a bitchy thing for her to do. After that, he really was furious at her – for what she said to me. He had it in for her, that's one thing I'm sure of. My boyfriend had no use for Lydia Tsarlev.'

Thirty-two

'Get a policewoman in there to sit with her as soon as possible,' I said. Now it was my turn to pace in the confined area of Don Ledger's office. I was talking to Rocco, Pug, Mike and Mercer. 'Find someone who's had some DV experience and let her or him talk to Jean.'

There were officers in the SVU and in every precinct who'd been trained on the issues that make domestic violence such a sensitive category of crime. There was no sense in sending Jean home to face the fury of her dangerous boyfriend.

'And they need to monitor her calls. Mercer, maybe you can go back in and get the boyfriend's name and run a rap sheet. She keeps checking her phone, expecting a call from him. I doubt he wanted her to open her mouth about this, but she took the leap. I don't want him to get to her till we figure this out.'

'I can't let her go home?' Rocco asked. 'The guys promised her a ride back before they brought her in.'

'Call Safe Horizon,' I said, referring to the city's best

victim advocacy group. 'They can put her up in Parrish House for a few nights. I don't think it will take much doing to convince her she'll be safer there than at home.'

The DV shelters the organization ran were state-of-the-art, meant to be actual apartments with civilized living space and amenities, and their locations were never disclosed.

'You get any sense from her he could have hurt Lydia?' Mike asked.

'I can't rule it out, but there's no thread to the other cases – to Corinne and to the mole. We'll know more after we've eyeballed his sheet,' I said. 'Who's left to send to the Peekskill campus, Rocco? We're more likely to find people there who knew her, had classes with her.'

'Checking on it, Alex. I assume more calls have come in since her photograph was in this morning's papers. Somebody back at the office is on it.'

Mercer stood up from Ledger's desk, where he'd gone online as soon as I came back into the room spouting commands. 'The group you're looking for is ALF – the Animal Liberation Front.'

'Never heard of it,' I said. 'Anyone?'

No one had. He handed me a printout of a news story.

'It's been around since the sixties. And it is international. Operates in more than forty countries abroad,' Mercer said. 'So it makes sense that Lydia's mother got involved in Russia.'

'Where do they meet?' I asked.

Mercer laughed. 'It's a resistance group, Alex. Leaderless.

Very sixties radical. They wouldn't meet anywhere you could find them. All underground.'

Pug wanted a piece of the action. 'Like the tunnel people? That kind of underground? That would link right in with that Carl kid's murder.'

Mike waved him off. 'That's not what it means, Pug. You just stick to the Waldorf.'

'But Jean said Lydia was totally into nonviolence. Does that fit with this group?' I asked Mercer.

'I just scanned that article I printed out for you. No violence against people or animals, but ALF is very much into property damage. Started in the US with the Silver Spring monkeys.'

'What?'

'Some ALF members broke into a lab in Maryland where university scientists were using animals for medical experimentation. Freed the monkeys, put them in safe houses, then blew up the lab to the tune of a million dollars. End of the experiments.'

'Is there a zoo in Grand Central we don't know about?' Pug asked.

'Everything but,' Mike said.

'The feds have targeted ALF as a terrorist group.'

'Terrorist?' I asked, shocked at the appellation.

'Yeah. Domestic ecoterrorism.'

'Don Ledger's been worried about terrorist groups that have targeted Grand Central before,' I said, looking over at Mike. 'And so have you.'

'Mike's got terrorists on the brain,' Pug said.

'Sit on it, Pug.'

'Just sayin' . . .'

'To use Alex's word,' Mercer said, 'it's not a "fit" for these crimes. No question this killer is moving from the outskirts right into the terminal, but if you've got this place targeted – I mean the building itself – you can't do that without hurting lots of people.'

'The commish says the feds have got that angle covered,' Rocco said. 'Agents were sent in overseas after the international train bombings. That's why they're coming here in force today. Scully's orders are to keep our focus on the three murders. Leave the terrorist theories to the feds.'

'Are there any similarities between those bombings and our investigations?' I asked.

'Madrid was 2004,' Mercer said. 'Ten bombs in gym bags all set to go off on commuter trains in the morning. One hundred ninety-one people dead, thousands injured.'

I should have known the transportation guru would remember those details. 'Basque separatists?'

'That was the first theory, Alex, but it turned out to be a branch of Al-Qaeda. And nothing like our cases, although the supposed target of the blasts was the train station itself.'

'Of course,' I said, thinking of our terminal, around which all these crimes had occurred. 'The Atocha.'

Madrid's magnificent steel and glass rail station was also a work of art, refitted with a glorious tropical garden on its main concourse. I had visited the shrine to the bombing victims – an olive or cypress tree planted for each of them – on a trip through the city.

'Then came London in 2005,' Mercer went on. 'Four suicide bombers, all homegrown. Three bombs carried on the Underground in rucksacks and the last one went off on a double-decker bus. Fifty-two dead.'

'Homegrown what?' Pug asked.

'Islamic sympathizers. Blew themselves up,' Mercer said. 'Moscow in 2010. Two rebels from the Caucasus – women suicide bombers, which is a far less common phenomenon.'

'So two dead women here,' I said. 'Maybe our killer was trying to enlist them, and they refused?'

'I get that,' Pug said. 'Once he told them his plan and they wouldn't go along with it, he had to kill them.'

'What was that horrible thing in the Tokyo subway?' Rocco asked.

'The sarin attack,' Mike said. 'Nerve gas.'

'Terrorists?' I asked.

'A religious cult, Coop. You just can't pigeonhole these things,' Mike said, skimming the article on the ALF that Mercer had printed out. 'More people were killed in South Korea when a taxi driver went on a rampage in the subway and set fire to a morning train, trapping and burning almost two hundred people.'

I shuddered. 'What was his cause?'

'No cause at all. Mental illness,' Mike said, dropping the paper and throwing his hands up in the air. 'The guy suffered from severe depression.'

'All right. That gets me back to what Jean Jansen said about Lydia's strange visitor. The guy hears voices.'

'How does she know?'

'Because that's what she heard him telling Lydia.'

'She heard the words herself?' Mercer asked.

'Yes. This guy was yelling at Lydia, and I guess that's when Jean started listening. He told Lydia there were voices in his head, talking to him, telling him what to do.'

'Schizophrenic,' Mike said.

'Someone trying to control his thoughts.'

'Way to go, Coop. Another guy, another notch on your belt.'

'What?' I snapped at him.

'I thought that's the defense in the cannibal cop case. You're trying to exercise mind control over Dominguez and half the male population. Telling him what he should think and who he should eat. Maybe you've taken hold of our perp, too,' Mike said, grinning at me. 'Remind me, Rocco, when I start hearing voices, if one of them is Coop's, I'm gonna have to get monster-strength earplugs.'

'She could drive you to drink if you weren't already there,' Pug said to Mike. 'No offense, Alex, but you give enough orders and directions to keep me going for a month.'

I held my hands up, palms out. 'Okay, guys. Pick it up from here yourselves. Next time you need a search warrant for a pair of soiled underwear from a homicidal maniac, call Battaglia. He'll find you some well-meaning rookie who'll get it right on the third try.'

'Calm down, Alex,' Mercer said.

I looked at my watch. 'Still time for me to catch a flight to the Vineyard. Somehow, the way I remember it, you guys – the lieutenant, actually – asked me to go in and talk to Lydia's roommate.'

'And you come out with a boyfriend who beats her,' Pug said, 'and—'

'Yeah, and he hated Lydia. Tried to force himself on her very recently,' I said. 'I got you a terrorist connection to the vic, and the fact that she's had a grounding in radical movements as far back as her childhood in Russia. And a known schizoid who's been pressuring her to do something with him. Did I come up short, Loo?'

'Sounds like you forgot to ask Jean the last time she saw Lydia,' Mike said. 'Last time she heard from her. You're slipping, kid.'

'That answer, Detective, would be Tuesday evening.'

'The night Corinne Thatcher's body was found in the Waldorf,' Mercer said.

'Yes, but remember it had been there for twenty-four hours,' I said. 'Jean isn't sure, but she doesn't think Lydia came home Tuesday night.'

'Was that unusual?' Rocco asked.

'Jean didn't really keep tabs on her. Says she sometimes stayed overnight – Jean has no idea with whom – when she had late meetings on the north campus and the buses stopped running. But they had no reason to sync up with each other. They weren't close.'

'Did Lydia call Jean?' Mercer said. 'Try to reach her?'

'Not once,' I said. 'So the first night, and even the second one, weren't unusual. Jean thought it was strange that she hadn't come home by last evening – when we know she was found dead. Then she saw the photograph online this morning and called in.'

'My dog's got better friends than that,' Pug said.

'They weren't tight, is all. Different lives, different lifestyles. The shared apartment was simply a matter of financial convenience.'

My phone had been vibrating in my pocket throughout my conversation with Jean Jansen. It started again, and I removed it to see who was calling.

'It's Battaglia, guys. Let me take this.'

I put the phone to my ear and plugged the other one with my forefinger so Rocco and the team could go on talking.

'I guess your desk can be recycled to another member of my staff, Alex.' The tone in the district attorney's voice was clipped and curt, not the syrupy one he used at political fund-raisers. 'You seem to have taken up residence at the Waldorf.'

'I thought you'd be pleased that I freed myself up to be on top of these murders twenty-four/seven.'

'Pleased, perhaps, if I knew what was going on up there.'

'What don't you know?' I asked. 'We're actually working out of Grand Central now, because of the third homicide yesterday.'

'I had to find out from the papers that she was only a college student. Tragic.'

'Paul, we didn't get the call identifying her till this morning. You had everything I did by the time I went to sleep.'

'So that's the bad news. Give me something good.'

I was tempted to say that fortunately, for him, she was foreign. He had not lost a voter. But I suppressed the temptation. 'Nothing yet. The roommate just gave us a bunch of leads.'

'How fast can you get here?'

'Here?'

'I'm at City Hall, Alexandra. Or are you just waiting at the terminal for the next body to drop? The mayor's asking me questions I can't quite answer.'

'I can be—'

'Tell Chapman to shoot you out of a cannon, for all I care. Lights and sirens, whatever it takes.'

'I'm on the way.'

'You're already too late. Scully and his team – the lot of you – should have had this wrapped up already. Now the feds are looking to divert the president's train on Sunday.'

Thirty-three

'The mayor wants you to come in, Alexandra,' the district attorney said to me, faking a smile as he held the door open for me.

'I thought we were going to wait for Commissioner Scully,' I said, smoothing my wrinkled shirt and concerned about the impression jeans would make in this formal setting.

'He wants to talk to you first, as long as you're here. I told you he's got his priorities all screwed up.'

Paul Battaglia couldn't hide his contempt for the new mayor. During my entire twelve-year tenure as a prosecutor, a brilliant, creative, if not somewhat idiosyncratic chief executive ran City Hall. He had been respectful of the DA and our staff and had a truly collaborative relationship with his much-admired police commissioner.

The new regime was proving to be a crapshoot. Too many campaign promises that made no sense except to curry favor with voting blocs, and meddling into a pending civil lawsuit that undermined long-standing police procedures – setting off a frenzy of picketing against the new mayor by the detective union.

'C'mon in, Alexandra.' He motioned to me to sit opposite him, in a chair beside Battaglia. He held out his hand and reintroduced himself to me. I'd met him after the resolution of the murders in Central Park two months earlier. 'Scully will be here any minute. I just wanted your take on something before we get started on these horrific crimes.'

'Certainly, sir. I'd like to apologize for my appearance. The cops and I have taken on the somewhat dusty veneer of the terminal regulars.'

'Dress-down Friday. No worries,' he said. 'Look, Alex – may I call you Alex? I wanted to ask about a case you've been handling. Nothing inappropriate, nothing off the record. I'd just like a better understanding of what makes it a crime.'

I looked at Battaglia, who seemed to have caught the same vibe I did. Someone to whom he owed a political favor was pushing for the mayor to intervene on the Gerardo Dominguez case.

'Oh, Christ. Don't play with me, Mr Mayor,' Battaglia said. 'You've got us here for a much more important reason. It's almost five o'clock. First day in four without a murder and we've only got seven hours till midnight. Don't sandbag me with this bullshit.'

The mayor feigned surprise. 'Sandbag you? You're a lawyer, Paul. I'm not.'

'Then what business did you have stepping in the middle

of a ten-year-old lawsuit? You're lucky you still have a police officer willing to walk a beat for you.' Battaglia stood up and walked to one of the tall windows overlooking City Hall Park. 'Whose dirty work are you doing now?'

'Not fair, Paul. You know better than that. I don't have a pony in this race. I'm just asking questions. What's the basis for your case, Alex?'

'It's not my case anymore. I don't think I should be speaking about it.'

'Really? I'd just like to know when it's against the law for me to be thinking about something really evil, and then getting arrested for it. What's the tipping point?'

The mayor looked like a goofy, overgrown kid. He couldn't have been more disingenuous, but then, he'd apparently formed his judgments about the workings of the city's criminal justice system by watching bad movies and TV shows.

'You can tell him, Alexandra,' Battaglia said.

Someday I wouldn't be working for a bureaucrat – even one I admired as much as Battaglia on most days – for whom I'd have to toady up from time to time. Someday I'd be free to tell the mayor that I thought he was a total asshole.

'Yes, sir,' I said. 'I think you have a teenage daughter, Mr Mayor. Don't you?'

'I do.'

'Suppose this – this man who has a different set of values than you do—'

'He's entitled to those, isn't he?'

'He certainly is. No problem for me there,' I said. 'Suppose in between doing a Web search for recipes that involve the use of chloroform and then buying a Taser online, suppose his next search is for the name of your sixteen-year-old daughter—'

'Let's leave my daughter out of this, shall we?'

'Sure, sir. Let's make it somebody else's daughter. It's always somebody else's daughter when you don't want the reality to seem quite so immediate,' I said. 'So Keith Scully has a teenager, too. And she might be harder to find than a girl who lives in Gracie Mansion. Everyone knows where to find that one.'

The mayor wasn't amused. But it wasn't my purpose to amuse him.

'So the guy with the odd thoughts searches out the name of the police commissioner's daughter. Then he goes one further, trying to find out her address and which high school she attends. All pretty easy stuff to do.'

'It is.'

'Then his next email to one of his fetish-friends talks specifically about what the best way is to kill a teenage girl.'

The mayor appeared to be uncomfortable. 'Still not a crime, is it?'

'No, sir. I just think it's a bit reckless, a bit out of control. But I'm still with you. No prosecution,' I said. 'Now, may I ask what your favorite restaurant is?'

'I'm a Brooklyn kid. Why?'

'So pick one of those chic Park Slope places.'

'Got it.' He was twiddling his thumbs now, moving them around faster than a wheel in a gerbil cage.

'Suppose one of the waiters told you that the chef had a powerful fantasy about poisoning his customers. That he'd been saying that one evening it was going to come to that.'

The mayor laughed. It was the same inappropriate kind of giggle that had come out of him late one night at a press conference about the sixth snowstorm of the season this past February, when he announced the city was just plain out of salt and rich folk on the Upper East Side should think about sledding to work the following day.

'Then, every few days your chef would engage in conversations with other people about his desire to poison his customers – especially the regulars – and that he had gone online and was pleasantly surprised to find how many recipes for hard-to-trace poisons were actually posted on the Internet.'

Battaglia had his hand on the edge of the dark-blue curtains, smirking at the mayor while he listened to me.

'Now one of the guys in his chat room came to see him in the kitchen a few times a week. The chef shows him the list of names he wants to target. Elected officials at the top. "Hates those whores," he says.'

'My chef wouldn't talk like that.'

'In my version, the chef has *you* in his sights. Says to his cyber buddy, "I just can't wait to watch the top dog drop dead. The mayor of New York City. Know those french fries he loves? Just a tablespoon of cyanide – it looks so much like salt crystals – he'll be drooling in his plate in fifteen minutes."'

'Got me on the fries, Alex.'

'You going back to that restaurant, Mr Mayor? You just going to play Russian roulette till the chef decides it's your night to die? Actually, I think not. I think you might want to come with me to Rao's or to Fresco for dinner. Much safer bets.'

'Give him the rest of it, Alex. Give him the facts.'

'She's making her point, Paul. She's—'

There was a sharp rap on the door, and Keith Scully walked in without waiting for an invitation.

'Mr Mayor, Paul,' he said. 'Sorry to keep you. I'm sure Alex has been filling you in.'

He patted me on the back before taking the seat on my other side.

'Actually no, Keith,' I said. 'The mayor doesn't like my take on Gerry Dominguez.'

'I told you he's a sick puppy, sir. You've got to stay out of that one. And you've got bigger issues on your plate. Way bigger.'

'I know that.'

'I was held up at Federal Plaza,' the commissioner said. 'My team was over meeting with the head of the Secret Service in New York. You won't like this, Mr Mayor, but the feds are closing down Grand Central Terminal for the weekend. They called me in to tell me the plan. My men are working with theirs right now.'

'They're doing what? That's impossible.'

'A little inclement weather and your constituents can all sled to wherever they've got to go, even in the summer. That line worked for you once,' Battaglia said.

Scully talked over Battaglia. 'The terminal closes at two A.M.'

'I know that.'

'The feds want to take charge of the operation and—'

'And you're willing to let them?'

'I'm willing to do anything to keep the public safe, Mr Mayor. Transportation hubs – and this one is the most beautiful in the world – they're magnets for trouble,' Scully said.

The mayor was practically foaming at the mouth. 'I'm in charge of running this city. It's what the people elected me to do.'

'Trains out of here go to a number of other states. That alone gives the feds jurisdiction,' I said. 'And all the way to Canada. That's international territory, in case you weren't sure.'

'Watch your mouth,' the mayor said, pointing a finger at me.

'I've seen the bodies of the murder victims, Your Honor. It's hard to swallow, sir.'

'The Service is also fighting with the president,' Scully said. 'But he's bound and determined to ride that train right into the terminal. Gateway to the Continent. He wants to connect to all that history. And I understand that he feels the need to show the country he's not afraid.'

'It's impossible to close the terminal,' the mayor said, stuttering and sputtering at the same time.

'As I started to say, it shuts down at two this morning. So there's a natural break in the train schedule, and that's when the police get to move all the stragglers out. It just won't reopen at five thirty A.M. on Saturday. That's the plan we're going to put in motion. Jointly, with the feds.'

'It's Saturday. The terminal should be crawling with tourists, full of people from the suburbs bringing their kids in to see Broadway shows and go shopping all over town. It's an enormous amount of revenue for the city every minute that building is open, do you get that?'

'It's better than doing this on a weekday, sir. It's better than having all the commuters unable to get to work on Monday morning. Chances are with a joint task force manning this operation, we'll have it solved within twenty-four hours.'

'You can't close it, Scully,' the mayor said, pounding his fist on the desk. 'I own Grand Central Terminal.'

There was silence in the room.

'Actually, Mr Mayor, you don't,' I said. 'You don't own it.'

'Not me personally, Alex. I realize it's a public-private partnership. But I have control of the Metropolitan Transportation Authority. Don't get in my way, Scully.'

'The MTA just rents the terminal, Mr Mayor. There's actually a landlord. There's actually a man who owns the entire Grand Central building itself, as well as the tracks below – seventy-five miles up to Poughkeepsie – and the air rights above it.'

'Commodore Vanderbilt is long dead,' the mayor said,

throwing one arm up in the air. 'It's like the old joke that the Brooklyn Bridge is for sale. Don't take me for a fool, Commissioner.'

Keith Scully stood up, ready to make his exit. 'The terminal was sold out from under you in 2006, sir. It's owned lock, stock and barrel by a fifty-five-year-old real estate developer. An hour ago we got his permission to shut the place down.'

Thirty-four

I took the short walk from City Hall to the DA's office with Paul Battaglia and his security detail. The cops who had driven me down from the terminal tailed us up Centre Street to the courthouse.

'I've got to confess to you, Alex, I had no idea that Grand Central is privately owned, but I damn well loved seeing Scully shove it down the mayor's throat.'

'None of us knew about it either till we had our introductory tour last night. Seems the developer and a couple of institutional investors bought the whole thing for eighty million dollars.'

'Are the feds doing the right thing?' Battaglia asked. 'I mean, closing it.'

'I think it's the only way to go. Rocco and both squads – North and South – are chasing down every lead, but this perp is moving faster than we are. There's too much at risk – too many lives – if he has the terminal as the centerpiece of his master plan.'

When we got to the eighth floor, I followed Battaglia

into his office to debrief him on my meeting with Jean Jansen and the story of what happened in the morning when we were trapped in M42.

'Have you had time to get a list of every employee in the terminal?' he asked.

'Mike asked for it last night. The stationmaster had it waiting for Rocco first thing this morning. Every task, like going through those names, takes so much manpower, takes so many men off the street. It's terribly discouraging.'

'What's your plan? Are you staying at Mercer's again tonight?'

'I guess so. The cops who are watching over me will drive me back uptown. I thought I'd pick up some dinner for the team, then go on to Queens. Vickee's off tonight, so she'll be home with me. The terminal should be saturated with law enforcement types from every agency under the sun by the time I get back there.'

'We'll be in town all weekend. Don't leave me hanging, Alex.'

'I'm on it, Paul. Have a good one.'

It was almost six P.M. Both Rose and Laura left before we returned to the office. I put the lights on and sat down at my desk, relishing the quiet.

I called Evan Kruger, who was still working. 'What are you doing here?' he asked.

'The boss called me down.'

'I've got this one, Alex. I went up to court and made a record of my appearance on the case. I've fielded four nasty phone calls from David Drusin about his client – and some venting about you, personally – and I've spent the afternoon reading the evidence.'

'Lose your appetite?'

'Completely.'

'I wanted to let you know this weird thing just happened,' I said. 'And you'd better watch your back.'

'What's that?'

'Battaglia and I were called over to City Hall with Keith Scully. Of course the main event is figuring out how to deal with Grand Central in light of three murders in its orbit, moving closer and closer to the main concourse. That should have been the only thing on his plate.'

'It's a scary situation.'

'But all the mayor wanted to talk about at first was Dominguez and why taking overt steps to find recipes to cook women in his cannibal café is a bad thing.'

'You're kidding, right?'

'Nope. So Battaglia just told me that not too long after the election, some preacher the mayor knows from Brooklyn got pulled over on a traffic stop. He had two outstanding warrants. So what does the mayor do? Calls the precinct and suggests to the CO that his buddy be released.'

'Before the man's arraignment? Before seeing the judge? Before clearing the warrants?'

'Used his mayoral "get out of jail free" card, Evan,' I said. 'Used it once and it worked for him. I don't want our case to be his second try at a fix. Just be on the alert. Somebody's put a bug in his ear about Dominguez.'

'Thanks for covering my back, Alex. Do what you've got to do. I'm good with this one.'

'Don't thank me. It's entirely selfish,' I said. 'If someone has the reach to get to City Hall about a cop with a serious death fetish, then Raymond Tanner might be hanging on his coattails, too. Keep your antennae up for me, will you?'

'Done.'

I thumbed through all the messages, crumpling and tossing the ones from journalists with questions about Corinne Thatcher and Lydia Tsarlev. Those from friends got pocketed, and inquiries from adversaries about pending cases would wait on the top of my desk until Monday.

It was 6:15 when I walked out of the revolving door onto the street. I told the cops who were waiting for me that I wanted to pick up some dinners at Forlini's, the family-run restaurant behind the courthouse that had fed and watered more generations of lawyers and judges than anyone could count.

One of them walked down Baxter Street with me while the driver circled the block. We talked about weather and wondered aloud if tonight's anticipated thundershowers might bring a break in the heat wave.

I didn't even venture into the dining room, which was beginning to fill up with a mix of courthouse regulars who weren't getting out of the city, but went directly to the bar. The room was cool and refreshing, with delicious smells wafting in from the kitchen and classic Motown sounds on the jukebox behind me.

'The usual, Alexandra?' the bartender asked.

'Nothing to drink, thanks. I just need a whole bunch of dinners to take out. Will you please do the order?'

'Sure thing.'

There would be a lot of hungry detectives working with Rocco tonight. 'Let's make it easy,' I said. 'Give me a dozen veal parm, and throw in every side you've got. Spinach, broccoli, fried zucchini. We're feeding a small army. And plenty of bread. Not garlic bread, please. Just Italian bread. And toss in a few salads.'

'You got a moving truck?'

'Better than that. Two cops waiting to drive me uptown. We'll get the smell of the last hundred prisoners out of the backseat of the patrol car.'

I spun around on the bar stool and walked to the jukebox. I pulled a couple of singles out of my pocket and played all the Smokey Robinson and Marvin Gaye the machine had to give.

When I got back to my seat, there was a very healthy-looking pour of Dewar's waiting for me. It seemed like a perfectly good way to relieve the day's tension.

'Thanks for the drink,' I said, letting the ice cubes rest against my lips before sipping the Scotch. 'I forgot to tell you I've got to put this on my tab.'

'You look like you needed a cocktail,' the bartender said, writing my name across the front of the computer-generated dinner bill and stashing it in a drawer behind the bar. 'I know you'll be back.'

Twenty minutes later, when I had practically sucked the life out of my drink, one of the waiters appeared with several shopping bags full of food and plastic utensils. I walked to the door to ask the two officers to help me carry the meals.

When we reached Grand Central, it took all three of us to carry the dinners into the Grand Hyatt entrance on the Park Avenue Viaduct, where my escorts left their patrol car, into the lobby and through one of the hidden hallways that fed onto the main concourse of the terminal.

The summer rush hour was winding down. There were certainly fewer commuters than there had been at this hour just the night before.

And there was a noticeable increase in uniformed officers on patrol. Not as many in view as Scully led me to believe would be on site, but perhaps that would come later. It could take hours to bring in all the manpower that the various agencies had promised to deliver.

'Dinner is served,' I said, leading my cops into Don Ledger's office.

'You can throw out your Chanel No. 5, Coop, 'cause you've never smelled better,' Mike said. 'Good thinking.'

'Spread it around, Rocco. I've got a dozen meals, and the portions are huge. Where's Mercer? I got the zucchini just for him.'

'He's back upstairs in the situation room. Scully wants us to run the PD part of the operation from there.'

'It's the best control position for the whole terminal. Good idea.'

'C'mon,' Mike said. 'Grab some meals and let's feed him.'

'Ready.'

He pointed to the two officers who had come in with me. 'Chow down, guys. As soon as Blondie has finished her dinner, the lieutenant would like you to take her out to Douglaston, to Detective Wallace's house.'

'We're cleared to stay with her the whole night.'

'No need for that. Wallace's wife is home. She's a detective, too. Just hang out here for an hour or so, and we'll get you on your way with your dangerous cargo. Just a warning, guys: She attracts whackjobs.'

'I really do,' I said. 'Help yourselves to some dinner. See you in a bit.'

We left the cramped office, carrying two bags of food out onto the concourse and across to the elevator that was out of sight, at the bottom of the ramp on the far side of the information booth.

The automated voice – even fresh at the end of a long working day – reminded travelers again to take all their belongings and to say something if they saw something. I was getting sick of her telling me to mind the gap.

Mike dangled a large key ring in front of my face. 'Keys to the kingdom, Coop.'

'Nice score.'

'Rocco got a set for Mercer and for me. Must be fifty keys here.'

'Marked?'

'Of course. You think I'd have to guess which one to use if I needed to get into one of these places in a hurry?'

He handed me the plastic bag while he fumbled for the key to the elevator with the unlisted seventh floor.

We snaked our way through the labyrinthine corridors lined with steam pipes, a far cry from the gleaming pink Tennessee marble of the concourse.

The door to the situation room was open. Rocco had called up to Mercer and Pug, who were expecting us. They had turned on the bank of televisions, setting each to a different channel so that they could stay on top of any news developments.

'Welcome back, Alex,' Mercer said. He didn't often appear to be restless, but this evening he was. He had opened the blind that separated the room from the operations command next to it, leaning against the large window, looking back and forth between the screens showing all the train traffic and the monitors displaying local news. Fourteen men were still at their posts, tracking the trains coming and going from the terminal.

'Traffic slowing?' Mike asked.

Mercer nodded his head. 'I'm not going to be happy till they shut this place down.'

'So you know?' I asked.

'Yeah, Scully talked to Rocco about it before he even got to City Hall. Less than seven hours to go, then we get in and give this station a clean sweep.'

I was unloading the plastic containers of lukewarm food, setting places at the conference table with paper toweling for place mats. 'I've brought a little something to get you through the night. Take a break, guys.'

Mike was already gnawing on half a loaf of Italian bread as he fiddled with one of the televisions. 'I hope the rain holds out till after the game,' he said. 'The Yankees really need this one.'

'It's terribly humid,' I said.

'You timed this right, Coop. Six minutes to the Trebek finale.'

Pug, Mike, and I sat at the table, but Mercer's eyes were riveted on the men running the trains.

'What is it?' I asked.

'I keep thinking of 9/11.'

I had been a young prosecutor the day the Towers fell, watching from my office window as every man and woman in uniform ran south, so many selfless first responders racing to a certain death. Mike had been one of the lucky ones, coming to my home that night, mourning the loss of friends of a lifetime.

'I was in Harlem that morning,' Mercer said, pointing into the operations center. 'Somehow, the guys who worked where those men are sitting now stopped every train coming in this direction from north of 125th Street — wherever they were on all those miles of track — reversed their courses, and then sent all the passengers back to outlying stations.'

'The bridges and tunnels were shut down immediately,' I said. 'The only way out of Manhattan was the railroad.'

'That's the last time this terminal was evacuated. They just loaded up the trains that were here — pulled every car out of the yard — and sent them on their way. People trying to get as far away from this city as they could.'

'Don't get all heavy on me, dude,' Mike said. 'These guys can still get it done, worst-case scenario. They control seven hundred and ninety-five miles of track from that little room next door, Mercer. They can stop a train on a dime – no matter what stretch of rail it's on – and they can empty this terminal whenever they need to.'

'Not if they don't have any outbound trains, Mike. Not in the middle of the night.'

It rattled me when Mercer, who was usually the epitome of grace under pressure, became unnerved. And he caught my reaction to his gloom as soon as he looked over at me. I had plated some food but was too nervous to eat.

'I'll feel better after I get something in my stomach,' he said, trying to cheer me, I was sure. 'You too, girl. Then I'll send you on your way.'

Having not had any dinner and with the drink having gone to my head, I took a few bites and worked my way through a salad. When it was time for the Final Jeopardy! question, Mike turned the volume up on Trebek.

'That's right, ladies and gentleman. Tonight's topic is nicknames. Famous nicknames.'

'Is this still your game, Chapman?' Pug asked.

'Yeah. You in for twenty?'

'I have trouble playing bingo. I'll just watch.'

Mike had devoured his veal parm and taken half of mine. 'Easy category. Could be anything.'

Mercer and I agreed. We continued eating through the commercials and talked about what had happened in my absence.

Trebek noted that each of their pens was down, and he stepped back to allow the answer to be revealed: IN PHYSICS, SUBATOMIC PIECES THAT GIVE MASS TO ENERGY, FORMALLY KNOWN AS HIGGS BOSON.

'Physics?' I said, stymied by the unfamiliar words. 'If I'd known that was the category, I wouldn't have bet a nickel.'

'If you hadn't stopped for a cocktail without bringing me a roadie, I might have left you off the hook.'

'Cocktail?' I could see the contestants struggling to write down a response.

'You are such a bad liar, Coop. And Scotch isn't a fraction as odorless as vodka.'

'Why, you know the answer?'

'Course I do.'

'Mercer?' I asked.

'No clue.'

'What is the God particle?' Mike said.

'What about God?' Pug asked. 'And mass? It's a religious thing?'

'Not even close, Pug. It's not that kind of mass, if you get my drift. And the nickname using God, well that's just ironic.'

I was watching Trebek confirm Mike's answer.

'I thought a bosun worked on a boat,' Pug said. 'Wish I had a cocktail, too.'

'Different kind of boson.'

'There's a really good wine store right off the concourse downstairs,' I said. 'I could go down for a couple of bottles.'

'We've got a long night ahead,' Mike said. 'I'll pass for now.'

'You don't know the first thing about physics. How'd you get that right?'

' 'Cause this stuff fascinates me. This guy Higgs? Super-brainiac. He's a Brit.'

'Oh, I guess you met him on your extended vacation abroad.'

'No fair, Coop. I told you there's an explanation.'

'So, Higgs?'

'Came up with this theory fifty years ago, explaining how particles smaller than atoms got mass, traveling through a field.'

'What field? Where's the field?'

'The Higgs field. You can't see it, Coop. He named it fifty years ago, but nobody found proof of it till 2012.'

'Like a field in his backyard?' Pug asked. 'A football field?'

'Stay tuned, Pug. I'll get to you next.'

'You can't see the field?' I asked.

'You're yawning at me in the middle of a Higgs boson moment, Coop? Didn't they teach you at Wellesley how rude that is?' Mike said. 'Anyway, you may be able to see the field briefly, but it's so unstable that it disappears.'

'Like you this summer. Unstable and disappearing.'

'I've got one word for you, Coop,' he said, changing the channel from *Jeopardy!* to another news network. '*Limerence.* It explains everything.'

'Lay off her, Mike,' Mercer said. 'Why don't you hit the road, Alex?'

'I will in a few minutes.'

'So I got hooked on Higgs, which led me to the string theory.'

'As night must follow day, I guess.'

'Hey, you know how strongly I feel about coincidence? That there's no such thing?'

'Yeah.'

'Well, string theory is like a genius's way of ordering the universe the same way I happen to think, okay? Simple as that.'

'The string theory says there are no coincidences?'

'No, no, no. It says all objects are comprised of vibrating filaments – strings. That the entire universe is made up of all these invisible strings, holding it together.'

'Really?' I said, pushing back my chair. 'I'll never drink again. This is so weird. I can't see these strings, either, can I?'

'They're subatomic, Coop. Smaller than the size of an atom. They're everywhere, and of course you can't see them. But they're the reason that nothing is random. All this energy is connected. There is no such thing as coincidence.'

'So will you guys think I only put in half a day if I call it a night now?' I asked. 'I feel more useless than a sub-atomic particle.'

'I'll walk you down,' Mercer said.

'Imagine, guys. I used to complain because Mike

wouldn't talk about anything except murder. In hindsight that was pretty stimulating compared to physics.'

'It's all connected to this pattern, Coop. There's a relationship here we just haven't made yet.'

'Strings?'

'Make fun of me, kid. None of what's been going with these homicides is coincidence.'

'I get that, Detective Chapman. Where's the string that ties all this together?'

We'd been talking so loudly that we didn't hear footsteps approaching the room. There was a knock on the door before Rocco let himself in.

'We got a game changer, guys,' he said, dropping a stack of papers onto the table with each hand. 'We got a name.'

It was as though an electrical charge raced through the room, slicing the tension and exhaustion, filling the space with energy.

'Yes!' Mike shouted at top volume. 'What'd you get?'

'A hit on the DNA from NDIS.'

'He's in the national data bank?' I asked.

Rocco Correlli pressed the fingers of his right hand onto one of the piles of paper. 'Yeah, they just faxed the results up to me via the stationmaster. Maybe you can walk us through this.'

'Happy to,' I said, my heart pounding as the adrenal started to pump. 'What's his name?'

'Nicholas,' Rocco said. 'Nicholas Blunt. Twenty-nine years old.'

'We're out of here,' Mike said, holding out his hand. 'You got addresses? Let's get this motherfucker off the street.'

'No address.'

'Can't be.'

'It is, Chapman. At the moment, that's what it is. No current address.'

'Do we just go back to figuring how he chose his victims,' I asked, 'or is there any reason to connect him to Grand Central? To think he's targeting it?'

'Every reason to connect him,' Rocco said.

Mercer didn't move a muscle. His left shoulder was against the window over the operations room, his eyes fixed on the men inside. 'Why's that?'

'Blunt grew up here, according to the stationmaster. I mean right here, in this terminal. His father was a hostler.'

'Hustler?' Mike said. 'What difference does that make?'

'I didn't say *hustler*. It's *hostler* – with an *o*.'

The four of us looked at Rocco with blank stares.

'His old man drove the locomotives from their platforms out to the roundhouse. Turned them around, tuned them up, and brought them back for the next part of the trip. That's all he did, every day of his working life.'

'You mean he was an engineer?' Mike asked.

'Hostlers never leave the station. They're engineers, but all they work on are trains in the rail yard. Grand Central was his life.'

'And his son?' I asked.

'Nicholas Blunt grew up in this place. Every minute he

wasn't in school, he was hanging out with his old man. He knows more about this terminal and each piece of track that runs in and out of here than anyone on the planet.'

'Sometimes I hate it when I'm right,' Mike said.

'Scully's on his way up with the city head of the FBI,' Rocco said. 'They won't wait till two A.M. to close Grand Central. We've got two hours to get everyone out of here, best we can.'

'It's not possible,' I said.

'It better be, Alex. By ten tonight, we're in lockdown.'

Thirty-five

'Let's get Coop on her way,' Mike said.

'I'd like her to tell me what this DNA stuff means first, okay? There's pages of it,' Rocco said. 'Then the guys can take her out of here.'

'I'm not going. I know these cases as well as anyone.'

'No time to get stubborn,' Mercer said.

'Let's see how this develops. I've still got my uses, don't I?' I smiled, trying to diffuse the tension.

'Then get an officer up here, Loo,' Mike said, turning to me. 'And you do have your uses. Loop in the Thatcher family, then we'll get you a laptop and you can be our researcher on whatever comes up.'

'Oh, great. You're looking for the killer, and I'm in charge of Google Alerts?'

'You stay close to anyone who's got a badge and a gun, okay?'

Rocco seemed surprised. 'No heat?'

'I've never had a gun, Loo. Fortunately, Battaglia doesn't

believe in letting his legal staff carry. I'd probably have taken Mike's head off by now.'

Each of the men had tried dialing out on his cell – Mercer to update his boss at the Special Victims Unit, Mike to check in with his lieutenant at Manhattan North, and Pug to notify his team who were still hunkered down at the Waldorf.

'There's no reception here,' Rocco said, pushing the spider-phone toward Mercer. 'It's built like a bunker on purpose. You've got a couple of different landlines to use.'

Mercer had one hand on the receiver. 'Do we have a plan, Loo? Are you going with Blunt as a person of interest?'

'What's his criminal history?' Mike asked, pointing to the sheaf of papers that Rocco Correlli had passed to me. 'How can he be in the data bank and not known to the department?'

'Too many questions at once,' I said, pulling my chair closer and starting to plow through the information about Nicholas Blunt. 'He's not KTD because he's never been arrested.'

'How's that possible?'

'The match isn't arrest-based. That much is clear.'

'Case-to-case?' Mike asked. 'DNA from semen in an unsolved rape?'

Rocco was talking over my head. '*Person of interest* is an understatement. We've got his blood on the curtain at the Waldorf and in the sink on Big Timber. Alex, can we call him a suspect? It's okay legally?'

'Go for it, Loo. I don't care if you tag him as the perp.

As long as the public puts a name and face to the guy who's running around out there, and they understand that he's horribly dangerous,' I said, scrutinizing the FBI lab records. 'It's not seminal fluid. The DNA came from a swab. From saliva.'

'An investigation?' Mike asked. 'What state?'

'Not an investigation. Voluntary. It's connected to some kind of job he was working about three years ago.'

'Keep reading.'

'NorthStar. That's the name of the company that submitted the sample,' I said. 'The DNA report itself is not very complicated, Loo. The paperwork is thick because it's all the lab notes confirming the matches. All they need is the headline you got. The blood found at two of the crime scenes belongs to Nicholas Blunt.'

'That's helpful. I thought I'd be swimming in double helixes all night.'

'So I guess finding out more about Blunt is my first Google assignment. Where's the laptop I'm supposed to use?'

'Coming up any minute,' Rocco said.

'You don't need a search engine for that,' Mike said. 'NorthStar. One word, right?'

'Yes.'

'It's a security contractor, mostly for overseas work in the most hostile territories in the world.'

'Like Blackwater?' I asked. I remembered stories about the private firm that was created to support government troops abroad after the bombing of the USS *Cole* in Yemen.

'A lot like it, but much smaller.'

'Tough guys, no?'

'Blackwater had a lot of former military experts,' Mike said. 'Smart founders who recruited some very experienced men – and yeah, some hard-hitters. At one point they were up to eighty thousand employees worldwide. They got into some hot water and had to rebrand.'

'But legit?' I asked.

'Mostly. They had a slew of government contracts,' Mike said, as the door opened and a Metro-North cop entered the room with three laptops. 'Blackwater actually trained Navy SEALs and military SWAT teams. I don't know if they're completely out of that business, after allegations of shooting civilians in Iraq, or if they just regrouped under a new name.'

The newly arrived Metro-North cop was obviously tech-savvy. He began setting up the laptops and connecting them to a power source under the table. I slid one over in front of me and turned it on.

'NorthStar hasn't been around for that long. Does the same kind of thing as the old Blackwater. High-threat protection. I don't think the government uses them much, but they provide security for a lot of business entities – like oil companies – that work in risky third-world countries or war zones.'

'NorthStar swabs their employees for DNA?' I asked. 'For identification purposes?'

'Yeah, in the event any of the workers go DOA. Their profiles are already in the data bank. The military does the same thing.'

'So what else can we find out about Nicholas Blunt?' I said, typing his name into the search function.

Mercer sat down opposite me. 'I'll do NorthStar.'

It was Rocco Correlli's turn for the landline. He called the head of the Metro-North police and asked his questions after the formalities were done. 'I need an officer to be assigned to a prosecutor working in the situation room tonight. Pronto. Got someone for me?'

'I get the feeling I'm going to have a new best friend any minute now,' I said, scrolling down through all the Blunts whose names appeared on my screen.

'Excellent. I'd like that as soon as possible,' the lieutenant spoke into the mouthpiece.

'I can't believe how many Blunts there are.'

'Nicholas?' Mike asked.

'I'm trying to eliminate by age. The people-finder search engine has more than thirty of them, and at first glance, nothing's a match.'

I reached for the stack of papers again and tried to find the original submission request.

'So NorthStar opened its doors about eight years ago,' Mercer said. 'Usual vague stuff on the website. More than fifteen thousand employees on missions around the world, mostly in Asia or Africa.'

'Would Blunt have needed military experience?' I asked. 'We could get a load of information about him that way.'

'Not necessary, the site says. In fact, most of the employees don't,' Mercer responded while writing numbers on a pad. 'Could you get a man on military records, Loo?

I'll call NorthStar headquarters, though I'm not likely to get anybody at a corporate firm after hours on a Friday night. The feds will probably cut through that faster than we can.'

'This will help, guys,' I said. 'Having a eureka moment.'

I stood up, waving the paper in my hand.

'What?'

'Surname Blunt. Given name Nikolay.'

'Don't we already know that?' Mike asked.

'Father's given name is Walter. Mother's given name, Zoya. The spelling of *Nicholas* is eastern European,' I said. 'Probably Russian. Zoya's a Russian name, too.'

'And Blunt?' Rocco asked.

'Could be just plain old English,' Mike said. 'Or Ellis Island neutral. Not everybody came through with all their vowels intact, Loo, like you did.'

'So?'

'So I'm getting from Coop the idea that we ought to look for a link between our Russian victim and Mr Blunt.'

'That's where I'm headed, Mike,' I said.

'That's challenging, don't you think? Lydia Tsarlev's from Russia, and it's possible this Blunt kid may have Russian roots. I can get that far. Next step is to see whether he's got a psych history of any kind, or other witnesses who've heard about the voices in his head. The whole scenario could get really scary with a schizoid Soviet who's been playing paramilitary enforcer. A Putin puppet with a grudge of some kind.'

'Slow it down, Mike,' I said.

'Hey, every one of those "Stans" has some disgruntled former Soviets. I was mostly just relieved that the name attached to this DNA wasn't Arabic.'

'The master of political incorrectness, Detective. The prosecution rests.'

'Strings, Coop. They're all coming together for me. Hustler, hostler. Nicholas, Nikolay. Same bastard, whatever he calls himself.'

'You're thinking the guy hearing voices in Lydia's apartment is Blunt?' Rocco asked Mike and me.

'Better than a long shot,' Mike said. 'We need a picture bad, Coop. We need to get the roommate to give us a scrip and to stick around to identify a photograph of him as soon as we get one. It can't be a coincidence that the guy fighting with Lydia in her bedroom, trying to enlist her to join his cause — well, it's got to be related.'

'Didn't the roommate say he had no accent?' Rocco asked.

'Yes,' I said. 'But who knows where he was born? Or his mother? I'm just telling you guys not to ignore that possible Russian background connection as we go forward.'

'Who asked me if there's a plan?' Rocco said.

'I did,' Mercer said.

'Give it another five minutes. Then we go back downstairs to meet with Scully, who expects to be here before eight thirty. Get me everything you find online.'

'Here he is on Facebook,' I said. 'Nik Blunt.'

'How do you know it's our guy?' Rocco asked.

'There are a few others, but all spelled the traditional

English way. And only one who listed the Animal Liberation Front as his favorite organization, Loo. How's that for a start?'

'Does he have any friends, or did he kill them all?' Mike asked. 'I knew putting you on Google was the right move. You're a total geek, Coop.'

'This Nik Blunt hasn't posted anything in two and a half years.'

'Not even photos that give an idea where he was then?'

'The Great Dismal Swamp.'

Mercer looked up from his laptop. 'You got to be kidding. There's such a place?'

Mike said, 'North Carolina,' at the very same moment I said, 'Virginia.'

'Which is it?'

'North Carolina,' Mike said. 'Acres of swampland. Like a national refuge now. If there's some kind of animal you never wanted to meet? It's there. Blackwater set up headquarters in the Great Dismal to train their men, prepare them for conditions in Iraq, if that gives you any idea of how dismal it is.'

'The larger part of it's in Virginia,' I said. 'It's probably where NorthStar trained its people, too. There are no clear faces in the photo, but lots of men in camo.'

'Suddenly stepping in on my military expertise?'

'It's my literary bent, Mr Chapman. The swamp was the subject of Harriet Beecher Stowe's second novel,' I said, knowing the subject would interest Mercer. 'The Great Dismal was a refuge for runaway slaves.'

'C'mon, guys,' Rocco said. 'Anyone come up with a photograph of Blunt's face yet?'

'Not finding one,' I said.

'What do the employee records show for his family's address?' Mercer asked. 'For the father?'

'He's dead, and the mother moved somewhere upstate,' Rocco said.

'I want the address from when his father worked here,' Mercer said. 'We can figure a high school location from that and maybe find a yearbook picture.'

Rocco flipped through the Metro-North employment file of Walter Blunt and found an address in Queens. 'Looks like Forest Hills,' the lieutenant said. 'Does that help?'

'I can give it a try.'

'Okay,' Rocco said. 'Three minutes and we're downstairs to meet Scully. We'll take off as soon as an officer shows his face to hang with Alex. One of you see whether Motor Vehicles has anything on their site?'

'I'm hunting, but most of the official stuff like that is only going to be available to us Monday morning,' I said. 'We'll be stiffed for now on government records.'

'Where else can we get photos?'

'The girl who was in today – Lydia's roommate,' Rocco said. 'Mike's right. Bring her back over here and nail down a description of the guy she saw fighting with Lydia. Drag her boyfriend in, too.'

'How come no one has mentioned the word "guns"?' I asked. 'With NorthStar in his background, he's bound to be armed.'

'That's our worst nightmare, Alex. It's on all of our minds,' the lieutenant said, wringing his hands. 'But at this very moment, there's not a thing we can do about it, except prepare all the details coming in on the search.'

'And clear the terminal,' I said. 'For whatever good that will do.'

'Monday morning may be too late to pull all this information,' Rocco said. 'I'll get a man assigned to contact all the agencies and business links first thing tomorrow. Somebody has to be minding the store on weekends. Meanwhile, the stationmaster is trying to find out where Blunt's mama is and to locate his siblings – see whether they're still around.'

'Anybody check Match.com? "Likes track rabbits; likes to dance. Could be terminal." There are all kinds of selfies on those sites,' Mike said. 'We can't meet the feebs without a photo. They're bound to have one they'll want to shove down our throats to show how superior they are.'

This time I heard footsteps approaching the room.

A young woman entered, wearing a Metro-North police uniform, with the nameplate Y. FIGUEROA on her chest, below several merit decorations. She held up a hand to all of us. 'Police Officer Yolanda Figueroa.'

The lieutenant introduced himself to her and to everyone else in the room.

'I'm your charge,' I said, eyeing the Glock holstered on her hip. She was shorter than I by two or three inches, with curly black hair and light brown skin. 'I'm Alex Cooper.'

'Good to know you.'

'Same here. Nice of you to do this.'

'All right,' Rocco said. 'Let's get you guys going. Time's running out on us.'

I shut down the computer and pushed back from the table, standing up between Pug and Mike.

'Not you, Alex,' Rocco said, pointing to the chair I'd been sitting in. 'Commissioner Scully was firm about that.'

'He was *what*?'

'You're to handle all the interagency contacts, if you want to stay here till we close the terminal. Do all the research you can for us online. Put your tail in that chair and Officer Figueroa here will make sure you've got everything you need.'

I couldn't protest to Keith Scully if he wouldn't give me an audience. 'The district attorney is so not going to like this,' I said, doing a slow burn as I seated myself again. 'You know how he hates to be the last to know what's going on.'

'Yolanda just needs to make sure you're boarded on the nine fifty-nine to Vickee's house. See if she can teach you to scramble up some eggs for breakfast. Chances are Mercer and I will be there in the morning for a victory celebration,' Mike said, flashing a grin at me. 'You've been grounded, Coop. Sit down and fasten your seat belt.'

Thirty-six

'Are you in a safe place?' Paul Battaglia asked.

'Completely fine,' I said. 'I've got a terrific policewoman keeping me company in the situation room, helping me surf the internet for more info about Blunt. I wanted to tell you what's going on here and give you the number for this landline.'

I was fiddling with my cell phone, which I'd placed on the tabletop, but it was showing no signs of life in this inner sanctum of the terminal.

'Thanks.'

'And that Scully has cut me out of the program, Paul. I was thinking maybe you could give him a call, let him know that you'd prefer I stay on the case, in the meetings with the FBI and all that, rather than sticking me up here in an isolation booth.'

'The commissioner's in a better position than I am to know what's going on. All I want from you is a steady flow of information. If Scully and his men get lucky, I need to be up to speed for the media. You understand that?'

'Of course I do.' I left out the observation that Battaglia was all about smoke and mirrors. The substance didn't matter at all if he had the appropriate sound bites when the time came.

The team had been gone only about ten minutes when I heard footsteps again. I turned my head to look in the doorway and saw that Mike had returned.

'Hey, did you forget something?' I said, happy to see him. 'Coming into the girls' locker room without knocking? Scully wants us up here because Yolanda and I are such delicate—'

'Scully's the man, Coop. You wanna step out here for a minute?'

'Is this my ticket to ride?'

Mike rolled his eyes and motioned to me. 'Over here, please.'

Yolanda was on her feet. 'Are you taking her somewhere, Detective? 'Cause I need to stay with her.'

'You sit tight. I just have some instructions to relay from the police commissioner. We'll be right here in the hallway, and I'll deliver her back to your capable hands.'

I got to my feet and walked toward Mike, talking to Yolanda. 'Didn't you ever see *High Noon*? The sheriff thinks he's the only guy who can save his town. Has to put the little woman on the last train out of Hadleyville to keep her away from danger. There's always a final speech with these guys when they suit up to meet the gunslinger,' I said. 'I guess I'm headed for that train.'

Mike grabbed my arm and pulled me into the hallway,

laughing at me. 'Don't flatter yourself, Coop. You're no Grace Kelly.'

'You find the gunslinger?' I asked, as Mike closed the door behind me. 'Is that what you've come to tell me?'

'I've got a confession to make.' He backed me against the wall, in between a pair of rusted steam pipes. 'I have to tell—'

'Just don't start with a "come to Jesus" speech now, okay? I am so not in the mood for that.'

'I know.' He was running his fingers through his hair.

'You've got serious work to do. You've got to find this sick bastard before he hurts somebody else. So if you're up here to feed me more bull—'

'I lied to you. That's what I want you to know.'

'Somehow, I think I did know that, Detective. I can't believe that I actually fell hook, line and sinker for the old "sick mother" bit.'

'Look, I did get the twenty-one-day rip, okay? That was all true. The commissioner wanted me publicly hung out to dry.'

'Thank you for that really pleasant reminder of your affair.'

'It's not fair to call it that, Coop.'

'No, but it's more tasteful than the alternative.'

'I went to Ireland first, okay? You know that part is real.'

'Phone calls from Dublin numbers. Postcards stamped and marked from Derry and from Ballydesmond. Brilliant tradecraft, Mr Bond. Must be true then, mustn't it?'

'You and that hair-trigger temper. If it wasn't so annoying, it would be almost attractive.'

'But it's not the least bit attractive. It's just all I've got in me at this point. So why not step aside,' I said, pushing against Mike's chest, 'and go find Nikolay Blunt. Why does any of this matter right now?'

''Cause it's been eating at me, okay? I hate to see you this way, this wound up. You've been working like a dog on these murders, and you should be with us when we get this guy.'

I raised my eyes to see if Mike was joking. 'For real?'

'Yeah. But I'm not in control of that. I'm working on Scully, Coop. I really am.'

'Thanks,' I said. 'Okay, I'll buy the part about the three-week rip in Ireland. And the lie?'

Mike leaned one hand against the wall, beside my right shoulder, while the other continued to brush back his hair. 'You know about the ILP?'

'Sure.' He was talking about the International Liaison Program, an intelligence initiative with the NYPD, formed after 9/11 as a counterterrorism plan. The department recruited officers from within specialized units to be stationed abroad in eleven cities – everywhere from Moscow and Lyons to Tel Aviv and Manila.

'I'm not a likely candidate for intel, am I?' Mike laughed nervously.

'Skip the false modesty, Detective. You're the smartest guy I know – about some things.'

'Turns out Scully had a plan for me. I mean, the rip could have been just for a week and he would have been satisfied. But he suspended me for three so guys in the department would know I really got stung.'

'Then the vacation?' I asked, still feeling my anxiety over the added separation. 'The four-week joyride with your cousin that you tacked on to it?'

'That part never happened, kid.'

'Want to tell me where you were?' I was tapping my fingers against the rusted pipe.

'Look, Scully made me—'

'Where were you?'

'Rhode Island. Newport, Rhode Island,' Mike said, almost sheepishly.

'Damn. I could probably have seen you if I stood on one of the tables at the Bite. A yachting adventure, perhaps?' Steam was more likely to come out of my ears than from the pipes alongside my head.

'The Naval War College. In Newport.'

'Really?'

'The college ran a special program this summer. A monthlong course in counterterrorism techniques. They offered Scully five spots, and I got lucky.'

'And I'm supposed to believe that—?'

'Secrecy was the hallmark of the whole thing. There are only two or three bosses in the entire department who know the names of the participants. The other detectives are the ones doing two-year stints abroad, brought back in from Singapore, Cairo and Mumbai. Nobody wanted to blow their cover, and connecting me to any of them could have served to do that.'

It was my turn to be sheepish. 'I – I wish I had known.'

'Do you understand what a risk Scully was taking? I stepped on my private parts with that psycho judge – all my own doing – and there was the police commissioner himself, wanting to rehabilitate and send me back to learn the most state-of-the-art techniques in fighting the bad guys. I mean the big bad guys.'

'Who better to train than you? So much of it is military, paramilitary stuff. You're ahead of the curve on that to begin with.'

'We did the first week in Newport,' Mike said. 'Then we were each sent out in the field. I was actually in a new office that opened in Kfar Saba.'

'Where's that?' I felt so petty and small for having held a grudge for the last few weeks.

'It's a suburb of Tel Aviv. The NYPD has a one-man office there,' he said, lifting my chin with his forefinger to get me to make eye contact with him again. 'I'm not kidding you, Coop. That's why I couldn't call or write to you. It was a crazy time for everyone involved.'

'I understand that now.'

'There was actually chatter about a threat from Hezbollah, with a very soft target, and I got to work through the entire operation.'

'That must have been great.'

'You know what it's like to save lives, Coop. Well, I don't. I always get there too late, you know? Damage done. Bring on the body bags.' Mike was trying to get me to smile, to lighten up. 'This time I helped do that, and I gotta tell you it feels better than anything else.'

'So you were successful.'

'And here's how we knew it. Because nothing happened. *Nothing*.' Mike paused, grimacing at my forlorn expression. 'How's that for a good day on the job, Coop?'

'It should make you very proud of yourself,' I said. 'It makes me proud of you.'

'Then stop sulking.'

'Why'd you choose this moment to tell me?'

''Cause the last thing I wanted to do the other night was to walk into that crime scene at the Waldorf and find you there. I – I didn't know what to say in front of everyone else.'

'Your mother's heart condition kind of rolled off your tongue.'

'Okay, okay. I owe you.'

'You owe me nothing. It just sort of unnerves me that you can be so facile when you lie.'

'I didn't think I had a choice. I figured you'd call me out 'cause I had no business being at a homicide in Manhattan South. Out of bounds for me. Not my jurisdiction.'

'You tap-danced around that pretty well, too.'

'Scully didn't want me there because of the dead girl. It's only that the president is coming to the hotel and he's going to have me working with the terrorist task force from time to time, whenever he hears there's new thinking, new methods of policing to bring to the table.'

'This killer,' I said, squirming a bit to get Mike to move

back from me, 'this Blunt guy, you think he's involved with terrorists? Is that why you came back to talk to me? Or are you just trying to tie up your string theory? Try and control me like a big puppeteer?'

'No strings on you, Coop,' Mike said, stepping away. 'Blunt's acting more like a crazy man, not that the two are mutually exclusive. But this is the greatest train station in the world, and if his plan is to paralyze this city, he's going to start that from right here.'

In the narrow hallway beyond the situation room, I was able once again to hear the loudspeaker system from the concourse below.

The lady with the automated voice had been given the night off. Someone from law enforcement had taken control of the microphone.

'*Good evening, ladies and gentlemen. I'd like your attention, please,*' the deep baritone greeted evening travelers. '*Due to some emergency repairs that need to be made on the tracks this weekend, Grand Central Terminal is going to be cleared earlier than usual.*'

'Thanks for coming up to try to make this right,' I said.

Mike held a finger over his lips, telling me not to talk.

'*The last train will leave the station at ten P.M. That is ten P.M. We suggest you check schedules for the next train to your destination. Again, please check the schedules. After ten P.M., there will be city buses outside the terminal on the Lexington Avenue side to take passengers to the outer boroughs, where you can pick up your connections. And remember, folks, if you see something, say something.*'

'That will make some commuters most unhappy,' I said.

'It's meant to start them moving and fill the trains without causing a stampede. Nobody wants to alarm them before we need to.'

'Hardly necessary to add any fuel to the fire after today's headlines and the news about Lydia.'

'Cops are herding people out of the food court already and planning to shut the doors – at least the ones that shut – a little before the clock strikes ten.'

I made an attempt at good cheer. 'Thank you – I mean that – for letting me know about the last month, about the great big white lie. It's for such an important reason that you were gone,' I said. 'I should have trusted you.'

'Ladies and gentlemen,' the voice broke in again. *'Time to step lively. Your attention, please. Grand Central Terminal will be shutting down at ten P.M. this evening.'*

'How about if I throw in some bacon with the eggs?' I asked.

'Crisp. You know the way I like it.' Mike patted down my hair and kissed me on the crown of my head. 'I'll see you on your way home. Thanks for listening.'

'Then you just wait here for him to do something else?'

'Oh, no. We've got some messages planned to go out over the loudspeaker shortly after ten o'clock, designed to rattle the cage of Nikolay Blunt, wherever he is in this maze. We need to smoke him out, Coop, and bring him down. His killing spree is over.'

Thirty-seven

I had given up finding any more information online about Nikolay Blunt and was about to call it a night. 'Ready to go, Yolanda. Who takes me down to the detail who's driving me to Vickee's house?'

She picked up the landline to call her command, spoke to someone on the other end, then answered me. 'My partner is on his way up to fetch us,' she said. 'Seems Lieutenant Correlli has the suspect's sister in the station. They want you to talk to her before you head home. Do you mind?'

'It's exactly what I'd prefer to do. It makes me feel useful.'

I thumbed through Walter Blunt's Metro-North employment records. It listed three children as his dependents at the time he was employed here. Nikolay was the eldest, with a younger brother and sister.

I studied the senior Blunt's file until Yolanda's young partner appeared in the doorway. 'I'm supposed to bring you two down to the stationmaster's office, okay?'

'Should we take the laptops?' I asked Yolanda.

'You can leave your stuff here, Ms Cooper. I think your supervisors want to fill you in on what's been going on. Then I'll escort you back up along with the young lady you'll be interviewing. They want you to keep working up here, 'cause it's good space and it's away from the commotion on the concourse.'

'Commotion?'

'You know. They're trying to shut this place down soon.'

I gave Yolanda a thumbs-up. 'Looks like I bought myself an invitation to work in the sandbox with the guys. Do you want to wait for me here?'

'I'm on you like glue, Ms Cooper.'

We wound our way back to the elevator. The young cop unlocked it with what looked like a master key, and it creaked its way down to the bottom of the ramp below the main floor.

The three of us exited and started our way up. At the intersection on top, where a right turn led to the old waiting room and the left toward the concourse, it was obvious that even more uniformed officers from a cross section of agencies had arrived.

Some of the men and women looked like SWAT team members, with guns and helmets and bulletproof jackets obvious to all. There were more K-9 patrols than I had ever seen in one place. Everyone seemed to be herding civilians to exits on the sides and ends of the vast terminal.

'Attention, please,' the rich male voice spoke sternly to the stragglers. *'Grand Central Terminal is closing down in fifteen minutes. You have fifteen minutes to get yourself to the*

platform if there is a train headed for your destination, or to make your way back onto the street. We apologize for the inconvenience this may cause. Watch your step, ladies and gentlemen. Watch your step and remember to mind the gap.'

We stopped for a minute to let a group of men who seemed slightly intoxicated weave past us prodded by two agents, who were in street clothes with their badges flapped over their pockets. They appeared to be coming up from the Oyster Bar, unhappy to have their revels interrupted.

'That voice sounds so familiar to me,' I said to the cops.

'It's one of the men from Homicide,' the young man said. 'He's taken over the controls in the stationmaster's office and seems to be having a mighty fine time of it.'

We made the left turn and headed for the concourse. There was indeed a commotion, and most of the officers seemed to be struggling to respond to angry and confused commuters who were standing their ground.

I had never been in Grand Central when the information booth that was in the center of the floor was empty, but those employees had obviously been dismissed for the night. Cops with dogs were standing along each of the departure gates on the far side of the room, guiding passengers to the last trains waiting to pull away from the platforms.

Police had even taken over the carts that sanitation workers used to scoot around the station. There was a small fleet of machines, zigzagging across the floor, trying to round up the more stubborn people who weren't moving toward the exits. They looked like a fleet of Zambonis clearing the ice after a hockey match.

I glanced up at the constellations painted on the ceiling. The majestic celestial figures seemed to be the only part of the terminal undisturbed by all the activity below.

As we crossed the floor, headed for the stationmaster's wing – out of sight behind the staircase to Vanderbilt Avenue – I was conscious of stares from many of the officers patrolling the terminal. I must have looked a bit bedraggled at this late hour, in my sloppy outfit, escorted by a pair of cops – more like a belligerent passenger than part of the law enforcement team.

Rocco Correlli saw me coming and waved me into the office.

'Good work. You found a sibling already?'

'Pug did it, believe it or not. I'm not sure it's such a good thing.'

'Why?'

'It's Blunt's kid sister, twenty-three years old. Same name as the mother, so she wasn't that hard to find. And she's a waitress at a joint in the theater district, six blocks from here.'

'What's the bad news?'

'She's refusing to talk. I got Chapman in there, hoping he can use some of his charm to weasel something out of her. Then I thought maybe you being a woman and all, she might open up to you.'

'Feels like that's the only use you have for me, Loo. It doesn't always work that way, but let me give it a try.'

Rocco walked me down the short hallway to the office in which Mike was sitting with Zoya Blunt.

'Hey, Coop. C'mon in. Meet Zoya.'

'Good evening. I'm Alex Cooper.' I held out my hand, but she wouldn't take it.

'Pug found her on Facebook. Drove right over to the west side and picked her up. Isn't that right?'

Zoya Blunt was slight and small in stature. Her dirty-brown hair was short, framing her pale, unsmiling face with waves. She was wearing a tight black skirt over opaque black stockings, a white T-shirt, and a short apron with pockets, which still held order slips from the restaurant at which she worked.

'I don't want to be here, miss. I want to go back to work.'

'I've explained to you, Zoya,' Mike said, 'you're not going anywhere until you talk to me about your brother.'

The girl couldn't have been here very long, but already Mike was short on patience.

'Maybe I could sit down with you for a while,' I said. 'There's a private room upstairs. We could just be talking there, out of the way of these – uh, bullies.'

She looked from me to Mike.

'Really, Zoya, Mike's got a tough job to do. He's not unreasonable. I can make you comfortable upstairs, where I've been working.'

'I'm not going to be comfortable anywhere. I'll get fired for leaving the floor during a Friday night dinner hour.'

'We'll see that you don't get fired,' I said. I leaned in toward her and tried to cut through the scowl on her face.

'Young women have been murdered, Zoya. We have every reason to—'

'I read the newspapers. I know about the murders.'

'If for some reason it's not Nikolay—'

'You can't even pronounce his name right.'

'Sorry for that. But if for some reason we're wrong, you can help clear him.'

Mike was standing behind me now. 'I've told her all that, Coop. She's determined to stand by him, I guess. If that's her game, there's nothing any of us can do about it.'

'Let me work with her a while.'

'Maybe she had a hand in it, you know? I never thought he got this done all by himself. Didn't I always say I thought he had an accomplice?'

Zoya Blunt threw her head back in disgust. When she faced me again, there were tears streaking down her cheeks.

I needed Mike to lay off the 'bad cop' stuff, but I feared that it might not be an act.

'Why don't you give us some time, Mike?' I said. 'Leave us alone in here.'

'Time isn't gonna change anything,' Zoya said. 'You're both too stupid to know that.'

'It's not the first time I've been called "stupid,"' Mike said. 'I usually like to know why.'

'You actually think I might have had something to do with these killings?' she asked. 'Or with my brother?'

Mike took his handkerchief from his pocket and passed it to Zoya. 'Maybe so. Maybe that's why you're all clammed up.'

'You really think you can keep me here against my will?'

'That's the last thing we'd want to do,' I said. 'But the commissioner might direct me to get a material witness order.'

'What the *F* is that?'

I wouldn't have a prayer getting one for Zoya Blunt at this point in time. 'It means a judge would agree with us that you have information about your brother that's too important to us to let you go.'

'Screw it. You can't find a judge in the middle of the night,' she said, blowing her nose, as her mood went from tearful to defiant.

'I can't tell you how good Detective Chapman is at doing just that.'

Mike pulled on the back of my shirt collar.

I let her take a few breaths before I went back to what she had said a minute ago. 'Why shouldn't we think you'd have something to do with your brother? Aren't you close?'

'Nobody's close to him.'

'When's the last time you saw him, Zoya?' I asked.

She lowered her head and twisted Mike's handkerchief into a ball.

'I haven't seen Nik in more than a year, okay?'

'You remember when it was?' I asked, pressing her harder than she wanted to be pressed. 'Do you remember if you've heard from him since then? We need to know everything about him we possibly can.'

'We need your help trying to find him,' Mike said.

'There are dozens of cops out here looking for him. If you don't give us a hand, he's likely to get hurt.'

'You think that matters to me, Detective?'

The tears were flowing again.

'He's your brother,' Mike snapped back. 'I'm sure it matters.'

'Here's why you're stupid, Detective. I don't give a damn if he gets hurt,' Zoya Blunt said. 'The last time I saw Nik was the night he raped me.'

Thirty-eight

'Why don't you leave us alone for a few minutes?' I said to Mike.

Zoya Blunt had put her head on the table and cried to the point that her shoulders shook.

'I didn't mean to be so rough on you, Zoya,' Mike said, kneeling beside her to try to get her attention. 'I – I didn't know.'

'You couldn't have known. I never told anyone.'

'I can get you all the help you need,' I said. 'We've got counselors who deal only with this issue.'

She didn't speak. I wanted to hold out the hope of psychological support but didn't want to waste a minute of time in the search for Nik Blunt.

'Would you like me to do that?' I needed to get a conversation started with the suspect's sister. I wanted to take her back up to the operations room with Yolanda and get her talking.

'There's only one thing I need, and you can't give me that.'

'What is it? I'll certainly try.'

'I lost my family, Ms Cooper. I lost my entire family because of Nik. You can't do a goddamn thing for me.'

I walked away from the table, to the far end of the room.

'You're right about your family. I can't change that. But I can do things for other people, for people who don't deserve to be damaged any more than you do.'

'Not my problem.'

'Would you mind getting one of the crime scene photos, Mike? I think the lieutenant has a folder of them. A picture of Corinne Thatcher is what I want.'

Mike nodded and left the room.

'I don't want to see any pictures, okay?'

'No, it's not okay with me, Zoya. I want you to look. I want you to pick your head up off this table and stop wallowing in your own misery. Tell us what you know about Nik and where he might be hiding. I'm not going to let go until you do that.'

'How would I know?'

'Have you ever met either one of the young women he killed?' I asked. 'Or the young man? Did you recognize their names and their photographs in the papers?'

'I'm not interested.'

'Did you know any of them? Do you know if Nik knew any of them?'

'More stupid questions.'

'I'm going to keep asking them until I hit one you know the answer to. I've got friends out in this terminal. Great friends, who cover my back every day of the week. And I'm not going to let a single one of them get cornered by your brother.'

Mike returned to the room with three eight-by-ten photographs in his hand. I took them from him and laid them on the table just beyond Zoya Blunt.

'This is what we do for a living, Zoya. Day in and day out. We see people who've been violated in the worst possible ways, who've been butchered and battered and left for dead,' I said. 'Take a look at this.'

She didn't move.

I walked around her, so that her head – still resting on the table – was facing me. 'Pick up your head, young lady,' I shouted in her ear.

Zoya's head practically bounced off the table, but still she wouldn't look at me.

'We know that Nik hears voices,' I said. I was hoping my bluff would work, counting on my intuition that the person Jean Jansen heard fighting with Lydia was Nik Blunt.

Her eyes opened and focused on me for the first time. My hunch was confirmed.

'Look at these photographs, Zoya.'

'No, no. You tell me what you know about the voices. How did you find that out?'

'We have a witness.'

'Then you don't need me,' she said. 'Tell me who the witness is.'

'Look at the pictures,' I said, grabbing the photos that showed Corinne Thatcher's throat, sliced open from one side of her neck to the other. 'Look at what Nik did to her.'

'I don't want to look.'

I slammed my hand on the table, next to her ear. She sat upright. I wrapped one of my arms around her shoulder and held her in place, sticking the image directly in front of her.

Zoya Blunt gasped.

'We're out of time,' I said, softening my voice. 'What happened to the boy who loved to come to this terminal with his father, Zoya? How do we find him before he does this to someone else?'

She shook her head from side to side. 'Nik could be anywhere. He doesn't have a home.'

'Everything he's been up to has been connected to Grand Central.' I didn't need to point out that the bodies were piling up closer and closer to the main concourse to make my point. 'If you tell me what you know about him, maybe that will help.'

She was silent.

'You say you want your family back,' I said. 'What happened to everyone?'

'My father was an engineer, like his father before him. A hostler. You know what that is?'

'We just found out tonight.'

'We came here with him all the time, especially my brothers, but I loved it, too. More inside the terminal, and riding with my dad on the train. Not so much the tunnels and tracks.'

'I'm with you on that,' I said. 'Tell me about your mother, Zoya.'

She exhaled and closed her eyes. 'I'm named for her – Zoya. She – she had a lot of problems, too. Nik's like her. A lot like her.'

'Was she from Russia?' Mike asked.

'What difference does that make?'

'Maybe none,' I said. 'But one of the victims was an exchange student from Russia. Maybe there's some – some cause that Nik believed in. That might have been the way they met each other.'

'No causes except himself. That's always been Nik.'

'In what way is he like your mother?'

'I'm sure the men who worked with my dad will tell you anyway,' she said. 'The mental illness. The voices. She heard them, too.'

I had handled cases with schizophrenics before, both as victims and as perps. I knew that in at least 10 percent of people with the condition, there is a first-degree relative – a parent, uncle, cousin – that the disease is most often inherited from.

'Was your mother ever diagnosed?'

'Pretty late in her life. But she was in denial. She blamed everything for the difficult life she'd had.'

'How was it difficult?' I asked. 'In what way?'

'She'd grown up in Russia. Her family was very poor. They couldn't feed all the children, so they actually encouraged her to leave. To emigrate here. She met my father, which is the only good thing that ever happened to her.'

'Why do you say that? She had three children, too – that must have been a happy thing.'

Zoya Blunt sneered at me. 'My father was a rock. Just a good solid guy, who loved his family, loved his work. Married my mother before she went crazy, he used to say. The kids? Yeah, we made them both happy at first, but I can't really remember a time that Nik wasn't a problem.'

'A problem in what way?' Mike asked.

'Hard to know where to start. Nik was a wild child. A daredevil, a fighter. My dad wanted the three of us to go to college. Nik's really smart. I mean scary smart about some things. He got into a good school on Long Island – but he was drinking and smoking pot – and dropped out the first semester.'

'Did he have an influence on your other brother?' I said, thinking of the middle child.

'You think,' Zoya said, sarcasm dripping from her tongue, 'that killing him was a bad influence, Ms Cooper?'

That answer got Mike's full attention. 'Nik killed your brother? How's he been this violent but never arrested?'

'If you want to know what broke my mother's heart, it was the night five years ago when Nik was twenty-four. He got my brother drunk, stoned – whatever it was – then put him behind the wheel on the Long Island Expressway and passed out on the backseat.'

Zoya Blunt paused.

'The car skidded on black ice and was crushed against a tree on the side of the road. My other brother – who

388

was really a sweet kid, like my dad – was killed instantly. Of course, Nik was thrown clear.'

'It's always that way,' Mike said.

'It's why I never went to college. My dad had already died of a heart attack a few years before that. My mother cracked up, and I was left to stay home and take care of her.'

'More than any teenager should have to cope with,' I said.

'Yeah. I didn't do it very well.'

'Nik's violence,' Mike said, 'when did that all surface? Did schizophrenia cause your mother to be violent?'

'Never,' Zoya said. 'My mom lost touch with reality. She'd watch television and think that characters on a show were sending messages to her, you know? She had delusions all the time, so she wasn't able to function outside the house.'

'That's what trapped you at home with her?' I asked.

'Yeah.'

'Were there ever delusions about politics?' Mike asked.

Zoya looked at him, giving the question some thought. 'Actually, yeah, there were. She used to have all these crazy thoughts that were about people she knew back in Russia. That they were trying to make her do things. Nightmares about her childhood there.'

'Was her family persecuted for political beliefs?'

'Depends on who you asked. When my mom started losing it, she claimed that was the case. That we'd all be killed – back in her hometown and here – because of political beliefs, from back when the Soviet Union broke up,' Zoya said. 'But my father told me none of that was true. I never knew if he said that just to keep me from being frightened, or because it was a fact.'

'What did he think?'

'What my dad thought, Detective, is that my mother's family were a bunch of thugs. *Gangsters* was the word he used. That what they did was smuggle tobacco in from Kyrgyzstan, and not one of them knew the first thing about politics. They weren't dissidents; they were thugs. And anything else she thought about her relatives was a total delusion.'

'The tobacco trade is really dangerous over there,' Mike said. 'Talk to me about NorthStar, Zoya. I know Coop wants your family history, but we'll work backwards for that after we find Nik.'

'All he ever told me is that it was top secret work,' she said. 'Look, Detective, I'm pretty sure that was delusional, too. He tried to get into the army after the car wreck. Tried really hard to enlist, but by then we all knew he was hearing voices. No one would have him. Except this NorthStar operation, whatever it is.'

The detective who had taken over the loudspeaker was ramping things up a notch. *Attention, Metro-North riders. The last trains have left the station. We are closing for emergency repairs. Anyone refusing to leave the concourse will be escorted out by force and arrested for the crime of trespass. Step lively. Find your local bus, hail a taxi, start walking to Fleetwood – it's only fourteen miles away. This station is closed for business till further notice.'

'You're doing well, Zoya,' Mike said. 'I'm going to see if there's anything my boss needs for a few minutes. If you can think of anyplace here, somewhere Nik would feel safe and could hide out for the night, that's our most urgent need at the moment.'

'He can hide out anywhere in this terminal that he wants to, Detective Chapman. Nik has the keys to every room in this building.'

Thirty-nine

'Where did he get those?' Mike asked. 'How'd he do that?'

'Like I told you, my father worked here for more than thirty years. Look at any of the old-timers and see what the key rings look like, hanging from their belts.'

Don Ledger had made that point to us.

'Over time, the supervisors would give my father access to anything he needed. Elevators to get upstairs, lounges to rest in, emergency backup in case there were problems in the basement.'

'I can understand that,' I said, 'but they must have taken them back. You don't retire with keys to the workplace. Nobody would let that happen.'

'My dad never retired, Ms Cooper. He had a heart attack on his way home. He got off the subway near our house, complaining of chest pains as he climbed the stairs from the platform. Then he collapsed on the street and died right there.'

'I'm so sorry.'

'A neighbor who was on the train with my father came

to the house to get us. Left him with a couple of strangers. Nik ran out and got to Dad first, even before the ambulance arrived.'

Zoya Blunt took a breath and a drink of water.

'We met the ambulance – my mother and I did – at the hospital. Nik rode with his body. After we said goodbye and the paramedics went to give her his belongings, Dad's wallet was missing. Mom got all up in their faces and accused them of stealing from him. Nobody gave any thought to his keys.'

'But it was Nik?' I said. 'At least, that's what you think?'

'He never admitted to stealing money, but it would be just like him,' Zoya said, wiping a tear away. 'A few days later, after the wake and after all the guys from Metro-North had paid their respects, Nik began to wear the key chain on his belt. Out in the open, everywhere he went. Thirty, maybe forty keys on it. I never gave it any thought, to tell you the truth. He idolized my father, and I figured it just made him happy to feel like maybe he'd be following in his footsteps. I didn't care if the bosses at Grand Central had the damn keys or not. Wouldn't make any difference to them. Now, I think they were . . .'

'What?'

'Like trophies, you know? Like a sign that Nik could go anywhere my father had been,' she said. 'Only he knew he wasn't a fraction of the good person Dad was. Nothing like him.'

Yes, Mike and I knew about saving trophies.

'You must know this whole terminal the way Nik does,'

Mike said. 'Did he have a secret spot? We've shut the place down now. The FBI was able to get a photograph of him from NorthStar a few minutes before you got here. The cops will find him if it takes all night.'

'I'm trying to help you. Really I am.'

'Try harder.'

'We always played in the ticket booths when it was slow in the middle of the afternoon,' she said.

'Not a very good place to hide. They were occupied all day, till fifteen minutes ago.'

'Well, there's a basement. Some kind of stuffy old place that I didn't like to be in.'

'Yeah,' Mike said. 'He found that.'

'The older he got, the more he liked creepier parts of the terminal, like the tracks and tunnels.'

'He was allowed to go there?'

'Depends on what you mean by *allowed*. My father used to let us ride with him sometimes when he drove the engines to the roundhouse. I could pull the whistle, the boys could take turns sitting on his lap. As Nik got older – and like I said, he was a daredevil – he'd jump down and take off into the tunnels. My father didn't want him to get hurt, of course, but by the time Nik was a teenager and tough to control, Dad figured it was just safer to teach him his way around. All the guys had kids who wanted to hang out in the train yards. It was one of the best perks of a job that didn't pay very much.'

'Attention Nikolay Blunt!' Both Zoya and I started at the sound of her brother's name. A new speaker had taken

over the microphone. *'My name is Keith Scully, and I'm commissioner of the New York City Police Department.'*

Zoya balled the handkerchief in her fist and pressed it against her mouth.

'We know you're inside this terminal. We know you've killed three people this week. We know what you look like,' Scully said. *'We intend to find you before you find us. I've got SWAT teams from several police departments, federal agents, United States Army troops, and dogs that will run you to the ground no matter what corner of this building you're cowering in. Time to surrender, Mr Blunt. Time to surrender.'*

'Does he have guns, Zoya?' Mike asked.

'Probably so, Detective. I really don't know. My father didn't like guns and wouldn't have ever had one in the house because of my mother's illness.'

'They must have trained him with guns – probably automatic weapons – to go abroad for NorthStar. When you saw him – other than that last time . . .' Mike said, leaving out the word 'rape.'

'He had a gun that night. He didn't threaten me with it. But when he took his clothes off, I saw that he had a gun, and he had a lot of ammunition.'

'Do you know what kind of gun?'

'I'm not familiar with guns, Detective. Nik had a gym bag, too. I have no idea what was in that, either. I was afraid it was more weapons.'

'Did he talk about the gun?' I asked. 'Why he had it with him?'

'I asked him why he did. You have to understand how

terrified I was about everything that was going on that night. I was – I was distraught.'

'We wouldn't have expected you to be anything else,' I said.

'He told me it was because of voices. He told me that there were – I know this sounds absurd – that there were two people living inside him. Nik said he was torn between the two people. That one was beginning to issue orders to him, commands to do things,' Zoya Blunt's head rolled forward. 'That's the one who made him rape me.'

'Did Nik tell you why he was commanded to hurt you?'

'My mother was from Chechnya, Ms Cooper. You know Chechnya?'

'I just know it's a republic of the Russian Federation. I know there are Chechen rebels and that there have been lots of terrorist attacks carried out in the name of Chechnya. Is Nik involved with them?'

Zoya dismissed me. 'Maybe one of his voices gets messages from the rebels. Not my brother. He was talking all kinds of nonsense that night. About my mother's relatives in Chechnya, about human right violations, about . . .'

Mike's antiterrorist antennae had been raised again. 'Are you Muslim, Zoya?'

She glared at him. 'That would make this easy for you, wouldn't it, Detective? Nik could be some kind of Islamic jihadist.'

'Easy isn't the issue,' Mike said. 'It may explain why he's on this rampage and how big a stage he's looking to set.'

'We're Christians, Detective Chapman. My mother's

family was Muslim, as much of that region is, but she was raised without any formal religion – like a lot of thugs – and converted to Catholicism when she married my father.'

'Has Nik ever been back to Russia? To Chechnya?'

'Not so far as I know. I mean, I don't know what this NorthStar thing is about. Could he have gone there with that group?'

'Let me see if the lieutenant has gotten through to anyone at NorthStar,' Mike said. 'I'll be right back.'

'While you're at it,' I said, 'see if anyone has found out what part of Russia the third victim's family lives in. Lydia Tsarlev. Maybe she's Chechen. And I want to see a photo of Nik, okay? Bring me a copy of what the feds came in with.'

Mike left the room.

Zoya had her elbows on the table, her face in her hands. 'I don't ever want to see him again, Ms Cooper. Not even a picture.'

'You don't have to look at this one. It's for me to get an image of Nik.'

'We look a lot alike. He's taller than I am – maybe about your height. But we've got the same hair color, the same shape nose. We both resemble my mother.'

'She must have been very pretty,' I said.

'It's hard for me to remember her before she deteriorated so badly. The madness altered everything, even her appearance.'

I thought I'd change the subject. 'I spent some time in the tunnels this week. I don't know how anyone finds their way around down there and stays safe. Not to mention how much all the rodents spooked me.'

'It was the same for me. I was never tempted to get off the trains and walk around. The rats never bothered Nik, though. He actually had two in his room when he was in high school.'

'Pets?' I couldn't conceal my disgust.

'Yes,' Zoya smiled. 'But he didn't get them from the tunnels. He bought them in a shop, mostly to keep my mother and me from snooping in his room. And it worked fine. Nik used to call them the lazy man's dogs.'

'I can't believe pet shops sell rats. That never occurred to me.'

'It wouldn't matter what they sold, Nik came home with some creature every time he had the chance. Gerbils, turtles, parrots, rabbits. My parents wouldn't let us have cats or dogs, so Nik made do with everything else. I should have known he was crazy when he wanted rats. But he was totally an animal lover. I don't think it ever bothered him to watch someone beat the guts out of another person, but talk about shooting a rat with a BB gun? Nik would make sure, one way or another, that it never happened.'

I thought of Lydia Tsarlev and the Animal Liberation Front. Was it possible that Nik had met her through an underground resistance group that trumpeted illegal means of saving animals by destroying government and private property? And that the reason he had confronted her in her apartment was to enlist her to his new cause, his apparent sudden interest in Chechen human rights violations?

'Have you ever heard of the Animal Liberation Front?' I asked her. 'Is it the kind of organization Nik might have belonged to?'

'Get it through your head, Ms Cooper. My brother Nik isn't a very social person. I don't think he belongs to groups and parties and liberation fronts, whatever—'

She looked up when the door opened and Mike reentered the room, handing me a Xerox of a photo of Nik Blunt.

'—whatever they are,' she said, finishing her sentence. 'My brother Nik is a lone wolf. That's what he's always been.'

'Any sign of him yet?' I asked Mike. 'Any response to Scully's "give it up" message?'

'Yeah, there's a sign of him all right. They just found two pipe bombs, planted directly underneath Big Timber. That fancy old private varnish was about to be blown to bits.'

Forty

I left Zoya Blunt with Yolanda Figueroa, the Metro-North policewoman, and hurried out of the office with Mike, jogging down the staircase to the lower concourse. All the shiny black wrought iron departure gates were closed and locked, except for the one farthest off to the eastern end of the terminal.

The officers were from so many different commands that the mixes of uniforms and military outfits and agents in suits was almost overwhelming.

Rocco Correlli and Keith Scully were standing with several men I didn't recognize. Mike elbowed through the group, and I followed in his wake.

'I thought she went home,' Scully said to Mike, pointing at me.

'May I speak for myself, Commissioner? I'm working for you.'

'Coop's good,' Mike said. 'She's getting nuggets out of the Zoya girl.'

'Pipe bombs,' Scully said. 'Now I've got to clear cops

out of here while the dogs nose around to see whether there are any more.'

Pug McBride was walking around the circumference of Big Timber. 'I think it was just a subterfuge.'

'Big word, Pug.'

'I don't even know what it means, Chapman. It's what the Bomb Squad guys said.'

'Are they here?' I asked.

'Been and gone. Took out the first two bombs that were under this train and they're being bused up to Rodman's Neck,' Rocco said. 'We've obviously engaged Mr Blunt, but he planted blanks this time.'

'Blanks?'

'Al-Qaeda has an online program. "Build a Bomb in the Kitchen of Your Mom."'

'Seriously?'

'I'm afraid so. Blunt must have downloaded the instructions, Alex, but didn't have time to make these operative. It would have been pretty tough for him to get past all the devices inside the terminal that sniff for explosives, not to mention this slew of dogs we've assembled.'

'How did you find these,' I asked, 'if not dogs?'

'Trainmen were readying to move Big Timber on its way. Spotted them on the tracks.'

Pug pulled up a snapshot on his cell. 'Bits and pieces from old clocks, a rope line of Christmas tree lights, scrapings from match heads, and leftovers from a hardware store. My tenth grader's more dangerous than this with his chemistry set.'

'Let's hope so.' Scully looked grim as he turned away from the platform. 'I've got too many men inside there to take chances that Blunt's not luring us in towards bombs that actually work. We'll clear some of the guys out to the street for a while and leave the K-9 patrols to go through the place.'

Mike and I started to retrace our steps as I told him what Zoya Blunt said about Nik after he left the room.

'I can buy the lone-wolf thing,' he said. 'I've just spent a month studying terrorists and this doesn't fit any of the patterns.'

'But the feds—?'

'The FBI defines terrorism as having political motivation. That's it. It's the Arab Spring; it's Hezbollah; it's what's happened in Syria. Domestic terrorism,' Mike said, 'is more likely a result of psychopathology than politics.'

'I never thought of it that way.'

'John Hinckley tried to assassinate a president of the United States, not because of Reagan's political views, but to impress Jodie Foster. Think of the Boston Marathon bombers.'

I couldn't remember any day, since 9/11, that I had been so heartbroken and felt so helpless as when I watched the aftermath of the bombing on television. Many of my Vineyard friends were running that race, and I scoured the crowd looking for familiar faces. The random loss of life – and the horrific injuries – were devastating.

'The Russian-born brothers who thought they were jihadists?'

'There's not a shred of evidence that they were, Coop. They were rampage killers, is all. Losers. Mega-losers. They could have just as easily targeted a shopping mall or a crowded movie theater as they did the marathon.'

Mike still wore his Boston Strong T-shirt to Yankees games and cheered the great victory – despite his fierce spirit of rivalry – of the Red Sox winning the pennant the year of the bombing.

'And we don't have many shopping malls in Manhattan,' I said.

'So why not Grand Central Terminal?' Mike asked. 'The world's sixth-greatest tourist attraction. That ought to call a bit of attention to himself.'

We had crossed the lower concourse and mounted the staircase, headed back to the stationmaster's office. At the top of the steps, we came to a standstill.

Scully must have given orders to move scores of the officers back out onto the streets while the K-9 teams sniffed for traces of explosives. Cops were trying to find their partners, National Guardsmen were looking to regroup with their teams, military men and women were using walkie-talkies to communicate. The terminal floor looked like rush hour on steroids.

'So Scully doesn't want to alert Nik Blunt that he's worried about the possibility of more bombs,' Mike said, shaking his head. 'He's not announcing the orders to evacuate on the loudspeaker. He's just creating a little chaos.'

'You don't approve.'

'I don't. My bet is Blunt is in a position to be watching

all this from some secluded vantage point that he knows far better than we do.'

I scanned the enormous space. I took in the entire concourse, which was slowly emptying of its uniformed crowd. I looked above us, both east and west, to the massive walls of windows – towering sixteen stories over the terminal floor – and remembered the walkways that connected them to offices in each corner of the building.

'Bombs?' I asked.

'I don't think there are any more. I think it's part of Blunt's mind game with us.'

'But the Boston Marathon brothers—'

'They actually had a mother with a kitchen, Coop. A place to put their bombs together. This hump lives on the street. Or in a tunnel, right near the mole he killed.'

'So what are you worried about?'

'Guns. How many guns Blunt has with him. Handguns, like his sister saw. Automatic rifles,' Mike said, also eyeballing the enormous terminal from top to bottom.

'But he slit the throats of his victims,' I said. 'He didn't shoot them.'

'Yeah, and you don't work for NorthStar unless you can hit a moving target from a speeding vehicle.'

We were waiting for the scattering troops to clear.

'You've got to think of the catalysts for radical behavior,' Mike said.

'War College stuff?'

'Yeah. There are obvious triggers that incubate this kind of behavior. On the economic side, a guy without a job and no means to support himself. Socially, a guy with the perception that he's alienated from everyone else. Personally, the death of someone very close to him – and Blunt's witnessed the death of his younger brother and the father he idolized, as well as his mother's mental deterioration.'

'And he knows he's got the same disease that ravaged her,' I said. 'So he's a poster boy for being radicalized, even if it isn't political.'

'But every bit as dangerous as if his cause was a jihad.'

We turned the corner behind the staircase and I saw Yolanda Figueroa's partner standing outside the stationmaster's office. He spoke first.

'Ms Cooper. I've been waiting for you. Commissioner Scully wants me to take you back upstairs to the situation room.'

'What about Yolanda?'

'She's already gone up there with Ms Blunt.'

I looked at Mike.

'The sister was refusing to leave until her brother's in custody. She's afraid because he knows where to find her. The commissioner figures she might be useful in coaxing him out.'

'I'm glad she changed her mind,' I said.

'Scoot, Coop. It's like a bunker up there. Safest place in the building.'

'Don't jinx it for me.'

'See you later. Keep excavating. You're pulling great stuff from the sister.'

'Where are you going to be?'

Mike threw up his arms as he moved away from me. 'Wherever Scully wants me.'

'Stay safe.'

'Have to. I have a hot date tomorrow night.'

'Mr Blunt. I want you to listen up.' Keith Scully's voice boomed over the loudspeaker from the stationmaster's office as Mike walked away from me. *'We found your toy bombs, Nik. You're just upping the stakes every time you do something stupid like that. We know you have a gun, Mr Blunt. We know you might have several guns. Time for the white flag. Time to surrender so we can make a deal with the district attorney's office. It's your best hope.'*

I turned in the direction of the elevator that had taken us up to the situation room earlier.

'Not that way, Ms Cooper. They've turned off that particular elevator. Scully and the FBI chief are concerned that Blunt might still have that key. We're going up on the east side of the building. There's an elevator in the far corner,' he said, pointing in the direction of the Lexington Avenue exit.

'Are you sure?' I asked, looking over my shoulder to see whether Mike was still in sight.

'Yes, ma'am. There are uniformed cops stationed at the elevator doors on every floor. I promise to get you there just fine.' He smiled at me, and I smiled back, despite my growing case of jitters.

'Lead the way.'

Dogs were guiding their handlers to all points on the concourse. We skirted the information booth in the center of the floor, going kitty-corner toward Lexington Avenue. I kept stride with the officer, passing the newsstand and walking through the arcade of shops that were shuttered tight, with metal gratings like those you see in third-world countries.

'You don't think any killer's gonna buy that, Ms Cooper, do you?'

'What?'

'That your boss is gonna give him some kind of a deal. Doesn't make sense to me, and I didn't kill nobody. Kill three people and think somebody's cutting you a plea bargain? He'd have to be insane. Forget surrender. I'd be so far away from this place you'd never find me.'

There were two NYPD officers stationed on either side of the elevator. Both were armed with shotguns, wearing vests and helmets. My Metro-North police escort held up his key, tin badge in hand, and they nodded to us as we got on the elevator.

The officer hit the button for the sixth floor.

'But it's on seven, isn't it?'

'Yeah, Ms Cooper, but the only way directly to the seventh floor – to the situation room – is that elevator they shut down. We'll walk up from six. Trust me.'

'Of course.'

The elevator moved at the pace of a machine built a century ago. I was beginning to feel oppressively confined by the time it groaned to a halt.

The small landing onto which it opened – which held the elevator as well as a wide stairwell with steps to the flights above and below – was also guarded by an NYPD officer. It was a desolate space, with chipped and grimy paint, and steam pipes running in every direction.

He held open the door to let us out of the landing. 'You know how to get there?'

'Not this way,' the Metro-North cop answered with confidence. 'We need to take the stairs one flight up, to the situation room. My partner's in there with a witness.'

'Go ahead.'

I followed the cop up the double-height staircase. The door at the top of it was locked, and he used some kind of master key to open it and enter. I took three steps in his wake, and then abruptly stopped in place.

It seemed as though I was suspended in midair. There were long windows – with panes of glass more than six feet tall – on either side of me. Most terrifying of all was that when I looked straight down, I could see sixteen stories to the floor of the terminal. The catwalk I needed to cross was made of glass brick.

'What's wrong?' the cop said, looking back at me.

'I – I feel like I'm going to fall. It actually makes me dizzy to be up here.'

'First time is tough for everyone, Ms Cooper,' he said, walking back to me. 'It seems like nothing's holding you up, I know that. Grab my hand and you'll be fine. It's just an illusion.'

I took baby steps, as though I was moving to the edge of a gangplank.

I was halfway across the catwalk, trying my best not to

look down, keeping my eyes on the back of the cop's head while he guided me across the glass floor. Pellets of rain were pounding against the windows to my left. The storm had started.

Suddenly, there was a new voice on the loudspeaker. The microphone crackled and screeched as whoever was at the controls increased the volume.

'Your turn to listen up, Commissioner. There's no white flag in your future.'

It was Nik Blunt.

The police officer dropped my hand and pulled his gun. 'Get down,' he screamed at me, as he placed himself in one of the windows, looking down over the concourse.

I followed his orders and lowered myself onto the floor, watching as he took hold of a huge metal wheel that was attached to the frame of the window and pulled on it. The glass pane next to me cranked open, almost two hundred feet above the terminal floor.

'Just so you know, Commissioner,' Blunt said. *'It's impossible to shut down Grand Central, no matter how hard you try.'*

I was flat out on my stomach, peering through the glass bricks to see what was happening below. The few remaining cops were scrambling for cover, as though they were trying to figure out where this madman was.

'Is he in the stationmaster's office?' I asked. 'Do you think something happened to Scully?'

'No, no,' the cop said. 'I can't quite see him, but I know where the other loudspeaker is. He's talking from inside the information booth.'

'*You want to put cuffs on me, Commissioner?*' Blunt's voice was sharp and angry. '*Come and get me, Scully. The shock and awe portion of your evening has just begun.*'

The next thing I heard was the rapid-fire repeat of an automatic rifle, spraying bullets onto the floor of the main concourse from the very center of Grand Central Terminal.

Forty-one

The noise stopped abruptly after forty or fifty seconds.

As soon as it did, the deafening sound of return fire coming from four or five police sharpshooters echoed up to the celestial ceiling, very close to where we were.

'Stay down,' the cop said. 'Crawl. Go behind me and get over to the far side, toward the situation room.'

I crossed in back of him and then shut my eyes, wiggling my way to the safety of the landing behind the massive wall that stretched above us, as high as the building went.

Now it was Scully's voice. *'Move in, men. If he's still breathing, bring him out alive.'*

The commissioner was challenging Blunt, trying to flush out his position as well as his physical condition.

I sat upright, slightly nauseous from the dizzying view but drawn to the drama playing out below. At least two officers had been wounded in Nik Blunt's surprise shelling. They were being dragged by other cops across the concourse floor in the direction of the old waiting room.

'Snipers, take up positions.' Maybe a Code Black was in

effect, affording Scully a screenshot of the scene, allowing him to give orders to the men on the ground. He shouted to them, a disembodied voice like the wizard behind the screen in Oz. *'Move in now.'*

Four of the SWAT team members approached the information booth, guns aimed directly at the glass partitions. All were coming from the same direction, obviously to avoid friendly fire.

I couldn't see the solid brass door at the rear of the information booth. I'd stood at it dozens of times in my life, asking for directions, checking for the next train to Stamford or to White Plains or to Pelham. I knew the door opened on the side closest to the departure gates, which was out of my sight line.

'Stand up,' the cop said to me. 'Let's run you over to Yolanda.'

I got to my feet, still edged against the wall, looking down at the concourse. 'Wait,' I said. 'I want to see if they got him.'

The officers were up against the circular booth, kneeling below the glass windows. One of them stood up, aiming to blast the lock on the door.

'C'mon, Ms Cooper. I need to get back down there. They didn't get him.'

I stopped to question my escort. 'How do you know? Why do you say that?'

'That's one of the best-kept secrets of the terminal,' he said. 'There's a hidden staircase inside the information booth. It spirals down to the lower level. Blunt got the jump on your men, Ms Cooper. Screw the lockdown. He's on the run now.'

Forty-two

'Put this on, Ms Cooper,' Yolanda Figueroa said. 'Your lieutenant sent us up here with these.'

She was helping me into a bulletproof vest, just like the ones she and Zoya Blunt were wearing.

Her partner had left the three of us together. I bolted the door behind him, then dialed the stationmaster's office from the landline.

'Let me speak to Chapman or Wallace,' I said to whomever answered, and waited while the phone was passed. 'Mike?'

'I guess I was a little quick to blow off our tour guide yesterday. We should have been the ones to know about the staircase.'

'Blunt really got out of there?' I asked.

'We caught a shot of him on the surveillance camera, although no one had any way to make him at the time, to know who he was.'

'What do you mean?'

'He's dressed in camo and assault boots, carrying an

413

automatic rifle. He looks like half the guys on the floor here, like one of the guardsmen. It was only when we hit REPLAY to see how he got into the booth that we spotted him. He just melted into the crowd.'

'We couldn't have given him better cover,' I said.

'When the information booth employees were let go at nine fifty, Nik Blunt came out of whatever hole he'd been hiding in, unlocked the booth while everyone around him was busy doing his or her own thing, and apparently crouched inside.'

'Then Scully sends half of the troops back out on the street—'

'And Blunt sat in the crown jewel at the center of the terminal, knowing he could escape by way of the spiral staircase and come out on the lower level, which had just been evacuated because of the pipe bombs,' Mike said. 'All cred to NorthStar. He's a wily little bastard.'

'Zoya says everybody's kids knew about the staircase. Her guess is that Nik went down to the lower concourse to get to the tracks, into the tunnels.'

'Those gates to the platforms and tunnels are all manned, Coop. Pretty hard to slip out that way. Pin her down for any other sweet spots she remembers, okay?'

'How badly hurt are the two cops?'

'One has a shattered kneecap, and the other one just got knocked down, saved by his vest. You suited up?'

'Yeah. We're good,' I said. 'You?'

'Mercer and I are itching to get into this, but at the moment we're chained to the commissioner.'

'Scratch the itch, Mike. Scully needs you. It's almost eleven o'clock and no one's dead,' I said. 'Let's make it a record-breaking day.'

We hung up and I repeated the conversation, including how Nik Blunt was dressed, to the two women. Zoya was chain-smoking the remainder of a pack of cigarettes, filling the room with smoke.

I was pacing back and forth. The operation center attached to the situation room still had four workers in it. I could see from the monitors that there were no trains moving south of 125th Street. They were watching the rail connections far to the north.

I sat Zoya down at the table and pushed her again. 'So none of us knew about the staircase inside the information booth. That's not your fault – and you couldn't have guessed that Nik would get into there any better than we did – but we want you to rack your brain to tell us about other places like it here. Nik almost killed several cops tonight. Doesn't the hidden staircase make you think of anything else?'

'Honestly not, Ms Cooper. For me, it's been more than ten years since I used to come here. I wouldn't have thought of that staircase until you told me about it.'

We went back and forth for another fifteen minutes. I picked up the phone again to call Mike. I told him about the Campbell Apartment near the Lexington Avenue entrance. It had been built as a private residence for one of the original railroad trustees, John Campbell, and was a luxurious sanctuary in the middle of the terminal.

Unoccupied for much of Zoya's youth, it was now a glamorous bar – closed for the night – that Nik knew well, too. It was the only other place the young woman could recall as a special hangout of her brother's.

'I'll check it out,' Mike said.

'Anything else?' I said, fidgeting with the snaps on my vest.

'Mercer just spoke with a man who worked for NorthStar.'

'How'd you find him at this hour?'

'We didn't. He found the NYPD hotline. Called in when he saw Blunt's photo on the news tonight.'

'Does he solve the problem of where in the world Nik Blunt was?' I asked. Zoya's head snapped to look in my direction. 'Was he ever in Russia?'

'Never. No Muslims, no jihadist mission. The US government had a contract with NorthStar to go into Uganda, looking for a rebel leader who was abducting hundreds of kids to turn them into child soldiers. That kind of thing.'

'And Nik?'

'Caught the fever. Lived there for eighteen months,' Mike said, 'and seemed to have enjoyed the danger, the license to kill.'

'Voices or no voices?'

'Yeah, voices, all right. At least for the last few months. Now don't go telling Zoya what I'm about to say to you next. Promise me?'

'Okay.'

'Just so you know what we're dealing with, Coop. Nik and another man went off the reservation after their compound was attacked by the rebels. They attacked civilians in one of the villages in the countryside.'

I kept a poker face. Zoya was trying to study my reaction to the information I was receiving.

'Yeah?'

'All the men were off pillaging somewhere else, so Nik and his partner took it on themselves to rape four of the wives who'd been left behind.'

'Like the other guy living inside him told him to do.'

'Then he must have also told Nik to slit their throats from ear to ear,' Mike said, 'because he did that, too.'

I was speechless. How many other killings had there been between the women in Uganda, Zoya's rape, and Corinne Thatcher's murder? And what ever put a woman like Corinne in his line of fire?

'Say something, Coop. Something normal so you don't freak the girl out.'

'So nothing about any political mission, right? No work in Russia?' I knew it would sound like I was babbling and repeating myself, but I didn't want Zoya to learn about the other murders yet.

'Nope. But NorthStar is where Nik picked up all his moves. Blinding security cameras, like he did at the Waldorf. Enlisting marginal types, like Carl the mole, to do his dirty work, the way he found recruits in the Ugandan villages. Killing for pleasure. You've got to sink pretty low to be fired from a place like NorthStar. They got him out of Uganda before he could be charged for the crimes there. Or executed. That's why he wound up on the city streets – or below them.'

'Okay, we'll keep on talking up here. Don't forget about us.'

'Much as I might like that, Coop, it would be hard to do.'

I hung up the receiver.

Zoya asked what Mike had been telling me about Nik. Before I could answer her, the entire room went black.

I walked to the wall and flipped the switch, but there was no power at all. The only light in the situation room was the glowing tip of Zoya Blunt's cigarette.

Forty-three

'I want to get out of here,' Zoya shouted.

For three minutes, PO Yolanda Figueroa and I had scoured the room for a fuse box or an alternative source of power. Even the brightly colored screens tracking train movements had gone to black in the operations center next door.

I unbolted the door and cracked it open to look in the hallway, to see whether it was simply our area that had lost juice, but the corridor was entirely dark, too.

'Don't you carry a flashlight?' I asked Yolanda.

'Something had to give. I rarely use one working days, and they kept me overtime tonight. I had these three vests to carry up here, my walkie-talkie, water bottles, notepads. I'm sorry. Nobody thought I'd need a flashlight.'

'You have matches, Zoya?'

'A lighter.'

'Better still. Let me have it,' I said.

'No. I'm keeping it. I want to go.'

I tried the landline again, but that was dead, too. 'Give

it five minutes. There's nowhere for you to go, and no sense going by yourself. The commissioner will have someone come up and get us as soon as possible. Generators usually kick in pretty quickly, don't they, Yolanda?'

Yolanda Figueroa was jumpy, too. 'Are you crazy? They've never been able to maintain a generator in Grand Central. Do you understand how much power would be necessary, between the train grid and the size of the terminal?'

I was trying to convince myself as much as the two women to remain calm. 'There's no generator? Maybe the rainstorm caused the blackout. Maybe that's what did it. Lightning has knocked out the train system many times. They'll get something up and running,' I said. 'They'll have to.'

'The only backup they have powers up the trains first,' Yolanda said. 'You'll know that when the lights go back on the screens in the operations center.'

I looked through the window, but it was as dark in there as it was on our side.

'Not so fast, Ms Cooper. That could take half an hour,' Yolanda said. 'There'll be no lights in the terminal till they figure how and why they went off. And no generator to serve as an intermediate power source.'

'You don't know about the button, do you?' Zoya Blunt asked me. She had stepped on her cigarette to put it out, and now there was no glow at all.

'What button?'

'My father used to call it the red button. It turns off all the power in the terminal with a single switch, and it stops

420

'every train that's on a track, as far off as they may be.'

I tried to control my anger that she hadn't thought about it during my questioning. I tried to control my fear at the idea that this blackout could have been caused intentionally. 'Where is it, Zoya? Where is that button?'

'You think I was holding out on you, Ms Cooper? I just don't know where it is. I was never allowed to see it. It's in a subbasement that nobody's allowed in. It wasn't a place for kids, my dad always said.'

'Is it in M42? The subbasement with the rotary converters?' That's where Nik had been sleeping, but Scully had stationed men there so he couldn't go back.

'No, no. It's not M42. But it's downstairs somewhere near there.'

I had to tell Mike and Mercer. 'Yolanda, let me have your walkie-talkie.'

'It's not getting any reception,' she said. She was slow in passing it to me. 'I think I ought to bring you two back to the stationmaster.'

'I want to go with you,' Zoya said. 'I don't like the dark.'

'Let me have your lighter, please?'

She lit another cigarette and passed me the small plastic tube. I flicked it on and tried to make a call on the walkie-talkie. I pushed the right buttons but couldn't get through.

I pulled the laptop to me and linked to my internet service. I typed an urgent e-mail to both of the guys – and to Nan Toth, who was undoubtedly safe at home. I clicked SEND, but the notice that my message could not be delivered until a later time came back immediately.

'You won't get anything on the internet now,' Yolanda said. 'And you can't call or text. We're in a dead zone, and once we lose power, it's hopeless.'

'It wasn't a lightning strike that did this, Ms Cooper. It has to be Nik. He's going to find me here,' Zoya said, growing more and more hysterical. 'I want Yolanda to take me back to the detectives.'

'There's no reason for Nik to even know you're in the terminal,' I said. 'No one wants him to know.'

'Well, what about you? He'd be after you, wouldn't he?'

'I'm nobody in all this, Zoya. He doesn't have a clue who I am, and that's how I want to keep it. Nik's bought himself a confrontation with the NYPD. That's what he seems to want.'

The young woman drew a deep breath. 'From the looks of things downstairs,' she said, 'I'd have to say that's suicide.'

Zoya Blunt was exactly right. Suicide by cop.

Suicide, though, that took with him as many innocent lives as he could muster on his way out.

Nik's madness, his murderous rampage, was most likely a desperate effort to call attention to himself. Not a cause, not a political mission. The psychopathology of a schizophrenic who was driven by the torment of an inner voice. The psychopathology of someone who had lost everything to live for.

The young woman walked to the door of the room and opened it.

'No!' I shouted. 'You can't try and figure out your way down alone. You have no idea where Nik is.'

'I'm taking her, Ms Cooper. I've got a gun.'

'He's got a bigger gun, Yolanda. Probably more than one.'

'I have orders not to leave you here alone. And two of us don't want to stay one minute longer,' the officer said. 'I have orders to keep Ms Blunt safe from her brother, too.'

'Are you telling me I have to leave this room?'

'I can't make you do anything, Ms Cooper. But I'm ready to go. There are NYPD officers with automatic weapons stationed at every landing between here and the concourse,' Yolanda said. 'You must have seen that on your way upstairs. I can send one of them back up to hold your hand.'

'I – uh, I saw one where we got off the elevator.'

'You can be a sitting duck up here,' she said, patting the decorations on her breastplate, 'or you can come with us. I didn't get these citations for cowering in the dark.'

I thought about letting the two women go and bolting myself into the room. Nik Blunt didn't know who I was. There was no point for him to target the situation room.

'Nik has no reason to come here,' I said. 'We'll be fine.'

'You know the most damage he could do, Ms Cooper?' Yolanda said. 'He could get inside the operations center, to those guys on the other side of this wall who've still got thousands of lives in their hands.'

People speeding north through the night to Hudson and Hartford, I thought, unaware of the monster in the terminal they'd left behind.

'Nik Blunt could get in that room and throw switches. He could derail trains all over the Northeast Corridor, if he's rigged that power button in a way that he can control it from wherever he is within Grand Central.'

And NorthStar probably taught him how to rig some controls exactly like that.

'So you can sit here on your ass, Ms Cooper, and watch for the neon glow of those distant train signals to light up the operations board again.'

'But—'

'You cross your fingers and hope those passengers won't know what hit them when the trains jump the rails while they're cruising along at sixty-five, seventy miles an hour tonight. Me? I'm going out to make sure the bosses send more men upstairs to guard the workers in that room. They're a little more important in the big scheme of things tonight than you are.'

Forty-four

Yolanda Figueroa was the first of us to step into the darkened corridor. Zoya was behind her, and I was third in line.

'I've been up in these hallways several times a week for nine years,' Yolanda said. 'I can find my way down easily and guide you there. For now, you should follow the pipes.'

'What?' Zoya asked.

'Some run vertically and others horizontally. Just keep a hand on the ones that travel lengthwise over your head. They go the full distance of the corridor. Holding on to one of them will steady you. Keep you from bouncing off walls.'

There was an eerie stillness in the short hallway that was even more unpleasant as we made the right turn into the longer one that led back in the direction from which I'd arrived. Earlier in the evening I had been able to hear voices on the loudspeaker from time to time – some of them familiar to me. Now, no one was speaking.

I flicked on Zoya's lighter again. It was a plastic disposable

Bic, and I had no idea how much butane was left in it. I could see that there were no obstructions ahead of us so I turned it off.

Yolanda was more sure-footed than we in moving forward. I reached up to grab the old piping overhead, which was dust-covered and rough with rust. It made me more comfortable than the prospect of stumbling as I walked. Zoya Blunt couldn't reach the pipes, so she held on to the bottom hem of Yolanda's uniform jacket.

We reached the end of the corridor, and Yolanda pulled on the heavy door and opened it.

'No officer here,' she said.

'There wasn't one when your partner and I came up,' I said. 'The last cop I saw was guarding the elevator door one flight down.'

I moved into place, around Zoya, to face Yolanda. For the first time since the blackout, I could see into the terminal.

'Oh my God,' I said.

'If you can't deal with heights, then don't look down.'

Off to my right, the pounding rain hitting the long windows over Lexington Avenue in sheets was now accompanied by ragged streaks of lightning. At that very moment, a clap of thunder caused Zoya's heels to lift off the ground.

The lightning illuminated the all-glass catwalk, focusing me on the dizzying effect of the translucent flooring we had to cross to get to the stairs that were next to the incapacitated elevator.

'I can't do it,' Zoya said.

'This is no time to be afraid,' I said softly. 'I can't stand heights, either, but it's our way out of here.'

'It's not about heights.'

'What, then?'

I was looking down through the glass at the floor of the concourse below us. I'd never seen it cloaked in darkness before. I could make out figures moving across the wide space but had no idea who they were or what they were doing.

'We played on these catwalks all the time when we were kids. My dad used to rest in the lounge. The engineer's lounge.'

'Quick, Zoya,' I asked. 'Where's that?'

'On the fourth level, southeast corner. We played hide-and-seek,' she said, trembling again. 'Nik will see me if I walk out on that glass. I know he will.'

Yolanda was determined to get us down. 'He doesn't know you're here, Zoya. He's looking for cops. He's looking for ghosts that don't exist. Besides, you can't glance up from down below and know who anyone is. Trust me, I've spent hours looking for trespassers who get in here. You gotta be face-to-face, not looking at the soles of someone's shoes.'

There was a flash of light that blinded me for several seconds. The three of us retreated from the lip of the catwalk back into the stairwell.

'Was that lightning?' Zoya asked, holding on to my arm.

Yolanda answered. 'No. Emergency Services must have gotten some floodlights set up. Looks to me that's what it is.'

'That will help,' I said. 'They'll do floodlights and bull-horns.'

'It won't help anything,' Zoya said, clutching on to me. 'They'll just make it easier to see us walking across up here.'

Yolanda was losing patience with Zoya Blunt. 'Tell you what. You two stay right here in this landing, okay? You can lock the door to the corridor we just came from till I get back. I'll go down to get the other officer and you can wait—'

'We don't split up,' I said.

'Shit. You're worried 'cause you don't have a gun, Ms Cooper? We'll get somebody up here with one in five minutes.'

'It's not about the gun, Yolanda. I just don't want you to be alone.'

'We patrol alone most of the time. We only have part-ners in the tunnels and for VIP security setups. I'm used to this.'

Yolanda Figueroa was determined to head out on her own. Zoya Blunt had seated herself in a corner of the dark landing. I was torn between how to handle both of them.

Just then, Keith Scully's voice shouted through a bull-horn. *Sorry for the glitch, guys. The stationmaster tells me that Mr Blunt put his finger on something called the red button, to rather dramatic effect. He's managed to jury-rig the power controls in the terminal, so I apologize for the loss of light and sound.*

I also apologize for putting so many of you men and women,

whom I respect enormously, in danger. So I'll give Mr Blunt
exactly three minutes to show the white flag. If not, then there's
no deal on the table. The district attorney has withdrawn all
possible plea discussions. And I'm reminding you that Nik
Blunt is armed and extremely dangerous. We'll get you some
light back as soon as we can.'

'Another ten minutes,' I said, 'and we'll be able to see
where we're going and who's around to help us.'

'I'll be back before then,' Yolanda said.

A crash of thunder cracked the quiet of our landing.

'Here's what I'm going to do,' she said, Glock in hand.
'I'm going down this staircase, just the way you came,
Ms Cooper. If you can bring yourselves to do it, just
inch out a bit and you can watch me cross over on the
catwalk. Right inside that door across the way, you said
there's an officer on patrol. You won't ever lose sight of
me.'

I peered out onto the catwalk. The improvised lighting
from below and the occasional streaks of lightning from
outside showed that it was empty, top to bottom.

Yolanda Figueroa stooped in front of Zoya Blunt, resting
a hand on her knee. 'You okay with this? Is this what you
want?'

The young woman bit her lip and nodded.

Then Yolanda smiled at her. 'My boyfriend's one of
those guys in the operation room, so you know I'll be
right back. Gotta keep him safe at all costs.'

No wonder the cop was so eager to get extra protection
for the men in control of the train lines.

She stood up. 'You get it now, Ms Cooper? Or are you heartless?'

'I can't fight with you, Yolanda. He's a lucky guy, so you'd better be careful.'

'I'm good at my job. I'll be back.'

Yolanda Figueroa took the staircase down, moving faster without us. When she reached the floor below, about fifteen stories over the main concourse, I watched from my vantage point, where the catwalk met the enclosed landing that shielded us from sight. I envied the confidence with which she strode over the glass bricks, backlit by an occasional lightning flash.

She pulled on the door and it opened. She disappeared inside.

Since the elevator was incapacitated, I knew it would take several minutes longer for her to jog down the many steps necessary to get to the ground floor, and several more to find Scully or our team.

'You okay?' I asked Zoya, lighting another cigarette for her.

'I just want to sit here. This is fine.'

The storm was passing right overhead. The lightning streaks and thunderclaps were coming much closer together in time.

But only ninety seconds later, the door that Yolanda Figueroa had entered, one flight beneath us, burst open onto the catwalk.

From the angle at which I watched, I could see the figure of the young woman – gone almost limp, her head flopping against her chest – being pushed back out over the glass flooring by a young man dressed in camouflage clothes and assault boots.

I knelt beside Zoya and put my hand up to signal her to stay back.

Nik Blunt had Yolanda in his arms. It appeared from the blood on both her upper body and on Blunt's clothing that he had already slit her throat.

I was helpless as I watched him drag her to the window he had opened over the concourse. 'Hey, Scully! Commissioner!' Blunt screamed out into the poorly lit space.

Someone played the floods until they caught the two bodies – one alive, one probably dead – framed in the giant glass box so high above them.

'Hey, Scully! You looking for your officer?' Blunt screamed. 'I told her to mind the gap, but she didn't listen to me.'

I watched as Blunt threw Yolanda's body to the concourse fifteen flights below. Before she hit the marble floor, snipers were firing at Blunt, bullets seemingly deflected by the thick panes of glass.

'I told her,' he yelled down, laughing as if he'd been seized by a demon, before he scurried back to the safety of the landing and let the door slam behind him. 'I told her to mind the gap.'

Forty-five

'We've got to move,' I said, pulling Zoya Blunt to her feet.

'What happened to Yolanda?'

'She's been hurt. We've got to go.'

'Nik? Was that Nik shooting?'

Maybe Zoya hadn't heard his voice in the recess of the landing. 'Probably. I think he's on his way upstairs. I think Yolanda was right about his goal. We need to get out of this space as fast as we can.'

I knew that we couldn't go downstairs. The risk of encountering Blunt on the way was too great. But he was headed in our direction and we had to change position as quickly as possible.

'Put out your cigarette, Zoya. Someone might see the light.'

'Attention, team.' There was a new voice on the bullhorn. It was Mike Chapman. He had undoubtedly seen Yolanda's body splatter on the concourse floor and knew Zoya and I were in trouble. *'Change of plans.'*

Now he had to talk to us without giving Blunt any idea who or where we were.

'Okay, Zoya. That's the detective who was working with us downstairs. We're going to be fine. He'll tell us what to do.'

'He doesn't even know where we are.'

'I think he knows where Nik is, though.' I opened the door through which we had entered the landing. I knew Mike wasn't going to send us across the glass catwalk and expose us to this maniac.

'*My team needs to report immediately to Captain Poseidon's son,*' Mike said, choosing his words carefully. '*Got that? To Poseidon's son.*'

This was not a time for Mike's dark humor. If there was a Captain Poseidon, I didn't know him. I took Zoya's hand to lead her, but I wasn't sure where to go. The beating of my heart seemed louder than the crashing thunder.

I kept repeating Poseidon's name to myself and all that surfaced in my mind was Greek mythology, not an actual police captain. Of course, Poseidon. God of the sea. Did Mike want us to make our way downstairs to the Oyster Bar?

'*Remember, men,*' Mike called through the bullhorn. '*The captain's son has wings. Wings.*'

'Did you and your brothers learn mythology when you were kids?' I asked Zoya.

'No. Not me. I never heard anybody talking about it. Is that a bad thing?'

'It's great. Right now it's great.' I couldn't compete with Mike's knowledge of the Greek and Roman warriors, but I'd learned a lot from listening to him over the years.

'Why is he calling us "men"? He's not talking to you at all.'

'Oh, yes he is. He's just trying to throw Nik off, not alert him to the presence of the two of us.'

Poseidon, god of the sea, was also the father of Pegasus. And Pegasus was the divine winged horse of Greek myth – and of the zodiac. The golden image of Pegasus was one of the larger figures in the mural of the celestial sky that stretched above us.

Of course it made more sense for Mike to direct us upward than to chance an encounter with Nik Blunt, who was at least one floor below when he encountered Yolanda Figueroa. One flight up and we would be in the corner of the building, directly below the painting of Pegasus.

'Repeating, gentlemen, that I will meet you by Captain Poseidon's son. Not where his son actually is, but where he should be. Where his son should be,' Mike said. *'As God is my witness.'*

I stood still and repeated Mike's last words. 'As God is my witness?'

He was telling me something. Something he was convinced I knew. I got who Poseidon was and from that had figured Pegasus. What did God have to do with any of this?

I played the words over and over again in my mind, until the clues finally locked into place.

The celestial ceiling had been painted in reverse, we had learned in our tour. The information had seemed irrelevant at the time but satisfied my curiosity about the magnificent aqua sky. The artist had made a mistake in creating his great mural. I tried to remember everything we had learned such a short time ago.

And then I recalled what happened when Commodore Vanderbilt's heirs had been informed about the mistake, the very week Grand Central had opened. They announced that the mural was not an error at all, but a view of the earth from the heavens. God's view. God was their witness.

'Mike will meet us on the other side,' I said to Zoya. Not where Pegasus really is, but where he's supposed to be. 'On the top floor. Let's retrace our steps and you can follow me across.'

I let the door to the landing close behind us, lighted the Bic to make sure the path ahead was clear, and started jogging to the far corner of the building. The winding corridor was the entire length of a city block, parallel to 42nd Street, taking us from the Lexington Avenue side of the terminal to the Vanderbilt Avenue side.

When we reached the opposite landing, both of us took thirty seconds to catch our breath. There were no sounds from the corridor behind us. No voices, no footsteps, no gunshots.

'Ready?'

'You think your detectives are out there?' Zoya asked.

'If not now, then any minute. It's a lot of territory for them to have to cover quickly. Sixteen flights or more up the staircases, most of them locked.'

Who knew what kind of carnage they faced in the wake

of Blunt's maneuvers, and whether he had placed other obstacles in their way?

'How will you know when they get up here?'

'I'll – I'll take a look. I'll open the door.' I was as anxious to see protection for us as she was.

'Are you sure we're in the right place?'

'As sure as I can be,' I said. 'I'm going to open it now, okay?'

'Yeah.' She had her back flat against the wall, out of sight of anyone who would be in a position to see inside.

I cracked the door a couple of inches. The concourse was still bathed in darkness, but floodlights were panning the entire room. Some were running horizontally, along the walls and back and forth on the catwalks on both ends, while others were scanning from the top of the vaulted ceiling back to the floor. I figured I had less than ten seconds to stay out of the spotlight.

Mike still had the bullhorn and now he was talking to the fugitive. *'We got your stash, Mr Blunt. Whatever ammunition you don't have with you, we've got most of it. So if you're running low, you might want to rethink your plan.'*

I closed the door, counted to thirty, and opened it again.

'All that ammo you left in your crib in the tunnel, Mr Blunt? That's gone. Thanks to Smitty, former mayor of the moles. Cleaned you right out.'

I wanted Mike or Mercer or Scully – anyone who knew Zoya and I were on the loose – to spot me and send cops to make us safe, but the last thing I wanted was for Nik Blunt to catch us. I placed my shoulder against the heavy door and looked again but saw nothing and no one. Mike wasn't talking to Blunt about Yolanda's death. I'm sure he didn't want to give the murderer the satisfaction of knowing how everyone guarding the terminal felt about the killing of a police officer.

I was getting as depressed as I was anxious. Maintaining a stiff upper lip in front of Zoya Blunt was becoming more difficult by the minute.

Why hadn't any of the cops reached our position yet? Had Blunt intercepted and killed more of them, or was it just the steep and circuitous route they had to take to get to us?

I thought Mike would have raced up the many flights of stairs himself, but it was more like him to stay on the loudspeaker, letting me hear his steady voice talking directly to me, communicating his presence and support. He would have dispatched other cops to come find Zoya and me.

I knew there were sharpshooters set up all over the terminal by this point. I hated the idea of sticking my head out into the open space at the very top of the catwalk.

'Attention, team!' Chapman's voice again. 'Meeting unavoidably delayed. I know where you are, team. Check the Edisons. Check the Edisons. Waiting for power, team. Waiting for four thousand bare bulbs to go on.'

I was fast becoming too exhausted to play Mike's word game. Edison and bulbs suggested lighting. We knew the power was out. And four thousand bulbs was another count that figured in the structure of the terminal. Architects wanted to show off the new technology of the day: electricity. Every bulb that ringed the circumference of the ceiling of Grand Central – thousands of them – was absolutely bare.

Mike was broadcasting something to me that I needed to know. It had to do with the innumerable bulbs that were just overhead outside the landing.

'What does he mean?' Zoya asked.

I put my finger to my lips. 'Be absolutely still, okay?'

'Are they nearby?'

I figured Nik Blunt was closer to us than the cops.

'On the way.'

I put my hand on the knob, bracing my arm against the door so it opened only slightly. I focused my eyes, which was hard to do going from total darkness to the combination of searching floodlights and bolts of lightning. Nothing.

I closed it and waited ten seconds. Zoya took another cigarette from the pack in her pocket and asked me for the lighter.

'You can't do that right now.'

'It helps my nerves.'

'You'll give us away when I open the door.' I didn't want to tell her that snipers must have been setting up every-where. 'Just wait.'

'You said that before. I've been waiting, okay?'

I shushed her again and cracked the door. This time, the spotlights all seemed to be aimed in the same general position. They were crisscrossing the giant molding that formed a channel from the catwalk on the east side – from which Blunt had thrown Yolanda – to the one next to us, on the building's west side.

I stood on tiptoe, so close to the ceiling of the terminal that my vertigo almost overwhelmed me.

In the man-sized gully – which appeared to be an architectural design element from the concourse below – where workmen stood twice a year to change thousands of light-bulbs, I could see Nik Blunt. He had crawled onto the deep space through one of the long glass windows – clearly fearless of heights, unlike me – and was creeping across the entire length of the terminal in our direction.

Spotlights from the floor tried to follow his movement, but most of Blunt's head and body were below the rim of the channel.

I had no idea whether he had spotted me when I saw him throw Yolanda off the catwalk, or whether she'd had a chance, before he slit her throat, to give up the fact that his sister was in the terminal, helping the police find him.

Someone from below yelled the word 'fire.'

A hail of bullets flew in the direction of Nik Blunt, who flattened himself against his sky-high gully and laid perfectly still. They struck the marble walls and burst scores of lightbulbs.

I pulled the door shut before someone mistook my shadow for the killer.

Forty-six

I had my back to the wall, next to the door.

'What do you have in your apron pocket beside the lighter?' I asked Zoya.

She had heard the volley of shots and was ten steps ahead of me, backtracking in the corridor.

'Nothing. Just a Swiss Army knife and a bottle opener.'

A waitress, of course. 'Let me have them, please.'

She fished in her apron and handed me the multitooled gadget first. I pocketed that, then held out my hand for the corkscrew. I pushed in the lock on the door – there was no bolt – then asked her to come back and hold the lighter so I could see well enough to jam the keyhole with the wine opener.

'Let's go. That should buy us a few minutes.'

'But the gunshots?'

'It's the cops. They think they see your brother up here.'

'Near us? Coming toward us?'

'I don't know, Zoya.'

She started to run in the dark, holding the lighter out

in front of her. 'He'll kill me,' she said. 'Why aren't the cops here?'

He'll kill anyone he encounters, I thought to myself. 'Where are you going, Zoya? You're heading back the same way we came.'

Nik could just as easily crawl back to the catwalk he'd started from as come out to the one we'd been standing near. I wanted to find a place to hide.

The young woman kept running ahead of me.

'Zoya, how well do you know this area? There must be supply closets up here, aren't there? Somewhere we can be out of sight.'

'I'm getting out.' She was frantic now, and I couldn't blame her. I wasn't thinking any more clearly, although there didn't seem a way to escape from the top of the building that had countless entrances and exits on the street level.

'We've got to stay together, Zoya.'

'I don't have to do anything you tell me. You'll get me killed. You'll get us both killed.'

Halfway down the corridor, she took a right turn, which was the way back to the situation room that we'd exited with Yolanda Figueroa.

'Where are you going?' I asked.

I caught up with her as she pulled on the door. It wouldn't open. She stepped aside to let me try, but I couldn't move it.

'Don't you have a key? Don't you have anything to help us?' Zoya had lost it, emotionally. She was unable to talk to me now. Everything she said was a scream or a high-pitched rant.

'I don't have keys. I never did.' This hadn't been the plan for the evening.

Zoya swept past me and continued down the narrow hallway. I looked back before I followed her. Blunt didn't appear to be coming yet, if he was still alive. There was no noise from the direction of the landing, where I'd blocked the keyhole – at least temporarily.

Ten seconds later, Zoya let out a shriek. I ran toward her in the dark space, farther away from the corridor that led to the two catwalks, and to the stairwells that eventually could take us down to the concourse.

There was a body on the floor, directly in front of the door to the operations command center. A man in some kind of military camouflage who'd been shot in the chest. He was African American, so I knew that it wasn't Nik Blunt.

Zoya was out of control. She began banging on the door of the operations center.

I knelt beside the soldier – a National Guardsman or reservist. I grabbed the Bic lighter from Zoya's hand to take a cursory look at his face and chest. The man was dead.

'Let me in,' Zoya yelled to whoever was inside.

Keith Scully and his colleagues had obviously stationed someone outside the room where the trains were controlled. It appeared that Nik Blunt had killed him and taken whatever gun – whatever kind of weapon – the dead man had thought would protect him.

'Nobody's coming in here,' a voice called back. 'Who are you?'

'I'm – I'm – just a woman. Just – just – help me. What's the difference?'

'I'm a prosecutor. I'm Alex Cooper,' I said. 'I'm so glad you're okay.'

'You got ID? You got a badge?'

'No, no, badge. But you can call the stationmaster. Call the police commissioner. They'll tell you who I am.'

'Lady, we can't call nobody. How the hell do I know who you are? Somebody was supposed to be outside this door keeping us safe. Sounds like he's gone. We're barricaded in here till I see the man I work for. All our furniture's against the door, so don't try anything.'

'The man guarding you is dead,' I said.

I didn't know whether I was talking to Yolanda Figueroa's boyfriend or not, but it wasn't the time to break that sad piece of news to him.

'I've got a gun, lady. Locked, loaded and perfectly legal. Try to get yourselves in here and you're dead, too.'

Zoya started stumbling forward again, farther into the dark hallway, into what was unfamiliar territory for me.

I stood beside the man who'd been killed, unable to move.

Then I heard noise, remote but audible. Someone was playing with the lock that I'd jammed with the corkscrew, jimmying it, trying to force it open.

I reached up for one of the horizontal steam pipes and

grasped on to it. It was so dark that I couldn't even see Zoya, but there was only one direction in which I could move.

In ten or twelve steps, I could hear her breathing. I practically bumped into her, where she had stopped at an intersection in the narrow passageway.

I drew next to her and whispered in her ear, as softly as I could. 'I think Nik's going to be coming back this way. We won't be able to talk. We can't use your lighter.'

'How do you know he's coming?' She was panicky, shaking like a leaf.

'There's someone trying to get through that door on the landing we just left. If it was cops, they'd be calling out to us by now. They'd be offering help.'

'But you said—'

'We had to leave the position Mike sent us to, so the guys don't know where we are anymore, Zoya. How can they help us till they do?'

'Well, I'm getting out. I'm getting out of here.'

'Where are you going? I'm trying to help you stay safe. There must be some hiding place you remember.'

She turned her back to me and started to walk briskly. It was too dark to run.

Zoya Blunt had no intention of answering me. She was simply trying to put as much distance as she could between her brother and herself.

She made a right turn at the intersection in the corridor. I had no choice but to follow her.

We must have taken another twenty or thirty steps. To

my right was a series of doors – probably equipment closets. I slowed down to twist the knobs, but nothing gave.

Zoya Blunt stopped short just ahead of me. To her left were only two choices: a steel-framed door or a wooden staircase located at the bottom of a dozen steps.

I watched as without hesitation she chose the door.

I was practically on her back as she worked the handle. There was no lock.

Zoya pushed on the door and it swung open.

I looked out and gasped. She had stepped out onto the sloping roof of Grand Central Terminal, twenty stories above 42nd Street.

Forty-seven

Rain pelted my face as I froze in the doorway, half of me inside and half out. Thunder rolled overhead.

'You can't do this, Zoya. You'll fall!'

She sat down on the copper plates of the rooftop and started scooting sideways like a crab, heading to the west side of the building. Clearly neither she nor her brother shared my fear of heights.

I followed her progression with my eyes but was too paralyzed to copy her moves. The tiles were slippery from the storm. Zoya's skirt ripped as she slid down to the edge of the roof, catching herself on the concrete trim that decorated the entire edge of the vast building.

Fear was a powerful motivator. She rolled onto her hip and clawed her way up the side of the incline, closer to the top, then continued to propel herself westward.

Zoya had left me behind. I understood why but didn't know which way to go to save myself.

Nothing was moving below me on 42nd Street. Undoubtedly, the massive police operation had resulted in the closure of all traffic routes around the terminal.

There was a flash of light that stunned me for a few seconds. *More lightning*, I thought.

But when I picked my head up, there was a row of Emergency Service floodlights aimed at this side of the roof. Some were on the roadway, and others were directed straight ahead, on the Park Avenue Viaduct that encircled the building directly below me.

I ducked back inside, rain-soaked and confused. I stepped out of my wet sneakers and left them next to the door.

It suddenly occurred to me that there were police snipers in every office building on the opposite side of the street. If Nik Blunt had chosen to escape on foot, on any one of the streets or avenues, the sharpshooters would have been waiting for him. And of course, the rooftop was another possible route for someone as nimble as Blunt.

I closed the door and tried to think about my options.

Then I heard footsteps. It was neither pounding rain nor the sound of Zoya Blunt scrambling across the roof of the terminal.

The steps came from the corridor we had just traveled, and since no one was calling my name, I assumed the person approaching me was Nik Blunt.

I went down the short wooden staircase, wondering why Zoya – who clearly had played in this vast attic as a child – hadn't taken this passage. I assumed it was because it did not lead out to the rooftop, which, to me, was a good thing.

At the bottom of the steps was an enclosure – also made

of wood, somewhat decomposed and rotted out – which was probably original to the old building.

'Who are you?' It was Blunt's voice. The same one I'd heard after he'd disposed of Yolanda's body.

I took another two steps and was inside the shed, out of sight.

'I saw you peeking out from the landing. Guess nobody told you it was a bad night to be working late.'

I was relieved that the killer had no reason to know my name or my role in this manhunt and seemed unaware of his sister's presence in the terminal.

I turned around to see where I was, whether entrapped in this wooden corral or if there was another way out.

My eyes became accustomed to the light and in front of me I could see the interior of a gigantic clock, the rear side of huge pieces of stained glass that fronted on 42nd Street.

The spectacular timepiece was, I knew, the largest clock ever made in the Tiffany Studios. It was part of the iconic statue *Transportation* that was Grand Central's face to the world.

Blunt was getting closer. 'I need you to take a walk with me,' he said. 'Come on out, wherever you are.'

I knew the clock faced due south. Its center was bright blue, with painted rays of sunlight dancing around the dial. Each of the Roman numerals was also gilded against a deep-red circular background.

Blunt was playing with the knob on the door handle that led to the roof, the same exit Zoya had used.

I saw a small plaque on the wall of the clock room. Next to the numeral VI on the giant face, which was probably a dozen feet in diameter or more, were the words OPEN HERE. It must have been the way custodians could reach the exterior clock face for maintenance and repairs.

'Well, well. You must have had a change of heart. There's a puddle at this door by the roof, so I'm guessing you decided not to take that slippery slope after looking out.'

I reached for the long handle next to the numeral VI. It opened inward. I squinted at my wristwatch, which said it was 12:26. I looked up and the tip of the minute hand on the Tiffany clock face – an enormous gilded pointer – was just coming into view in front of me.

It was a heavy piece of steel, taller than I was, with a soldered-on extension that stuck out on both sides of the sharp point. Just beyond the minute hand, I could see the bottom of the famous sculpture that surrounded the clock – a thick rim bordered with oak leaves and cornucopia.

I didn't like my odds, but I had no intention of waiting for Nik Blunt to put his hands on me. I lifted one leg over the outer edge of the circular window – numeral VI on the giant clock face – grabbing hold of the minute hand to stay in place. I was tempted to use that long hand to anchor me, but I was afraid it wouldn't hold my weight. Then I swung my other leg out, so that I was seated on the window's metal frame, facing south across 42nd Street.

I pulled the casing closed behind me. Now I was alone on the rooftop of the terminal, outside in the furious storm, rain cascading down my head and shoulders while

I tried to figure out how to find a safe place to conceal myself.

I couldn't see anything because of the darkness and the blinding spotlights of the NYPD. It was probably better for me that way. I hoped the night-vision goggles of the snipers afforded them greater sight than I had. I needed them to establish that I was a disheveled-looking woman – barefoot, in jeans and a vest – and not the killer they were ready to take out.

I tried to channel Mercer's steady voice. I had never known anyone with the serenity that he always displayed. I imagined him standing behind me, steadying me, talking me into a way to save myself.

I heard the metal door that led to the roof, the one that Zoya had escaped through, open. Even if Blunt looked out there for either of us, she had long ago rounded the corner of the building, and I was too far in front of him, blocked from view by the statue above the clock.

'Maybe you slid right off the roof,' Blunt yelled out into the night. 'What a mess you'd make all over the sidewalk.'

Lightning split the sky in two. My hair and clothing were soaked from the heavy rain.

I closed my eyes and had my silent conversation with Mercer. I needed to get off the frame of the clock. I had to move away from this opening, which was likely to be Nik Blunt's next point of approach.

I counted on Mercer to calmly coax me to move, even though he was in another part of the building. *Time to go, Alex. Just step yourself down on a piece of that granite,* I imagined his voice in my ear. *Hold tight. Don't look down. I'll come and get you soon.*

I felt for the base of the great sculpture with my toes. The shape of the oak leaves that formed the bottom of it made a perfect foothold. The rough-hewn granite, exposed to the elements and weathered for more than a century, was far less slippery than the panels on the roof of the building where I'd watched Zoya struggle and slide.

I put one foot ahead of the other, bending over and reaching for the next garland in the elaborate carving.

I looked up. I had stepped a few feet away from the face of the clock. Directly overhead was the statue of Mercury, and almost within my reach, the giant draped leg of the reclining goddess, Minerva. I was desperate to pull myself up beside her and be sheltered by her strong, still figure. Then I thought of Mike and how he could tell me what each of these gods represented – Hercules, Mercury and Minerva. I smiled at that connection.

Then I heard the metal casing on the clock scrape against itself as the circular numeral VI window opened. I could see Nik Blunt stick his head and neck through the hole, and I pressed myself against the cold, wet stone so that he couldn't make out my position.

I didn't move. I watched as he threw one leg over the frame at the bottom of the circular window. The minute hand was about to cross through to the next numeral.

Nik Blunt grabbed the neck of the minute hand – which was longer than he was tall – and hoisted himself up on

451

it, swinging his other leg out onto the granite base of the sculpture. He appeared, again, to be fearless.

When he came to rest on the foundation of the sculpture, he balanced himself by grasping a piece of the granite, his cheek resting against the bottom of the clock.

Within seconds, he started to take in his surroundings. When he changed the angle of his head – looking to the right – we locked eyes immediately.

Nik Blunt laughed. 'You must be a cop.'

I couldn't speak. I shook my head violently from side to side.

'You've got the vest,' he said, stepping closer to me and extending his right hand in my direction. 'And that desperate look about you.'

I was above him now, slowly working my way up the pediment of the sculpture. He didn't appear to have a gun – or at least not one in his hand. I had no idea how many rounds of ammunition he'd already discharged in his spree.

I reached into my jeans' pocket. The small Swiss Army knife that I had taken from Zoya was closed, but with the nail of my forefinger, I pulled at the notch in the tiny blade and opened it. I doubted it was even two inches long.

'Not so fast, girl,' Nik Blunt said as he reached up and grabbed my left ankle. 'Another notch for my dead cop belt. Ladies' day. Wouldn't that be nice?'

I shook my leg and broke loose. He was not quite close enough to get a good hold on me.

There was a cornice of the pediment over my head. I

reached for it with my right hand – the one holding the tiny, red-encased blade – and then passed it to my left hand, clinging to the wet granite with both of them.

Nik Blunt swiped at me again, and this time connected. He was holding the leg of my pants with his right hand. He repeated his mantra. 'My good fortune, Officer. It's ladies' day.'

I looked down at him. I held the knife tightly in my hand, then leaned over and swiftly plunged the tip of it into the skin of his wrist.

He recoiled in pain, the knife sticking in place.

Blunt swiveled, trying to flick it off his right hand, still clutching a piece of the granite carving with his left.

As he turned his head away from me, the night sky blazed with floodlights. The snipers in the building across the street opened fire, five or six of them at once.

I shuddered and clutched at the granite as tight as I could, praying the bullets wouldn't miss their mark.

Blunt stretched out his hand to reach for my foot again – to take me down with him. Blood gushed from his mouth as he tried one last time to speak.

I kicked him away, grasping at the stone hem of Minerva's robe to keep my balance. I didn't know how many times Nik Blunt had been shot by the sharpshooters, but I had no doubt that he was dead before he hit the street.

Forty-eight

'Ladies' day, my ass,' Mike said.

He and Mercer were standing at the base of the pediment, as soaking wet as I was. Each of us was holding on to some decoration on the enormous statue. I was too shaken to try to climb down and into the terminal again. I didn't trust my own footing.

'Here's what's going to happen,' Mercer said. 'I'm going to step back inside, through the clock.'

'Please don't. You're the only one who keeps me calm.'

'I won't leave you until Emergency Services sets up out here. Mike and I—'

'Sorry, but Mike makes me too nervous.'

'What?' Mike said. 'Stick with me, kid. I'm going to break into that Shake Shack and make you a great big chocolate—'

'Don't tell me what you're going to do. Get me down off this roof now.'

'They've got rappel ropes and a harness, Alex,' Mercer said.

'Are you crazy? I'm not rappelling anywhere.'

'Just a precaution. I told them you'd feel more secure that way.'

'I almost died. Nothing's going to make me feel secure tonight.'

'How about if I put some brandy in the shake?' Mike asked.

'Stop talking to me. Mercer's trying to explain what I have to do.'

'You don't have to do anything,' Mercer said. 'You know these guys are the best.'

Emergency Service cops talked jumpers off bridges and saved people trapped in elevators. They plunged into the Hudson River after boats overturned and dragged folks out of burning cars. I had seen dozens of rescues on the news, but I still didn't want to be their next guinea pig.

'I must have to do something. That's what scares me. I'm tired and wet and cold and terrified.'

'You can just stand where you are,' Mercer said. 'They'll wrap you up and take you in. They'll carry you.'

'With my luck the ropes will break.'

'They hold water buffalo, Coop,' Mike said. 'You'll be fine.'

'Please make him wait inside.'

Mercer waved a hand at Mike.

'You'd have a quicker time of it,' Mike said, 'if you got one of those animal tranquilizer darts. She'll be easier to move if she's not croaking at you.'

Mike disappeared through the large circle on the clock face. Mercer stroked my shoulder and counted the minutes with me until the Emergency Service cops reached my side.

Forty-nine

Power was restored in Grand Central Terminal shortly after one A.M. Nik Blunt had indeed tampered with the red button that controlled the power and the rails. It took an electrical crew more than an hour to undo the problem.

Most of the officers – city, state and federal – were doing damage control and cleanup of the concourse by the time I reached the stationmaster's office to see Commissioner Scully.

On the way downstairs – by elevator, to avoid the glass catwalk – Mercer told me that Zoya Blunt had been rescued from the rear of the rooftop before I was brought inside. She had been taken to a hospital to be examined – for both physical and psychological injury. Beyond the scrapes and bruises she'd sustained in her effort to escape, the most profound effect of the evening was the emotional trauma she'd suffered in confronting the scale of her brother's pathology and monstrous nature.

Mike was waiting for me with Keith Scully. He wrapped

a blanket around me and brought me a steaming hot cup of tea.

'How do you feel?' the commissioner asked.

'Numb. Totally numb.'

'That was smart.'

'What?'

'Luring Blunt out on the roof so the snipers had a clean shot at him.'

'Smart?' I shivered uncontrollably as we talked. 'Zoya and I were backed into a corner. She took the lead and I assumed she knew where she was going. Climbing out on the rooftop was never a part of my plan, but if it's what kept me alive, I'm glad I did it.'

'I'm sure you would have liked the shots to have come more quickly,' Scully said, 'but there were so many guys in camo tonight, they couldn't be sure it was Blunt until he turned his head in the direction the snipers were aiming from.'

I'd have nightmares for months, I knew that. Any bad dreams about my fear of heights and falling would be trumped by all of the images of the night's bloody deaths.

'He's dead, isn't he?' I reached for the tea, but my hand was shaking too much to hold it. 'I didn't just imagine that, did I?'

'Yes, Alex. Nik Blunt is dead.'

I thought of Corinne Thatcher first. Her slit throat was the earliest sign I'd had of this killer's brutality.

'Has any more information come in?' I asked.

'Let's get you dry clothes and something stronger than

tea,' Scully said. 'There's plenty of time for questions tomorrow.'

'I want to know about the Thatcher girl first,' I said. 'Why did he target her?'

Keith Scully had been busy piecing the puzzle together in the short time he'd had, in preparation for the media assault that would follow in the morning. 'The squad finally found her boyfriend in the DR.'

'Paco?' I asked.

'Exactly. The guy with the grudge against the president.'

'Because his brother lost both legs in Afghanistan, right?'

'Yeah,' Scully said. 'Paco met Nik Blunt at the VA hospital.'

'The Veterans Affairs hospital?'

'Yeah. East 23rd Street. Paco was there taking his brother for treatment. Blunt was visiting a guy he'd worked with overseas. They both got to talking about political beefs. Paco figured Corinne might be an ally for Blunt because she worked with returning vets and their families. He connected the two of them.'

'Because she'd become disgruntled,' I remembered her parents saying to us.

The invisible strings that tied random people together weren't so coincidental in the end.

'So he meets these girls – at least these two, that we know of,' Scully said. 'At some point he gets bold enough to tell them he has a plan—'

'Do you know what plan?'

'No, but some kind of fireworks in the most public setting he can think of.'

'Grand Central Terminal. With the president on the horizon.'

'You know how it is, Alexandra. Every Tom, Dick and Harry will come forward tomorrow with a sighting or story about an encounter they've had with the killer. A theory or a motive that the journalists and profilers will jump on. Bottom line? Nik Blunt's a psycho. Meets these young women. Thinks they sympathize with him.'

'About a cause,' I said. 'Only Zoya told us he's never really had a cause, other than himself.'

'What sends him over the edge?' Scully asked rhetorically. 'Maybe the moment finally comes for his big plan to be realized, and both women turn him down. He figures they know too much and might betray him. So the voices in his head tell him to kill.'

'The way he's killed before – civilians in a village in Uganda. Maybe others,' I said. 'It was so obvious to us all that he had to have done something as violent, as extreme, before these murders. But he had no criminal record in the States.'

'NorthStar will be answering for that.'

'I know where Corinne and Lydia wound up, Keith. But where did he meet with them? Where did he take them to drug them?'

'There's a whole cache of materials in one of the little "caves" in the tunnel,' Scully said, 'near the Northwest Passage.'

'Surely neither one of these victims would have set foot in the tunnels.'

'I'm not suggesting that. But we found a lot of ammo in one of them, and a whole lot of journals with rants and diatribes. Some receipts from flophouse hotels he might have gotten them to visit, if they were bleeding hearts.'

'His cave in the tunnel,' I said, 'is it anywhere near the one that Carl lived in?'

'Very close by. We'll be working that area, too. Seems pretty clear he met Carl somewhere around the Northwest Passage – above or below the streets. And that he used Carl to do errands for him – probably like stealing the trunk from in front of the Yale Club.'

'So Carl became Blunt's runner-boy, too.'

'Seems that way. When he got too nosy or too greedy, it must have been easier for Nik Blunt to silence him. Use Carl as part of the tease to get us agitated about the train terminal.'

'Carl was disposable,' I said.

Mercer came into the room. 'Nan Toth just dropped off some dry clothes for you. She was watching on the late news, Alex. She said as much as you like shopping, she didn't think you'd find anything open at this hour.'

'Thanks. It'll feel good to change.'

'She also wants you to know that Evan went back to the judge on your cannibal cop case. Told him about the Raymond Tanner connection and what Tanner's been up to.'

'He didn't need to do that,' I said, massaging my temple with my fingers.

'Good thing he did. The judge was pretty outraged. He's

got your cannibal wearing an ankle bracelet from now till the case goes to trial, restricted from leaving home and lots of other tightened-up rules,' Mercer said. 'And the judge signed a subpoena to dump Dominguez's cell phone to try to track down Tanner.'

I picked my head up and smiled. 'Not that I don't like your hospitality, Mercer, but it would be awfully nice if they nailed Tanner before I hit retirement age.'

'I've got some pull with the commissioner,' Mercer said, pointing a finger at Keith Scully. 'He might free up some manpower now to get your man.'

'Count on it,' Scully said. 'You'll be in charge, Detective Wallace. Pick your own team and get it done.'

'There's still so much to figure out about Nik Blunt,' I said. 'Look at the resources you had to marshal to solve these crimes. Not to mention the follow-up everyone will be doing.'

Scully patted me on the back as he stood up to leave the room. 'These crazies are self-radicalizing, Alex. But we've got to spend just as much time running down every one of them as we do a terrorist threat. Mike'll tell you more about that, I'm sure.'

I looked up at Mike, sad that I had been so distrustful. 'Sorry, Detective. I didn't mean to doubt you.'

'As long as you didn't doubt that I was trying to get a crew up to the top of the terminal to bring you and Zoya down.'

'Well, I did wonder a bit,' I said, drawing the blanket tightly around my shoulders. 'You just wouldn't let go of the loudspeaker, would you?'

Mike cocked his head and looked at me, to see whether I was serious. 'I thought you'd like the sound of my voice, wherever you were. And I'm impressed you figured out my mythological clues. Jeez, kid – any rookie can run up all those flights of stairs. I wanted to save my strength for you.'

'I did like hearing your voice, Mike. Just not so far away.'

'Blunt had actually booby-trapped some of the stairwells, Coop. NorthStar tricks, I guess. I had every faith in you till the troops got there.'

Mercer was still holding the clothes that Nan had sent over to me. 'These are for you, Alex. Mike will take you out to shower and change. There's a special train set up by gate 100. Let's get you warm and dry before we take you home. Your teeth are chattering.'

'A special train? I'm too tired for a pajama party, even on steel wheels. Just take me home, guys. I'll stop shivering if you let me go home.'

'The president insists, Coop.'

'The president of the United States?' I said, mustering a laugh. 'Really? I'm way too stressed out for your sense of humor. Unless there's a bar car on this special train.'

'There's all the bells and whistles you can handle. POTUS wants to thank you for making the terminal safe for his arrival.'

Fifty

'Why is this train here?' I asked. I had showered and was warming up, sitting in a gleaming silver railroad car that was parked next to the track, adjacent to the terminal, where Big Timber had been.

'Consider it like Air Force Two, Coop. The president's been whistle-stopping on his main machine, which consists of four cars for his entourage and staff. This is the fifth piece, which is actually brought into Manhattan whenever POTUS stays at the Waldorf. It backs up to Roosevelt's armored car, in case there has to be an emergency evacuation from the city.'

'And tonight?'

'The head of the Secret Service saw Mercer and the guys bringing you down from the roof. Scully told them who you are. They thought you needed some TLC.'

I was dressed in a white robe with the presidential seal on the pocket, part of the guest accoutrements of this elegant private varnish. There was a complete setup of personal items in the lavish bathroom, where I had showered and washed my hair.

463

A waiter had served me a Dewar's and offered a sandwich. I curled my feet up beneath me and settled on the sofa next to Mike.

'Is the president going ahead with his plan to ride into Grand Central tomorrow evening?'

'Apparently with more purpose than before. He'll meet the families of the cops who were killed. The Thatchers and the Tsarlevs, who are being flown in from Russia, too. He'll make a speech about the need for vigilance on the part of every citizen and express his gratitude for the work of law enforcement and first responders.'

'That's such a good thing for him to do. Pay respect to those who lost their lives this week and restore confidence in the use of this great terminal.'

'You feeling any better?'

I nodded. 'It's crazy to be so chilled in the middle of this heat spell.'

'It's your emotional thermostat that's out of whack. Getting drenched – and frightened near to death – while you were on the run from a maniac just topped it off.'

'Thank you, Dr Chapman. And who do you think has been fiddling with my thermostat this last month?' I asked. 'Please don't tell me I have to spend another week with Vickee and Mercer till somebody puts the cuffs on Raymond Tanner.'

'Nope. You're no longer banished to Queens.'

'How'd you take care of that?'

Mike took a slug of his martini and then grinned at me. 'I'm taking you home tonight. I'm staying with you until—'

'You're what?' I was flushed with embarrassment, or perhaps excitement.

'I said I'm—'

'I mean, after all the horrors of this week,' I said, playing with strands of my wet hair, 'and the way things have been between us lately, it doesn't seem the best moment to try to put this together.'

'I need to fix that, Coop. I need to start working on that as soon as possible.'

'But tonight?' I picked up my Scotch, my hand shaking, and tried to move it to my mouth.

'Tonight you're going to sleep,' Mike said. 'End of story. I'm just going to watch over you, kid. Make sure the night terrors stay out of your head.'

The train started to move and I lurched forward. Mike reached out to grab my arm so I didn't tumble off the sofa.

'Where's this thing headed?' I asked.

'Put your clothes on. Come out on the observation deck with me while you finish your drink. Then I'm taking you home.'

'But how are we getting home if we've left the station?'

'Hey, don't you know about Freud and railroad trains and tunnels? I need to get you out of this tunnel before I get an irresistible impulse.'

I looked at Mike and laughed. 'I'd say "take your best shot," but I'm way too tired and wobbly to be much of a challenge. And where are we going, anyway?'

'I figure you'll only get to ride on the presidential train once in a lifetime, right?'

'And the tunnel doesn't end till we hit 97th Street,' I said. I stood up to take my clothes inside to change. Mike lifted the drink from my hand and rested it on the side table, standing to embrace me.

'Mercer will meet us at 125th Street and drive us to your place. I'll let you get some rest, I promise. It's just important for me to be there.'

'I'm going to study up on my Freud,' I said, leaning my head against Mike's chest. 'I kind of like it here in the tunnel with you.'

Acknowledgements

'Is it not cruel to let our city die by degrees, stripped of all her proud monuments, until there will be nothing left of all her history and beauty to inspire our children? If they are not inspired by the past of our city, where will they find the strength to fight for her future?'

Jacqueline Kennedy Onassis wrote those words to the mayor of New York City in 1975, when she learned of plans to demolish the majestic Grand Central Terminal. Her handwritten plea in support of the Municipal Art Society's valiant efforts to save the iconic Manhattan building helped turn the tide. And now, in the second century of its storied life, Grand Central is the thriving centerpiece of the city.

Some of my most vivid childhood memories involve train trips to Manhattan. I remember arriving on the lower concourse, walking up the ramps with a tight grip on my mother's hand. We would always stop to take in the enormity of the great space, look up at the magical celestial ceiling, watch the images on the massive Kodak Colorama screen, amuse ourselves for a moment in the Whispering Gallery, and marvel at the masses of people at the beginning or end of a day's journey.

I love Grand Central Terminal. And I was pleased to find how many others – New Yorkers and citizens of the world – share my passion for its design, its purpose, and its intrigue.

The brilliant architects who revitalized and restored Grand Central Terminal in the 1990s were with the firm Beyer Blinder Belle. It was through the eyes of one of their visionaries, Frank Prial Jr, that I got to see the building from top to bottom, learn riveting details that could make up an entire book, come to understand the meticulous care that went into the project, and walk the glass catwalks. It was one of the most thrilling days of my professional life.

Then I was fortunate enough to be introduced to Daniel Brucker, who included me in a most unusual tour. Danny started working at Metro-North in 1987 as a press secretary and is the terminal's best ambassador to this day. Tracks, tunnels, presidential private trains, hidden staircases – they all come alive because of his passion for the history, and mystery, of GCT.

The Municipal Art Society, in conjunction with Metro-North and the MTA, offers tours by docents every day. I walked them frequently and learned something new on every visit.

Sam Roberts is a great journalist and the author of many fine books. He is also a longtime friend. His 2013 book – *Grand Central: How a Train Station Transformed America*

– is not only a fantastic read but was my go-to source for facts, stories, photographs and inspiration.

Other interesting works I relied on for research include *Grand Central: Gateway to a Million Lives* by John Belle and Maxinne R. Leighton, *Grand Central Terminal: 100 Years of a New York Landmark* by the New York Transit Museum and Anthony W. Robins, and *Grand Central Terminal: Railroads, Engineering, and Architecture in New York City* by Kurt C. Schlichting.

One of the most fascinating books I read in preparation for writing was *The Mole People* by Jennifer Toth, a compassionate and frank look at life underground.

As always, I endlessly clip good news stories from my favorite papers. The *New York Times* is a wonderful source for metropolitan life pieces, especially Corey Kilgannon's story on the ratters, this time out. And the *Boston Globe* staff piece titled 'The Fall of the House of Tsarnaev' was informative and compelling. To all those who survived the marathon bombing – Boston Strong – my boundless respect.

I don't know the federal prosecutors who tried the actual cannibal cop case, but I have great admiration for their work and words. To assistant United States attorneys Randall Jackson and Hadassa Waxman – my gratitude.

My real-life heroes remain the prosecutors and police officers who work on the side of the angels every day, especially in the Manhattan District Attorney's Office and NYPD. Melissa Mourges and Martha Bashford – you two keep my forensics honest.

My team at Dutton is extraordinary – and patient. It all starts at the very top with Brian Tart and most especially buoys me up under the leadership of my superb editor, Ben Sevier. My thanks always to Christine Ball, Jamie McDonald, Jessica Renheim, Stephanie Kelly, Carrie Swetonic, and Andrea Santoro. To David Shelley and my Little, Brown UK family, cheers always.

Esther Newberg is first and foremost my friend. That she is a formidable force in my corner at ICM Partners is an added starter.

As always, my family and my friends are my greatest joy. There are several muses who hover over me whenever I sit down to write – Justin Feldman, Bobbie and Bones Fairstein, Karen Cooper. Stay close.

And this one is for Michael, whose friendship of forty-five years is a gift beyond imagining.